PRAISE FOR PAUL E. HARDISTY

'A solid, meaty thriller – Hardisty is a fine writer and Straker is a great lead character' Lee Child

'A stormer of a thriller – vividly written, utterly topical, totally gripping' Peter James

'This is a remarkably well-written, sophisticated novel in which the people and places, as well as frequent scenes of violent action, all come alive on the page … This is a really excellent debut' *Literary Review*

'A page-turning adventure that grabs you from the first page and won't let go' Edward Wilson

'An exceptional debut, beautifully written, blisteringly authentic, heartstoppingly tense and unusually moving. Definite award material' Paul Johnston

'This is an exceptional and innovative novel. And an important one. Hardisty appears to know his territory intimately and describes in mind-grabbing detail its culture, its beliefs and its hopes. I can't praise it highly enough' Susan Moody

'The author's deep knowledge of the settings never slows down the non-stop action, with distant echoes of a more-moral minded Jack Reacher or Jason Bourne. A forceful first novel by a writer not afraid of weighty issues and visibly in love with the beauty of the Yemen and desert landscapes his protagonists travel through' Maxim Jakubowski

'A trenchant and engaging thriller that unravels this mysterious land in cool, precise sentences' Stav Sherez, *Catholic Herald*

'*The Abrupt Physics of Dying* is compelling reading and tackles subject matter not often encountered … it is both dynamic and different and I enjoyed it immensely' Grab this Book

'From the beginning to the end – both of which are played out at gunpoint – this novel is non-stop action. It's thrilling, but also highly sophisticated, and offers a startling look at what developed countries will do in their hunger for resources' Crime Fiction Lover

'I was a big fan, in 2013, of Terry Hayes's *I Am Pilgrim* and I hadn't up to now read a conspiracy thriller which came close to it in terms of quality. But Hardisty's book was an excellent read with a similar sweep across the politics of international money-making' Sarah J. Ward, Crime Pieces

'Just occasionally, a book comes along to restore your faith in a genre – and Paul Hardisty's *The Abrupt Physics of Dying* does this in spades. It's absolutely beautifully written and atmospheric – and it provides an unrivalled look at Yemen, a country few of us know much about … appreciate intelligent, quality writing' Sharon Wheeler, Crime Review

'This thrilling debut opens with a tense, utterly gripping roadside hijacking … Hardisty's prose is rich, descriptive and elegant, but break-neck pace is the king … an exhilarating, white-knuckle ride' Paddy Magrane, Crime Book Club

'A great page-turner with all the elements that make a cracking thriller. There's plenty of action, twists and turns, skulduggery and an evil oil company – what more could you want? This is one of those books that makes you want to turn to Google and find out how much is fact and how much fiction' Novel Heights

'At heart this is first and foremost a cracking good thriller … a lot of good stuff here not often found in a crime novel' Crime Novel Reader

'Fast-paced and cleverly written, this novel has bestseller written all over it' Writing WA

'Hardisty details Yemen, the political climate and the science with an authority that's never questionable and with a delivery that's polished enough to make you wonder whether he hasn't secretly been publishing thrillers under a different name for years … as assured, gripping, well paced and finely detailed as they come' Tony Hill, Mumbling about Music

'*The Abrupt Physics of Dying* is a tense thriller, the violence and corruption is vividly portrayed, yet there is nothing in the story that shouldn't be there … If you enjoy a story that is well-written with a plot that twists and turns, and leads you astray, then I'd recommend this. If you want a hero that is a little bit unusual, with his own issues, but is determined and so well created, then I'd recommend this. If you want a complex and intelligent thriller, then I'd really really recommend this' Anne Cater, Random Things Through My Letterbox

'For *Abrupt Physics of Dying* to be a debut novel, a brilliant debut novel, there's surely only exciting things to come from Paul E. Hardisty, starting with next year's sequel *The Evolution of Fear*. A sensational first novel' Sophie, Reviewed the Book

'A well-crafted, admirably constructed, and convincing tale of modern corruption, touching on topical issues, *The Abrupt Physics of Dying* has introduced Hardisty as a serious player in the (eco-) thriller genre, and I expect impressive things from him over the coming years' Charley Barnes, Mad Hatter Reviews

'An exceptional debut thriller … well-written, the prose clear and crisp, the voice clear and authentic. Tense and moving, it grabs you by the throat' Atticus Finch

'A knowledgeable and intelligent thriller which, despite being set two decades ago, feels fresh and thoroughly relevant to today's geopolitical situation ... We can hear the noise, feel the heat and even taste the poisoned water. Hardisty clearly knows his stuff and has created an evocative portrait of Yemen' Louise Reviews

'It is clear that the author's background and experience has enabled him to write a thriller that is so rich and detailed in description that you can almost feel the searing heat and visualise the vast endless desert ... a very powerful and compelling message of corporate greed and the deliberate destruction of life and land' Karen Cocking, My Reading Corner

'Where this book stands out is the fantastic writing, the stunning imagery ... the heat, the fear, the colour, smells, and tension of each scene. The intrigue is gripping, the characters complex, the denouement satisfying' Jackie Law, Never Imitate

'I seriously cannot remember the last time I was this gripped by a thriller ... Mr Hardisty brings Yemen to vivid, colourful life, the people and the hardships, the politics and the realities and wraps it up in a beautiful package of really exceptional storytelling, with an authentic edge which means you honestly believe every moment of it ... a modern thriller with a literary edge, one that could equally win the highest awards' Liz Loves Books

'In true Bond and Bourne tradition, Clay is a maverick who often operates outside the rules. The novel's plot is fiercely gripping yet labyrinthine; each time you think you're nearing a solution, you find instead another twist ... his experience shows in the urgent authenticity of his writing. Here we have a novel, a writer to watch' Claire Thinking

'The sex, violence and corruption had shades of Robert Ludlum, and the relationship between Clay and Rania was reminiscent of a Bond romance (of the Daniel Craig, as opposed to Sean Connery, era). If you fancy a fast-paced thriller to brighten up this winter, this is it' Amy Pirt, This Little Bag of Dreams

'This epic story is a spell-binding read. Highly atmospheric, it is grounded in the Yemen landscape, with the tension of a country on the brink of civil war sparking from every page … a thought-provoking and heart-wrenching book. A real page-turner with a pulse-poundingly fast pace' Crime Thriller Girl

'Well-paced with plenty of action … I look forward to reading more from this author. Definitely a cracking debut' Bleach House Library

'A gritty, at times violent and gripping eco-thriller, life on the edge in Yemen – the clash of cultures, the oil industry and the locals' Trip Fiction

'International intrigue, sophisticated treatment of non-Western cultures – which means neither demonised nor romanticised, abundant grey areas where there are no simple choices, and peopled with the sorts of psychopaths addicted to adrenaline. The science reminds me of Patricia Cornwell's Scarpetta novels. This is a modern treatment of a centuries-old conflict between indigenous peoples and usurpers bent on exploitation, us and them' Texas Book Lover

'The well-written almost-poetic vivid descriptions are unusual in a book of this genre, showing how the author Paul E. Hardisty has a gift for detailed but fast-paced writing' Victoria Goldman, Off-the-Shelf Reviews

'Civil war, terrorism, corporate ruthlessness and corruption, and harsh global realities are examined in a thrilling action fuelled style that has enough authenticity and atmosphere to sink the reader into the story' Crime Thriller Hound

'Think Jack Reacher and then some. This book is adventurous and fascinatingly topical. The author brings home to us the realities of the world today with themes of global exploitation and discomfort' Tracey Book Lover

'Hardisty writes with incredible passion and technical precision and the reader can never be quite sure who is good and who is bad, which keeps the reader gripped to the end ... an epic reading experience that will have them yearning to know what happens next' Segnalibro Blog

'What I thought was going to be a forgettable page-turner actually turned out to be something far more thoughtful, both on a wider scale and at a more personal level as the story examines the dehumanising effect of conflict on Straker. The writing is beautifully descriptive, Yemen is vividly and evocatively brought to life yet alongside this the action is often unflinchingly and brutally violent' Karen Cole

'Far from being your average page-turner, Hardisty has a superb command of language, creating evocative images of land which many will be unfamiliar with. The issues covered are very contemporary with seemingly impossible battles against overbearing figures and organisations. It's an exciting, absorbing and provocative stormer' Kevin Freeburn

'Think Jack Reacher and then some ... adventurous and fascinatingly topical' Tracey Walsh

'A brilliant thriller, with so many twists and turns it will make you dizzy' Tracy Shephard

THE EVOLUTION OF FEAR

Canadian by birth, Paul Hardisty has spent 25 years working all over the world as an engineer, hydrologist and environmental scientist. He has roughnecked on oil rigs in Texas, explored for gold in the Arctic, mapped geology in Eastern Turkey (where he was befriended by PKK rebels), and rehabilitated water wells in the wilds of Africa. He was in Ethiopia in 1991 as the Mengistu regime fell, and was bumped from one of the last flights out of Addis Ababa by bureaucrats and their families fleeing the rebels. In 1993 he survived a bomb blast in a café in Sana'a, and was one of the last Westerners out of Yemen before the outbreak of the 1994 civil war. Paul is a university professor and Director of Australia's national land, water, ecosystems and climate adaptation research programmes. His debut novel, *The Abrupt Physics of Dying*, received great critical acclaim and was shortlisted for the CWA John Creasey (New Blood) Dagger. Paul is a sailor, a private pilot, keen outdoorsman, conservation volunteer, and lives in Western Australia with his family.

The Evolution of Fear

PAUL E. HARDISTY

**ORENDA
BOOKS**

Orenda Books
16 Carson Road
West Dulwich
London SE21 8HU
www.orendabooks.co.uk

First published in the United Kingdom by Orenda Books 2016

A catalogue record for this book is available from the British Library.

ISBN 978-1-910633-24-3

Typeset in Garamond by MacGuru Ltd
Printed and bound by CPI Group (UK) Ltd, Croydon CRO 4YY

SALES & DISTRIBUTION

In the UK and elsewhere in Europe:
Turnaround Publisher Services
Unit 3, Olympia Trading Estate
Coburg Road
Wood Green
London
N22 6TZ
www.turnaround-uk.com

In USA/Canada:
Trafalgar Square Publishing
Independent Publishers Group
814 North Franklin Street
Chicago, IL 60610
USA
www.ipgbook.com

For details of other territories, please contact *info@orendabooks.co.uk*

For Gary Pulsifer

'There exists no limit to the blindness of interest and selfish habit'
Charles Darwin

'Our fears do make us traitors…'
Macbeth, **Act IV, Scene ii, William Shakespeare**

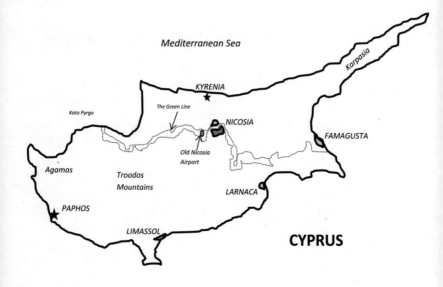

Part I

1

No Difference the Instrument

30th October 1994: North coast of Cornwall, United Kingdom

It was a good place to hide. From almost any vantage the cottage was invisible. Notched into a wooded draw at the top of the bluff, accessible only on foot, the place looked as cold and dead as the Devonian slate and mudstone cliffs from which it was made. Forty minutes now he'd been watching the place, as dusk faded and night came, but he'd seen no one, nothing to suggest danger. Just the crash of the waves on the shingle beach below, the whip of wind through the trees.

Claymore Straker shivered, pulled up his collar and watched the storm come in off the Irish Sea. Rain clouds scuttled overhead, low and fast, moving inland over the gorse and the stunted, wind-bent trees. The first drops touched his face, the cold fingertips of a ten-hour corpse. Winter was coming, and he was a fugitive.

Eight and a half weeks he'd been here, anchored into the cliffside, staring out at the grey solitude of the sea, watching the depressions deepen. Fifty-nine days, one thousand, four hundred and twenty-two hours not knowing where she was, not knowing if she was alive or dead, uncertainty burning away the very fibre of him. And today he'd cracked. He'd succumbed to worry and fear and he'd walked all the way to Crackington Haven, fifteen miles across the national park. Defying Crowbar's orders, he'd gone into the village, found a public phone, and he'd made a call. Just one. And now he was more worried than ever.

Clay hefted his bug-out bag onto his shoulders and started towards the cottage. The path tunnelled down through a tangle of wind-shaped scrub, the branches closing over him as he went. Hands reached out from the darkness, snatched at his clothes. A thorn caught his cheek, nicked open the skin under his left eye. He cursed, bent low and followed the track as it swung back towards the cliffs. By the time he emerged from the thicket, the rain was coming hard and flat, squalling over the bluffs. He raised the stump of his left forearm over his eyes, trying to shield his face from the icy darts. There was the dark outline of the slate roof, the chimney pot just visible, the low stone wall that enclosed the small courtyard.

He had just moved into open ground when the clouds broke. Moonlight bathed the cliffline like a parachute flare. And there, just outside the cottage door, the back-lit silhouettes of two men.

Clay stopped dead. A gust raked through the scrub, a loud tearing as a sheet of rain whipped over the bluff. The men were only metres away, blurs in the slanting rain. They were looking straight at him. Seconds passed, slowed to the tick of insect wings in a childhood dream, then stalled completely in chrome-white illumination.

Surely they'd seen him.

One of the men shifted, shook the rain from his coat. A voice rose above the wind. Clay couldn't make out the words, but the tone was calm, unhurried. As if commenting on the weather. Or the football scores. And in that moment, as the realisation came to him that perhaps these men were simply lost, walkers strayed from the park, he thought how powerful are the doubts we carry inside, how strong these prisons we make for ourselves.

He was about to raise his hand in greeting when the two men turned away and walked the few paces to the cottage. One bent to the lock, worked it a moment, then pushed open the door. The other pulled a gun and burst inside.

It was as if a gallows door had opened beneath his feet.

Adrenaline hammered through him. He wavered a moment, then sprinted to the wall and dropped to the ground. A loud bang from inside the cottage amped out through the open door – a gunshot? A door being kicked in? Clay pulled the .45 calibre Glock G21 from under his jacket, cradled it dry in his lap, worked the action. He remembered Crowbar slamming the gun on the table the day he'd left him here. Stay put, his old platoon commander had said. I'll come get you when things calm. Whatever you do, stay clear of town. With that bounty on your carcass, every *poes* from here to Cape Town will be hunting you.

Clay swallowed hard then started along the base of the stone wall, keeping low. He reached the cottage, crouched and looked seaward across the courtyard. The door was less than five metres away. It was the only way in or out. He waited, listened, but all he could hear was the pounding of the surf and the wind buffeting the cliffs, and above it all the drowning crash of his own heart.

How the hell had they found him, here of all places? Had someone recognised him in town? He'd been in and out in less than twenty minutes. Who, other than Crowbar, knew about this place? Knew he was here? Questions boiled in his mind.

But he didn't have time to think them through. The door opened and one of the men stepped out into the rain-swept courtyard. He was short and stocky, powerfully built, and wore a black, thigh-length raincoat and a black baseball cap. He took a few steps towards the wall, shoes crunching on the gravel. They were city shoes; must have been wet through. A pistol with a long silencer hung from his left hand. He stood for a moment looking out to sea. Clay raised the G21, steadied it on the stump of his left arm and aimed for the middle of the man's chest.

Just then, the second man stepped out into the rain. He was taller, wore a dark jacket and was bareheaded. Slung across his chest was a Heckler and Koch MP5 machine pistol. As Clay shifted his aim to take out the more heavily armed man first, the shorter man reached for his cap and pulled it off his head, slapping it against his thigh as he turned to face his companion.

'*Hy is nie hier,*' he shouted above the wind. '*N' volledige opfok.*'

Clay's heart lurched. The sound of his native tongue pierced something inside him. He's not here, the man had said. A complete fuckup. He'd said it in Afrikaans.

'*Ja, maar hy was hier*,' said the taller man, looking out towards the bluff. But he *was* here.

The other man nodded. '*Kan nie ver wees.*' Can't be far.

Clay knelt behind the wall, the Glock trained on the man with the MP5. His hand was shaking. These were his countrymen, Boers by their accent, men who by their look and demeanour had in all probability fought against the communists in Angola and Southwest Africa, as he had. Their presence here, in the foresight of his gun on an autumn night on the north coast of Cornwall, seemed impossible, the ramifications a nightmare.

Clay knew he had to act quickly. He could run, disappear into the heathland, go west along the coast, give himself a head start. But they'd already managed to get this close. If he ran, they'd follow, just like they'd done with the SWAPO terrorists all those years ago, tracking them like Palaeolithic hunters, wearing them down with calloused feet, pushing them hour by hour towards the quicksand of exhaustion. It made no difference, the instrument: helicopters or spears, stones or high-powered assault rifles. Even, as he'd learned to his horror, back then during the war, the cocktails of muscle relaxants and incapacitating agents that shut down everything but your brain, suffocated you as you fell to the sea from four thousand metres, a silent scream drowning in your throat. Clay shuddered at the memory.

The tall man turned, looked down the track, readjusted the sling of his weapon so its muzzle pointed down, and said something to his companion that Clay could not make out. A gap opened in the clouds. Moonlight flooded the gravel courtyard again, pale as a false spring day. The two figures stood silhouetted against the hammered steel background. Clay breathed in, steadied his aim.

I did not ask you to come here, he said. I did not will this or want it in any way. I know why you are here, and I cannot let you leave. You have given me no choice. No choice.

He exhaled, squeezed the trigger.

The large-calibre slug hit the tall one between the shoulder blades, severing his spine. His legs collapsed under him and he sandbagged forward, inert, hands limp at his sides. Before the dead man's face hit the gravel, Clay shifted left, aimed for the other target and fired again. This time to wound, to incapacitate, not to kill. The man spun right, fell to the ground. But then he was up, scrambling towards the cliffs, his feet flailing and slipping in the gravel. Clay was about to fire again when the lights went out, the moon suddenly obscured by a thick bank of cloud. The target was gone, black on black. Clay could hear the man scrabbling on the crushed stone. He aimed low along the wall of the cottage, fired blind once, twice, aiming at the sound: deflection shooting. Slowly his night vision returned. The tall one was where he'd fallen, face down, the rain pelting his back. Otherwise, the courtyard was empty.

2.7 Seconds of Nothing

Clay scanned the open ground beyond the wall. Nothing. Had he hit the other guy? The way he'd spun and fallen, Clay guessed yes. But he couldn't be sure. Unarmed, the guy would try to run, if he could. But did he have a backup weapon? He might be hiding on the cliff side of the cottage, hurt, bleeding, waiting for Clay to come to him; or perhaps he was moving around the building now, trying to flank him.

The clouds had thickened, and the world was every shade of black, liquid and heavy, screaming out its anger at these desecrations, this waste. Clay leaned into the wind, almost blind, soaked. The cliff edge was a pace away. Waves exploded against the rock below sending chutes of sea spray hurtling up towards him, the foam black like the sky, the salt coating his lips, stinging his eyes. He turned and crouched, tried to cover his eyes, peered along the cliff edge. Nothing. Just the dark outline of the cambered roof, the low front wall built into the cliffside. Clay knew he had to move fast. By daylight, his chances of getting clear would fall away rapidly. Any hope he might have had of getting some information out of his would-be assassins was gone. At this point it was about one thing: survival.

Clay sprinted back to the courtyard and knelt beside the corpse. The rain had washed the bullet wound clean, sluiced the blood away over the gravel. He pushed the Glock into his waistband, flipped the MP5's strap over the dead man's head and pushed him over onto his back. The man's eyes were open but his nose and teeth were smashed. Pieces of gravel pushed into the skin, the mouth, pierced through the bottom lip. It would have hurt like hell if he'd been able to feel anything when he hit the ground.

Clay grabbed the machine pistol, checked the action and flipped off the safety. The other man's handgun was there in the gravel too. Clay picked it up, thrust it into his jacket pocket and sprinted towards the back of the cottage. Rounding the corner at a crouch, he moved along the landward wall. Here he was in the lee of the wind, shielded from the rain. At the far corner he paused, took a deep breath, raised the MP5 and rested the forestock on his stump. This was the fourth side of the building, the only place he hadn't checked. If the guy was still close, this is where he'd be. Clay breathed out and pivoted around the corner, swinging the MP5 around and down the line of the wall, into the full fury of the wind.

No one. Just the slate and the dark grass grown up around the stone foundations, and beyond, the dark, godless anger of the storm. Clay looked out across the rain-swept gorseland. If the man had fled out there, Clay would never find him. He moved along the wall towards the cliff and peered over the edge. It was forty metres straight down (d), with only a narrow, slippery ledge of slate and an involuntary $\sqrt{(2d/g)}$ = 2.7 seconds of nothing but gravity (g) and empty space to the shingle below.

The man had disappeared. Perhaps he'd fallen off the cliff and been dragged out to sea, taken by the storm. Or, with his friend down, he'd panicked and run. If so, he was probably making his way back to wherever they'd left the car. The nearest paved road was about three kilometres inland, paralleling the coast. Either way, Clay could be sure of one thing: word would be out fast, and they'd be closing in.

It was time to go, time to get back to Rania, find her and disappear for good. Keep that promise he'd made to her, to himself. Maybe change the trajectory of his life, find some of those things he'd been looking for, atone for the wrongs, one more just done.

Clay let the MP5 hang on its strap, turned back and made his way to the courtyard. He'd grab a few things from inside then sprint to the road. If he could find the car, he'd take that. If he couldn't, he'd go overland on foot.

The men had left the cottage door open and the swirling wind had carried rain and dead leaves across the old slate floor tiles. Clay slipped as he came in, caught himself, started towards the fireplace. He'd taken three steps when a flash of movement caught the furthest edge of his vision.

Clay's instinctive turn towards danger was less than one-eighth complete when the blow caught him high on the left shoulder, knocking him off his feet. He crashed to the floor, the MP5 flailing about his neck. A dull ache spread through his arm, replaced almost immediately by that acute precision of screaming nerves, hot and wet. He turned to see his assailant slam down hard onto the slate, forearms breaking the fall with a crack, a bloodied blade in his left fist. It was the gunman, the Boer from outside. He'd slipped as he lunged in attack, and now he grunted in pain, scrambled to his knees and dived at Clay, the blade flashing. Clay rolled left and whipped his arm across his body and down onto the man's forearm, deflecting the blade and sending his attacker twisting to the floor. Clay followed through, driving the man's knife hand down hard onto the slate flag. The knife spun across the floor. Clay groped for the MP5's pistol grip. His finger found the trigger. He was about to raise the weapon for a shot when the Boer lunged. A burst roared out in the enclosed space. Rounds clattered off stone, splintered wood. The Boer hit him with a full body tackle, punching the air from his lungs. He came down hard on the slate. The Boer's full weight was on him now. The pistol grip was gone from his hand. The Boer grabbed for the MP5's forestock, wrenched it hard, jerking Clay's head forward. They were face to face, inches apart, the smoking weapon wedged between their bodies. The Boer was trying to pivot the MP5's muzzle down into Clay's chest. Clay could feel the thing digging into his ribs. He twisted his torso and drove his hand into the space between their bodies and grabbed the weapon. As he did, the Boer bared his teeth like an enraged hyena, snapped his head forward. Clay turned his head just as the Boer's jaw cracked shut, an enamel snap and the kiss of lips against his cheek. A kiss that would have taken away half his nose. Clay's hand was on the pistol grip now. He found the trigger guard, prised away a finger, crushed it against the curved metal of the guard. The man screamed in pain. Then the shallow-grave rip of the MP5, its detonations muffled and drummed up through two chest cavities. Bullets shredded the kitchen cabinetry. Cordite stung his nostrils. For a fraction of a second they stared at each other, realising that somehow neither had been hit. Clay had his thumb wedged into the pull space behind the trigger now and jerked back hard on the pistol grip, hammering his knee into the man's body. The Boer grunted, clamped down hard on the MP5. The guy was strong. Clay was winning the battle for the trigger but losing the fight for the gun. He tried to roll out, but the Boer outweighed him. He could feel the bastard's breath on his face, smell the cigarettes and crap coffee. The gun's barrel was coming down onto Clay's throat, touching now, as the Boer levered his weight, still trying to pry Clay's fingers from the trigger. Clay gasped for breath, pushed back with all his strength. He could feel the barrel crushing his windpipe. Pain seared through his brain, began its too-quick metamorphosis into panic. The Glock was there in his belt, he could reach it with his stump. If he still had two hands this would be over. But he didn't, and it wasn't. The Boer shifted his balance forward, putting all his weight into the MP5, trying to choke Clay to death, going for the kill.

There are moments in any struggle, any battle, when outcomes hinge on the thinnest line, a fraction of a degree. *Now*, Crowbar used to call it back then, during the war. The moment when winning or losing, living or dying, depended on what you did right *now*. Whatever Crowbar was, he was no fatalist. *Nou, seuns*, he'd yell, charging forward, R4 dispensing single-shot judgement on any who chose to stand and die. Now.

Clay raised his knees and pushed up hard against the floor, a powerful hip thrust that over-balanced his attacker, momentarily releasing the pressure on his neck. Clay arched his back, lined up the man's head, and with every joule of energy he could summon, whipped his neck forward.

Clay's forehead made contact with the man's nose. The cartilage collapsed as if it were raw cauliflower. He could hear the crunch. Clay rolled away, twisting the MP5 on its strap and sending his attacker crashing to the floor. Clay gasped for air, fumbled for the MP5's grip. By now the Boer was up, blood streaming black over his lips and chin. He stood a moment, frozen. A stab of moonlight flicked across the room. The man was fair-haired, with big, pale eyes set in anxious sockets and a heavy, farm jaw, a goddamned *voortrekker* if he'd ever seen one. Clay raised the MP5. The Boer's eyes widened.

'*Wat julle gestuur het?*' said Clay. Who sent you?

The Boer blinked twice. '*Fok jou.*'

'Who sent you, damn it?'

The Boer glanced towards the open door, the gale howling outside. Then he looked back at Clay and smiled through the blood. '*Mandela het my gestuur,*' he slurred. Mandela sent me.

Clay pulled the trigger. Nothing. A jam. Or out of ammunition. He dropped the MP5, reached for the Glock in his waistband. And then the light was gone, and so was the Boer.

Clay scrambled to his feet, Glock out, the MP5 flapping about his neck, and staggered to the door. The man was already across the courtyard. Clay raised the G21, took aim through the slanting rain. The Boer hurdled the low wall and stumbled into the gorse just as Clay fired. Clay ran across the courtyard to the wall. A dark shape was lurching towards the cliff edge, about thirty metres away now, barely silhouetted against the sea. Clay steadied himself, raised his weapon. The Boer stopped, turned. He was right there, the abyss before him. Clay fired. The Boer pitched back and was gone.

A Talisman of Sorts

Clay walked back across the courtyard, the pain in his arm rising now as the endorphins and adrenaline burned away. The rain had relented and the cloud cover thinned. Moonlight sent shadows twitching across the landscape. He knelt once more beside the dead man and went through his pockets, extracting a wallet, three extra magazines for the MP5, a set of keys with a BMW ring, and a mobile phone, its standby light blinking red. Clay flipped open the phone and thumbed the scroll button. Nothing. The phone was password protected. He pulled out the SIM card and threw the phone over the cliff.

Back inside the cottage, he lit a lamp and inspected his arm. The knife, still lying on the floor, had sliced through the sleeve of his leather jacket and into his deltoid. He walked to the bathroom and opened the big cupboard. Crowbar's idea of a medical kit resembled a military field hospital. There were giving sets, IV kits, every size and shape of bandage and compress, sutures, tape, morphine, coagulants, antibiotics by the carton, splints and slings. Clay took off the jacket, winced as he pulled the grey hooded sweatshirt over his head and pulled off his shirt. It was a clean slice across the arm, about three inches long, at least a couple of centimetres deep. Not too bad. He'd been lucky.

He stood and watched the blood ooze from the wound. As he'd lunged for Clay, the Boer had slipped on the wet floor and missed his target. Those new city shoes he'd been wearing, the shiny wet leather soles, had probably saved Clay's life.

Which shoes you put on in the morning.

The side of the helicopter you got out of.

Where you decided to step. Here, or here.

These were the things that determined if you lived or died, whether you ended up in a coma for the rest of your life, lost your legs just above the knees, went home in one piece, physically at least. The brute physics of it – in retrospect always so pure and clear, something you could calculate, but in the causation so utterly unpredictable and, in the end, so spectacularly unfair. And for so long it had been for him the ultimate argument *against* the existence of God, and since he'd met Rania the ultimate argument *for* Him. For without His arbitrage, what possible explanation? What meaning?

One thing was certain. Allah, if he was out there, had a warped conception of justice, but a hell of a sense of humour.

Clay washed and dried the wound, snapped open a vial of disinfectant and doused the upper part of his arm, letting the sting nudge away this pointless philosophy. Soon he had the wound passably sutured and bandaged. He was getting good at working one-handed, much better than the bumbling frustration of the first weeks. He grabbed a box of painkillers, extra sutures, gauze and compresses, more disinfectant, a box of morphine, two clean towels and a box of surgical gloves, carried them into the kitchen and put them on the table.

Time was running. Clay threaded on a clean shirt, a dry hoodie, and hunched into the wet leather jacket. He opened up his bag, stuffed in the extra medical supplies. Then he grabbed the MP5 from the table, cleared the chamber, pulled out the magazine, and slid weapon and ammunition in with the supplies. From the drawer under the sink he fished out a box of .45 shells for the Glock and dropped them in with the other stuff. He walked to the fireplace, opened the flue, reached up and worked loose the blackened brick just above the baffle, pulled out a metal tin and extracted a fold of cash, sterling and euros, and two passports: Marcus Edward, Canadian, from Vancouver; and David Jackson, a Brit born in Shepton Mallet, Somerset. Both documents contained the same photograph of Clay, taken two and half months ago, the day after the killings in London, the eyes narrow, the mouth drawn, the hair chopped back. He looked like someone else, someone older. Clay stashed the money and passports in the inside breast pocket of his jacket. He glanced at his watch. Just gone seven. Maybe ten and a half hours of good darkness left. He pulled a rain poncho from a hook near the door and pulled it over his head.

Not for the first time he wondered about this place he'd come to know so well. Hints of its recent past were everywhere. The half-used boxes of ammunition under the counter, the shredded railway sleepers in the buttressed shed outside, old copies of the South African *Sunday Times* yellowing in the coal scuttle, cupboards stocked with enough lamb stew and tuna to last a year. And now a dead man outside the front door.

He breathed, closed his eyes a moment. Then he walked to the bookshelf, pulled out an old hardback volume of *Macbeth*, stuffed it into his jacket pocket, killed the lamp and walked out the door for the last time.

Clay set off down the footpath at a run, the wind at his back, the rain gusting in sheets that flayed across the open blufflands, the gorse shivering with each whip of the lash. The car couldn't be far. He was going to find it and put as much time and distance between himself and this place as he could.

As he ran, the telephone conversation of earlier that day replayed itself in his mind, the words finding cadence with his footfall.

Crowbar had answered first ring.

'It's me, *broer*.'

'I told you to keep quiet,' Crowbar – Koevoet in Afrikaans – had said. He'd sounded drunk.

Clay switched to the language of his childhood. 'I haven't heard from you.'

'Where are you?'

'Town.'

'*Kak*, Straker. I *fokken* told you–'

Clay cut him off. 'Have you heard from Rania?'

Silence, and then: 'No. No, I haven't. But there have been–'

'What, Koevoet? Have been what?'

'Articles in the paper. Written by Lise Moulinbecq. That's her alias, isn't it?'

He'd told her to keep quiet, stay hidden. Irony flooded through him, that particularly brutal nausea. 'What articles?'

'Something about Cyprus. Some sort of scam involving stolen antiquities.'

'Get me out, Koevoet.'

'Look, Straker.' Crowbar coughed, deep and bronchial. 'I have connections in the police. They don't know who plugged Medved and his two thugs, but they know it happened in your hotel room. They want you for questioning.'

Killing Rex Medved had been the first right thing Clay had done in a long time, the first unselfish thing. But even as he'd pulled the trigger, something inside him had been pulling the other way, that promise he had made to himself a decade ago, after he'd fled the war, the insanity of a country tearing itself apart: no more killing. And then, deep in the wilds of Yemen, just five months ago, his day of reckoning had come. He'd met Rania. And that night when he'd killed Medved, it had been for something that mattered. It had been for her, for all those people in Yemen that Medved had screwed over, the dead kids, all the poisoned villagers whose minutes and hours and years had been chewed up and shit out into the open sewer of exploitation.

'Be patient, *broer*,' said Crowbar. 'It's going cold.'

'Cold? A hundred thousand pounds cold?'

Crowbar laughed. 'Not anymore, *broer*. Medved's sister raised the reward to a million, just last week. And that's just for information. She's offering twice that for the hit, *ja*.'

Two million pounds. Enough to change a life: pay debts, buy freedom, solve problems. It changed everything, for him and for Rania, raised risk to the sixth power.

'Congratulations, Straker. You're finally worth something,' slurred Crowbar. 'If it wasn't for this new job in Angola, might even take it on myself.'

After all these years, Crowbar was going back to Africa, this time to fight someone else's war. As he'd said on the drive down to Cornwall, he didn't know how to do anything else, and wouldn't want to if he did. He'd even tried to recruit Clay into 'The Company' as he'd called it.

Clay heard Crowbar light a smoke and exhale.

'This Medved woman is not the kind of person you want to get mixed up with, mind.' The clink of glass, pouring. 'Maybe you can just wait her out.'

'You're not listening, Koevoet.'

'She'll be dead in six months, by all accounts. Some degenerative liver disease. One failed transplant after another. She's now convinced that the only thing that can save her is this lost icon thing she's searching for.'

'Icon?' he said.

'The Patmos Illumination, some twelfth-century Eastern Orthodox trinket. They say it was carved out of wood from the cross.'

'Which cross?'

'*The* cross, for *fok*'s sake, Straker. They say Christ's blood soaked in, that you can still see the hole where they drove in the spike for his hand.'

'Koevoet…'

'They say it has the power to heal. You know, make the blind see, all that *kak*, *ja*.'

'Koevoet.'

'They say that it vanished, years ago. Wonder if it could help me.'

'God damn it, Koevoet.'

'Never been the same since I took that FAPLA bullet.'

'I don't have six months, Koevoet. I'm leaving. With your help or without it.'

'Okay, *seun*. Go back to the cottage. Now. Stay put a while longer.'

'I've got to get off this island, Koevoet. The weather's killing me.'

Crowbar laughed, the rasp of his cigarette lungs. 'Look, Straker, it'll take a while to organise, a week maybe.'

'A week? No way, *broer*.'

'For *fok*'s sake, Straker,' growled Crowbar through the line. 'For once in your life can you just do what you're told?'

He had trusted this man with his life so many times. Never had he known anyone cooler under pressure. Clay could see him there now, R4 gripped in one burly hand, massive golden-haired forearms bare in the Ovamboland sun, those blue eyes shining their battle light through the dust and the smoke, striding along the line as if he were on manoeuvres, the rest of them all scared shitless, staring up at him from the bottom of their holes, the metal ripping through the air all around like arcing electricity, him urging them up – return fire lads, steady now – like some old-time Regimental Sergeant Major. If you hadn't seen it you would never have believed it, understood what courage that took, to expose yourself to that horrible mutilating reality, to see other men fall with shattered limbs and holed, jellied skulls, to will yourself into that cathedral of horrors. And Koevoet had done it repeatedly, routinely, until the men in the platoon came to look upon him as invulnerable, a talisman of sorts, immortal even, as others more careful were killed and maimed all around him.

'Look, *oom*, I'm serious.' Clay let the Afrikaans word of respect sink in. Uncle. 'If they're after me, they're after Rania, too. I need to *ontrek*.'

'Okay, Straker. Two days. Just get back to the safe house. Sit tight, *ja*. I'll set it up.'

'Air?'

'No way, *broer*. You wouldn't get past check-in. The airports are still being watched.'

'How then?'

'I'll come down to get you. Tell you then.'

'I'll set another place for dinner. We can discuss Shakespeare.'

Koevoet grunted. 'How you liking the place?'

In truth, the solitude of the little cottage had done Clay good. He missed Rania more intensely than he had ever thought possible, none of his defences, the thousand mile deserts, the numb Atlantics of disavowal, the sheer fucking *hate*, able to resist her. And after a while he'd stopped trying to fight it, started to live with it, this thing lodged inside him like some exquisitely jagged trajectile. Thus armed, each day without her became a second chance. He started drinking less, suffering at first, pushing through. He took long walks along the coast, avoiding towns and villages, covering twenty or thirty miles a day over chevron bluffs and shingle beaches, watching the gulls whirling in the breeze, the sun strobing through shot-holed cumulus onto a sheet-metal sea, getting strong again, daring to think about the future. Evenings he pushed makeshift weights, did sit-ups, chin-ups, push-ups till his muscles screamed. He practised in the shed with the silenced Glock. He read, hours by the fire, the rain washing the hours and nights away.

But that was finished. And as he ran through the night, he recalled his final words to Crowbar. 'Two days,' he'd said. 'If you don't show, I'm gone.'

Two days. A lifetime.

He'd done as Crowbar had asked. He'd gone back to the cottage, only to be met by these assassins. And now he was running for his life, half-blind through the gorse. It was raining hard, thick drops that crashed through the hedgerows and streamed from his eyes. Up ahead, a beam of light flashed across the cloud and was gone. The road was close.

He came to a gap in the hedgerow, pushed through and stepped onto a narrow lane, the tarmac sunk deep into the ground, a grass-edged rut in the landscape. He stopped and peered through the rain, looking west, but there was only the dark, water-slicked road. He turned east and started walking. He'd covered fifty metres when he saw the outline of a car tucked into a pullout on the laneside. It was facing away from him, a large saloon, wide tyres. A BMW. Clay exhaled, relief surging through him. He took the keys from his pocket and started towards the car. Plans started forming in his head, destinations, routes. He'd head south to the coast. Find a boat. Try for the continent by sea.

He was within touching distance of the car when a light flared inside the passenger compartment. Clay froze. Then the sound of a window motor, the flick of a red cigarette end. One man, alone in the driver's seat, waiting.

4

The Chasm between Now and Then

Clay stood next to the car, the ruts in the road streaming black water, the driving rain heavy in his eyes. Three miles behind him was the cottage on the cliff, which Crowbar had used as a safe house for the last five years of his tenure as chief European operative for the old DCC – South African Military Intelligence's secret Directorate of Covert Collection. And a metre away, miles from the nearest village or farm, sat this black 500 series BMW with its lone occupant.

Clay pulled the G21 from his waistband, held it close, checked the magazine. The ember of the driver's cigarette end glowed red inside the car then died. Clay approached at a walk, the Glock pointed to the ground. He didn't rush. The rain was coming harder now. He could hear the drumming of the raindrops on the car's roof, see the back of the driver's head, the green light of the dashboard clock. He tapped on the driver's side window with his stump.

The driver jumped, whipping his head towards the sound. Through the rain-washed glass, Clay could see the man's face, the eyes bulging white with surprise, the two-day stubble on his chin, mouth open in a curse. Clay signalled that he should lower the window. The man composed himself, moved his right hand to the control panel and lowered the glass about an inch. A bloom of cigarette smoke wafted out and dissolved in the rain.

Clay leaned towards the gap in the window. 'Lost, mate?'

The man shrugged, tried an ugly smile and leaned forward. There was a black handgun on the seat next to him.

In that instant, the outline of the Heckler and Koch handgun clearly imprinted on Clay's retina, the rain running cold down the back of his neck, the Glock's trigger safety coming off, a .45 slug sitting dry in its chamber, the firing pin millimetres away, Clay wished that the man was lost, that he'd simply pulled to the side of the road in his expensive car, wipers going, interior lights on, a roadmap spread over his knees, fingers tracing the web of narrow, hedgerowed ruts, that he was late getting home perhaps, was visiting a friend, a mistress even, anything but this. But there was no map. The interior of the car was dark. He wasn't lost.

They looked at each other, a blink. It took only a fraction of a second. The man knew Clay had seen the weapon. His eyes widened. Clay could see his body tensing, preparing itself for a grab at the gun. Clay pushed the muzzle of the G21 into the gap between the window glass and the frame. The man froze.

'Move and you die,' Clay said. And then in Afrikaans: '*Verstaan jy?*' Do you understand?

The man nodded once. Of course he understood.

'I don't want to kill you,' Clay said, again in Afrikaans. 'Don't give me a reason.' Please, don't give me a reason.

Another nod.

'Get out of the car.'

The man sat, unmoving.

'Do it.'

The man nodded again.

Clay was about to step back when the man jerked forward in his seat, pushing his head down towards the door. As he did, the window motor engaged and the glass started coming up. A fraction of a second later the car's engine gunned. Clay just had time to pull the Glock free and jump back as the car lurched forward. Clay fired. The bullet blew out the side window. The car swerved right, stabilised for a moment then surged away, the engine screaming. It had travelled about fifty metres along the lane when suddenly it jagged hard left and ploughed up into the hedgerow.

Clay ran to the car and peered inside. The driver was unconscious, slumped over the steering wheel. Clay scanned the laneway right and left. No one, no lights anywhere. He opened the door and dragged the man free. Then he got into the driver's seat, restarted the engine and backed the car down the lane and into the pullout. The rain had stopped now and faint moonlight shone on the wet tarmac and danced in the rivulets flowing down the gutters. Clay got out and ran back to where the man was lying, grabbed him under one shoulder and levered him up so that he could slide his stump under the other arm. As quickly as he could, he dragged the man back to the car and laid him in the grass of the verge. From here, the car would screen him from anyone who happened to drive past.

Clay dropped his pack, pulled out his torch and ran it over the man's body. He was thin, wiry, with a closely shaved head. Clay pulled away the man's jacket and tore away his shirt, exposing the wounds. There was a lot of blood. It looked as if the bullet had passed through the meat of the shoulder and then grazed the side of the neck, not deep enough to hit an artery. The *oke* had been lucky.

Using the supplies from his pack, Clay bandaged the wounds as best he could. It took valuable moments, but by the time he was done he was pretty sure he'd stopped the bleeding. If the man received proper medical attention in the next couple of hours, he'd be okay. Clay checked the man's pockets but found nothing. He stood by the car, the rain pelting his skull again, running rivulets over his face, and looked down at the man's motionless body, and he felt it come: the empty horror, the physical pain, the shaking, the buzz. His hand was trembling, his heart rate spiking, irregular. He felt the cold rain snaking down his spine, and the dark chasm between now and then, the infinity that separated one moment from the next, one living and one not.

He threw his pack onto the passenger seat, jumped behind the wheel, reached across the centre console, grabbed the H&K from the passenger-side footwell and stashed it in the glove box. It wouldn't be long before Medved's people were notified of the failure. For these *were* Medved's people, here for the reward. Of that he had no doubt. And soon they would be coming after him.

In Angola he had always been among the hunters, tracking SWAPO through the bush, chasing them across the miles, assaulting them from the air, deep inside the border. Now, he was the prey.

Clay grabbed the steering wheel, closed his eyes, concentrated on his breathing and tried to calm himself. He adjusted the seat, the mirrors, got comfortable. It was a beautiful automobile.

He was about to start towards the A38 when he saw a blinking green light under his feet. He reached down into the footwell and retrieved a mobile phone. It was open, paused in mid dial, active. Clay scrolled through the recent call numbers, but saw nothing familiar. He was about to close the phone when his thumb stopped, hung twitching on its tendons. A string of digits burned in the display, a string whose pattern he recognised. He checked the number again, read it aloud. The London 0207 prefix, the uncanny string of primes. It was the number he'd dialled from the phone box earlier that day. Crowbar's flat in Kilburn.

5

Their Glorious Youth

The BMW was fast and smooth, the roads empty.

Crowbar's words came to him in a flash: *might even take it on myself*.

Jesus Christ Almighty. Crowbar had betrayed him. He'd tried to use his own guys to collect Regina Medved's three-million-pound reward. The tip-off and the hit. Clay could not bring himself to believe it, would literally have wagered his life against it. In so many ways, he already had. But there they were, lying dead and injured in the gorse, Boers like Koevoet, bloody Natal farm boys, lately of the DCC or 32 Battalion or some such outfit, guns for hire, mercenaries, using their years of experience to fight other people's wars now that their country no longer wanted them.

Clay turned on the stereo, an expensive Blaukpunt. A CD loaded. He eased back the seat and settled in, the night air buffeting cold through the empty side window. A tinkling synthesised intro filled the car, building, mournful, that long single chord lasting and lasting in the background, and it made sense, really, that the men he had just killed would have been listening to this on the way here, anticipating perhaps the payoff and all it would bring. All of them of the same era, fighting that same race war. Now they were fighting each other. And then that haunting guitar and those four notes that always seemed to be asking him: *where are you now?* All of it always reminding him of Eben and that cheap tape deck and the *Wish You Were Here* cassette he played over and over in their tent at the Kunene River encampment, and the way Koevoet always came round and told Eben to turn it off, threatened to shoot the thing, run it over with a Buffel, give them all extra guard duty, and the way Eben always laughed and turned it right back up as soon as the old man had gone, and those long nights on standby, sitting by the fire, screaming the lyrics they were living out into the night with all the strength of their glorious youth: *caught in the crossfire, blown on the steel breeze*. Then, like now, none of it real, somehow. As he gazed through the trembling tunnel of light, the confused shadows of his memory twinned then trebled, the embers from the fire spinning skyward then blurring, *come on you target*, dissolving in the rain until they were gone and he was no longer sure that they had ever existed. He drove on through the night, sang it out at the top of his lungs until his already bruised throat ached. How I wish you were here.

The rain had intensified now and was falling in a continuous sheet. Dark hedgerows flew past, road spray hissing from the wheels and past the open window. He passed the first farmhouse, a distant light across the fen, and joined the B road for Launceston. Soon he was trundling along with the evening traffic, a light rain falling, the lights of the cars swimming across the wet pavement. He stopped at a newsagent and picked up a fifty-pound phone card, paying cash.

A few miles down the road he pulled into the carpark of a Tesco supermarket on the edge of town. The place was busy with after-work shoppers, the lot almost full. Outside the main entrance was a bank of public telephones. He searched the eaves of the building. A single CCTV camera watched the automatic doors. Another was perched atop a lamppost at the far end of the lot. Clay pulled up his hood, wandered to the opposite end of the carpark and circled back towards the phones, avoiding the cameras' eyes.

Closing the phonebox door, Clay brushed the rain from his jacket then cradled the receiver between his shoulder and ear and dialled the number. The line clicked, fuzzed and finally rang. Clay imagined the telephone on the little pinewood table next to the kitchen window, her walking from the lounge, looking out across the valley, the Dents du Midi towering in the distance, perhaps in cloud now, early snow falling at altitude. She was safe there, he told himself, veiled by a new name, a new identity, a place to live free from questions and intrusions. The ring tone pulsed for the fourth time, a fifth. Clay looked down at his boots, the rain falling across the pavement, the shoppers scurrying past with fists clenched over straining plastic.

'*Allo?*' A woman's voice. Not Rania.

'Is Rania there?'

'Who is calling, please?' A strong French accent, an older voice.

He decided to take a chance. 'It's Clay, Madame.' He doubted that they would be monitoring her calls, that the police had made any sort of connection between them, yet.

'*Monsieur Clay?*' the woman gasped.

Clay knew the voice now. It was the old lady who'd led him to Rania after the violence in Yemen. The violence that had brought him here. Madame Debret.

'She is not here, I am afraid.'

'Where is she?'

Silence. Caution. Good.

'Do you remember the Café Grand Quai in Geneva?' he said. Where he and Madame Debret had met for the first and only time.

'*Oui.*'

'You held my hand. Told me about Rania's father.'

A deep breath. 'I am worried, Monsieur Clay. I told her that she should not leave, but she insisted.'

'Where has she gone?'

'*Chypre.*'

'Cyprus?'

'Nicosia, yes. Her editor has given her this assignment. He contacted her two weeks ago. At first she did not want to go. But he was insisting very much, calling her many times.'

'LeClerc?'

'She did not say his name.'

It had to be LeClerc, the man Clay had met in London, the one who'd finally published Rania's story, the one who, in doing so, had helped to blow the casketlid off Medved's corrupt and deadly oil production activities in Yemen, helped expose the murderous cover-up entrusted to the Bulgarian mercenary, Zdravko Todorov.

Soon after publication, the Medveds had lost all financing for their Petro-Tex venture in Yemen and were forced to sell the company at a loss.

'When did she leave?' Clay asked.

'More than two weeks ago. You might see one of the stories she has written in the *journaux*.'

'Did she say when she'd be back?'

'No.'

'Have you heard from her since?'

'*Non.*'

'Forwarding address?'

'None.'

'Telephone number? Mobile?'

'I am sorry.'

'Thank you, Madame.' He was about to hang up when he heard her call out.

'Monsieur Clay, please. Wait. She left a message for you, if you called.' Noise down the line, scraping, a drawer being opened and closed. 'I have it here. She wrote it for me.'

Clay waited, said nothing.

'It says only: '*Ecoutons la confession d'un compagnon d'enfer.*''

Clay understood only one word: *enfer*. Hell.

'It is Rimbaud, I believe,' she said. 'Listen to the confession of hell's companion.'

A tumour of ice materialised in Clay's chest. He knew this, from the boy-poet's *A Season in Hell*, the chapter entitled 'The Infernal Husband'. He curled his lip, hung up the phone and stared out into the half-light of day. She'd chosen carefully, knowing he'd read this prose-poem over and over while he was in Geneva searching for her, this lament, taken by its power: *I am lost. I am impure, a slave of the infernal husband. A widow.*

Why this? Something was wrong. Clay pulled in a half breath, let it flow back out as vapour, then looked long both ways along the storefront pavement, out into the carpark, through the big front windows into the fluorescent glow of the supermarket, the patch-work of vivid primary colours, his insides roiling in a Southern Ocean gale.

☾

Shoppers raced for their cars, newspapers and umbrellas over their heads. Raindrops drummed on the stretched skins of car roofs and pelted the tarmac like bullets. Clay stared at the rain guttering down from the roof.

He picked up the phone and dialled his Cayman Islands banker. It was the first time he'd made contact since the killing. Clay gave the password and his account number.

There was an urgent message for him, the banker said. It had arrived only three days ago. Clay jotted down the name and tele-phone number. The prefix was for South Africa, the area code Johannesburg. He put down the phone, checked his watch, took a breath and dialled.

A receptionist put him straight through to the clinic's director.

'This is Declan Greene,' he said. His new identity, a recent and unintentional gift of the Yemeni secret police, complete with off-shore bank accounts, an Australian passport and an apartment in Perth, Western Australia. 'I had a message to call.'

The director paused, as if searching his memory. 'Yes, thank you for calling, Mister Greene. We were expecting to hear from you sooner.'

'I've been busy, Doctor.' Doing nothing. Waiting.

'I am very sorry to disturb you like this, but you see…' The direc-tor stopped, cleared his throat. 'There is no easy way to say this, I am afraid, Mister Greene.'

The line crackled, empty.

'Then you'd better just tell me.'

'Yes, of course. We traced you through the payment you made

to the clinic earlier this year, Mister Greene, and since there are no direct living relatives, not any more, you were the only person we could contact.'

Clay's throat tightened.

'I'm very sorry to inform you that Eben Barstow died four days ago.'

Clay's legs quivered. Eben, the best friend he'd ever had, wounded in action in Angola all those years ago, a bullet to the head. Clay had carried him to the helicopter and he had survived, if you could call it that, physically functioning but otherwise dead. How many times had he tried to convince Eben's parents to let him die? Now it was done. Relief surged through him, a decade of regret. It took him a moment to catch his breath, to fully process this information. 'Did you say no living relatives?'

'That's right.'

'What about his parents?'

'They died the same day.'

Jesus. 'The *same day*?'

'Yes. Tragic. But there is something you should know, Mister Greene. The circumstances of Mister Barstow's death, were – how can I put this – unusual.'

Just say it, for Christ's sake. So many times he had anticipated this moment, such had always seemed the inevitability of it, but now that it was here he couldn't quite believe that Eben was gone, that the tiny shard of hope he had carried with him all those years – wrapped up in a teardrop, a pearl, hidden away somewhere so secure he'd almost forgotten it was ever there – had turned out to be the folly he always knew it was.

'Mister Greene, are you there?'

'Tell me.'

'He was shot, Mister Greene.'

Clay thought he had misheard. He was hot. Died of fever.

'Someone broke into the hospital at night, went to his room, and shot him three times. Twice in the chest, and once in the head.'

Clay's blood stopped pumping. Jesus Christ.

'And whoever it was, they also broke into our records department. It seems they were after information about Eben, about our accounts.'

'What did they get?'

'Everything, I'm afraid, Mister Greene. The police said it was a very professional job. The perpetrators were in and out without being seen by any of our staff, or waking any of the other patients.'

Jesus. 'And Eben's parents?'

'They died in a car accident. As I said, a tragedy.'

Clay's mind blanked, raced. All three of them, on the same day?

'Mister Greene, are you there?'

'Yes.' No, not really.

Outside, the rain was coming down again, hammering against the thin steel of the supermarket's cantilevered roof. He pushed the receiver onto his ear.

'There is a sizeable credit on Mister Barstow's account,' came the voice, faint against the din, 'which you paid in advance, if you recall. What would you have us do with it, Mister Greene?'

Clay stood staring out at the cars and the rain coming in trembling panes. 'Are there any others?'

'Pardon me, Mister Greene? Others?'

'Any others like Eben.'

'Sorry, I don't follow.'

'Vets.' Fucked up unfortunates. The half-digested shit of a forgotten war, a failed system. Him.

'Yes, of course. There are three others.'

'Give it to whoever needs it most.'

Silence there, so far away, in a place he used to call home. And then: 'That is very generous, Mister Greene.'

Clay said nothing, waited a moment, was about to hang up, when the director's voice came again, urgent: 'Mister Greene, before you go. There is something else.'

'I'm listening.'

'You must understand. We are all very shocked here.'

Clay waited for the director to continue.

'When we found him…' The director paused, cleared his throat. 'You can imagine. It was a horrible sight.'

Yes, he could imagine. All too well. Did so on a nightly basis.

'The killer, or killers, left a message. We have no idea who it was intended for, or what it means.'

'Tell me.'

The director paused, then continued, his voice wavering. 'It was written on the wall, in Mister Barstow's blood. It said: "*She's next*".'

Clay stared down at the wet concrete, the implications of this moving through him now like a slow dose of poison. 'Are you sure, Doctor? Absolutely sure that's what it said?'

'No question at all, Mister Greene. The words were very clear, well spelled out, as if they had taken their time. They used a brush.'

'Did you say *brush*?'

'A paint brush, yes. They left it in the room.'

6

Three-Day Head Start

It was an hour short of dawn when he reached the outskirts of Falmouth on Cornwall's south coast. The first morning commuters painted the roads with sleepy headlights. Clay knew that with each minute his chances of being detected grew. He needed to get rid of the car, quit this cold, damp place. He left the motorway, turned towards the sea and worked his way along the coast road, scanning the warehouses and shops that cluttered both sides of the road, grey brick walls, fenced yards choked with machinery, chandleries, glimpses of the broad estuary opening up on his left as the sky lightened. After a few miles, the first boatyard, full of gleaming white fibreglass craft bobbing in ordered ranks within a dockwork lattice, the freshly paved parking area dotted with expensive German cars, and then, a few minutes later, another marina, well-tended and prosperous.

Clay drove on.

After a while, the buildings began to age noticeably, brickwork faded and crumbled, the first bruised Fords and rusty Hillmans appeared. Twenty minutes later he slowed and followed a narrow laneway down towards the water. At the end of the cul-de-sac was a stretch of clapboard fence about fifty metres long. The boards sagged between listing posts. Grass and weeds choked the verge. A few corroded aluminium masts poked above the fence. To the right, beyond a tangle of bare trees draped with bramble and ivy, a chain-linked equipment yard, rusty machinery, stacks of wooden shipping pallets. To the left, an old brick warehouse building, windowless, empty-looking. Clay slowed the car and approached what looked to be the entranceway to the place. The sign, hanging from a bar over the gate, looked decades old, grey, peeling lettering on a once-blue background. It read simply: *Pearson & Son. Vessels bought and sold.* It was worth a try.

Clay turned the car around and tucked it tight beside the brambles at the far end of the fence. The dashboard clock showed five fifty-eight. He turned off the engine, opened the door, stood and stretched. The air was heavy with that dead smell of the sea, of things recently expired, washed ashore. He closed the door and walked along the verge to the gate, scanning the laneway back to the coast road. There was no one about. The gate was wire link with tarpaulin stretched behind, ragged and torn. A rusty, padlocked chain held the gate closed. Clay peered through the gap between the gate and the fence post. A gravelled lot, brambles thick on all sides, an asbestos-roofed shack, a few dilapidated sail boats up on blocks, the grey fibreglass hulls of land-ridden power boats, stacks of weathered lumber, a few drums, the flat, grey estuary in the background. The whole place had that marginal, break-even look. Clay looked back down the still-deserted laneway, wedged the toe of his boot into the fence, grabbed the wire, pulled himself up and over, and landed with a smooth flex of both knees.

He looked at his watch. 06:07. The boat ramp was quiet, the haul half out of the water as if someone had forgotten to pull it out after a launch. There was no wind. Half a dozen craft dozed on buoys under a close, grey sky. Gulls cried low across the glassy estuary, wingtip perfect. Clay stood for a moment and looked out across the muddy water towards the sea.

'Buying or selling?'

Clay turned towards the voice, startled.

A man stood on the boat ramp. He was short, not much over five feet, clad in a grey wool jumper, faded, loose-fitting jeans and black lace-up boots. He was clean-shaven, the skin lined, weathered. His hair was spiked, straight-up punk, platinum. He looked Clay up and down, fixed for a fraction of a second on his stump.

'Both,' said Clay.

Punk shuffled down to where Clay was standing and stood, hands on hips, looking up into his eyes. 'Bit early for boat buying, innit?'

'Couldn't sleep.'

Punk glanced at Clay's shoulder, narrowed his eyes. 'I can see that.'

Clay raised his hand to his arm. The sleeve was wet with blood. 'Clumsy.'

Punk's mouth curled into a thin approximation of a smile. 'I'm not buying.'

'What about a trade?'

'You thinking perhaps that nice new BMW out front?'

Clay smiled. 'Could be. Depends.'

'Shame about the window.'

Clay said nothing, insides tumbling.

'What're you after?'

'Something sea-going. Sturdy.'

Punk sniffed the air, looked out across the estuary. 'If you're in a hurry to go out there,' he jutted his chin towards the sea, 'you should think again. Storm coming. You an experienced yachtsman?'

Clay pointed to a powerboat moored about fifty metres out. It looked sleek and powerful, with twin inboard-outboard engines. 'What about that one?' He had about thirty thousand pounds cash left. That was it.

'Not for sale.'

There were a couple of old-style boxwork cabin cruisers that looked as if they hadn't moved in decades, an open whaler and a compact sloop with an aluminium mast – too slow, too light and small to make the crossing. Nothing else back in the yard had looked even remotely seaworthy. Clay turned and started walking back to the car. He would have to try somewhere else.

'Where you going?' said Punk.

Clay kept walking.

'Ey there, guv, what you want for the car?' Punk called after him.

Clay stopped, looked down at his boots, at the oiled gravel of the boat ramp.

'Don't worry,' Punk continued. 'I can clean it. I have friends.'

'I'm happy for you.' All mine are dead or in deep shit. Clay stood, not looking back. He had a decision to make. And he had to make it now. Trust the guy, or leave. Problem was, he was running out of time. Time and options.

Punk was alongside him now. 'Let me show you something,' he said. 'Come with me.'

Punk led him to a steel door in the warehouse wall, through a darkened loading bay and out through another door. He walked slowly, deliberately, with a pronounced limp, as if one leg was shorter than the other. They were on a raised wharf, looking out over the water.

Punk pointed to a boat swinging on a mooring about a hundred metres out. 'She's old, but sturdy,' he said. 'France?'

'No.'

Punk nodded. 'Good. France is too obvious.'

Clay glanced at the guy, looked away.

'Full set of sails, working diesel engine, charts, even food on board. I never manage to get out in her anymore. My life's story.'

A crossing to Normandy by sail would take three days. Punk was right. France was too easy. Medved, the cops, Crowbar's mercenary friends, they would all be watching. 'Straight swap,' said Clay.

Punk took in a short breath and laughed. 'You'll have to do better than that. My friends are good, but they take a big premium.'

'I can give you ten grand more. Cash.'

Punk turned away and started back to the building. 'Make it twenty.'

Clay considered this. He didn't have much choice. 'Done,' he said.

'I'll unlock the gate. Bring it in quick. We can get to work cleaning that blood from the front seat.'

Clay's heart lurched, hung up an instant, restarted. He stared down at the crumbling concrete of the disused wharf. Without looking up he said, 'Once I'm gone, give me a three-day head start. I don't care what you do after that.'

7

A Hundred Hours

They moved the BMW inside the compound and hid it behind one of the wrecked cabin cruisers at the back of the yard. Cleaning out the car didn't take long. Punk had done this before. Afterwards, he led Clay to a small, brick cottage nestled in a riot of elm and brambles behind the corrugated asbestos office building. The rain was falling now, thick sheets of it, winter oblique, cold. Punk stamped the wet from his clothes, slicked up his hair and closed the door behind Clay. Inside it was warm and dry. A coal fire burned in an open hearth. The walls of the small lounge were covered in guitars, polished wood acoustics, electrics of every shape and colour, even an old banjo.

Punk looked up at Clay. 'You play?'

Clay raised his hand, his stump. 'I listen.'

Punk frowned, reached down and hiked up his right trouser leg almost to the knee, revealing a polished metal prosthetic, structure only, jammed into a boot. 'I watch football.'

Clay smiled.

'You should get yourself one, amazing what they're doing with titanium these days.' Punk dropped his trouser leg.

'I prefer the natural look.'

Punk grinned, huffed something Clay couldn't make out, and led him to a small kitchen. 'Have a seat.'

Clay sat on the only chair. Punk put the kettle on and stepped back out into the lounge. Clay looked out of the kitchen window across the rain-swept estuary and heard the click-click dialling of an old rotary phone, Punk's voice.

When Punk returned, the kettle was whistling on the stove.

'My friends will be here by ten,' Punk said, handing Clay a steaming mug of tea. 'They'll have that thing dismantled and on its way to Russia before tomorrow morning. When they put it back together, it'll be a brand-new car. Impossible to trace. Incredible what these blokes can do.'

Clay looked at his watch. If Punk had called the cops, they'd be here in five minutes, less. There was still time to get out. But where to? He looked at Punk, watched him fussing over the stove, decided to trust this man. He didn't have much choice.

It was just gone seven in the morning, nine in Cyprus.

'When can I get out to the boat, check her out?' This was all going to take a lot longer than Clay had hoped.

'How about some breakfast?' Punk pulled off his sweater to reveal a still-muscled torso clad in a frayed singlet that looked like it hadn't been washed in years. His arms were heavily tattooed; a thick gold chain hung from his neck.

Clay nodded. He hadn't eaten since the previous afternoon. 'Mind if I use your phone? I can pay.'

Punk swung a cast-iron frying pan from a hook on the wall and pointed to the front door. 'Phone box on the main road, towards town.'

Clay stood, slung his pack. 'I'll be back in a bit.'

'Breakfast in twenty minutes. You like eggs?'

'Hundreds,' said Clay, starting to like this old guy. 'See you in twenty.'

Outside, the lane was still quiet. Clay started walking towards the main road, a red-and-white blur of streaming lights about half a kilometre distant. About two hundred metres along, a clutch of ragged hawthorn and wild-sown elms sprouted like adolescent fuzz from the side of the warehouse. He stopped alongside the copse, looked back along the lane to Punk's yard, a part of him expecting Punk to be standing there, watching him, but the lane was empty. Clay pushed through the rain-bent branches and pressed himself into the angle of one of the brickwork buttresses that ran like whale ribs along the building's Victorian wall. Protected against the rain, hidden from the road, he waited.

It was going to take him at least six days, more like ten, to reach Rania. Nicosia, two weeks ago – that's all Madame Debret had said. Clay knew the place well, had lived there for almost three years, would still have had an apartment and a business there if he hadn't died, been resurrected as Declan Greene, been forced to leave that life behind. There were only three or four decent hotels in the city. He had to try.

Fifteen minutes later, satisfied that Punk hadn't called the cops, Clay pulled his hood around his face, left his hiding place and walked to the intersection. The rain was coming down harder now, slowing the traffic. He stood on the pavement with the cars flying by, peered through the road spray, and scanned the road for the phone box. Nothing. He started walking towards town. This was the last place he wanted to be, in full view of a steady train of eyes, soaked to the skin already, conspicuous. Then he saw it though the traffic, across the road, about a hundred metres away, an old red phone box. He put his head down and trudged along the pavement, checking over his shoulder for a gap in the traffic. After a sprint he was across, into the dry cocoon of the phonebox. He pushed in the phone card and dialled, looking out at the river of cars.

The phone clicked and a female voice answered. His Cyprus accountant's secretary. He'd known her for years, a sweet old woman with a pure heart. Clay disguised his voice, brought it up half an octave and tried to put on a neutral English accent. Within a few minutes she had read out the phone numbers of the four Nicosia hotels he'd asked for. He jotted down the numbers in his notebook, thanking her in Greek. The traffic had slowed. Clay watched the cars, the people staring ahead through streaked windscreens and flailing wiper blades. He was about to dial the first number, the Holiday Inn near the Green Line, when something he saw made him stop. By the time it registered, the car was past, gone in the rain. It had been more than a glimpse, a good two

or three seconds, more than enough to be sure. The Afrikaner from
the cottage, the pale-eyed Boer who'd knifed him then escaped, disappeared at the cliff edge. In the passenger seat of a big Mercedes.

Clay thought back, brought up the image. Profile only, the square
jaw, the big Dutch forehead, the swollen nose. He was sure he
hadn't been seen, but Jesus Christ, how had they caught up to him
so quickly? Was Koevoet guiding them? It had to be that. He still
couldn't believe it, fought against it, this betrayal. But it was Koevoet
who had told him not to fly. On the long drive to Cornwall two
months ago they had spoken of getting out by sea. Falmouth had
been the obvious choice. Damn it. They were here, and they were
looking for the Beemer, looking for him.

Clay took a deep breath, punched in the next number and enquired
after a registered guest, name Lise Moulinbecq. No such person. Again,
the Intercontinental this time. No luck. He was down to less than ten
pounds on the card now. Rain pounded like fists on the phone box.
Cars swept by. He tried the Hilton. Hiss, click. Wait. Lise Moulinbecq? One minute please, Sir. Money flowing, numbers flickering, a
countdown. Connecting you now, Sir. Adrenaline surge. A big one.

The phone system churned through to her room. Nine-thirty
there, no way she was still in this late. He let it ring, imagined the
device pealing on her bedside table, the bed perhaps still unmade,
the cast of her body pressed into the mattress, her smell in the weave
of the sheets, the down of the pillow, that finely evolved chemistry.

'*Allo?*' She was out of breath, as if she'd just burst into the room.
It sounded like sun, like warmth.

'Hello, beautiful.' He felt dizzy.

The line was silent for a moment. He could hear her breathing,
imagined the rise and fall of her chest, the delicate whisper of her lips
near the mouthpiece.

'Claymore? Is that you?'

'I don't have long, Rania. Please listen.'

It always seemed to be this way with them. Never enough time:
a precious few days in the chalet in the Alps, both of them broken,

needing the other's strength; and before that, in Yemen, caught up in a spiral of death and vengeance, just those two nights before they'd been torn apart, flung in different directions. One dark evening alone on the Cornish coast he'd calculated that they'd spent no more than a hundred hours together, ever. Nothing. Not enough to feel like this, heart racing at the sound her voice, the thought of her touch. But it was fear now that coursed through him, thick and heavy, a cholera of doubt.

'You have to get out of there, Rania,' he said. 'Now. Leave Cyprus, go back to the chalet and keep quiet, out of sight.'

He could hear her taking this in, thinking about it.

'Rania?'

Nothing.

'Rania, please. We don't have long.'

'I have not heard a word from you in nine weeks,' she said. Her tone was strained. She was crying.

Clay steadied himself. 'Do you understand what I'm saying, Rania?'

'Was it you, Claymore? Did you kill Rex Medved?' Her sexy Algerian French accent was tainted with fear.

'We don't have time for this now. Listen to me, please.'

'No time? After two months not knowing if you are alive or dead, you tell me that you do not have time? Answer me, Claymore. I want to know.'

Clay watched the time running away. Where did it go, he wondered, drifting again. He fought back to now.

'Yes,' he said.

She didn't reply. It sounded like she was holding her breath.

'They've found me. Tracked me down. Medved's people.'

She gasped.

'They know who I am, Rania. They know who you are, too. You're in danger. I want you to get out now. Go home. I'll be there soon. Then we can disappear. Together. Go to Africa like we planned.' He still had the tickets to Cape Town in his pocket.

'Do *not* tell me what to do, Claymore.' Her tone was stern, a cleric's. Time disappeared. 'Look, I'm sorry, Rania. Just go home, please.'

A pause, seconds vanishing, and then, her voice breathless, 'Things have changed, Claymore. What we talked about in London, what we did, it was … it was premature.'

Clay said nothing, waited, sank.

'I have work to do here. I know you want to go back to Africa. Go, Claymore. Do whatever you have to do. Make peace with yourself.'

Her words ripped through him like hot shrapnel. He stood staring at the raindrops tracking across the phone-box glass, blind sperm flicking their tails in a futile journey to barren ground. All his dreams lay massacred on the wet concrete floor. The line was open. He could feel her there on the other end, hear her breathing.

'Please, Rania,' he choked, overcome. 'You're in danger.'

'No one is after *me*, Claymore–'

He interrupted her, spoke over her. 'They wrote it in blood. On Eben's hospital room wall after they killed him: *She's next.*'

But she wasn't listening, just kept talking back at him. 'There is something happening … Something big … sinister … getting close. I … a few more days.' Their words collided across the line, leaving a wreckage of shattered vowels, amputated syllables.

'A few relics aren't worth dying for, Rania.'

Silence.

'I'm serious.'

'So am I. This goes a lot deeper than religious artefacts. It is theft on a massive scale, cultural genocide. Extinction.'

'Jesus Christ, Rania. Even more reason to get out. Pass it over to the authorities.'

'I cannot, Claymore.'

Money clicked away in the display. They didn't have long, seconds. 'Why the hell not?'

'I think the authorities are involved.'

Clay swallowed hard. They were almost out of time. 'I'll be at the chalet in ten days, maybe less. Meet me there.'

'No, Claymore.'

'Okay,' he snapped. 'Just promise me you'll get out.'

'I will return when I am finished here.'

'How long?'

'I do not know. A week perhaps. Maybe longer.'

'For God's sake, Rania, please.'

Less than a pound left, the last few pence draining away.

'Clay…' she stumbled, broke off. He could hear her crying. 'You broke…'

The line went dead. The phone card had expired.

Clay smashed down the receiver handle, stood shaking, staring into the winter sea of the phone's toll screen as if the time could somehow be recaptured, credited to his account, reversed. So much more he needed to say.

After a while he stopped staring at the phone, opened the door and stepped out into the rain. Five minutes later he was back at Punk's place. The BMW was still where they'd parked it, awaiting its imminent dismantlement and resurrection. He knocked on the door and stepped inside without being asked. The smell of frying bacon and hot toast filled the place. Despite everything, his stomach started working, anticipating.

Punk peered out from the kitchen, a floral-print apron slung over his neck, a spatula in one hand, an H&K nine millimetre parabellum in the other. 'Make the call you wanted?' he said.

Clay stopped, staring at the handgun.

'Found it in the glove box,' said Punk. 'Yours?'

'Keep it,' said Clay.

Punk put down the spatula, worked the handgun's action, slid out the magazine, ejected the round from the chamber and put it all on the table.

'No thanks,' he said, putting a plate in front of Clay. Fried eggs, bacon, tomato, fried onions, two thick slabs of dark toast, dripping butter.

Clay devoured the breakfast, for those few minutes concentrating only on the food, on the slaking of his hunger. It had been the same in the bush, even during the worst days: opening the rations, forgetting everything, the blood, the fear, the danger. An animal fulfilling its basest instinct. Survival. He ate quickly, methodically. Did not look up. Did not speak. Ignored the weapon there beside him.

When Clay had finished, Punk tossed something onto the table. It rattled to a stop next to Clay's plate. Metallic, about the size of a pack of smokes.

Clay looked up at Punk, questioning.

'Found it in the Beemer. A custom extra.'

Clay turned it over, examining it.

'It's a transmitter,' said Punk. 'Don't worry, I've disabled it.'

'Shit.'

'They're here, aren't they?'

Clay nodded. Punk must have killed the signal just before the Boer drove past.

'How long do you have?' Punk leaned against the table.

'Not long.'

'Let's get you on your way then, Guv. The tide's right.'

Clay stood, looked Punk in the eyes. 'If they come, tell them I forced you.'

Punk smiled, waved his hand. 'Don't worry about me, mate. I can look after myself.'

Clay was sure he could.

8

Candaules' Queen

Punk rowed him out to the boat. The wind was coming in strong now, furrowing the estuary, pushing the muddy water into a criss-cross of brown chop. The little dory's bow flung up spray as Punk leant into his strokes, head to wind. From a distance, the yacht looked settled and sturdy, unworried in the rising wind, a streaming wake emerging from her stern and swirling out across the rippling surface. Low clouds scuttled in from the west, heavy with moisture, an Atlantic distillation, one part water, three parts pure energy, dew point and latent heat ready to collide in the dark boiling hammer-heads massing on the horizon.

'Wait till the storm blows through,' said Punk between clenched teeth, straining at the oars. 'You'd be a nutter to go out in this, unfamiliar boat and all.'

Clay looked past him, out towards the ketch and the headlands to the battlefield of the horizon. 'If you had a chance to go back and do it over, would you?'

Punk looked him in the eyes, slowed for a moment, then dug the oars in and pulled hard. 'Not a day I don't think about it,' he said between clenched teeth. 'Not a day.'

Clay nodded, realising that he would never see this man again, never call him friend, never hear the stories of his life, the choices, the history, the losses and victories. Such isolation. We're not islands, he thought. We're fucking comets, hurtling through space, trailing the fiery plasma of our own destruction, at the mercy of our own fearful wanderings, ephemeral homeless visitors. And there, moving closer, was the vehicle of his peregrination. Saint Exupéry had it right, disappearing in his P38 over the Med, burning up in his own fiery chunk of the cosmos.

'She's called *Flame*,' said Punk as they drew alongside. 'Named her after Negley Farson's boat. Heard of him?'

Clay shook his head, no.

'*The Way of a Transgressor*. Great book. You'd like it. There's a copy on board, I think.'

Clay grabbed the toe rail, pulled them close. Her hull was wood; the decking, cabin, cockpit, all made of gleaming, cared-for teak.

'She was built in Bombay in 1965,' said Punk. 'The hull is one-and-a-quarter-inch planking all around, two-by-three-inch frames every fourteen inches. All teak. You could run a Centurion tank over her, wouldn't bother her in the slightest. Ever sailed a ketch?'

Clay shook his head. His sailing experience had come as a boy, summers off Durban with his mother's brother, a keen ocean racer. He'd crewed several races, learned a lot. On his last leave before jump school he had raced from Durban to Cape Town with his uncle. That was the last time he'd sailed.

'The mizzen is a treat, once you know how to use it, especially in rough weather. Experiment with it, you'll figure it out.'

Clay tied off the dinghy's bow line and climbed aboard. The cockpit was small, functional. The decking gleamed in the flat light, the fittings looked as if they had been polished only hours ago. This boat was loved, adored.

Punk hoisted himself aboard, swung his leg over the lifeline, whispering something to himself, or was it to this object of his affection? A lover's greeting, an invocation. Punk unlocked the main hatch, slid open the gangway cover and ushered Clay below.

It was like stepping inside a museum, a shrine to nautical tradition. Oiled teak, brass Clay could see himself in, his face warped and disfigured, copper. Heavy brass instruments adorned the bulkhead panelling, a ship's chronometer running to time, a thermometer, an elegant barometer that read one thousand and one millibars. Books lined both sides of the cabin behind teak rails. A fully equipped galley, navigation station with new electronics. It was all here.

Clay stood for a moment and listened to the water rippling against the hull, surrounding him, amniotic. He felt like an intruder, being shown things he should not see, Gyges hiding in the shadows, watching Candaules' queen undressing, the thin silk of her dress falling across her breasts and over her round hips, pillowing to the floor, Punk the proud, soon-to-be-murdered king. A shiver ran through him, cold like the October wind moaning outside.

'This was going to be my escape,' said Punk. 'Estelle and me. Get out, go live in the Greek islands. Never worked out that way.' He pulled open the engine compartment, revealing a beautifully maintained diesel engine. 'There's a full tank of fuel, a hundred gallons of fresh water in two tanks, fore and aft, plenty of food, as long as you don't mind baked beans and sardines.'

Clay smiled. 'I can't take her,' he said.

Punk turned, stood there with the foam-insulated engine panel in his hands. 'I'm not coming down from twenty,' he said. 'The deal's struck.'

'It's not the money, *broer*. You got anything else?'

Punk looked out the starboard porthole at the building weather. 'Nothing that's going to survive what's coming. If you're set on going, this is the best you can do. Believe me.'

Clay could see what the boat meant to this old guy, the love he'd poured into her, the years of faithful care, the hoped for adventures.

'Look, guv,' said Punk, 'my friends are going to be here soon. It's all in motion now, as we used to say back in the day. Nothing for it now but to push on.'

He was ex-army, Clay was sure now. Maybe a para like him. He wasn't going to ask, just like Punk wasn't going to tell.

Punk produced a set of keys, flicked them by like pages in an unwritten book. Engine ignition, padlocks for the hatch cover, starboard cockpit locker, safe under the port saloon locker. Clay took the keys and pocketed them. Sails forward, full complement, labelled.

Extra sheets and warps in the starboard cockpit locker. Self-steering gear. Tool kit, emergency tiller, planking for repairs in the forward port-side locker. Full set of charts in the nav station, Baltic to the Med, radio, lights, transponder.

'No GPS, mind,' said Punk. 'I'm a bit of a purist that way. How's your celestial navigation?'

'Rusty. Sextant on board?'

'Included in the price. That's about all.' Punk looked at Clay and held out his hand. They shook. Clay counted out the cash.

'Oh, and one more thing,' said Punk, shoving the wad of bills into his trouser pocket. He crouched down, reaching up and under the nav table. A teak panel swung open. 'Priest hole.'

Clay peered inside. It was about the size of a kitchen freezer.

'Me mate's a master cabinet maker,' said Punk, arms crossed, smiling with pride. 'Join work is perfect. Completely invisible once it's closed up. There's an air vent to the outside, even a foam base for your arse.' He looked Clay down and up. 'Might be a little tight for you, mind. But you never know, do you?

Clay smiled. 'You never do, *broer*.'

Punk reached into the compartment, withdrew a polished wooden instrument and closed the door. He stood for a moment looking down at the thing, a miniature guitar. He looked up at Clay and handed him the ukulele. 'Nights can get long,' he said with an oblique scowl, half grin, half frown. 'Especially single-handed.'

'I'm getting used to it.'

Punk grinned wide, pushed the ukulele into Clay's hand. Like the rest of this place, the instrument gleamed as if it had been freshly, lovingly polished.

'Play left-handed,' Punk said. 'Strum with your stump.'

Clay looked into Punk's eyes and smiled.

'Rhodesia?' Punk said.

Clay shook his head.

'When'd you leave South Africa?'

'Eighty-three.'

Punk nodded, turned and climbed the companionway steps. Clay followed him up to the cockpit. Above decks, the wind had risen. Waves thudded against the hull. The rigging sang. A few drops of rain spattered the deck, dotted the murky water.

'Look after her for me,' Punk said with a catch in his voice as he clambered down into the dinghy. 'She needs to get out, do what she was made for.' He untied the line and started back to shore.

Clay stood a moment and watched Punk row for shore. He considered calling out, something about bringing *Flame* back to him, when this was all done, then thought better of it and turned away.

He jumped below, found the small jib bag and pushed it up through the forward hatch onto the foredeck. In a few minutes he had the foresail hanked on and ready to go, the sheets made good and lined back to the cockpit. He pulled off the main cover, attached the halyard, checked the main winch and made ready the unfamiliar mizzen. The engine started first go, that comforting diesel rattle, not fast, but could go all day. He walked forward, looking back towards Punk's yard, the chimney of the cottage trailing a wisp of smoke, and let go the mooring buoy.

Soon *Flame* was motoring seaward, the estuary opening up broad and flat on both sides, the breakwater passing astern now, the breeze fresh in his face, the heads at Penlee looming to starboard, Haybrook bay to the east. The wind was strong but steady, eighteen knots by the anemometer, gusting twenty-five he guessed, the swell coming in strong now, *Flame*'s bow ploughing through the waves, the big, full keel steady and heavy, all that steel ballast holding her centre straight like a compass, a conviction.

Clear of land now, Lizard Head off distant to the west, the Spanish coast somewhere over the horizon, through the black clouds and the grey sea, five hundred nautical miles distant. If he pushed, with a bit of luck and a following wind, he could be in Santander in four days.

And somewhere out there, another thousand miles away again, across yet more sea, mountains, coastlines and frontiers, Rania.

❲

By noon, *Flame* was foaming along at ten knots under foresail, reefed mainsail and mizzen in a force four westerly. Clay made west as hard as he could, knowing that, in the northern hemisphere, the wind would back as the storm moved south. He was making good time. The weather had closed in, the clouds close and heavy, visibility still reasonable. Just after one, a small freighter appeared then tracked away off to the north, heading for the coast. He had long since lost sight of land.

Trimmed up, the wheel lashed, *Flame* heeling nicely, he moved around the cabin, stowing his few things in the priesthole – the money, the guns and ammunition, all sealed in plastic inside a duffel bag – exploring the food stores, laying out the charts, plotting a dead reckoning position he had taken half an hour earlier. He opened a can of baked beans and ate it cold sitting in the cockpit.

He was estimating distance made good, *Flame* foaming along, close-hauled in a rising wind, stays and sheets strumming like guitar strings, when a pounding chop cut through the symphony. His body tensed, reflexed, knew what it was before his brain had time to compute, and he was back in Ovamboland, the Alouettes roaring in above the treetops, door guns blazing, the whump of the blades detonating in his chest, the white dust spinning all around, blinding, leaves and branches swirling in the storm, the atmosphere jumping with electricity, lead and steel ripping through the air, tearing at its very fabric, shearing the molecules he breathed. The noise was getting louder. At first he thought it was another of his hallucinations, another post-traumatic spell to ride out. He grabbed the gangway-hatch guide plate, steadied himself. The metal strip fixed into the teak decking was vibrating, the frequency matching the pounding beat. It was real.

He clambered into the cockpit and searched the clouds. And then it was there, right above him, fifty metres above the masthead, no more, in a gap in the clouds. A Bell Jet Ranger, hovering tail up, jerking in the scuttling cloud like a hornet in a wildfire.

9

The Difference between Living and Dying

The helicopter hung in mid-air for an instant, the pilots fish-bowled inside their Perspex bubble, headphones over their ears, working the pedals, the stick, struggling with the rising wind, peering down at him through the rip in the cloud. The machine pitched and yawed, battered by the gusts, the turbine screaming. As the tail swung around, Clay glimpsed the civilian registration markings, the blue stripes on the fuselage. The clouds were closing in, racing across the sky like crazed greyhounds. He could see the pilots' mouths working behind the headset microphones as they fought to keep the little sailboat in view, the gap in the cloud narrowing. They were right above him now, staring down at him. The pilot had dark hair, a dark moustache, green-tinted Raybans. The man beside him was bulkier, fleshy, pink-faced. Clay could see the perspiration shining on his forehead, a wisp of platinum hair jutting out from under the headset strap. Their eyes met. It was Crowbar.

Clay held his old platoon commander's gaze for an instant, he there on the pitching deck, the other no more than thirty metres above, swirling in the gale, dancers parting on a crowded floor. Then he raised his hand, made a gun, flicked his thumb. Son of a bitch, he mouthed. I trusted you. Loved you even, as a boy loves an older brother, a father.

Before Crowbar could react, Clay wrenched the wheel hard to port, falling off with the wind. *Flame* responded instantly, the sails driving the hull through the water. The compass spun as *Flame* went from close-hauled to broad reach in a matter of seconds. Clay opened up the main, let *Flame* flatten out, then eased the jib and mizzen, cleated the sheets and felt the surge of speed as she ran with the wind and the sea. He looked up over his shoulder just as the clouds closed, swallowing the helicopter. In a matter of seconds the dull concussion of rotor blades faded and was gone, leaving only the blood echo of empty, pounding loss.

With *Flame* trimmed up in a searing broad reach, Clay noted time and heading and went below. He sat at the nav station, the chart spread before him, the dead-reckoning track jerking across the paper, bearings, times, estimated distances. Current position was about forty-five nautical miles south of Falmouth, give or take. With any luck, Koevoet had seen his course change and would be projecting a direct downwind run across the Channel to Normandy. He had to assume that they were calling in his position right now, that a chase boat would soon be on its way. That gave him a couple of hours at most. There was no way to outrun them. The storm was his only ally.

Clay tuned the radio, dialling in the continuous marine weather report. It didn't take long to get the news: severe gale warning, deepening depression tracking south and east across the Channel towards the Bay of Biscay, a secondary low developing over Ushant, the westernmost part of France, expected winds force five gusting to six or seven, seas four to six metres. Jesus. He'd never been in anything like this before. But there was no question of running for shelter. As Punk had said, it was all in motion now. He would head straight for the storm, lose himself in the heart of the depression, dare the bastards to follow him in. Clay looked at the chart, up at the barometer. Nine hundred and ninety-two, a fall of nine millibars in three hours. It was coming, fast and furious, and he was riding its whip edge. Time to dive in. Just try to catch me.

Clay set about preparing. He found the kettle, half-filled it with water, fired up the stove and clamped the kettle down tight on the burner. The stove swung on its gimbals, the kettle perfectly happy despite *Flame*'s corkscrewing shimmy. He broke out a tin of beans, dumped them into a saucepan on the second burner then opened a can of sardines and dropped two of the salty darts into his mouth. He drank a litre of water, the taste clean aluminium. With the food warming, he went forward and rummaged in the wet locker. Punk's heavy-weather gear was two sizes too small. Clay found an old wool sweater and pulled it over his head, tore the cuffs of the oilskin jacket up to the elbows along the seam and stuffed himself into it. He was too broad. It wouldn't close across the chest. He found a pair of fingerless wool gloves, pulled on the right one, threw the left back into the locker and donned a black wool skullcap. It wasn't going to keep him dry, but it was the best he could do. It would get cold in there.

Soon the beans were steaming. He gulped them down straight from the pan with the rest of the sardines, poured the hot water into a steel thermos and sanded in a handful of instant coffee and a slug of sugar. He stowed the pot and kettle, stuffed a handful of muesli bars into his jacket pocket, wedged the ukulele tight between the settee cushions and climbed above deck.

Coming out of the warmth and relative peace of the cabin into the fury of the rising storm was like waking up to a firefight, an awakening as rude as birth. His stomach lurching, more from fear than the increasingly violent motion, Clay stashed the thermos in the small aft locker, checked the compass, his watch, and looked up at the rigging, the too-dark sky close, boiling. He had too much sail up.

It took him the best part of half an hour to put another reef in the main, shorten the mizzen, hank on and raise the storm jib, everything so much more difficult with just four fingers and one thumb. Then he brought *Flame*'s bow reluctantly to wind and set course for Ushant and the dark eye of the storm.

☾

As the depression tracked south and east, the wind backed, pushing *Flame* along in rising seas. Night fell, cold and brutal. By 21.00 the barometer had fallen another seven millibars. Clay estimated the winds at force five, howling through the taut rigging like wounded

jackals. By 22.30 he had to douse the main, fighting with the flapping canvas as *Flame* pitched and yawed in a universe that seemed
to have no end and no beginning. Punk was right. She was a strong
little boat, this thirty-two feet of teak and brass, surfing the frothing
wavetops, grinding through the black troughs.

Just after midnight he caught a glimpse of lights somewhere off
his starboard bow, a freighter perhaps, steaming south. He watched
it a moment, imagining the well-lit bridge, warm and dry inside,
the comforting rumble of the big engines underfoot, and then it
was gone. Under storm jib and mizzen trysail, *Flame* hurtled into
the depression. With the glass at 993 and falling, Clay closed up the
hatch, took the wheel and tied himself into the cockpit.

By 0300 hours, the last of the coffee gone, *Flame* was reaching
in heavy quartering seas. Clay's arms and shoulders ached with the
continuous effort of keeping *Flame* on some sort of course. The wind
seemed to have stabilised at something like force five, a deafening,
almost human cry. Even under shortened sail, they were making ten
knots, maybe more. With only the dull phosphorescent glow of the
compass to guide them, they rode the contours of the storm. Clay
peered out into the darkness. Somewhere out there was the eye, the
dark centre of the depression. Fear came hard. Koevoet's people were
out there. Clay had accepted that now, the wound of betrayal, the
death of friendship. The company, Crowbar had called it, guns for
hire. Just business. But this was a new kind of fear, sharper, more
discriminating, seeping from deep within his cortex, Neolithic,
ungovernable. And he knew that it was not like anything he had
ever felt before. Fuck Koevoet. And fuck Medved – the bastard had
deserved it. No, it wasn't any of that. And it wasn't the storm, this
uncaring thing he was offering himself to. Nor was it death itself, or
even the manner of dying, or the totality of all of this, the aggregated
power swirling all around him, the pure indifference of it. It was
something else. And as he wrestled with the tiller, his shoulders and
arms burning with the effort, the icy wind tearing into the core of
him, he knew. It was *her*. The impossible vulnerability of her. The

power. God, just don't think about it, he said to himself. Focus on this wave, this wall of black water, just get it behind you. Get there. Get to her first.

He pushed the little boat on through the night, skidding and pounding through the chaos, riding the isobar as it spun towards the continent. With each wave, *Flame*'s bow pitched high until Clay was staring up into the swirling cloud. A star winked and was gone. Time stopped, hung there a moment, cresting a mountain, the bare mast just visible against the cloud. And up there, on the top of the world, songs came in the wind, screaming ballads. He could see Rania's face, her mouth open wide so he could see her teeth and the black emptiness at the back of her throat, her midnight hair a hurricane about her head, and the rhythm of it was hard and adrenaline-fast, like a frightened heart, and she was sitting there cross-legged like a schoolgirl on the cabin roof, singing to him, a dirge all her own, the notes ragged and torn so that he could make out neither melody nor lyrics. He blinked the rain from his eyes, closed them hard. Go away, please, he said out loud. Not now. And then he felt it in his feet, his guts, the start of the fall, and down he went, eyes wide, nothing before him but the deep brine, pulling him in. And on that long ride down it was as if he could see into the cold depth of it, below that mean, slicked surface, down to the calm currents and the big, ancient bottom fishes, the sea-floor vents, the mud of aeons lying quiet and thick and so heavy. And then the shuddering impact and they were under, the bow buried. A cold sheet of brine knocked him to the cockpit floor, burying him. Water swirled all around. He reached for the wheel, pulled himself up spluttering and coughing, the salt burning in his mouth, the little ketch shedding water in thick streams as she struggled back out of the wave and began her climb up the next.

Together they fought. She tough and responsive to his commands, he fighting to protect her from the full fury of the waves as best he could, urging her on, the storm sails powering her through the maelstrom even as conditions worsened.

As he tired, his mind wandered. Crowbar had said the hit had been on for a week. That's the way he'd said it, as if they already knew the target. The doctor said Eben had been killed four days ago – five now. By examining the clinic's files, the assassins had deduced that Eben's benefactor, Declan Greene, was in fact his friend and brother parabat, lately of 1 Parachute Battalion, South African Defence Force, Claymore Straker. His cover was blown. Regina Medved had known this for five days. But only Crowbar knew that Clay was her brother's killer – he'd been there with him, watched him pull the trigger. All the other witnesses were dead. And only Crowbar knew he had been hiding in the cottage. Only Crowbar had all the pieces, and those had surely been his guys come for the hit. So why the attack on the clinic, the cryptic message in blood? Crowbar hadn't needed that information, could have provided Regina Medved with everything she needed without ever mentioning Eben. It only made sense if Crowbar had betrayed him for more than just money. The whole thing in the clinic reeked of spite, revenge. Koevoet was a lot of things – arrogant, contemptuous of weakness, hard-headed, auto-cratic – but until a day ago he had been Clay's definition of honour. Money was one thing, but revenge?

Before Medved's killing, Clay had decided to go back to South Africa and testify to Mandela's soon to be established post-apartheid Truth and Reconciliation Commission. He'd told this to Koevoet, who'd accused him of disloyalty, threatened to terminate their friend-ship. Clay had sworn, along with the others, never to reveal what had happened that day in Angola, the day Kingfisher was killed. Even during the inquest he'd kept quiet, stuck to the story they'd all agreed. Could Crowbar really have decided to betray Clay to prevent him from testifying? Eben had been there too, that fateful day in Angola, had been one of the actors in that unspeakable tragedy that still haunted Clay's days and turned his nights into ultramarathons of regret. Was that why Eben had been killed? Eben had been in a coma for ten years, more. He could no more talk about what had happened that day than he could walk out of the clinic.

And so, why the delay? It had been at least four days between Eben's murder and the appearance of Koevoet's mercs at the cottage that night. Maybe it wasn't Koevoet at all. Maybe it was the PSO, the Yemeni Secret Service. The CIA. Maybe the two events – the attempted hit at the cottage and Eben's murder – were unconnected. Clay shook his head, opened his eyes wide to the wind. Jesus, he was losing it, wasting his energy on an insoluble problem. A problem with too many variables and not enough equations.

Fatigue swept through him, pushing his mind over false peaks, into blind troughs. And as he hurtled through the night, the fears and possibilities merged into a single density, churned by the storm, components irretrievable.

A dull dawn came, revealing towering seas whipped with wands of foam, evil spells of grey cloud. Clay shivered in Punk's ill-fitting jumper and jacket. He was weak from hunger. Sleep beckoned, whispered to him, tugged at his eyes, luring him to the warmth of her bed. He scorned her, pushed on through the storm. Mid-afternoon the rain relented. Shortly after, the wind dropped a little. It was barely perceptible, perhaps only a knot or two, but he could feel it on his face, hear the change in the rigging. A lull. Clay took the opportunity. He brought *Flame* head to wind, backed the storm jib, lashed the wheel and with *Flame* hove to, went below. The little boat tracked into the wind and then fell off, lashed rudder and backed jib nudging her back and forth in a slow, nodding dance that kept her bow into weather but slowed her to no more than a knot. The cabin pitched like a rollercoaster. Bracing himself against the aft bulkhead, Clay ate a tin of cold beans, thought about trying to heat water for coffee but abandoned the idea. He plotted a dead-reckoning position, a best guess, assuming a relatively constant course of SSW at about ten knots for the best part of twelve hours. It put *Flame* about fifty nautical miles north and west of Ushant, a place of deadly reefs and fickle weather. Beyond, the Bay of Biscay, notorious for its winter storms and big seas. The barometer had continued to fall, sat now at 987. The full power of the storm was still a few hours away.

Clay crabbed his way forward, lay on the main berth and pulled the blanket around his shoulders. He hadn't slept for two days. He closed his eyes. To the furious cry of the sea, he let sleep come. He'd learned that in the war. Sleep whenever and wherever you can. Days of this to go. It could make the difference between living and dying. That's what Koevoet had always told them, the young guys just out of school, eighteen and nineteen, wide-eyed, hyped on adrenaline and fear and blood. Sleep, boys. Tomorrow you might not. The 'short sleep' he called it. The other sleep was the one you never woke from.

Time strobed as he shuddered between unconsciousness and waking dream. The flow of moments seemed to lurch between crest and trough, and it was as if the sea and time and the ragings of his subconscious had become one, a comingled fluid racing laminar and clear and then suddenly rupturing, dimensions blurring, friends long dead laughing now in the eddies, their teeth smashed, skulls opened up in the sun, then the concussion of an RPG, the hammering of steel on steel, the sucking of an open wound, the last breath of a dying man, oh shit I don't fucking believe it, and then looking away, anywhere, up into the too-blue sky and the emptiness of it and that hollow, sewer-pipe feeling inside like there never was anything in there anyway.

After a while the dreams stabilised, and he could hear the screaming of the wind in the rigging and the choking gurgle of the water over the hull. He recognised it as such and yet he was there, on that patrol, and it was that day, and it was real, and he knew what was to come but could not escape it. Kingfisher is there walking ahead of him, five metres, no more, just like he'd been taught. Sweat stains Kingfisher's back. His browns are torn and ragged after ten days in the bush. The strap of his R4 cuts into the back of his sunburned neck. Clay can see the skin chafed raw, Kingfisher's bush hat pushed back on his head the way he always wore it, and the sun so fierce now, and him so goddamned thirsty because they'd missed the resupply that morning due to some foul-up with the Pumas, and one second he's staring at Kingfisher and the next second, no, less, a blink, Kingfisher's head disappears, just vanishes in a mist, and a piece of something hard rips into his cheek and sticks through so he can feel it sharp and jagged and strangely porous with his tongue as the world around him explodes, and he is hurled through the air.

Clay landed with a dull thud as his shoulder and hip hit the ground. He looked up, startled, reaching for the thing in his cheek, but it was gone and he wasn't in Angola but on the floor of *Flame's* little cabin, and the noise wasn't the screaming of rockets but the wail of tearing fabric.

Clay jumped to his feet, staggered to the hatch and pulled it open. He was met by a blast of cold rain. He stuck his head out, looked up at the rigging. The storm jib was in shreds, the heavy canvas torn from tack to head. Without the stabilising push of the jib counteracting the guide of the lashed rudder, *Flame* now lay ahull, drifting in the storm. Clay climbed into the cockpit, closed the hatch, centred the rudder, let go the foresail halyard and staggered forward. Blinded by the sheeting rain, clutching at the boom and the shrouds with his hand, he crabbed his way across the pitching foredeck. The storm jib was gone, useless. Bracing himself in the pulpit, he gathered in what was left of the sail, detached the sheets and the halyard, and let it go over the side. It flew away like some deranged octopus, tentacles tiptoeing across the surface of the water, and then was gone, swallowed by the sea. In the polarised half-light the waves towered over the little ship so that it seemed impossible that it would not drown, be smashed into splinters. The air was thick with spume, the tops of the waves shorn off by the wind, atomised. Gone now were the smaller patterns on the surface, ripples and undulations. The whole heaving surface was morning-smooth, like moulded plastic, hammered clean of any texture by the wind.

Clay started to crawl back to the cockpit. He was halfway across the coach roof, his left arm cradled around the boom, when he saw it. It wasn't a wave. That's not what he saw. What confronted him then, surging towards them from astern, was a cliff face, a wall of dark-grey water that filled the horizon. He glanced down at the deck of Punk's little ketch. A pang of sorrow flooded through him. She wouldn't survive. It was almost upon them now. There was no way to make it back to the cockpit. He found the vang line and grabbed it in his hand, hugged the boom. And then he was standing on the mast and the last thing he saw before he closed his eyes was the boat's stern high above him.

10

Just a Deep Breath Away

When the spin broke, finally, after a breathless eternity, the first thing he noticed was the light. Not some distant beacon; he was inside it, a cold womb every shade of green, from algae to gemstone, churning like the rapids of an African river. And then the sound came. Even here, so far down, protected from the surface fury, the concussion of pounding water thrummed inside his head, his chest, his bones. And as the oxygen in his bloodstream burned away and the sealight began to dim, thoughts came to him, fractured pictures, voices, things indeterminate and without substance. And he was so deep now, his head ready to implode with the weight of it, the cold inside him, numbing the pain, the paintings in his brain fading, the end just a deep breath away.

Then he smiled. He could not feel his face but his eyes were open and he knew he was smiling, and it was just like the dreams that came most nights since he had put a bullet into Medved's skull, an imminent end blown to pieces by a flash of realisation: Rania was out there somewhere, smiling with those unforgettable eyes, gracing whatever part of the world she was in. And that was enough. He closed his throat and opened his lips, bared his teeth at the implacable deep, electricity arcing through him. Like waking from a coma of years. If he could have he would have laughed. He started swimming towards the light.

When he burst to the surface, the world had not changed. The sea towered over him, waves upon waves, crests truncated by the wind's scythe, bleeding white spume so that the air was wild with it. The sky was as it had been, noon dark, screaming violence, everything as it was except that *Flame* was gone. And without Punk's lost little dream, he was dead.

Clay scanned the chaos, peered through the driving spray, raised the stump of his forearm as a visor, tread water, finned with his right hand. Numb with cold, he struggled in the heavy oilskin, turning circles as the waves raised him up, resting in the deep troughs. Up he went, the boiling surface opening out as he rose, spray whipping across the crests, but there was only water, and the whole world was liquid, every colour of black and white. Down again, prison walls closing in, and he knew he was tiring, could feel it in every part of himself. He slipped off Punk's oilskin, too numb with cold now to feel his hands or feet, hypothermia setting in. He had a couple of minutes left, no more. A whole life condensed into this, perhaps two hundred seconds to come to terms with it all, to come to some kind of resolution, find some sort of truce. Carried up again, he knew that those things were unreachable, lost to him forever, drowned in the hate of war, in his own regret, and that if he searched for two hundred years he would not find them.

At the crest of the next wave he took a deep breath, looked out across the grey desert one last time and summoned his courage.

And there she was.

Two wavelengths away. Perhaps fifty metres. Dismasted, low in the water, her deck a tangle of splintered spars and cable, but upright and still afloat.

A wave of adrenaline surged through him, a last burst from some unknown reservoir. He tried to swim, willed his legs to move, but they were dead, lifeless, and it was that same feeling after he had lost his hand, his brain's signals ignored, ridiculed. Spluttering and coughing, he pounded his legs with his stump, beat them into action, forced them to kick. He pushed himself through the water, timing the next wave, spotting *Flame* again, adjusting course. Breathing hard, he clawed his way over the next wave, slid down the back side of it. *Flame* was close now. He could see the extent of the damage. Both the main and mizzen masts were shorn stumps. The bowsprit was gone, torn from the deck. The wheel had been swept away. The main boom trailed in the water, hung over the side in a tangle of steel cable. It was acting like a drogue, slowing *Flame*'s progress through the water, stabilising her.

Clay reached out and touched her wooden hull with his fingertips, the reassuring solidity of her, an island of hope in a liquid nightmare. But she was sinking. He grabbed one of the stay cables that hung over the side and pulled himself aft, inspecting the hull. Cold as he was, he knew he would have to find and seal the breach to keep her afloat. He took a deep breath, went under, the cable still firm in his right hand and scanned the hull for any sign of rupture. Slowly, he worked his way forward, riding the swell with the boat, timing his rise and fall with the boat's own cycles. When he reached the bow he could see the open wound where the sprit had been torn away, the splintered planking, the water pouring into the hull with each down-ward pitch. He worked his way aft along the starboard side. The rest of the hull looked intact. By the time he reached the stern he knew he was on the edge of hypothermia, if not already there. He needed to get aboard. He forced himself under one last time to confirm that the rudder was still intact. It was. Thank Allah. He emerged splut-tering as the boat rolled, snapping the cablework hard through his hand. He felt a sting in his palm and then nothing, just the cold as he followed the boat crashing down the side of a huge wave. The boat hit the trough hard, shuddering to a stop as the wave crashed over her, ten tons of green water hammering into her superstructure. Clay only had time to brace his legs against the hull before the water hit.

Later he would calculate that he must have been flung through a tethered arc, picked up and somersaulted onto *Flame*'s coachroof, saved from the anvil face of the teak decking only by the give of tangled rigging cable strung above the deck like a spider's web. He could just as easily have been impaled on the shorn stump of the main mast, broken his back on one of the spreaders.

For a moment he lay staring at the sky pitching above him, assess-ing what was working and what was not. There was a ringing in his head. The knife wound in his arm was seeping blood. His limbs were numb, wood. But otherwise, he was okay, functioning. He looked down. The coachroof was intact, incredibly, but the cockpit was full of water, and the main hatch was stove in, a gaping black hole. *Flame* was taking on water steadily. She now lay with decks almost awash. In a few minutes, the situation would be unsalvageable. He had to plug the holes and start pumping soon, or she would be under.

Clay got to his feet, scrambled back to the cockpit and jumped down into the cabin. The water was chest-high, covered in a slick of diesel fuel. He sloshed forward through a layer of floating cushions, pulped paper, splinters of teak planking, the boat rolling beneath his feet. He found the forward starboard locker, reached down through the murky water and dredged up the tool box. He found a cord-less drill packed in a watertight plastic container. Punk's store of repair planking was down there somewhere, too. What foresight the guy had. So much preparation, a lifetime getting ready to go, and never going. Clay reached into the locker, feeling around with numb fingers, bumping around like a blind man, his mouth below the water line, breathing through his nose. Nothing. He pushed his head under, reached down to the base of the locker, felt a hull spar, a planking joint, and then the stub ends of a bundle of planks. He pulled them free, broke the surface just in time to see a deluge of white spray pour in through the gaping hatchway.

Clay waded aft to the nav table, which was still above water. He set the toolbox and the drill and the planking bundle on the table. Then he stepped back to the galley, reached below the water, opened the main storage cupboard door, held its edge in his hand and kicked hard with his heel. First one hinge then the other gave way. He pulled up the door and put it on the table, ripped out another. Then he carefully opened up the drill case. The drill was still dry. He touched the trigger. That wonderful whirr, like music. In a few minutes he had fashioned the cupboard doors into a sturdy hatch cover and fitted it in place. Using spare rope to make a hinge so that it could be opened and closed, he pulled the new hatch shut.

Although he stood chest deep in water, the storm was now on the outside. Inside, it seemed almost quiet. It wasn't perfect, there were gaps, but most of the water was staying out. He turned and half waded, half swam forward and crawled up into the forward berth. The hole in the deck was about the size of his outstretched hand, almost at the point of the bow, just aft of the anchor locker, difficult to get at. Planking was not going to fit, not without cutting and fitting. He didn't have time. Clay grabbed one of the floating cushions and jammed it into the hole. It took a few seconds to force the foam into the opening, then he wedged it into place with the boathook. He couldn't count on it for long, but it fit well enough and for now it was keeping most of the water out. With the hull sealed, the next priority was bailing. He tried the electric pumps, knowing that they wouldn't work. They didn't. The electrics were shot. So no radio either, no chance for rescue. Not that he would have taken it anyway. Crowbar's men would be out there, listening. Some rescue: a bullet through the head.

Clay waded aft, grabbed the pump handle from its cradle near the nav station and clambered out into the fury of the gale. He stumbled through the cockpit feeling for the attachment point, slammed in the handle and started pumping.

Clay had always found something soothing, something transformative, about repetitive action. During the long patrols deep inside Angola, putting one foot in front of the other, watching the dust swirl from under his boots, the horizon unchanging, time would slide by and for a while there was a measure of peace in the green bushes and trees. And after the – what did you call such a thing? Massacre? Slaughter? He realised he'd never named it; for all these years it had always just been there, barely buried beneath that thin layer of denial, a regolith of self-delusion – so yes, massacre, recovering from his wounds in the Bloemfontein military hospital, doing his rehab exercises, he would work his body until his muscles burned, anything to keep the screams away, keep his mind from what had happened, his role in it, quiet the open wound of his conscience. And now, here, with the sea rising around him, he moved the handle through its strokes, imagining the rubber diaphragm pulling in water, pushing it out through the seacock, a cup at a time, a litre, a gallon, not thinking of Rania or Medved, of Crowbar or any of them. Despite the roar of the wind and waves, he could hear the pump working, feel the water surging under his feet. Like walking, you think you'll never get there, but you do. Just keep going.

He pumped until his arm was trembling with the effort. In the hospital in Oman, the staff had offered to fit him with a prosthetic, a short, flesh-coloured device that he could strap on to his stump. The doctor told him that, with practice, he would be able to grip and manipulate objects, perform basic tasks. But it was ugly, an offence, and his first attempts at using it were clumsy, embarrassing, and he'd torn the thing from his arm and thrown it across the room. Now he wished he'd kept it. His shoulder muscles were burning. He kept pumping.

After a time he noticed that the rain had stopped, and he dared imagine that the wind had slackened, just a bit. The sky still swirled with menace, but the pitch of the wind's scream had changed perceptibly. He looked at his watch. An hour, maybe two since they'd been pitchpoled and dismasted. More than an hour of pumping. Clay clambered to the hatchway, slid back the makeshift hatch cover and peered down into the cabin. Lying ahull in the storm, without the stabilising inertia of the masts, the ketch rolled violently across each wave. Water sloshed back and forth in the cabin, carrying a growing tide of flotsam, Punk's ukulele was there, floating amidst all the other junk, strings up. But the water level had dropped. Not by much, maybe ten centimetres, but it was something. A start. Energy flowed through him. He pushed back the hatch, searched the port locker for a bucket, stood in the gangway, started bailing. Twice he was knocked off his feet by the roll, but he kept going, scooping up bucketfuls of diesel-tainted water and tossing them over the side. After a while the tops of the main cabin lockers emerged. Clay stood a moment, bucket hanging in his hand, feet planted wide against the roll, water sloshing around his thighs, tilted his head back and stared up into the swirling sky. Then he opened his mouth wide and screamed above the wind, howling his defiance.

11

Instruments of Darkness

He bailed to exhaustion.

By evening he had managed to remove most of the water from the cabin. In the last of the day's light, the boat still pitching in wild seas, he winched the boom back aboard, lashed it to the deck, retrieved what was left of the mizzen rigging, and made fast whatever could be salvaged. He scanned the eastern horizon: no sign of land.

As darkness fell, he retreated below deck and collapsed into the main berth. He was asleep before his head touched the sodden cushion.

When he woke the starboard portholes glowed yellow, filling the cabin with morning. Waves lapped the hull. Clay closed his eyes and felt the ketch rock gently beneath him. Shaking off a forgotten dream, he swung his feet to the floor, winced at the pain in his arm. He pushed open the makeshift hatch, stood on the second gangway step and stuck his head outside. *Flame* bobbed on a sea almost calm under a blue cirrus sky, yesterday's storm just a distant rumour on the northern horizon. The breeze was fair from the northwest. He was alone, rudderless, adrift and without power, the universe of the sea stretching away to every distant meridian.

First, he needed to look after himself. Every part of his body ached. He tore the wet bandages from his arm, examined the wound and applied a fresh dressing. Soon he had the stove going, water heating. He opened the food locker and rummaged through the jumble of disintegrating packaging, smashed glass and diesel-smeared plastic. The labels of most of the tins were either gone or indecipherable, so he picked a big can that didn't look like beans and opened it. Peach slices in syrup. He gulped them from the can, the juice running down his chin and shirtfront. Amazing. He grabbed another tin, larger. It was some kind of meat stew, thick and rich. He dumped the contents into a pan and put it on the stove, his body quivering with the promise of healing protein.

After eating he set to repairs. Basic steering was the next priority. It took him the best part of the morning to hack away the shorn wheel sleeving and flange the emergency tiller to the rudder shaft.

With the sun nearing its zenith, it was time to start determining just exactly where he was. Clay found Punk's sextant and took a noon sight. His calculations put him at approximately 6° 15′ W longitude, about sixty-five nautical miles west of Ushant, latitude uncertain. From here, any course east of south would land them on the north coast of Spain, anywhere from A Coruña to San Sebastián.

By late afternoon he had rigged a makeshift mast by lashing the boom to the main mast's shorn stump, cannibalising stays from the tangled wreck of the mizzen and making them fast to the deck plates that had survived the dismasting. Soon he had the smallest of the reserve jibs up and flying as a mainsail in a reaching wind. It gave him less than a third of the original sail area, but with careful trimming and adjustment, he soon had *Flame* foaming along at what he estimated to be four knots, bound for Spain. There was still a long way to go, but it was a start.

As the sun set over the Atlantic, he sat at the tiller and sipped a mug of strong, sweet coffee, guiding *Flame* down the back of a following wave. At this rate, he could be in Spain in three days.

By now, Koevoet would have realised he hadn't landed in France. Not at any of the major ports, anyway. How many places could they watch? Did they have a line into French customs? If the company was working for Regina Medved, which seemed almost certain now, they could bring their combined forces to bear. He wondered how long it would be until they shifted their attention to Spain. Koevoet already knew Rania was in Cyprus – had told Clay so himself. Maybe they wouldn't even bother trying to intercept him on the continent.

They'd just wait for him come to them. Clay imagined Eben's killers, brush in hand, painting that horrifying message in blood on the clinic wall. Suddenly, three days seemed like an eternity, stuck on a crippled ship in the middle of nowhere, at the whim of winds and tides, travelling at four nautical miles per hour. He could run faster.

What had Rania said on the phone? He replayed their conversation in his head, the words she'd used: genocide, extinction. What the hell was she mixed up in? He couldn't have made the danger any more clear. Surely she had seen sense and was by now back in Switzerland. At the chalet in the Alps, holding a cup of herbal tea, the early-winter snow thick already on the mountains, icicles hanging from the eaves. He wiped the image away. Premature. Go, she'd said, go make peace with the one person you can never forgive.

The barometer was rising steadily now, the air warming, the wind steady from the west-north-west, the aftermath of the storm moving away towards France. He sailed on through the night, south across aeons of stars. Once, he spotted a ship's running lights on the horizon, but she was moving fast, and soon there was only darkness again and the shimmer of distant planets reflecting on the black waves. Towards midnight he trimmed the makeshift rig, found he could gain an extra knot by rigging another stay and bracing the foot of the sail. Later, the sky cleared enough for a crude fix on Venus, allowing him to plot a position 170 nautical miles north-north-west of Santander.

And in this reduction of the universe and his place in it into the calculus of sidereal hour angles and distances from the first point of Aries, there was no lessening of the mystery of it. No diminishment of awe.

Sometimes just to be alive seemed the miracle it surely was.

☾

The westerlies held till sunrise, strengthened through morning. By midday *Flame* was humming along, doing five knots on a broad reach. Clay sat in the cockpit, tiller under his left arm, Koevoet's copy of *Macbeth* open in his right hand. As the water slipped away beneath him, he read until night came.

The instruments of darkness tell us truths.

The next morning Clay stood at the bow, searching through the binoculars for the northern coast of Spain. The star sights he'd taken just before sunrise had given him a reasonable fix. If his navigation was on, Santander's approach beacon should be coming into view soon. Trimmed up in a following wind, *Flame* slid noiselessly through the morning calm. Clay looked down into the clear, cold, Biscay water, watched the swell of *Flame*'s bow wave flexing like a translucent muscle. He was about to raise the binoculars again, scan the horizon, when a pair of sleek grey backs surged up through the water and finned into *Flame*'s bow wave. It was a pair of Atlantic bottlenose dolphins, pale and sleek, hitching a ride. Clay sat in the mangled arms of what was left of the pulpit and watched the dolphins, legs dangling over the side, water splashing on his bare feet, just the three of them in an empty morning world, speeding along together to some unknown future. The dolphins were close enough to touch, inches from the hull. They looked up at him. Where are you going? their eyes seemed to ask him.

They stayed with him for a long time, dancing for him, talking to him in a language he did not understand. And then, all at once, they exhaled in a double burst, *pfough pfough,* snatched breaths of air, held there for a moment and dove deep. Clay watched them fade from view, waited a while hoping they'd come back. After a while he looked up. There was the coast, big and close and dirty.

12

Leave Me in the Sun for the Vultures

Clay stood tiller in hand and piloted *Flame* into the channel leading to Santander harbour, the timeless gratitude of landfall warm inside him. Despite hours trying, he hadn't managed to get the engine going. It was cool, a late-autumn day on the northern coast of Spain, a light breeze blowing in off the sea, feathers of cirrus wisping in a hazy sky. The old port city opened up before him, the sand spit and lowlands of the eastern shore, and to the west, ridges of whitewashed buildings, turn-of-the-century façades cascading down to shingle beaches. He brought *Flame* about, made for the protective embrace of the Punta del Puerto, a cluster of masts half-hidden behind a rocky islet.

Twenty minutes later he glided *Flame* past the rocks and into a narrow embayment, a notch in the limestone bluff. Big pines clung to the slopes, an amphitheatre of boughs, and above, the rooftops and dormers of the city. Two dozen boats hugged both sides of a single plankwood dock that bisected the cove. The dock ramped up to a small stone building. A man was standing outside the doorway, hand raised to shield the sun from his eyes.

Clay let the mainsail luff. The man started down the dock towards him. He walked slowly, with a slight limp. As he approached, Clay could see that he was older, slightly stooped, with a thick grey beard. He wore a colourless woollen jumper and black cloth cap. The man reached the end of the dock, stood for a moment looking out at *Flame*. Then he smiled, raised his hand and waved. Clay raised his bandaged hand. The man pointed to the west side of the dock. Together they guided the battered ketch to a safe standstill. Clay jumped down, making fast stern and spring lines, the old man the bow.

They stood together looking at the wreckage of *Flame*'s deck.

'*Madre de Dios*,' said the man, crossing himself, running his fingers through his beard.

'*Allah akhbar, broer*. Absolutely.'

The man smiled, shook Clay's hand. He had soft brown eyes, kindness there, history. '*Inglés?*' the man said.

'*Si, inglés.*'

It turned out that the old man, Señor Gonzales, owned the place, had for years, his father before that. His son soon appeared. He had a La Liga haircut, wore a Barcelona football shirt and had the kind of good looks that older women swoon over. Soon, they'd led Clay up to the building, installed him before the hearth, got a nice fire going, poured him a cup of hot coffee and wrapped a blanket around his shoulders. The son, who spoke passable English, explained to Clay that he could clear customs tomorrow. No rush. The family doctor showed up shortly afterwards, checked Clay's bruised ribs, the blue under his left eye and put ten stitches in the knife wound in his arm, the son watching all of it, staring intently at Clay, at the sewing. After a while Gonzales and the doctor left and walked down to the dock. Clay watched them through the window, the two of them standing there gazing at the battered little ketch.

'Your hand,' said the youth.

Clay pulled up his sleeve, let the boy look at the stump.

'How?'

'Trying to help some friends.'

'From a danger?'

Clay nodded.

'And you did? Help them, I mean?'

'Some. Some not.'

'It hurts?'

Clay looked at the boy, considered how to answer this. He wanted to tell him some of what he'd learned. That no one ever walks away from a fight without damage. That the pain never leaves you. Ever. That he'd lost so much more than a hand. Instead, he said, 'Yes.'

The boy nodded.

The doctor and Gonzales returned. Clay offered the doctor a fifty-euro note, but he waved it away, said something to Gonzales that made the old man laugh.

Clay thanked them for their hospitality and asked directions to a good hotel.

'No,' the youth said, translating for his father. 'You must stay with us. Our home is just here, beyond the trees. We are crowded there, but here there is a bed in the back room, a toilet and shower around the back. My father says you will eat with us and tell us of your crossing through the storm.'

Clay nodded to these good, kind people, thanked them. He pointed at the telephone on the desk, looked at the father, the son. 'Please,' he said, 'I can pay. I must call someone, long distance.'

Son and father smiled together, nodded. 'My father says of course, please, as you like.

The old man and the doctor left. Clay gave the son the fifty-euro note and asked him to bring an English newspaper, buy him a razor, a toothbrush, shaving cream. The kid smiled, took the money and left.

The crossing had taken six days. Long enough for his pursuers to know he hadn't landed in France. Long enough, he hoped, for Rania to have finished whatever it was that she had to do and get back to Switzerland. He picked up the phone, dialled the chalet and waited with a loping heart.

Silence. Nothing. No connection.

He replaced the receiver, tried again.

Same thing – a few random clicks, then dead air.

Cradling the receiver between his shoulder and neck, he dialled the Nicosia Hilton. Three ring tones, an immediate connection. Reception. Ms Moulinbecq checked out two days ago. No forwarding address.

He tried the chalet again, checked each digit of the number as he dialled, the same number he'd used to reach Madame Debret a few days ago from England. Again, no ring tone, no busy signal, nothing – as if the line had been disconnected, had never existed. He filled his lungs, let the air go, closed his eyes, felt the floor pitch beneath him. For hours and days he'd thought of nothing but this one call, the rush of her voice on the other end of the line. Had she quit Cyprus as he'd asked? Or had she simply changed hotels, checked in somewhere else under an assumed name, understanding his warning that she was in danger, but not heeding his advice to leave the island? And why was the line to the chalet down? What had happened there over the last six days to cause this? Fear marshalled in his chest, nightmares making ready to escape their starlit prison.

He put down the phone, walked outside, tried to do his breathing, stood looking down along the dock, the boats there shimmering in the midday sun, halyards flapping in the breeze, the cloud-strewn harbour beyond, all of it pure in its indifference.

When he went back inside the boy had returned with a copy of *The Independent*, the other things and whatever money was left. Clay thanked him and gave him a ten-euro note. The boy smiled. Clay spread the paper on the table, pinned the fold with his stump and peeled open the front page. He scanned the headlines. The eighth of November 1994: the Space Shuttle Atlantis mission, Ronald Reagan's Alzheimer's, Johan Heyns, long-time critic of apartheid, assassinated at his home in Pretoria. Clay was surprised it had taken them this long. And, on page eight, just below the OpEds, a piece by Lise Moulinbecq, byline Nicosia. As he read it the youth stood behind him, gazing over his shoulder.

North Cyprus Development Threatens Turtles with Extinction
Neo-Enosis, an ultra-right wing Cypriot militant group, has lashed out publicly at the UN and the EU claiming that illegal development in Northern Cyprus is driving Mediterranean sea turtles to extinction. In a communiqué delivered to AFP, Neo-Enosis claims that new

*tourist resorts in the occupied north are being built on land stolen
from Greek Cypriots when the Turkish Army overran the northern
third of the island twenty years ago. The developments, which the
group claims violate the 1974 Geneva accords, will allegedly disturb
turtle-nesting beaches protected by the United Nations as World Heritage Sites. The group is threatening direct action against the developers if the UN and Turkish governments do not immediately halt
construction of the resorts. Neo-Enosis has been unofficially linked to
at least two recent murders of prominent businessmen in the north.
Several major new resort proposals have been put forward by developers on both sides of the border seeking to cash in on the tourism
boom in Cyprus. Dr Hope Bachmann of the University of California
has been studying turtles in the Mediterranean for over a decade.
Her research reveals a steady decline in turtle numbers since 1970
due to illegal harvesting, accidental drowning in fishing nets, and
the destruction of nesting beaches. The green turtle is now threatened
with extinction. Despite anonymous death threats, Cyprus-based
Bachmann has continued to call upon the UN, the European Union
and the Governments of Cyprus to enforce bans on coastal development near the remaining pristine nesting beaches. Accusations of
theft, murder, environmental negligence and the lure of huge profits
have heightened tensions between north and south to a level not seen
on this island since the 1970s.*

Clay put down the paper, looked out across the water.

'In Spain also this happens,' said the youth.

Clay looked at him.

'When I was a boy there were many fish here. Now to catch one
is difficult.'

Clay guessed the kid at seventeen, maybe eighteen, the same age
he'd been when he'd made his first kill, watched that SWAPO fighter
collapse in the dust. 'My hand will the multitudinous seas incarna-
dine,' he said.

The boy frowned, not understanding.

'Something I just read.'

'What does it mean?'

'We do things,' Clay said. 'And then we can't change them.'

The boy thought about this, nodded.

Clay pointed at the telephone. The boy smiled at him, nodded, turned and left, closing the door behind him. Clay picked up the handpiece and tried LeClerc, Rania's long-time editor at AFP. The receptionist said he was not available, was in meetings all day. Three more times Clay tried the chalet, each time met by that same empty silence, that absence. He checked his watch. If he was going to find her, wherever she was, he needed to get out of these rags, get cleaned up, buy some new clothes and get going.

After a hot shower and a shave, he walked down to the dock, collected his passport and cash from the priesthole onboard *Flame*, closed it up tight with the guns and ammunition inside and threw Crowbar's old leather jacket over his rags. When he emerged from below deck, Gonzales and his son were there on the dock, refuelling a pretty little sloop. They looked up at him and waved. He waved back.

Clay walked back up to the office, scribbled a quick note of thanks, a promise to call and discuss repairs to *Flame*, laid out two thousand euros in cash as a down-payment, folded the note around the bills, placed it all on the desk where they would see it, and started into town. As long as he was here, they were in danger.

After five days on a churning sea he rolled like a lost drunk, his inner ear still compensating for the swell. He walked west, along the tree-lined esplanade of the Avenida de la Reina Victoria, the empty beaches of the Punta de San Marcos on his left, the harbour spreading grey and muddy beyond. He watched the road ahead, stopped and turned every now and again to look back. He had no reason to believe that Medved or Crowbar knew he was here, but the fear was there.

After the best part of a kilometre his sea legs settled, and soon he was into the old city, treed streets lined with buildings from the turn of the last century, wrought-iron lamp posts standing like elegant reminders of another time, a time of gas light and belief, tradition. He found the Mercado del Este and walked into a men's clothiers.

They were not happy to see him. The sales assistant looked ready to call the cops, had even started to pick up the phone when Clay set a pair of heavy drill canvas trousers and five one hundred-euro notes on the counter. The clerk looked down at the cash, up at Clay, an obsequious smile blooming on his face. Forty-five minutes later Clay emerged wearing a dark, good-quality wool suit, a white collared shirt, dark tie and a pair of black leather brogues. In a bag slung over his shoulder he carried the trousers, a heavy flannel shirt and a new pair of sturdy boots. They'd even thrown in three pairs of boxers and sewn up the arm of Crowbar's leather jacket. He stuffed his torn and bloody rags into a plastic bag and dumped them into a roadside bin fifty metres from the store.

Not far away he found an Iberia office, bought a return ticket to Geneva for Declan Greene, and in a nearby travel agency another to Nicosia made out to Marcus Edward. The Geneva flight left at 23.30 that evening, the Nicosia flight the next morning. He stopped at a streetside café, ordered a coffee and watched the people go by, the cars, thought about Rania, where she was right at that very moment, what images her retina were processing as if by knowing these he could somehow divine her whereabouts. The sun was low now and the wind came cold from the sea. A young couple walked by, his arm around her bare shoulders. The girl had long, dark hair like Rania's, a pretty upturned nose. She was laughing at something her man had said. Clay could hear the ring of her voice, the joy there. And then they were past, swallowed by the city.

It was just after five pm. He bought a phone card, found a public telephone and tried the chalet again. He was about to hang up when the line opened. A woman answered, automated, formal. A recording. This number is not available. Clay checked the number, dialled again. Same result. He put the receiver back into its cradle, a hollow place opening up inside him.

He keyed in another number.

LeClerc answered immediately.

'This is Declan Greene.'

There was a pause, the sound of papers shuffling. 'Ah yes, Monsieur Greene.'

'Where is Rania? It's important.'

'Will you wait a moment, please?'

Clay could hear voices, footsteps, a door closing.

'Monsieur Greene?'

'I'm here.'

'The last time I heard from her she was in Nicosia. That was two days ago.' His voice was tense, half an octave higher than Clay remembered it. 'She filed a story shortly after we spoke.'

'I read it.'

'Yes, the turtles. A good piece.'

'Did she go home?'

'This is all I know, Monsieur Greene. Now if you will please–'

Clay cut him off. 'She's in danger, LeClerc.'

Silence.

'Regina Medved wants her dead.'

The line burned empty, just air. Clay let the silence hang between them. Finally LeClerc spoke. 'I am sure she is fine.'

'Fine? Did you hear what I said? They're going to kill her.'

'Surely it is not as bad as you suggest.' LeClerc's voice sounded thin, coming through walls and glass.

'You know what her story did to them. The story *you* published.'

Silence.

'LeClerc, are you there?'

'Please. This is all I know.' The guy was seizing up. Clay could hear the cold terror in his voice.

'Jesus, LeClerc. What the hell is going on?'

'Nothing is...' Shaky. 'Nothing is *going on*.' An attempt to stabilise. 'I am trying to run a news agency. Now if you will please allow me–'

'I need your help, LeClerc.'

Another pause. And then: 'Please, Monsieur Greene, if that is your name. I have told you what I know.'

'You sent her to Cyprus. You insisted she go. Why? Why this story in particular?'

'Do not insinuate.'

'Answer me.'

'It was her interest. Hers.'

'When do you expect to hear from her?'

'I don't know. Tomorrow perhaps. I don't know.'

'Expect a call from me tomorrow, then.'

'Please, *non*. I will be in meetings all day. I cannot.'

'Convince yourself.'

'*Pardon?*'

'Tomorrow, LeClerc.'

Clay expected LeClerc to hang up but he did not, just stayed there on the line, the silence thick between them. 'There is something…' LeClerc stopped dead.

Clay waited. 'I'm listening.'

'Something, something difficult…'

Clay let the line hang, gave him time.

LeClerc stalled a moment, restarted. 'I'm sorry, Mister Greene. I…'

Now he had Clay worried. This was not the decisive, confident LeClerc he knew, the one Rania held in such esteem.

Clay pulled in oxygen. 'What's wrong LeClerc?'

Nothing back.

'Tell me. I can help. Is it Rania?'

More silence. Clay could hear him thinking it over. And then: 'Something has just come across my desk.'

Relief in his voice; this not the something he had started to tell.

'A suspect in the murder of Rex Medved has just been appre-hended by police in England. He was caught on the south coast, trying to flee the country by boat. He is now in hospital under close guard, recovering from a gunshot wound. The police haven't released his name, but apparently he's South African.'

Well, leave me in the sun for the vultures. The police must have picked up the Boer he'd wounded near the cottage, the one he'd seen in the passenger seat of the Merc in Falmouth. It had to be him.

The line went dead.

Clay put down the phone, considered this a moment, the obliquity of things. After a while he picked up the phone again and punched in the number for his Cayman Islands bank. He was going to need more money.

A ring tone, far off, the line engaging. Clay gave his name and codeword.

He was put on hold, a thin, drifting melody.

Then: 'There is a message for you, Mister Greene.'

'Read it to me please.'

The sound of paper being shuffled, the bank clerk clearing his throat. 'It says only: "*I know where she is.*"'

Clay took a breath, his heart arrhythmic. 'That's it?'

'Nothing else. No sender identified.'

13

Purgatory

A few hours later Clay boarded the Iberia 737 non-stop to Geneva, managed a flat smile to the pretty stewardess, adjusted the tie that felt like a noose around his neck and settled into his business-class window seat. In his new suit and black brogues he looked like any of the other three dozen or more businessmen on the flight, off to make deals, sign contracts, pitch for sales. As the doors closed and the engines started, Clay thought of the little ketch that had delivered him through the storm, now lying in her cradle at Gonzales' boat yard. Over the phone from the airport departure lounge, Clay had agreed to pay the old guy nine thousand euros to step a new mast, fit new rigging, fix the hatch, service the engine and make her seaworthy again. After some intense bargaining via Gonzales junior, Clay had agreed to wire three thousand euros direct to Gonzales' account, plus four thousand more once the work was complete. Gonzales promised to have the ketch safely in Larnaca harbour in Cyprus in three and a half weeks, in a secure pre-paid, six-month berth. Punk's queen would make it to the Med after all.

With all the tourists coming and going, access to Larnaca harbour was easy and anonymous. The Suez Canal was within a couple of day's sailing. He would find Rania, wherever she was, and they'd sail south, to Africa like they'd planned. Through the canal, down the Red Sea, past Yemen, down the east coast, maybe stop for a while in Zanzibar. He'd always wanted to see the Spice Islands.

His nerves tingled at the thought of her, a deep biological faint that seemed to bloom from within the fibre of him, the sinew grafted to his bones, the cartilage of his joints. She knew he was coming. A matter of hours, now. He reached for his soda water, took a long drink, wished it was whisky, let the ice cubes rattle his teeth.

After a while he fell into a stuttering sleep, edging in and out of consciousness, still urging himself to stay lucid, clawing at the fuzzy threshold of what was real, the need to keep *Flame* on course, guide her safely over the surging waves. The plane hit the runway and jerked Clay awake. He opened his eyes, looked out at the rain, the low grey cloud. Geneva.

After clearing customs he found a phone box, called the chalet again and listened to the same mechanical female voice. An hour and a half later he was in a new rented Renault Laguna, hurtling along the E62, Lake Geneva spreading grey and unsettled on his right. He checked the rear-view mirror. The same black Mercedes had been with him since before Lausanne, almost forty minutes now, two cars back, steady like a star turning in the sky. At Vevey, where the autoroute bifurcated, the black Merc stayed with him towards Montreux. He hadn't seen anyone following him in the airport, but if Medved or Crowbar had access to flight passenger records or even customs clearance data, they would know that he had surfaced. The message sent to the bank had been designed to rattle him, push him towards Rania, flush him out. They needn't have bothered.

Just outside Villeneuve, the Merc steady two back, Clay braked hard and swerved from the outer passing lane across three lanes of traffic, rumbling across the hatched warning median onto the exit sliproad for the Shell Villeneuve services. The black Merc flashed past, unable to follow. Clay watched it pass, two kids in the backseat, mum checking her makeup in the vanity mirror. Jesus Christ.

After a plastic sandwich and a cup of coffee, Clay was back on the road. He rejoined the autoroute at Lavey-Les-Bains, took the Colombey exit and started the climb towards Champéry, the countryside familiar now but changed from when he was here with Rania in the last bloom of summer, the frosted anticline of Pointe-de-Bellevue looming now through the clouds, the forests thick-covered in fresh white, the roads high-banked with graded snow.

Traffic slowed to a walk behind heavy trucks panting up switch-
backs thick with slush. He willed them forward, his impatience for
her burning a ragged hole in his chest. By the time he reached the
outskirts of Champéry, the air was thick with big, spinning flakes
and the cloud hung low in the valley. At the *téléphérique*, Clay left the
main road and started up, past the old hotel, its window-boxes piled
with snow, icicles hanging like rows of silver teeth from the eaves,
then over the one-lane bridge, the road climbing through dark forest,
snow thickening under the Renault's tyres.

In his mind he could see the chalet, the pitch of the roof, snow
corniced along the eaves, smoke wisping from the chimney, light
glowing through frosted windows. And she would be inside, expecting him perhaps, sitting by the fire, her hair down, and if not there,
then somewhere just like it, solitary and safe.

Emerging from dense woodland, Clay peered out through cloud
and driving snow into the swirling beams of the headlights. He had
walked this road so many times during that short time that he and
Rania had spent together here, after Yemen – she still weak and
recovering from the gunshot wound, he struggling with the loss of
his hand – that despite the snow he could feel himself anticipating
every curve and rise as he contoured the mountainside. Rania's chalet
stood alone looking out over the valley, set into the slope just below
the road. He stopped the car and stared out through the windscreen
and the flapping wipers at this place that he did not now recognize.
At first he wasn't sure. The snowburst and the cloud and the throw
of the headlights in the deepening gloom distorted everything: the
layer of fresh snow frosting the confusion of bare black beams; the
wisps of smoke that rose from the dark open middle of the place; the
smell of charred timber reaching him now.

He pulled the car to the side of the road, shut down the engine,
opened the door and stood looking out through the flying snow. A
chill shuddered through him. He took a few steps forward, stopped,
kept walking, the soles of his shoes sinking into the powder as he
trudged down the drive, the full extent of the damage now clear to

him, the old oak beams and trusses blackened and burnt away, the roof caved into the wet, charred guts of the place, the gleaming pine floors gone, the hand-laid stone chimney rising from the ash, and everywhere the fiery taste of purgatory.

Part II

14

The World Can Go and Fuck Itself

7th November 1994: Somewhere over Bulgaria

Transiting Europe at ten thousand metres, Clay considered again the circumstances of his position. Before he was killed, evading capture near the Omani border no more than three months ago, Claymore Straker had been wanted for at least eight murders in Yemen, had been officially labelled an Ansar Al Sharia terrorist by the Yemen Government and the CIA. Despite LeClerc's surprising news that someone had been arrested for the murder of Rex Medved, Clay was far from safe. He would have to be doubly careful back in the Middle East. He had spent more than six years working in the region as an independent consultant on oil and gas projects, mostly in Yemen, Egypt and Libya. He'd also done work in Turkey, spent time in Istanbul. For three of those years he'd lived in Cyprus, and his Cyprus-registered company, Capricorn Consulting, was still in existence, its affairs still, he supposed, nominally handled by his Cypriot accountant. His flat in Nicosia would surely have been rented out by now, his possessions boxed up and disposed of – however the system dealt with a dead man's stuff when he had no next of kin.

At least he now had some idea of Rania's whereabouts. He'd stayed at the chalet for a long time watching the snow fall into the black pit – a mourner at a grave. Then he'd trudged the couple of kilometres up the road to the Auberge des Arcs, the place where he and Rania had spent a couple of summer afternoons drinking beer and looking out over the valley at the glaciers of les Dents du Midi shimmering in the sun. Clay spoke with the *patron,* who remembered him, remembered Clay's very beautiful wife. That's what he'd called her: *femme.* Clay didn't bother correcting him. The fire had been two days ago, he said. It had started at night, and by the time *les pompiers* arrived it was too far gone, a total loss; such a shame, a beautiful place, very old. Clay nodded in agreement and enquired about the occupants. The *aubergiste* answered that no one was home at the time, and no one had seen or heard of Madame Debret, the elderly owner, since before the fire. Clay thanked him, ordered something to eat, which he only picked at, then called LeClerc from the *patron*'s phone. The conversation had gone something like:

LeClerc: I am very sorry. I have made a terrible misjudgement. I should never have sent her. Forgive me.

Straker: Jesus.

LeClerc: I know where she is.

Straker, heart seized – those words, the anonymous message: Tell me.

LeClerc: Istanbul.

Straker:

LeClerc: Monsieur Greene?

Straker: What the hell is she doing in Istanbul?

LeClerc: Following a story. Several stories, actually.

Straker: Where is she staying?

LeClerc: We don't know. She hasn't checked in yet.

Straker: They torched her house.

LeClerc: *Pardon?*

Straker: Burned her house down. (But maybe you already know that.)

LeClerc: *Mon dieu.* (A long pause, LeClerc thinking something over, coming to a conclusion.) What will you do?

Straker: I'm going to find her. (I'm going to find her and get the hell out. Go back to Africa, sail off the map, just the two of us, untraceable. You and the rest of the world can go and fuck yourselves.)

LeClerc: Our Istanbul station chief will meet you at the airport. Let me know when you have flight details. I will do everything I can to help. Be careful, Monsieur Greene.

Clay had driven through nightfall, following strobe-lit snow ploughs and sanding trucks, the roads otherwise deserted, the snow gradually turning to sleet then freezing rain as he lost altitude. He joined the autoroute for Geneva and the airport, not caring who might be following. His mind was clear as the dark surface of the lake. LeClerc was hiding something. Of this, Clay was sure. What had he meant by 'terrible misjudgement'? Unwittingly or not, LeClerc had used the lure of a story he knew Rania couldn't resist to draw her from safety. And now he was driving them both to Istanbul.

☾

Five hours later Clay stood in the cavernous arrivals hall of Atatürk Airport, queuing for passport control. The place looked and smelled like the jumbled chaos of the city it served, a faded, yellowing museum suffused with cigarette smoke and the blanketing thrall of burnt kerosene. Clay cleared customs, pushed his way through the arrivals hall and joined the human river moving towards the exit, just one more soul carried along in the flux. At the far end of the chute, he saw a white A4 placard held above a sea of bobbing heads. Scrawled on the paper were the initials DG.

He'd decided on the plane. He'd walk whatever pathway LeClerc set him. He had no other choice. Clay scanned the crowd and pushed toward the placard. The man holding the sign had sallow skin and bulging thyroid eyes. He introduced himself as Hamour, AFP Istanbul station chief. LeClerc's man. In an ancient Egyptian-made El Nasr Fiat 128 copy, he launched them into the city.

Everything was as Clay remembered: the royal blue of the Bosphorus, the watercolour minaret skyline, the clash of culture and belief echoing along every confused alleyway, seeping from each palace museum and place of worship. The grey hulk of Sultan Ahmet mosque rose on their left as they sped along Kennedy Avenue, the Bosphorus calm and flat beyond Clay's open window, brilliantly blue after the washed-out grey monochrome of the northern winter. He could smell the place, the sea, the exhaust of a million vehicles, and strong from the east, all of Anatolia, that vast Turkic heartland of wheatfields and winter rains.

Clay turned in his seat and faced Hamour. 'Has she checked in?'

Hamour frowned, glanced into his rear-view mirror. 'Not yet. But we know she is here.' He reached over the seatback, pulled a sheet of paper from a battered leather briefcase and handed it to Clay. 'She filed with Paris this morning. You see? The byline is Istanbul. She is to contact me. That is protocol. I expect to hear from her today.'

Clay scanned the single-spaced typeset page: A campaign of assassinations and intimidation in Turkish-controlled Northern Cyprus, bribery and corruption in the South, an island in turmoil. At the centre of it, Neo-Enosis, advocates of union with Greece, by force if necessary, and led, the story claimed, by wealthy businessman Nikos Chrisostomedes, whose family was forced from its ancestral lands in the north during the 1974 invasion. The story went on to describe allegations that companies owned by Chrisostomedes had for years been engaging in bribery and blackmail to ensure a near monopoly of the south's lucrative upscale tourist industry, controlling hotels, resorts, catering, commercial districts and beachfront property. In an exclusive interview with Lise Moulinbecq, Chrisostomedes defended his record, pointing instead to the north, where he claimed illegal and systematic large-scale theft was virtually wiping out all traces of Greek society – an act of cultural genocide. Most damagingly, he claimed that the genocide was being bankrolled and directed from Turkey. If the government, the UN and the EU would not act, others would, he was quoted as saying. The Turkish Government was incensed and had immediately issued a stern denial and a comprehensive rebuke against what it called 'irresponsible and dangerous radicalism' in Cyprus.

'When will this go to print?' asked Clay.

'Tomorrow, God willing.'

Hamour glanced again at his rear-view mirror. 'I do not wish to seem paranoid, Mister Declan, but I think we are being followed.'

Clay adjusted his wing mirror.

'The black one, three cars behind. He has been there since the airport.'

There it was, a late-model German sedan, an Audi A6, two men. Perhaps LeClerc's man was not the stooge Clay had presumed him to be. Then again, maybe he was smarter than he looked.

'Next street, turn left, up into the city,' Clay said. 'Don't indicate.'

'In Turkey, no one is indicating, Mister Declan.'

Clay smiled. 'Well don't start.'

Hamour nodded. 'Perhaps I am imagining.'

'We'll see.'

Two minutes later, Hamour moved into the outer lane, waited for a few oncoming cars to pass then turned hard left across traffic into a narrow street lined with old, grey apartment blocks strung with wires and studded with decrepit, inefficient, first-generation air-conditioning cubes. The Audi followed a few seconds later, surging to catch up.

'You weren't imagining, *arkadaşım*,' said Clay. My friend.

He brought up the map of Istanbul in his head, the old paper tourist one he'd used on that first visit, years ago now, when he was working in the east out near Diyarbakir and Van, the one he'd used to walk the tangled streets for hours and days till the paper was soaked in his sweat and the folds and corners had pulped and worn through.

'The *buyuk kapalı* is close, yes?' he said in Turkish. The Grand Bazaar, a dozen miles of arched and pillared labyrinth, a confusion of shops and stalls selling every kind of trinket and antique and adornment ever conceived.

Hamour nodded and urged the El-Nasr up a steep hill.

Clay reached into the backseat and grabbed his bag. 'Drop me outside. Any entrance. It doesn't matter if they see me.'

'Where will you go?' said Hamour, the folds of his neck quivering as he darted through the traffic. 'I have a reservation for you at the Hilton.'

'I'll be at the Seglik Merkezi Hotel in Tepebaşi. Do you know it?'

'I can find.'

'Good. As soon as you hear from Lise, tell her to go there and ask for Mister Edward.'

Hamour nodded, opened his mouth, paused, closed it.

'Got that?'

'Mister Edward, yes.'

'*Sağol.*' Thanks.

'The bazaar is near,' Hamour gulped. 'Less than a kilometre.' His voice was strained, fearful.

Clay checked the wing mirror. The Audi was still there, five or six cars back now, struggling in the thickening traffic.

'There is one more thing: Monsieur LeClerc asked me to tell you that Zdravko Todorov has escaped.'

Clay spun in the seat, stared at Hamour.

'A deal was made between the Yemeni terrorists who captured him and the French government. Apparently something went wrong during the handover.'

'Jesus. When?'

'About one month ago, according to our sources.'

A month. 'Where is he now?'

'We have no idea,' said Hamour, slowing and pulling to the side of the street behind a small delivery van, its back doors open. Stacks of cut flowers filled the cargo space. Petals littered the gutter.

Clay had the door open before Hamour brought the car to a stop. '*Çok teşekur ederım,*' he said, swinging his feet to the pavement. Thank you. He paused, hand on the edge of the door, glanced at the Audi drawing near, leant into the car. 'I'll be waiting for Lise at the hotel.' And before Hamour had a chance to reply, he closed the door and strode through the crowd toward the big Ottoman archway and the entrance to the market.

15

Weapons Ready, Hearts Racing

By now Clay was pretty sure that LeClerc had been compromised. His erratic behaviour on the phone, the fear in his voice, the sudden change from recalcitrant and defensive to apologetic and helpful – all suggested something was seriously wrong. Was he being manipulated? Had he been paid off? Knowingly or not, and for reasons Clay could only begin to guess, LeClerc had sent him into a trap. Rania, too, most likely. The tail from the airport was proof enough. Whether Hamour was a willing participant or a witless pawn made little difference. Medved's people were here, and they were closing in.

But in chaos was safety. The bazaar was packed. He had a sixty-second head start and a thousand possible routes. Clay calibrated his internal compass for east, veered left into a narrow-arched passageway and emerged into a snaking artery walled with oriental carpets. Medved's people – he was assuming that they were Medved's people, or Crowbar's, working for Medved – would have no idea where to start. There were too many alleys, too many people, too many shops and turnings, and far too many exits to watch. He moved quickly through the throng, turning right into the broad, high-arched gold souk and quickly left again into the clutter of brasswares, moving steadily north and east. Ten minutes later he emerged, eyes blinking, at the Nurosmaniye Mosque, the domes and minarets on his right, the gardens green and cool, the trees ancient, trunks as thick as cars. His pace was quick but unhurried as he came out onto Bezciler Street. It took him less than thirty seconds to hail a taxi. He jumped in, haggled a price and sank down in the back seat for the ride through the Golden Horn and across the Galata Bridge.

Twenty minutes later the taxi dropped him in one of Tepebaşi's narrow side streets. Rubbish overflowed from ancient bins ranked along the pavement, stinking even in the cool of late afternoon. A cat limped from behind one of the bins, scurried across the road, disappeared down a laneway. Clay found the door he was looking for, pushed it open and moved along a dimly lit corridor, his eyes adjusting to the gloom. The lobby was small, an extension of the corridor, but better lit. He'd stayed here a few years ago, and it didn't look any better now than it did then: the same few plants along the front windowsill, the faded one-star tourist-hotel emblem on the door, the badly laid tile floor, the DIY wood veneer front desk. Clay booked a single room with a phone, one night, paid cash.

The second-floor room was small but clean, with a view of the street. He flung open the shutters and scanned the street below, the modest façade of the Seglik Merkezi Hotel directly opposite. Like most of this part of the city, the buildings were a monotony of grey stone, monuments to another era. Diesel fumes wafted through the open balcony door. A bray of car horns. Clay positioned a chair near the window, placed the telephone nearby, sat and started his vigil. He thought of lighting a cigarette but he didn't smoke now, hadn't since the war. Instead he pulled out a cheap switchblade he'd picked up in the bazaar, weighed the thing in his hand and flicked out the blade, turning it over in his fingers.

The street was busy, cars trundling past, a trickle of pedestrians. An hour passed. At dusk a troika of tourists returned to the hotel, an older couple slung with cameras and umbrellas, a younger woman, their daughter perhaps. Later a taxi pulled up, discharged another couple, idled there a moment and continued on its way. The *Akşam* came, the evening prayer, the first he'd heard in months, a thousand voices scattering shards of hope across the city, the sun lost now to the world, the start of a new day in Islam: God is Great.

Waiting was always the worst part. Those hours before an op, the chunks of time that stuck inside you like a tragedy, endless moonlit wanderings through forests of doubt, blown away once you were in the Puma's open cargo bay, the Angolan bush tearing away below you so close and green, a blur, the wind in your face, all of you packed in tight, shoulders and arms and backs pressed close, men's bodies fused, weapons ready, hearts racing.

God, he could use a drink.

Zdravko free. Jesus Christ. It had been Zdravko, ex of the Russian war in Afghanistan, who had done Rex Medved's dirty work in Yemen: money laundering, assassinations, murder of unarmed villagers. After Clay had put the nine-millimetre slug into the bastard's knee, one thing was sure: he'd be limping.

The room was dark. Passing cars painted the walls with drifting wedges of yellow light. Clay stood, stretched his legs and was about to call down to the front desk for a bottle of water when a lone figure appeared at the corner opposite and started towards the hotel. A woman, covered head to foot in a *burqa* – not nearly as common a sight here as in Yemen, but not unusual. Her stride was steady and smooth, her head still as she swayed beneath the black cloaking. Clay watched her approach, slow, stop then stand facing the entrance to the Seglik Merkezi Hotel. She was carrying a small case. Her back was turned, her shape silhouetted against the yellow lights of the hotel's windows. She glanced quickly left and right and disappeared inside.

Clay grabbed the phone and dialled the number for the Seglik Merkezi's front desk. The number rang.

A clerk answered in Turkish: '*Iyi Akşamlar.*' Good evening.

'Good evening,' Clay repeated in Turkish. '*Lütfen,*' he began. Please. 'A woman has just walked into the hotel. Can you see her?'

'Yes. She is here.'

Just then, a taxi pulled up in front of the hotel. A man stepped out onto the pavement. He was broad-shouldered, dressed in jeans and a dark jacket. The black spearpoint of a pronounced widow's peak split the pale expanse of the man's forehead, signposting a wide, much-damaged nose.

'Please ask her to come to the phone,' Clay said. 'I need to speak with her.'

Clay heard the clerk put down the phone and call out something.

Spearpoint paid the taxi driver, turned and disappeared into the hotel's entrance. Clay stood, heart and blood and breath stalled, the receiver to his ear.

'Sir?' came the clerk's voice, unsure. 'She, the woman, she has gone, Sir.'

Clay dropped the handset, grabbed his bag, flung open his door, took the stairs four at a time. He burst out onto the street and sprinted to the hotel. The lobby was small, a narrow foyer flanked by a reception desk set along one wall. Beyond the desk, towards the back of the lobby, a single elevator and a windowed service door. Rania was nowhere to be seen. Spearpoint was standing at the front desk talking to the clerk. He looked up as Clay entered. His eyes were grey, the colour of weathered concrete. He looked youngish but stressed, prematurely aged somehow, as if he hadn't slept for a long time. He looked Clay up and down with a quick flick, then lowered his eyes and returned his attention to the clerk. Clay continued across the lobby towards the desk at a slow walk and stood behind Spearpoint as if waiting to check in, bag in hand.

The clerk pointed to the back service door. Spearpoint nodded and started towards the door with long, steady strides.

Clay looked at the clerk. '*Bayan?*' he asked. The woman?

The clerk gave him a quizzical look.

'Where did she go?'

The clerk pointed again towards the service door.

By the time Clay burst through into the corridor, Spearpoint was three-quarters of the way to the rear exit. Clay called out to him. Spearpoint slowed and glanced back over his shoulder. Then he stopped, turned and faced Clay, squaring himself.

'*Problem?*' Spearpoint shouted, the same meaning in Turkish as English.

Clay didn't answer. Just kept closing the fifteen metres that separated them, his hand in his jacket pocket closing around the switchblade's grip, watching Spearpoint's shoulders coil, the fists starting to take shape, and in that action telling Clay everything he needed to know.

Clay was about five metres away when Spearpoint turned and ran, crashed through the back door and into the night. Clay followed, out into the alley. Spearpoint was running east towards Tepebaşi Street, his footfall echoing across the brick. Clay checked back in the opposite direction. Here, where the rooftops were higher, it was dark. But further along, dim city light rinsed one side of the alley. In the facing shadows, a black shape emerged from behind a rubbish bin and moved away towards the intersection. The woman. Clay swivelled round just in time to see Spearpoint reach Tepebaşi Street and disappear into the traffic. By the time he turned back again, the woman was gone.

Clay sprinted along the alleyway to the intersection. A narrow street with a few shops, the occasional tree, a mosque further up, a couple of pedestrians. He scanned the street up and back. More shops, a couple of delivery vans parked half up on the narrow concrete pavement. And just beyond, a flash of black passing under a streetlamp, a shrouded figure moving away at pace.

Clay looked back along the length of the alleyway, the leaking bins and talus slopes of rubbish, the stained concrete, the windowless rear walls of buildings serried like ranks of half-held secrets. He started after the woman.

She was moving quickly but he closed the gap, the sound of his boot soles on the pavement reverberating between the close-built, balcony-studded façades. He'd reached the vans when the woman stopped. She was alone, the next intersection still twenty metres away, the traffic lights burning green, waiting cars painting the tarmac with their headlights. Then she turned and looked back at him.

16

Constantinople Electric

They moved like assassins through the dinnertime streets. Just before the main road they turned down a narrow lane, all Ottoman facings and overhanging balconies, electric light banding through shuttered windows. The lane narrowed, split. They veered south across scattered islands of lamplight, through wide channels of darkness. The laneway ended at the high wall of an anonymous mosque, ancient even here, another of the many converted Christian churches, the minarets grafted afterthoughts, prosthetics. He swung open an iron gate. She reached for his hand. He led her through the unlit grounds, under centuries-old cypresses swaying among the first stars, past tombstones with names long since erased, up through the empty courtyard to the eastern gate. From there they followed a stonework footpath to a narrow stairway that twisted up through the lithic guts of the city until they emerged at a promontory.

All of Istanbul lay below.

The Golden Horn pulsed like a diode, electrons pouring in through the Galata Bridge, Constantinople electric.

They were alone.

'*Magnifique*,' she said.

He looked into her eyes. '*Ja*, definitely.'

Her eyes smiled.

He reached up for her veil but before he could pull it aside she took his hand, moved it away. 'I am being followed,' she said.

'I noticed.'

She looked down, still holding his hand. 'I know, Claymore. Please do not say it.'

Clay glanced back along the pathway. 'There is a place we can go. The proprietor is a friend. We'll be safe there, for a little while anyway.'

She nodded.

He glanced at her case, smiled. 'Planning to stay the night?'

She tutted, took his hand. 'Let's *ontrek*.'

He smiled again, couldn't stop smiling. The French-accented Afrikaans sounded sweet from her tongue. *Soos engele*. Like angels.

After half an hour of backtracking and careful halts, she – the one trained in counter-surveillance – was sure they were not being followed. Ten minutes later they slipped into the service entrance of the Pera Palas hotel and made their way to the lobby. Kemal Atatürk glared down at them from his portrait above the reception desk as if he were still here, plotting the revolution from these very rooms, from the Long Bar across the lobby.

The proprietor was happy to see Clay, agreed it had been some time, and with a discrete nod agreed that he was in fact not here at all, nor had they ever met, then passed him a room key without registering them. Clay led Rania to the old, wrought-steel, open-cage lift. The uniformed operator touched his fez, closed the grille and pushed the lever, starting the cables hissing up to the fourth floor.

Clay dumped their bags on the floor, bolted and chained the door, walked to the balcony and opened up the big French doors. Night air streamed in, the sounds and smells of the city, all of its layered chaos.

He turned to face her.

Rania pulled off her *burqa*. She was the same woman he'd first met in the wilds of Yemen barely seven months ago, the one who'd uncovered in him a few dim coals of hope for the future, the same, but different somehow, older, more bruised, despite the heart-stopping beauty. Two metres separated them. It felt like two kilometres.

He was about to ask her why she'd said what she'd said – about going back to Africa on his own, about it all being, what was the word she'd used? *premature* – when she raised her finger to her lips. Then she stepped towards him, wrapped her arms around his neck and pulled him down to her, her lips micron close so he could feel the pulsing heat of them.

'*Hurry*,' she whispered.

❨

Later he woke to the sounds of the street. She moulded to him, head on his chest, naked thigh drawn up over his knees. He breathed her in, filled his lungs with her to overdose from it.

She stirred.

He kissed her head.

'*Chéri*,' she whispered. 'Thank you for coming.'

'Thank *you*,' Clay said, expecting a rebuke.

'*Tu es impossible*,' she said, delivering it. She ran her hand along his torso, down to his stomach, taking him in her hand. Then she pressed her lips to his ear, as if frightened that someone might hear. 'Do it again,' she whispered.

Afterwards, Clay picked up the phone, ordered some late dinner to the room: salad, dolmades, roast chicken, bread, fresh lime juice, water. Rania rose, put on a hotel housecoat and started unpacking her case.

'Don't get too settled,' he said, watching her. 'We may have to leave in a hurry.'

She stood facing him, a small book cradled in her hands. The page edges had been gilded once, the silver text-block now a worn, tarnished grey. She looked up at him. 'It was my father's Koran,' she said. 'I always have it with me.' She held it out for him.

It was a small leather-bound volume, the Arabic script dense, impenetrable. On the inside front cover was a handwritten dedication, also in Arabic. All Clay could make out was the year, 1980. He closed the cover and handed it back to her.

'Madame Debret told me your father was killed when you were young,' he said.

She took the book, held it in both hands. 'I was twelve.'

'Algerian Islamists, she told me.'

Rania combed one hand through her hair and placed the Koran on the bedside table. 'They came into our house, herded my mother and me into the sitting room, made my father kneel in front of us and shot him in the head.'

Clay felt his heart stop. 'Jesus, Ra, I'm sorry.'

Rania looked at him for a moment as if she was going to say something, hung on it, frowned, then picked up her bag and disappeared into the bathroom. Moments later, the sound of a bath being run, steam wisping from the half-closed door. He lay back on the bed, closed his eyes. He heard the taps squeak, the rush of water slow then stop, the lap as she stepped into the tub, sank in. Then water lifted in cupped hands, poured over bare shoulders, laving over breasts, dripping from nipples. He could feel the hormones swimming through his body, the echo of her touch, the adrenaline there too. He was hard again, aching. He stood, walked naked to the balcony, gripped the rail as if it were a lifeline and looked out over the city, all the distance there, a half-moon rising over the Sea of Marmara, big and red through the smog and the haze from the sea.

She called to him, her voice echoing off the bathroom tile.

She was lying in the tub, wet hair plastered over her skull, her chest. Her breasts bobbed on the surface. They were big. Bigger than he remembered.

'Times like this I wish I still had two hands,' he said, staring.

She smiled up at him, lowered her eyes. 'You do well enough with one.'

He pulled up a stool and sat next to her.

She ran her hands through her hair, wrung out one of the tresses. 'You should marry me,' she said.

Clay ran his gaze from her eyes to her feet and back up again, slowly. He did not want to ask her about what she'd said on the phone, why she'd pushed him away. Not now.

'I should,' he said. 'It's late, now. How about tomorrow?'

'Yes,' she said, not smiling. 'Let's.'

'And then we'll *ontrek*, wife. Disappear.'

Rania crossed her arms across her chest. 'After,' she said.

'After what?'

'After I finish this story.'

Clay sat a moment staring into the water. 'They burned your place down,' he said, his tone flat.

She looked up, confusion in her eyes. 'What did you say?'

'I was in Champéry two days ago. Your chalet burned to the ground. It wasn't a coincidence, Rania. I was trying to tell you on the phone, they're on to you.'

Rania gasped, put her hand to her mouth. '*Mon dieu*. Heloïse. Madame Debret. Is she safe?'

'The *aubergiste* said no one was home when it went up.'

'*Al hamdillulah*,' she muttered. 'That explains why I have not been able to reach her. I hope she is alright. She must be very sad. It was her grandfather's house.'

'I looked everywhere for her. All over the village. No one has seen her since the fire.'

'Hope warned me this would happen,' she said.

'Hope?'

'Hope Bachmann. We have been working together in Cyprus. Or rather she has been providing me with information. We…' she hesitated, crossed her legs under the water, 'we have become friends.' Rania reached for a towel. Clay passed one to her. She stood and wrapped herself, did the same with her hair.

'University of California?' he asked.

Rania nodded. 'She said that sooner or later, if I wrote those stories, I would be threatened.'

Clay sat looking at her. Sooner, then. He didn't say it.

'She has had death threats, Clay, just for speaking out.' Rania stood before the mirror, wiped away the condensation with a hand towel and considered her reflection.

Clay looked down at his feet, the steam beading on the marble floor. 'It's not because of what you've written, Rania. I've been trying to tell you. It's Regina Medved. She wants revenge.'

Still staring at his feet, he told her about Eben, the threats delivered through his bank, about Crowbar's betrayal, his escape across the Channel. 'I think LeClerc sold us out.'

Rania turned. '*Impossible*,' she said.

'He told me you were here. His Istanbul station chief is the only one who knew about our rendezvous at the Seglik Merkezi Hotel.'

'Hamour, yes. He passed on your message. Marcus Edward. He did exactly what you asked him, Claymore.'

'And that thug arrives at the hotel moments after you.'

'He was following me before I got the message from Hamour.'

'Broad shoulders, pronounced widow's peak?'

She nodded. 'I thought I had lost him.'

'LeClerc was the only person who knew I was coming to Istanbul. I was tailed all the way from the airport, for Christ's sake.'

Rania scowled at him in the mirror. 'Medved has informants everywhere, Clay, in the customs services, in the government, the airlines. It could have been anyone.'

There was a rap at the door. Clay turned, closed the bathroom door behind him, walked to the suite's entrance and looked through the door lens. A liveried bellboy stood in the hallway with a trolley, blown out, spherical. He was alone. Clay opened the door, ushered the bellboy in and watched him open up the table, spread white linen, centre a single rose in a crystal vase, remove the silver cloches and lay out the food. Clay signed the bill, palmed him a tip then bolted the door behind him.

Rania emerged fifteen minutes later, radiant, wearing a clinging, white silk nightgown. Clay poured them some fresh lime juice.

'Not drinking?' she asked, eyes like black obsidian.

'Trying to stop,' he said.

'Are you changing for me?' she asked, smiling. 'I hope not.'

'For me.'

'Good, then.'

He tried to eat, watched her. He wasn't hungry.

☾

Later that night they woke, bodies entwined. The curtains streamed in a cold breeze and the shutters banged on their hinges. Clay rose and closed the shutters, then slid back in beside her, soaking up her warmth. Lying there in the darkness, she told him everything that had happened since London.

After fleeing the hotel room with only the clothes she was wearing, her passport and her purse, she'd booked the first flight from Heathrow to Geneva, gone back to Champéry as he'd asked and stayed put, expecting to hear from him. A week passed, two. Then she'd heard Medved's murder reported on the radio, and while she'd hoped he hadn't done it, she knew he had. She was angry, she said. Angry with him for leaving her, angry with herself for doing as he'd asked, angry with that conservative Muslim part of her that reflexively sought to defer to a husband she didn't have. She used the word without irony or artifice, as if it were fact. After six weeks, she'd resolved that it was over. That he didn't love her. That the whole thing had been stillborn, nothing more than a short-lived chemical reaction born of fear and proximity and lust and shared purpose.

Clay said nothing, let her speak. The infernal husband.

'And then LeClerc contacted me and asked me to cover a story about stolen religious artefacts in Northern Cyprus. I have always been fascinated by the clash of cultures in the Levant. I grew up with it. So I took the assignment, started researching and flew out there. It was good to have something else to do.' She shifted up onto her elbow, ran her hand across his chest.

'Madame Debret told me that LeClerc insisted you take the job.'

'He was very *résolu*, very keen.'

Clay said nothing, remembering the last time he spoke with LeClerc, his voice clear of the hesitation and fear Clay had heard through the phone in Santander. He wondered what had changed and why.

'On my first trip to Nicosia, I met Nikos Chrisostomedes,' Rania continued, 'a powerful, ridiculously wealthy Cypriot businessman. He is rumoured to be the money behind Neo-Enosis. Greek Cypriots see him as something of a hero, tilting at the nasty Turks and the UN. He is very popular at the moment.' She traced her hand towards his shoulder blade, touched the pendant that hung from a leather string around his neck, turned it over in her fingers, just as she had months ago in that little village in the Yemen hinterland. 'You never told me what this was,' she whispered.

Clay looked out into the darkness, the city glow coming like a blurred memory through the shutters. 'Chrisostomedes is a property developer, isn't he?'

'Correct. According to him, the thefts of religious artefacts in the north are a coordinated effort led by one man, Mohamed Erkan, a Turk who has built up huge business interests in Northern Cyprus since 1974.'

'I've seen pictures of him in the paper. Lots of them.'

'Not recently. His money has brought misfortune. Three years ago his wife was blinded in an acid attack. His son was killed shortly after in a helicopter crash. Since then, he has rarely been seen in public.' Rania snuggled closer, still fondling the pendant, tracing the flat curvature of it with her thumb. 'It is so, how do you say, *déchiré*, as if it were torn from something. What is it from, Claymore?'

He moved her hand away, propped himself up against the headboard. 'What's driving the market for the religious stuff?'

'Most of the demand is coming from Russia. Communism is dead, faith has returned, and there is a new class of super-rich seeking to express themselves. The old illuminations are particularly prized, apparently.'

'I've been following your stories,' he said, too loud for the darkness. 'Whenever I could.'

She kissed his chest. 'I interviewed government ministers on both sides of the Green Line, spoke to museum curators and Greek Orthodox priests. Everyone knows it is happening, but no one seems to know how to stop it. Most just do not seem to care. It was quite

depressing, actually.' She took a deep breath. 'It also became apparent that artefacts are not the real issue.'

'Land?'

'*Exactement.* Ever since 1974, every reunification plan has included
the stipulation that land in the north owned by Greeks should be
returned, or appropriate compensation offered.'

'And every plan has failed,' he said.

'*Oui.* It has always been the main sticking point in the negotiations.'

'That's because before '74, Greek Cypriots owned ninety percent
of the land in the north.'

Rania glanced at him sidelong.

'I lived there for three years.' He wasn't sure he'd ever told her. 'It's
all you ever hear about.'

She pushed herself up against the headboard, pulled the sheet up
over her breasts. 'Hope says Chrisostomedes is using the plight of the
turtles to focus international attention on the theft of Greek land in
the north. After all, it is the beachfront property they all want, the
turtle-nesting beaches currently protected by the UN.'

She reached up for the pendant again, traced her fingers along the
kudu leather strap around his neck. 'Why won't you tell me? What
is it?'

He looked her in the eyes, square. 'Bone.'

'It is so jagged. So *heurté.*'

'That's what happens,' he said, taking her hand gently in his and
holding it tight. Something lurched inside him and he recognised
it as fear, surfacing again, a recurrent malaria from whose delirium
respite was only ever temporary. Fear, and something else.

'Why are you here, Rania?'

'Chrisostomedes is behind two of the biggest proposed seafront
resort developments in the south, including one near Lara Beach,
a major turtle-nesting site. Hope says he does not give a–' Rania
stumbled, stopped. 'She says *shit*, about the turtles; that all he cares
about is the land.' The word seemed incongruous in her mouth,
bitter of taste. She winced. 'I have been up there, to Karpasia in

the north. The TRNC Government people I spoke with were tentative and unhelpful. Everywhere I went, I was "escorted" by Turkish police. In Karpasia I tried to interview some of the locals. It was bizarre.' She said it the French way, *bizarre*. 'No one would speak to me. As soon as I mentioned the beaches, the turtles or the planned development, they would go quiet. And Erkan has already started work. New roads are going in, land is being cleared. It should not be happening – those beaches are UN World Heritage Sites – but it is. Chrisostomedes blames Erkan. Both governments seem to be blind to it, or worse. And people are dying – eight unsolved murders in the last month, all in Karpasia, usually the quietest, most out-of-the way place you could imagine.'

'I've been,' he said, recalling the sweep of deserted, white-sand beaches, the towering dunes, green wooded hills, his lonely campsite in the trees, everything, until now, untouched.

'Erkan blames Neo-Enosis for the murders. That is why I came to Istanbul.'

Clay turned to face her.

'I came to interview Erkan,' she said. 'I am meeting him for lunch tomorrow.'

17

It Could Have Been Any of Them

They lay together in the darkness for a long time, her hand in his, their bodies touching. Outside, the city fell deeper into its ancient REM. The sea air, purged of diesel, flowed through the shutters, iodine clean.

She reached up, ran her finger along the scar on his cheek, traced it down again to the pendant. 'Before, you said: "that's what happens",' she whispered. 'When what happens? Tell me, Claymore.'

And then he was there again, for the hundred thousandth time, shafts of sun blasting through burned grass, a cosmos of dust swirling in a blue universe, covering him over, filling his mouth and his eyes, the sound of it moving inside his head, pushing from the inside against his ears so that there was no other sound, only the soft roar of the dust in his head. And then a face, haloed in smoke, the mouth moving, a hand reaching down to his face. Crowbar looking down at him and then turning away, calling out something, his chest rising and falling and the veins in his neck turgid, the heavy, blond-stubbled jaw working, though Clay could hear only the dust. And then Crowbar pulling him to his feet, looking him in the eyes, pushing his weapon into his hands. Straker, you're good, he heard through the smoke and dust. You're okay. And then his cheek afire, his tongue exploring the new, jagged topography inside his mouth, and then Crowbar reaching up to his face and pulling hard so that he almost knocked Clay over. And then the intrusion was gone and for a moment a hole opened up in his face and Clay could feel the air flowing over the side of his tongue. Then Crowbar pushing a compress against his face and tying it around the back of his head and holding up the thing for Clay to see.

'Claymore,' she whispered, the sound of his name unfamiliar to him in her accented lilt. She kissed his cheek, the scar there. '*Chéri*, are you alright?'

He looked at the wall. 'That's what happens, Rania, when a twenty-three-millimetre anti-aircraft shell travelling at 980 metres per second hits a human body,' he said. Clay closed his eyes, drank in the sound of her breathing, the touch of her skin. 'It's a piece of Kingfisher's skull,' he said, staring straight ahead. 'A friend.' He reached up and touched the scar on his cheek. 'It caused this.'

And then Crowbar had grabbed Clay's jaw, looked into his eyes, turned his head left then right. Ambush, he said. Assholes got Cooper, too. The slap on the back. You're okay, Straker. Come on. Firing's coming from that village. And then Crowbar was gone through the smoke towards the white church on the edge of the *chana*.

'After it happened,' Clay said, listening to his own voice in the darkness of the room, echoing from the glass, not him somehow, 'I just stood there looking down at him.' Standing on shaking legs, swaying in the hot sun, staring at Kingfisher's headless corpse in the grass. The body was strangely unscathed, the arms splayed wide, palms to the sky as if he were taking an afternoon nap in the sun, the webbing bulky around the waist, the nutria brown uniform covered in dust and dark patches of sweat. It could have been any of them.

'Why keep it here, *chéri*,' she said, 'reminding you of something so horrible?'

'Why do you keep your father's Koran, Ra?'

'It was the last thing he gave me.' She wiped her eyes. 'It is all I have left of him.'

Eleven years ago he'd put the piece of bloodied skull into his pocket, checked his R4 and, crouching low, started out across the grass towards the white church, the crack of rifle fire coming from the treeline, the mechanical hum of de Koch's MAG loosing off burst after burst, AK47s banging in response, the air above him alive with metal. And afterwards, standing there in the smouldering ash of the village, the bodies of the Himba women and the children and the old bushmen scattered about like discarded toys, they had agreed, all of them, never to speak of it again. They knew the fire had come from here, had found five FAPLA fighters dead among the bushmen, as many weapons, the anti-aircraft gun. It had been a mistake, they'd agreed, although they all knew it hadn't, had realised almost immediately that the village was inhabited. But they hadn't stopped. There was never any chance of it. Swept up by rage, only blood would slake them. Clay had charged in with the rest, screaming and yelling 'cease fire' till his larynx burst, but they hadn't stopped. And when Bluey detonated a FAPLA mine, blowing his legs off, everyone just went berserk, Clay firing too now, emptying magazine after magazine into everything that moved until the barrel of his weapon smoked red hot. And at the tribunal he'd stood up in his dress uniform in turn and sworn that there had been no civilians killed that day and that the Bosbok crew who'd overflown later and reported the massacre must have seen the result of a FAPLA retaliation on their own people. That's how it had stayed for twelve years now, hidden away in the SADF Provost General's archives, just another episode in a shitty war that few had heard of and no one cared about.

He told her all of it, every detail, painstakingly, knowing that with every word of truth he was pushing her away. And when he was finished she lay there for a long time and all he could hear was her breathing and the sound of her tears, the dim outline of her so close.

'It's there,' he said finally, 'because I never want to forget.'

18

Likelihood and Consequence

He woke early and lay watching her sleep, an Orient of regret marshalling in the colourless dawn. It had not been a dream. He'd told her everything, all of it. And if she decided now to exile him from her life forever, he would understand, embrace it even, as just but wholly insufficient penance. And he realised, as he watched the gentle rise and fall of her chest under the blanket, that no other dreams had come that night, and that in the telling of it something had been released. For the first time in a decade, he'd slept, really slept.

And she was still here.

When she woke, much later, she turned and looked at him. Morning prismed through the windows, lit her eyes. She smiled at him, took his hand. Two such simple things: a contraction of facial muscles, the fingertip touch of her hand; and in them a million chemical pulses to overload his senses, like reversing polarity on one of his PTSD freaks, as good as the worst were bad.

'Wow,' he managed.

'What, *chéri?*'

He took a breath. 'You're beautiful.' No words were adequate.

She smiled big. 'I have something for you.' She reached for her Koran from the bedside table. As she did, the bedsheet fell away, exposing her naked breasts.

The effect on his body was immediate and violent, a morning surge of testosterone that mixed with whatever else she had already triggered in him and made his head spin. She sat up and leafed through the pages as if unaware of the impact she was having on him.

Making no attempt to cover herself, she read the passage aloud in Arabic, tracing right to left with her index finger. Then she closed the book, put the same finger under his chin and lifted his head up so that he was looking into her eyes. 'Concentrate, *chéri*.'

'I am.'

She smiled, pulled the bedsheet up over her chest. 'Do you know Sura forty-seven?'

Clay fought to clear space in his mind. 'Surat Muhammad?'

She nodded.

'Those that disbelieve and avert people from the ways of Allah – He will waste their deeds,' he said. 'Something like that.'

'Near enough,' she said with a flick of a smile. 'Do you know the second verse?'

Clay shook his head.

'Those who believe and do good works, He will rid them of their ill-deeds and improve their condition.'

Clay said nothing, stared back into her eyes, fighting against the riptide of desire pulling him in.

'Do you not see? You can be forgiven.'

The effect of her words was immediate and complete. The euphoria was gone, replaced by the cold clarity of the graveside. 'No,' he said, looking away. 'I can't.'

'*I* forgive you, Claymore.'

Clay lay on the bed beside her for a long time without speaking, watching the sun angle higher across the hotel room walls, trying to process all of this. After a while she slipped from under the sheets and padded to the bathroom. He heard the toilet flush, the taps open, the sound of water streaming over naked flesh, falling to the tile. This was not something he had ever considered. How was forgiveness by another possible, when he had long ago decided that he would never bestow it upon himself? And even then, did it matter? Would it change anything? If he hadn't checked into Hell quite yet – if such a place even existed (and he was pretty sure it didn't, despite Rania's fervent belief in both it and its logical opposite) – he damn sure had a reservation.

After a while Rania reappeared and sat on the side of the bed, a single white towel wrapped around her body. Her hair hung in wet tresses across her shoulders. She looked into his eyes. '*Chéri*,' she said. 'I–'

But he didn't let her finish. He pulled her to him. Her lips met his, parted. Time slowed. Existence compressed into this – only this. Her. He pulled the towel from her body. He did it roughly, pushed her down to the bed, still kissing her hard. She moaned into him. He took her. She yielded. He was rough with her, not like the night before, when he'd been gentle and tender, but with abandon. He turned her over and pushed her head down hard into the bed and the more she opened herself, the more she took, the harder he was, the meaner, until at the end he was cursing under his breath as he emptied himself into her and hating himself for it.

After, Rania kissed him. She was gentle, as if the storm he'd unleashed were of no consequence, as if she *understood*. She rose silently, sat at the mirror, applied her makeup, dressed before him. He watched her from the bed, still grappling with everything she had offered, part of him still not understanding, not wanting to understand. She chose a dark pencil skirt and matching jacket, the blouse cut low enough to notice. Then she sat at the desk and picked up the phone. After a brief conversation in French she hung up and tried another number. After a few more calls she turned in the chair and looked at him.

'There is no trace of Heloïse,' she said. 'I tried everyone who knows her. It is very unlike her to disappear like this, absolutely unheard of.' She walked over to the bed, sat next to him and put her face in her hands. '*Mon dieu*, Claymore, what has happened to her?'

Clay put his arm around her.

She looked up at him. Tears welled in her eyes, beaded on her mascara-thickened lashes. 'After I have finished this interview, we will go home.'

'After *we've* finished the interview,' he said.

She ran her fingers along his cheek, along the scar there.

'I'm coming with you,' he said.

☾

As the taxi creaked along the Çirağan road, the Bosphorus flashing between the turrets and domes of teetering Ottoman houses, Rania there beside him, silent under the black burqa, Clay assessed risk. It was something he did routinely in his work as an engineer, back before he'd met Rania, just eight months ago when he still had a job and the prospect of rebuilding some kind of semi-normal life. Risk as a simple mathematical analysis; hazard described as the product of likelihood and consequence. The fact that Rania had come to Istanbul intending to interview Erkan, had set it all up beforehand, meant that anyone with access to Erkan knew she was here. Spearpoint's appearance in the lobby of the Seglik Merkezi Hotel the night before was proof enough. Likelihood: high. Despite Rania's remonstrations, he was more convinced than ever that LeClerc had sold them out, almost certainly to Medved and Crowbar. Erkan already knew Rania was coming to him so had no need to have her followed. Or did he? Clay intended to find out. Whichever way he considered it, the consequences were potentially catastrophic – possible loss of life. Multiply the two, and it was clear that they were in a situation that a risk-assessment specialist would technically describe as *in the shit*.

They arrived at Erkan's place twenty-five minutes later. Rania was sure they hadn't been tracked, but that did little to settle the churning rapids of worry eroding Clay's insides. The taxi dropped them on the street before a steel gate set in a ten-foot stone wall topped with razor wire. Clay pushed the call button and scanned the street. A moment later the gate opened and a uniformed guard ushered them into the compound.

The house had an elegance that no longer seemed possible. Ottoman, wood, beautifully restored, its three balanced stories gleaming white, the blue Bosphorus sparkling behind, lush, treed gardens in front, it was a place built for a prince, a princess perhaps, another relic in a city of relics.

Rania pulled off her burqa. '*Superbe*,' she whispered.

Erkan met them at the front door, flanked by two bodyguards. He was not much taller than Rania, with greying, too-long hair and a truck-driver's moustache. His expensive silk suit was too wide in the shoulders, pinched and drawn around the middle. He reached for Rania's hand, kissed it.

'*Mademoiselle*,' he said, '*vous êtes bienvenue.*'

'*Merçi.*' Rania smiled, glanced at Clay, replied in French. 'This is my colleague, Monsieur Greene.'

'I was expecting—' Erkan stopped mid-sentence, shot a disappointed glance at Clay. 'I thought we had agreed that you would come alone, Lise. May I call you Lise?'

'I made no such promise, Monsieur Erkan.' Rania smoothed her jacket. 'A pious Muslim woman does not meet strange men alone. You should know that. And please, Mademoiselle is fine for now.' Rania glanced at Clay a moment.

Clay took a step towards Erkan, already not liking this guy. 'And is this the committee?' he said, in Turkish, raising his chin towards the bodyguards.

Erkan looked at him, confused. 'Pardon me, Mister Greene?'

'The welcome committee.'

The bodyguards, a six-foot-five monster with bulging neck muscles and a prominent early homonid forehead, and a woman with dark, scrub-brush hair, wide hips and swimmer's shoulders, glared at him in unison. They both wore black military-style trousers and black t-shirts. Neither appeared armed, but Clay suspected weapons would appear quickly if needed.

Erkan turned up the intensity of his smile a notch, held it for a couple of seconds then let it slide away. 'Your colleague is a comic, Mademoiselle,' he said in English.

Rania glanced at Clay, the edge of a frown showing. 'Not a very good one, I am afraid.'

'No,' said Erkan, offering his arm to Rania, leading her through the main entrance into a grand foyer dominated by a swirling carved balustrade, a ton of crystal hanging high above like a partially

condensed cloud, then over hardwood parquet through a tapestried
sitting room out to the seaside patio. Clay followed; the body guards,
Ho (♀) and Hum (♂), a few paces back. A table for two set against
the sea rail, a parasol flapping in the breeze, potted palms, boats
plying the channel beyond, the iodine sodium-chloride tang of the
sea twitching in the air. Erkan clapped his hands, called for another
place setting, pulled out a chair for Rania, helped her sit then took
his place across from her. Clay stood admiring the view. The bodyguards stood by the doorway admiring them.

A uniformed waiter came and set out *rakı* and water. Erkan offered
some to Rania. She declined.

'I want you to know, Mademoiselle Moulinbecq,' said Erkan,
pouring himself a glass of *rakı,* adding water, 'that I have agreed to
this interview as a courtesy to your respected organisation.' The two
clear liquids clouded like a winter sky.

'Thank you,' said Rania.

The waiter brought salad, grilled fish and a chair for Clay. They
ate, watching the boats moving over the water, wakes like comets'
tails. After the plates were removed, Erkan lit a cigar, leaned back
in his chair. 'Before we begin, young lady, I want it understood that
this conversation must be kept entirely off the record. That is why I
wanted you to come alone.' He glared at Clay.

Rania nodded. 'I understand. You have my word.'

They both looked at Clay.

'My word also,' said Clay.

'If any of this is published I will deny it as pure fabrication. Do
you understand?'

Rania nodded again.

Erkan tipped ash from his cigar into the ashtray. 'Good,' he said.
'What you have written about me over the past days, quite frankly,
is slander.'

Rania blanched.

'I suggest you check your facts, in future, before committing such
rubbish to print.'

Rania made to speak but Erkan held up his cigar hand.

'Neo-Enosis, young lady, these are the criminals. In the last two weeks, four of my employees have been murdered, and you write about a few religious icons, about some sea animals? Where is your sense of perspective? The real issue is this: Turkish Cypriots are once again being terrorised by a callous Greek majority.' Erkan took a long drink and wiped his moustached lips with finger and thumb.

'What do you know about the collection and sale of historic religious artefacts from Greek Orthodox churches and shrines in the north?'

Erkan waved his cigar, glanced down Rania's top. 'From time to time I buy pieces from local collectors and sell them on to foreign buyers.'

Rania straightened in her seat. 'Local collectors?'

'Individuals acting of their own accord.'

'And your buyers?'

Erkan frowned, hesitated. 'Confidential, of course.'

Rania flipped over a page in her notebook. 'Can you comment on the illegal appropriation of Greek-owned land in the north, Monsieur Erkan?' Rania's voice was steady, all business.

'Everything I do in Cyprus is legal. I have land titles, permits, environmental approvals from the government.'

'A government that no country in the world except Turkey recognises,' said Clay.

Rania shot him a shut-up look.

Erkan's face creased. 'I am not a politician, thank God. I follow the laws, I do not make them.'

'There are those who suggest otherwise,' said Rania.

Erkan examined the length of his cigar, took a puff. 'If you want to understand Cyprus, young lady, you must first understand that it is the Turkish minority who are the victims, despite the loud noises made in the press by the Greeks about invasion, pillage, cultural genocide, and so on. It is exactly the opposite. If you want a real story, look into the dealings of Laiki Resorts and Properties in the south, for instance.'

'One of Nikos Chrisostomedes' companies,' said Rania, flipping open her notebook.

'Exactly. Whose land do you think they built the Alassou Resort on, last year, near Polis? Look into the records and you will find it was Turkish land, appropriated after the war. Illegally, I stress. Chrisostomedes bribed several government ministers to get approval to build inside a national park, to waive the Turkish-owned land titles.'

Clay had driven past the place several times on his way to the Agamas peninsula, Greek Cyprus's rugged last frontier, its mountains and steep coastlines gradually being whittled away by development.

'Do you have proof of this?' said Rania.

'My own eyes.'

Rania glanced over at Clay, waiting for Erkan to continue.

'In July of 1990, Christos Dimitriou, then Minister of Tourism and Development, received 250,000 euros, paid to an offshore account. In return, he approved the Alassou development the following month.'

Erkan picked up the teapot, offered Rania some. She nodded.

'In the past there has been, how shall I say, some measure of cross-border cooperation in business,' he said, pouring her a cup, one for himself. 'I myself made the transfer to the Minister's account, Mademoiselle. In return I received an interest in one of Chrisostomedes' ventures.' Erkan paused for effect, sipping his tea.

'*Mon dieu*,' breathed Rania.

'Come now, young lady,' smiled Erkan. 'Don't look so surprised. Business knows no boundaries. Chrisostomedes and I have done several unofficial deals together in the past. But that is all over now.'

Rania scribbled in her book. 'What has changed, Monsieur Erkan?'

'Neo-Enosis. That is what has changed. A group dedicated to the re-establishment of Greek dominion over the entire island, by any means possible. Chrisostomedes is one of the leaders of this new movement – or should I call it a revival.'

Enosis. Union with Greece. Clay had heard it discussed many

times when he was living in Cyprus. In 1974, the Turkish Government had used it as the pretext for invasion, invoking its duty to protect the Turkish-Cypriot minority.

Erkan continued. 'Chrisostomedes, garbed in his newfound Hellenic purity, wants to erase any evidence of past cooperation. In short, Mademoiselle, he wants me dead.' Erkan waved over his shoulder towards his bodyguards. 'Hence, these.'

Clay regarded the pair, a complete mismatch. Hum tall and brawny, dull-eyed, Ho squat, all hips, but with a delicate, small-boned, almost girlishly pretty face.

'Can you provide me with proof of this, Monsieur Erkan?' said Rania.

Erkan closed his eyes a moment, bowed his head. When he looked up again there were tears in his eyes. 'Other than the murder of my son, the disfigurement of my lovely wife?'

Rania reached across the table, touched Erkan's hand. 'I am very sorry, Monsieur Erkan.' Clay knew she meant it.

Erkan blinked hard and looked away, out to sea.

'Were the perpetrators found, tried?' Rania asked.

Erkan raised his chin and tutted. No.

'This is a story that needs to be told, Monsieur Erkan. And I can tell it.'

Erkan poured himself another raki and downed it in one go. Then he reached into the breast pocket of his jacket, produced a business card and set it on the table. 'Come to my office tonight,' he said, composure regained. 'I can show you documentary evidence: contracts, correspondence, bank transfer statements. All the proof you need.'

Rania took the card and pressed it into her notebook. 'Thank you. I will.'

Erkan tried a smile, if you could call that flex of his facial muscles a smile.

'And one last thing, Mademoiselle. Chrisostomedes is not alone in this. It has been the same story for centuries. The Greeks camouflage their own greed by blaming the Turk. Chrisostomedes and Neo-Enosis are trying to divert attention away from their illegal activities by garbing themselves as conservationists and accusing us of exactly the crime they themselves are perpetrating.' Erkan stood, bowed to Rania and motioned to the waiter. The interview was over.

'One last question,' said Clay. 'If I may?'

Erkan nodded.

'Why now, Mister Erkan? Why keep this to yourself all this time and reveal it now?'

Erkan took in a lungful of smoke, poured it back out, looked at Rania. 'I am trying to help you, Mademoiselle. The truth. It's what we all seek, no?'

Clay looked out over the channel. The truth. That most elastic of properties, so easily deformed, but so hard to break.

'Now, please allow me to offer you my car and driver to take you back to your hotel.' Erkan handed Rania another card. 'If you contact my driver this evening, he will collect you and bring you to my office.'

Erkan led them out across the lawn to the drive. A big silver Mercedes 500SL rolled slowly towards them, wheels crunching over the white quartz gravel. The uniformed chauffer got out and opened the back door.

'Oh, and Mademoiselle Moulinbecq,' said Erkan. 'One more thing. Tonight, now that I am no longer a stranger, please come alone.' Erkan frowned at Clay, tugged at the cuffs of his suit. 'Then write your story and go home. Cyprus is a dangerous place these days. I would stay away from it if I were you.'

'Strange advice,' said Clay, 'coming from the owner of a tourism company.'

Erkan looked at Clay and smiled, that same forced smile he'd met them with. 'And as for you, Mister *Greene*,' he said in Turkish. 'Fuck off.'

19

Maybe It Had Never Been There at All

Clay settled into the soft leather seat beside Rania, letting the chauffer close the door behind him. Rania took his hand, said nothing. The chauffeur walked around to the driver's door, got in and started the engine. The door locks engaged and the car started forward. Erkan stood on his manicured lawn and watched them go. When the car turned out of the gate he was still standing there, rooted to the same spot, staring.

'The Four Seasons Hotel in Sultanahmet,' Clay said to the driver.

'Please,' said Rania.

The Four Seasons was a long way from their hotel, on the other side of the Bosphorus, in the Golden Horn, the heart of the city's busy tourist district. A good place to disappear.

The Bosphorus slipped past in silence as they shunted towards the Golden Horn. It wasn't until they were just past the Boğaziçi Bridge, the big suspension bridge that links Asia with Europe, that Rania spoke.

'Why did you not call?' she said.

Clay thought about this a moment, wondered why she was broaching this now. 'I did.'

'Three months.'

'Fifty-nine days.' Each day forever.

'It was too long,' she said. 'Too much has happened.'

As usual she was thinking eight steps ahead, all this they were doing now already processed. Clay said nothing, looked into the rear-view mirror. The chauffeur was watching them, talking into a hands-free pickup clipped to his chest, a bud in his ear. Clay had been wary about getting into Erkan's car in the first place, but had figured that no matter what their means of conveyance, Erkan would be watching. This was simply the most convenient arrangement for everyone. Clay glared into the mirror and the chauffeur looked away.

After a while Rania said: 'Are you not going to say anything?'

He'd only half heard. The driver moved the Merc into the right lane, signalled. 'Too much for what?' he said, scanning the road signs.

She was looking away, out of the side window. 'Too much for us.'

The driver slowed the Merc and turned inland towards the Beşiktaş tunnel.

Clay leaned forward, Rania's words only half registering. 'The coast road is the fastest way to the Golden Horn,' he said to the chauffeur. 'Over the Galata Bridge.'

The chauffeur either didn't understand or pretended not to hear, completed the turn and accelerated inland. Rania glanced over at Clay. She'd noticed too.

'We're going to Sultanahmet,' said Clay. 'You're going the wrong way.'

'I take you other route,' said the chauffeur in thickly accented English. 'This time of day, quicker.'

'I doubt that,' said Rania. She turned to Clay, lowered her voice. 'It means tracking all the way up to the Haliç Bridge and then back down.'

'Yes. Faster,' said the chauffeur.

A little punch of adrenaline hit Clay low down, in his knees and quads. The car sped on. Wherever this *oke* was taking them, he was pretty sure it wasn't the Four Seasons. He looked over at Rania. She was thinking the same. He could see it in her eyes.

The Mercedes sped through the tunnel then turned west onto the expressway, still heading in the wrong direction.

Rania looked at him a moment, raised her eyebrows, then unrolled her burqa and threaded it over her head, adjusting the black veil down over her eyes.

The chauffeur guided the Merc onto a slip road and left the expressway. They were moving north now on a main thoroughfare, in exactly the wrong direction, kilometres from where they should be. The pavements were crowded with shoppers. The car slowed in the building traffic. Up ahead, Clay could see the congestion from what looked like a bus station spilling out into the road, a grinding mass of honking steel and glass.

Clay took Rania's hand. 'استعد' he said in Arabic. Get ready.

She nodded. The movement was almost imperceptible, more an exhalation. She reached into her purse, withdrew a small pair of hard-soled slippers and without changing the posture of her upper body replaced her heels with them. The car ground to a halt. Traffic piled in behind, locking them into a lattice of smoking Toyotas, Fords and Opels – moving, but only just.

Clay grabbed the door handle, looked up into the rear-view mirror. 'Thank you,' he said to the chauffeur. 'I think we'll just walk from here.'

'It is still far from the hotel,' said the chauffeur.

'We don't mind. It's a nice day.'

The car was at a standstill now. Clay pushed the door lock release button. Nothing. The master was engaged.

'This traffic not much,' said the chauffeur. 'Clearing soon.' He looked worried.

'Unlock the doors. Now.'

The chauffeur inched the car forward as a space opened up. Clay tried the window button. Nothing. Locked, too.

'Did you hear me?' Clay said, raising his voice a notch. 'I said let us out.'

The driver said nothing, just stared motionless at the traffic. An electric motor whirred inside the car. A glass panel emerged from the ridge of the front seat bench, closing them in.

It wasn't a conscious response. No analysis flashed through his brain. His limbs simply moved, vaulting him forward into the remaining gap. His back caromed off the roof, pitching him face-down into the front passenger seat. At the last instant he rolled right, crashing shoulder first into the front footwell, pulling his feet free of the rising partition. The chauffeur stared at him, surprise bulging his eyes. Rania was pounding her fists on the glass. Clay could see her mouth moving, her voice muffled by the heavy, bullet-proof polycarbonate. The chauffeur glanced back at her, blinked, reached a hand down beside his seat, started pulling out a handgun. It was small, black, some sort of .22. Clay twisted his shoulders and hips, pulled back his right knee almost to his face and let go a kick.

Clay's boot made contact with the chauffeur's head just as he fired. The detonation exploded like a pipe bomb in the enclosed space, the bullet ricocheting from the windscreen and off the partition before embedding itself in the door upholstery inches from Clay's head. The chauffeur's head snapped back instantaneously, slamming into the side-window glass. Rania was hammering on the glass partition. The car started to roll forward, the chauffeur limp and motionless in his seat, his foot no longer applying pressure to the brake pedal. As Clay scrambled to right himself the car crunched into the vehicle in front and lurched to a stop. Car horns blared. He reached over the chauffeur's body and hit the door lock switch. As he did, the man gasped. He was still alive. Thank God. Truly.

Rania was already out of the car and moving away through the gridlock. He thought of trying to find the gun, but decided time was more important. He opened the car door, stepped out into the sea of stranded, exhaling vehicles and started after Rania.

☾

It was mid-afternoon by the time they returned to the Pera Palas hotel, weaving and backtracking their way through the labyrinth of the city before finally reaching Tepebaşi and the hotel.

Rania flung her burqa onto the bed, picked up the phone and ordered up some tea.

Clay walked to the balcony, opened the doors and looked out

over the city, the cradled intersection of Europe and Asia sparkling gas-flame blue and gold through a veil of smog.

Clay turned his back on the city, leaning against the railing. 'Erkan is protecting himself.'

'Protecting someone,' said Rania.

Clay nodded. 'I had assumed it was against reprisal from Chrisostomedes. But the timing's wrong. His wife and son were attacked three years ago, you said. That's when Erkan and Chrisostomedes were doing deals together – mutually beneficial deals.'

'Perhaps,' said Rania, thinking this over. 'But you heard what he said. Neo-Enosis has changed everything. If they weren't enemies before, they certainly are now.'

'You know who Erkan's buying for, don't you?'

'He has many buyers.'

'Regina Medved among them. She is scouring the region for the Patmos Illumination. She thinks it'll cure her.'

Rania sat at the desk, pulled out her notebook and started writing.

'We've got to leave, Rania. We're not safe.'

'Not now, Clay,' she said.

Clay watched her work, the sun angling into the room, refracting off the window glass, through the cut crystal of the old chandelier, the light that seemed to drip from her hair onto her arms, her fine-boned hand working the pen in fluid loops, sending snowflakes of light spinning about the room. He stood behind her, put his hand on her shoulder. 'We have to disappear.'

'I need to file this story,' she said, not looking up from her work.

'I thought you agreed to keep the interview off the record.'

'I will.' She kept writing.

'Okay. File it. We'll leave tonight.'

Rania put down her pen. 'It will be filed once I have looked at those documents, and not before.'

Clay took a deep breath, not quite believing what he'd just heard. 'You're actually thinking of going back there, after what just happened?'

Rania didn't answer.

'If I hadn't – Jesus, Rania. God knows where he would have taken us, what they would have done to us.'

'You go, Claymore,' she said, not looking up. 'I can look after myself.'

He put his hands on her shoulders, turned her around in the chair so that she was facing him, crouched down and looked into her eyes. 'That thing you said in the car,' he whispered. 'That it was too much for us.'

She stared back at him as if from some faraway place. 'I thought–' she stopped. 'It was. It *is*.'

'Is that why you're telling me to go, sending me away?'

'Me? Sending you away?' She laughed, cold. 'Oh, Claymore, *chéri*. You were never here.'

He was quiet for a long time, staring into her eyes, considering this truth. 'Maybe if we'd met thirteen years ago,' he said finally. 'Before.'

Surprise in the widening of her eyes. 'Maybe what?'

'Maybe I could have loved you.' He'd never come close to saying anything like that before. The words stung leaving him.

She sat looking back at him, very quiet. 'Could have?' she managed after a while, a croak. Hurt boiled in her eyes.

'That part of me…' He looked out the window. He didn't know how to say it. That it had died a long time ago, out in that little village in Angola, in that C-130 over the Atlantic, shovelling those poor bastards into the void, that maybe it had never been there at all, that he'd been born without it, whatever it was, that place in the cerebrum where those things happened, where those chemicals were produced, or just that it was stunted too early, atrophied to scar tissue before it had ever had the chance to grow. 'It's gone, Rania.'

20

Things You Do Not Know

She'd stormed from the room, locked herself in the bathroom. She was in there a long time. When she finally opened the door she pushed past him without a word, went straight to the desk, started writing.

He lay on the bed, watching her work.

After a while he went and stood behind her, took her hair in his hand.

'I am finishing this story,' she said, not looking up. 'And then I am going back to Cyprus.'

It took him a long time to reply. 'Cyprus is the worst place you could go,' he said finally. 'You heard what that asshole Erkan said.'

'I will not be intimidated, Claymore.'

'We pissed a lot of people off with what we did in Yemen, what we did to Medved. And I'm telling you they want us dead. Both of us. There's a two-million-pound hit out on me, Rania. Do you understand what that means? Every hired gun for a thousand miles is looking for me, looking for *us*. I was followed from the airport. You were followed yesterday. We were almost taken just now. It's only a matter of time till they find us.'

She turned to face him. She looked scared. Good.

'I must go to Cyprus,' she said.

He put his hand on hers, tried to be gentle. 'I'm known there, Ra. So are you now, by the sounds of it.'

'Can you not see how important this is?'

'This thing you're getting mixed up in, this feud between Erkan and Chrisostomedes, there's no high ground, Rania. Let them go and screw each other. They'll do fine without any help from you. It's not worth risking your life for.'

She looked down, closed her eyes, dark lashes trembling. 'I promised, Claymore.'

'Promised who?'

She tried to spin away, but he held her fast.

'Who, Rania? Who did you promise?'

'Hope,' she said. 'I gave my word that I would help her, Claymore. She is all alone, fighting for the survival of a species, a whole race of creatures who have lived here for hundreds of millions of years.'

'They've had their run, then,' said Clay. 'That's a hell of a lot longer than we'll have, I reckon.'

'Do not say that, Claymore. It is not worthy of you. What else matters, if not life?'

'Jesus, Rania. They're only fucking turtles.' He regretted it as soon as he said it.

Rania jerked her head up, eyes blazing. She whipped her free hand up and open palmed him across the face, snapping his neck back.

Clay stumbled back, put a knee down, raised his stump to his cheek. 'Jesus. What was that for?'

'For everything,' she hissed. 'For not trying hard enough.' Her gaze ripped into him.

Clay said nothing, just stared back at her, trying to understand.

'*Good*, Claymore. That's what this is about: good.'

He wanted to ask her exactly what this obscure notion of good actually was. A decade ago, he was told that dead SWAPO terrorists made the world a better place, and he was rewarded for killing them. For a while, he'd even believed it. Then, in his work, he'd helped the clearing of forests to feed the multitudes, justified the dredging of reefs for new marinas, helped permit factories that made near-new junk, which was chucked into landfills within weeks of being produced, which meant more factories producing even better replacements, keeping thousands of people busy. It was all 'good'. But he did not say any of it. The streets outside ran a current of steel.

The air was thick with a haze of ozone and diesel that seemed to dematerialise buildings only car-lengths away. The sun's disc, faint and forlorn in what should have been a blue sky, fought to pierce the blanket that strangled the city. All of this, but he said nothing.

'It was you who did this, Clay. You.' She jammed her free hand into his chest, tried again to push him away. 'And you were right. I know now what my life is for, why I have been put on this earth. You helped me see it, even if you seem to have forgotten.'

'For God's sake, Rania. The Greeks and Turks have been killing each other for centuries. Do you really think you're going to change anything?'

She was crying now, tears falling from her eyes like broken glass, hard and angular. 'Do you remember what you said to me, when we were piecing the Yemen story together?' She moved her face closer to his, inches only between their lips. 'You said, "*this matters*". I can see it as clearly as if it was now, sitting together on that rock overlooking the glacier.'

Clay stared into the depths of her eyes, the swirling nebula.

'Well *this* matters, Claymore. And because this matters, so do I. Do you understand? Good is rewarded ten-fold. It is in the *Al-Anaam*, Claymore. I have repeated it since I was a little girl, but I had never really understood what it meant. You showed me. And I will always love you for it. Even if you don't.' She pulled her hand away, turned back to her desk.

Clay walked out to the balcony, breathed in a lungful of Istanbul smog, watched the sun starting to slant long across the Bosphorus, Asia Minor falling into darkness. The call to prayer drifted across the Golden Horn, a hundred voices raised to God. Clay wondered if He was listening.

After a while he heard her pick up the phone, dial. She asked for Hamour. A moment of quiet, car horns complaining from the street below.

Perhaps they could send Hamour to have a look at the documents. He was the senior AFP person in the country, after all. Then they could hire a car, drive overland into Greece, take a ferry to Cyprus or get someone to deliver *Flame* to Athens, then sail to Egypt and through the canal. And then? Suddenly the world seemed a very small place. He could hear her describing the outline of the story now, that newspaper language she spoke so well. She was excited, knew she was on to something, a crusader. Then, mid-sentence, she stopped. He heard her gasp, the distorted voice on the other end of the line speaking rapidly. He turned. She was sitting at the desk, the receiver clamped to her ear, her mouth agape, shock in her eyes, confusion. Her lower lip started to tremble. She raised her hand to her mouth and shut her eyes. Then she mumbled something into the phone and placed it gently in its cradle, sat staring at it.

Clay stepped forward. 'What is it, Rania? What's wrong?'

She looked up at him as if she wasn't sure who he was.

'LeClerc,' she mumbled.

Clay said nothing, waited for her to continue.

'He is dead, Claymore. Murdered. They found in him in a flat in Paris this morning, castrated, disfigured. Oh, *mon dieu*.' She buried her face in her hands, sobbing.

Clay stood a moment watching her cry. Then he walked to the armoire, pulled out Rania's case, opened the bureau and started packing her things.

Rania looked up. 'What are you doing?' she managed through her tears.

'We're leaving. Now.'

'Where?'

'I don't know. Anywhere. Africa.'

'No. Cyprus.'

'We'll find a place. Get married.'

'I cannot.'

'Yes you can.'

No answer.

He stopped packing and turned to look at her. 'Understand, Rania. Please. They burnt your house down. God knows what's become of your friend Debret. Now they've killed LeClerc. You're next. That's what they wrote on the wall, in Eben's blood, with a fucking brush for God's sake: *she's next.*'

Her eyes widened a moment, fixed him with a stare full of realization, horror. Then she turned away. 'She is not my friend, Claymore.'

'Who?' he stumbled. 'Who isn't?'

'Héloïse. Madame Debret.'

'What do you mean?'

'She is my aunt, Clay. My father's sister.'

Clay paused for a moment, thinking back. 'All the more reason to go.'

'I have to go back to Cyprus. There are things … things you do not know.'

Clay looked down at his feet on the Turkish carpet, back into those eyes. 'Jesus, Ra, you could fill a planet with them.'

'I am serious, Clay. I should have told you sooner, but…' She looked out of the open windows.

'What is it, Rania? Tell me.'

She picked up the telephone, looked at it a moment as if not quite sure that it was working, that the message it had delivered was real, then replaced it. She sat on the end of the bed. 'When you were away, when I was in Cyprus, I met someone,' she said, her voice flat, as if she'd given up on something.

Clay's insides turned to calcite. This, then, was the 'too much'.

'I was lonely. I was angry. I did not plan it. It just happened. I should have ended it, right then, after that first time, but,' she sobbed, wiped her eyes, 'but I did not. I had convinced myself that it was over between you and me, that there was nothing for us, Claymore, no future.' She lay on the bed and curled up on her side, foetal, her hands covering her face.

Clay stood looking down at her, calculating, trying to wrap logic around something that had no substance, no boundary conditions. Finally he said, hard: 'Is it over now?'

She sobbed. 'No.'

'Do you love him?'

She lay crying, didn't answer. Then she mumbled, 'There is something else.'

'Answer me.'

She lowered her hands, looked at him through eyes streaked black with mascara. 'Not him, Clay,' she whispered. 'Her.'

21

It Can't Hurt You

Clay stared down at the woman on the bed, this woman he thought he knew, unable to process the information being shunted through the war-torn pathways to his brain. Eben dead, Medved and Crowbar closing in, LeClerc tortured to death, Rania's aunt missing. And this. This dagger. Jesus Christ. He clasped his hands behind his head, no, his hand, put the stump over it, flexed his arms, took a deep breath, fought for control.

The telephone rang.

It was the hotel proprietor, Clay's friend. 'Mister Clay, *Efendi*. Please can you come down to the lobby? Something has just occurred which I … I am unsure of … but…' He sounded shaken, spooked.

Clay put down the phone. 'I'm going down to the lobby,' he said, his tone harsher than he wanted, stained with hurt. 'Stay here. Lock the door.'

She looked up at him from the bed, through tears. 'What is it, Claymore?'

'I don't know. Just pack and get ready to leave. I'll be back in a minute.'

He left her curled up on the bed, closed the door behind him, walked down the creaking hardwood corridor to the wide, carpeted stairway, down four flights, watching the steel counterweights and cablework of the lift hissing through the stairwell's hollow core.

The proprietor was waiting for him in the lobby. His hair – normally perfectly parted – was a mess, his tie askew, buttons missing from his jacket.

'What the hell happened?' Clay said in Turkish.

The proprietor did not answer, led him instead behind the main desk, past an equally frightened looking clerk and into his office. He closed the door, sat behind his desk. His face was pale, moist. He looked up at Clay, straightened his tie and swept his dark hair back out of his eyes. 'A man came into the hotel a few minutes ago, *Efendi*. He was asking for a Mister Greene. Declan Greene. He had a gun.'

The proprietor fumbled a cigarette out his pack, put it between his lips, struck his lighter once, twice, and held a trembling flame to it. 'He showed me a photo of you, *Efendi*,' he said, letting the smoke stream back out through his nostrils. 'He asked if I had seen you, if you had been in the hotel.'

'I didn't want to involve you in this, my friend,' said Clay. 'I'm sorry.'

The proprietor waved this away. 'Of course, I said I'd never seen or heard of this person. But then he became angry. He came behind the desk and pushed me into the wall, told me that if I saw you I should call him immediately. He threatened my family.' The proprietor slid a card across the desk. 'He gave me this.'

Clay picked up the card. Just a plain piece of white card with a handwritten string of digits. 'What did he look like?'

'He was well built, tall. *Çirkin*. Ugly. Foreign, by his accent.' The proprietor pointed towards the front door. 'He turned left, walking towards the bridge, no more than five minutes ago.'

'Thank you my friend,' said Clay. 'I promise you won't have any more trouble.'

'*Beyfendi*, please, there is something else. I have telephoned some of my colleagues. It seems this man has been making similar visits to other hotels in Tepebaşi.'

Clay turned the card over in his fingers and handed it back to the proprietor. 'He doesn't know where we are. Not yet, anyway. He's guessing. Can I ask you for one last favour, please, *arkadaşım*?'

The proprietor exhaled smoke. 'Not, I hope, the last. It is my business after all.'

Clay smiled. 'Of course. *Teşekur*.'

'You will be careful, yes?'

'Of course. Please can you phone one of the hotels nearby, one that he's just been to, a friend you can trust. Ask him to call the guy, tell him he's seen me, that I'm there now wanting to book a room.'

The proprietor picked up the telephone. It was an old-style rotary model with a built-in cradle, black, heavy. He dialled, spoke, listened. Then he replaced the receiver.

'An old friend,' he said. 'The Erdoğan hotel. On Tepebaşi Street, towards the bridge. Not far. He's making the call now.'

Clay took his friend's hand and clasped it. Looked into his eyes. '*Teşekur*,' he said. Thanks. '*Çok*.' Much.

Outside the air was cool, benzene fresh. Clay pulled his cap down low over his eyes, pushed up his collar and started towards the bridge. Whoever was tracking them was getting close. The proprietor had deflected them, but for how long? Clay needed to know who was hunting them and why, and he was going to find out. And then they were going to leave.

Cars rolled past. Shop lights flickered, pulsed. He scanned the street, people moving along the pavements, a businessman swinging a folded umbrella, a couple of Turkish teenagers dressed like American kids, Keds sneakers and jeans. He kept to the shadows, moving quickly.

She. Hope. Hope Bachmann. It was obvious. Not that it made much difference who it was. The hole inside would feel just as raw-sided, just as big. The Erdoğan hotel was close now, its blue neon sign glowing up ahead. He quickened his pace as he passed a string of shops dug into the grey granite bases of nineteenth-century monoliths and soon came to the wall of a mosque. He stopped there, in the shadow of the wall, the minarets soaring above him, lay back a moment against the headstone cold surface and tried to focus on the street, the people coming in and out of the hotel. All of the buried loss, the forlorn hope that had shadowed him like a wild dog over days and years crystallised before him. That feeling of being so close to something, almost able to reach out and touch it, and then to watch it disappear and there's not a thing you can do about it. Lights blurred. The street began to warp and distend, a flexing chainmail of interlocking plates. He rocked, steadied. Jesus. He had no right to this, this indulgence. No right to her. Any part of her. Or her forgiveness. What a *dof* he'd been. Fucking idiot. Putting himself into a situation like this, breaking the rule he'd given himself all those years ago, the promise he'd broken in Yemen, broken for her: *don't care, and it can't hurt you*. Vertigo came. He bent double, tried to breathe, to steady himself. A thousand screaming voices rose in his head, pierced its thin, insufficiently evolved shell of bone, burst into the air around him like shrapnel.

His hand found the rough cutwork of the wall. He breathed deep, pushed his back into the stone, clawed at it, fighting to hold on to its solidity. This way he rode the storm, bore its phases like the habits of an old friend. The first few years after the war, young still, each episode had been a new experience in isolation, confusion and fear. It had taken him years to learn how to cope. It hadn't been till much later, in London, that he'd sought medical help, been formally diagnosed. PTSD the doctors had labelled it, back then something that medical science was only just starting to understand.

You could run and keep on running. But for how long? At some point you had to turn and face up, fight. That was what Rania was doing. She'd decided to stand up, put herself between evil and its consequences. He'd seen the determination in her, felt it strong like an ocean current, couldn't help but admire it, didn't even want to try to swim against it. And in that thought he realised that he'd already forgiven her, that he'd never had to forgive her because there was nothing to forgive. Can you love someone you hardly know, truly, with madness? And if so, can you love more than one?

He shook his head, trying to obliterate the gentle violence of this speculation. He propped his hands on his knees, looked up, blinked and watched his vision clear. An old woman walked past him, close on the pavement. She glanced at him sidelong, pulled her shawl close around her shoulders and hurried away. About a hundred metres along, just beyond the hotel, a man stood outside a pastry shop, hands thrust deep into the pockets of a dark leather jacket. He was staring through the traffic, as if searching for someone. Their eyes met.

It was Spearpoint.

Without averting his gaze, Spearpoint pulled a mobile phone from his pocket, flipped it open and put it to his ear.

A battle jolt of adrenaline shot through Clay's body. Within seconds he was in full stride, darting between moving cars, bearing down on the man. He was twenty metres away now, sprinting along the pavement, coming straight at him. Spearpoint dropped the phone to his side, looked left and right, turned his back, took a couple of steps and disappeared into a side-street. Clay reached the corner a few seconds later, breathing hard. He stopped and peered along the crowded market lane. The place was choked with people, cluttered with produce stalls, fire-escapes, aging awnings with bent poles, food stands. Heads twisted and turned, mouths opened, hands offered and received, coins clattered to the ground, bills were counted, folded. Painted electric bulbs swung from bare cables strung between the close-pressed buildings, bathing everything in movie-reel flicker. One head, taller than the others, bobbed above the cobble of multi-coloured crowns. Spearpoint. Clay pushed after him, gained ground, got caught up in the crowd, ploughed his way past dowdy Turkish matrons and grey-suited shopkeepers, and finally reached an inter-section. Market stalls strung away in both directions, the banks of a river swollen with people. Spearpoint was gone.

Clay looked at his watch. He'd left the hotel no more than ten minutes ago. He turned back, shouldering through the crowd until he reached the main road, then set off at a sprint. Five minutes later he burst into the lobby of the Pera Palas.

The proprietor looked up at him from behind the front desk. 'Is everything all right, Mister Clay?'

'Has anyone else come into the hotel since I left?'

'No, my friend. I have been here the whole time.'

Clay's pulse slowed. He wiped the sweat from his temples, the back of his neck. '*Teşekur,*' he said. 'We will be leaving now, my friend. Quietly. Thank you again for your hospitality.'

The proprietor bowed formally.

Clay took the stairs two at a time. That was it, he thought. Spearpoint had seen him, had called it in. They knew where he was. He'd carry Rania out if he had to.

The corridor was quiet. He knocked on the door to their room, stood listening. Silence. He knocked again, tried the handle. The door was unlocked. He pushed it open. The room was as he'd left it. He called her name, closed the door behind him and bolted it. The bed was empty, just the depression where she'd lain, the dark stains of her tears still visible on the bedspread.

The desk where she'd been working was clear of papers. He opened the bathroom door, peered inside. Empty.

Rania was gone.

22

English as a Foreign Language

Clay stood in the empty room trying to process this gaping absence; her missing bag, the weight of her body lifted from the mattress, her perfume and the smell of her tears calling out to his senses like an echo, a shadow. The *burqa* was gone, her clothes and case, her toiletries from the bathroom. He walked to the balcony, looked down to the street below. No sign of her. She couldn't have been gone long, minutes only. He ran to the door, spotted her Koran still on the bedside table, a piece of hotel stationery folded and laid on the front cover. He snatched up the paper, stuffed it into his pocket, ran down to the lobby.

The proprietor was still at the desk. No, he hadn't seen Madame. No one had entered or left the hotel. Clay ran out onto the darkened street. Cars trundled by, a few pedestrians. He pulled the paper from his pocket, unfolded it and tilted it to the light:

It is no good.
Go home.
Please do not try to find me.
Hope you will understand.

He stuffed the paper back into his pocket. There was only one place she could have gone – to Erkan's office, to see the documents, the proof of Chrisostomedes' treachery.

He hailed a passing taxi. Twenty minutes later, the cab dropped him outside the Turkish Airlines office, just behind the towering domes of the New Mosque, near the abutment of the Galata Bridge.

Erkan's office was just up the street, a big floodlit sign declaring Star Crown Resorts. Two stores down, the sprawling displays of a local hardware and dry goods seller spilled onto the pavement, diverting the evening stream of pedestrians, the city coming to life. Clay paid the taxi driver, stepped through the crowd and into the hardware store. Dark, musty, everything about the place reeked of time, obsolete powertools covered in layers of dust, the smell and feel of mineral oil everywhere, original manufacturers' cardboard packaging decaying in every corner. Five minutes later he left the store and strode down the pavement towards Erkan's office, one-and-a-half metres of sixty-fathom, heavy-gauge chain in a paper bag cradled in the crook of his left arm.

Clay pushed open the glass door and strode up to the reception desk. A pleasant-looking young woman in a black cover-up and headscarf smiled at him.

'Mister Erkan, please,' Clay said in Turkish.

'May I say who is calling?'

'Tell him it's a friend of Minister Dimitriou.'

The woman picked up the phone, spoke briefly and replaced the receiver. 'Please wait,' she said, her smile gone.

Clay stood, looked at the display posters: vapid tourists with perfect smiles and airbrushed bodies frolicking in impossibly blue water, idyllic unspoiled Cyprus coastline stretching away behind them like another age. The elevator chimed, the doors opened. Two security guards emerged: Ho and Hum.

Clay smiled and held out his hand. 'What a pleasure,' he said in Turkish. 'Is the boss in?'

Hum frowned. It only intensified the jut of his forehead.

'Shut your fucking mouth, cunt,' said Ho in English. Her voice was almost husky but half an octave too high, like a teenage boy's.

'*Hou jou fokken poes, bek,*' Clay replied in Afrikaans, smiling.

Ho stood for a moment as if unsure how to respond. 'Fuck you,' she said, pointing to the door. 'And get the fuck out.'

The veins on Hum's steroid neck throbbed.

'I only need a minute,' said Clay, striding towards the lift. 'I have an appointment.'

Hum moved to block his way. Clay stopped, kicking distance away.

'I'm looking for a young lady – the one I was with when I visited the boss's place. You remember. Is she here?'

Ho, clearly the one in charge, or at least the one who could speak, took a long look at Clay's left arm. 'If she was here, do you think we'd tell you, asshole?' Not a native speaker, she'd certainly picked up a comprehensive knowledge of English invective.

Hum clenched his jaw, flexed his deltoids. Maybe he thought it made him look mean. It did.

'Look, I don't want to cause trouble,' said Clay, holding his ground. 'I just want to find my friend. Let me talk to the boss.'

'What would a hot whore like her want with a fucking cripple like you?' said Ho, smiling. Hum liked this, laughed.

'You'd be surprised,' said Clay in Turkish. 'Look, please. I only need a minute. That's all. No one needs to get hurt.' He meant it. He didn't give a damn about these two idiots, their slurs. Finding Rania was all that mattered, and time was flowing faster than it should.

'That's right, pussy. You don't want to get hurt, do you?'

Clay said nothing.

'You were told to leave, motherfucker,' barked Ho in English, drawing out a nightstick.

Clay filled his lungs, exhaled slowly. 'I've got a gift for your boss,' he said, sticking with Turkish. 'Here in this bag.'

Ho laughed, looked over at Hum. 'Get out, you fucking stupid cunt,' she barked, 'or we'll break your fucking legs.'

Clay smiled a moment, raised his right hand. '*Tammam*. Okay. I'll just it leave it here, then. You can take it up to him for me.' Clay turned his back, crouched, put the paper bag on the floor. Hum took a step forward. Clay reached into the bag, grabbed one end of the chain then burst low from his crouch, pivoting through one hundred and eighty degrees, whipping the chain through a scything arc. The heavy links took out Hum's ankles, wrapping them tight. Clay jerked back hard on the chain. Hum toppled, a hundred and twenty kilos of him smashing to the floor. Clay dropped the chain and brought his boot heel down hard on Hum's upturned face. Nose and teeth gave way with a sickening crunch.

Ho stood staring, the nightstick hanging from her hand.

'My appointment?' said Clay, voice flat like morning.

Ho took a step back, unsure, looked down at her motionless companion. Blood flowed from Hum's nose and mouth, pooled on the floor around his head. Fear dawned like a bad day on her little girl's face. For a moment it looked as if she would back away.

Clay hoped she would. 'Turn around and walk away,' he said. 'Please.'

Ho stared back at him as if she'd never heard a polite word used in her life. Then she raised the nightstick, held it there a moment in both hands at waist height, as if trying to extract courage from it. Clay could see her thinking it over, glancing left and right, perhaps hoping for backup, the sudden arrival of an ally.

No, he thought. Don't.

Hum opened his mouth, groaned, bubbled red foam.

It was as if the sound of her partner's voice steeled Ho to act. She moved towards him, the nightstick coming up. She probably thought that he'd back away. But Clay did the opposite, closed on her before she could raise the nightstick for a strike. Nine inches taller than Ho, he fended the nightstick with his stump and open-palmed her in the side of the face with his hand. She twisted with the blow. In one motion, Clay drove his stump into the small of her back, slid his hand over her eyes and jerked her head back, doubling her over. Then, holding the back of her head like a newborn, he brought her face down into a rising uppercut from his left elbow. He did it almost gently, at half speed, less, just enough to stun.

Even though he'd pulled the strike he felt her jawbone go, heard it crack, the female mandible so much lighter, so much easier to break, his calibration wrong. He'd never hit a woman before. Ho crumpled to the ground, blood pouring from her mouth. The whole thing had taken less than a couple of seconds. Clay stepped forward, looked down at her. Unable to speak, she looked up at him through an ocean of pain, wading on the edge of consciousness. Her eyes fluttered and she was gone.

He looked over at the receptionist, shame coursing through him already like grassfire. The girl's mouth dropped open as if she was in a dentist's chair. Clay raised his finger to his lips and walked into the elevator. His pulse, frighteningly steady until now, spiked as the realisation of what he'd done hit him full force. Later, he would rationalise that he had done it because she'd decided to strike first; and that in this career she'd chosen, violence was just part of the job. But just as quickly would come the blunting knowledge that he'd had options, that the powerful must always have a responsibility to the less so, and that in truth this was the only criterion of mercy.

But now, there was just the shame.

The lift opened up on to a fifth-floor wood-panelled waiting room. Beyond, an empty secretarial station, big double doors, closed. Erkan's office. Clay pushed open the doors and walked in. Erkan was sitting behind an oak-topped desk. His tie was askew, collar open, his suit jacket crumpled. He looked like he'd just been flying coach class all night.

Before Erkan had time to react, Clay marched around the desk, grabbed him by the neck and applied pressure to his windpipe. 'Where is Lise, you son of a bitch?' he said.

Erkan looked up at him, uncomprehending. 'I ... I told her to come alone,' he choked. 'Please. You are hurting me.'

Clay pressed his thumb harder into Erkan's windpipe. 'Bullshit. Where is she?'

Erkan spluttered. 'I ... I told her that if she wanted to see the documents she should come alone.' His eyes flitted from side to side, as if searching the room. 'Where are my security people?'

'I gave them the afternoon off,' Clay said. 'Now where is she?'

Erkan's eyes widened. 'What...?' he gasped.

'Message repeats.' Clay pushed Erkan back into the chair and stepped away. 'Look, just tell me where she is, and I'll go. I don't want to hurt anyone else.'

The reek of fear filled the room. Erkan's eyes widened, confusion vying with terror. Clay waited, wondering how long he had before the cops arrived.

'I…' Erkan glanced down at his desk drawer, moved his hands from his neck to his lap.

'Don't,' said Clay.

Erkan froze, stared at Clay a while. Then he put his hands palms down on his desk. 'I haven't seen her since you left my house.'

Erkan was a prick, but Clay could see he was telling the truth. Where had she gone? Had Clay made it here before her? What would she be thinking if she was stepping into the lobby downstairs right now? Clay couldn't believe that she'd leave without at least trying to get a look at the documents.

Clay set his face, a blank, crouched down and brought his eyes level with Erkan's. 'Something's happened to her,' he said. 'Do you understand?'

Erkan stared at Clay, nodded once. 'I'm sorry,' he blurted.

'Have you spoken to your chauffeur recently?'

Erkan spluttered, fear and confusion mixed two to one in his eyes. 'No, I … What?'

'Where was he taking us?'

Erkan looked at him as if he was crazy. 'Your hotel, of course.'

'Bullshit. Tell me.'

'I … I don't understand,' wheezed Erkan, starting to panic.

Clay leaned closer, stared into his eyes. The bastard didn't know about what had happened in the car. That was clear. Someone was playing him. His chauffeur must have been acting under other instructions.

Clay glanced around the room, out of the window. 'I want those documents, Mister Erkan. You wanted Chrisostomedes to fry. I promise you he will.'

Erkan's eyes fluttered, closed a moment. 'I can't give them,' he said. 'Off the record only. Please.'

Outside, the plaintive cry of sirens. Clay pushed the lid down hard on the anger boiling inside him, brought his lips to Erkan's ear. 'Give me those papers. I'll make sure she gets them.'

Erkan nodded once, pointed to a filing cabinet to the left of his desk and lifted two fingers. Clay stepped back and pulled open the second drawer.

'The red one,' Erkan said in Turkish.

Clay scanned the files. There was only one red tab, labelled 'Alassou'. Clay pulled it out and began flipping through the pages. Correspondence, a contract of some sort, in English, bank transfer statements. It was all there.

Erkan sat watching, massaging his neck.

'Don't worry, *bru*,' said Clay gathering up the file. 'Off the record.'

❰

Outside, Clay crossed the road, walked down to a small tea house, sat on one of the small, wooden-framed, reed-weave chairs set out on the pavement and ordered a glass of *çay*. From here he had a good view of Erkan's building. If Rania was still on her way he could intercept her, find out what the hell was going on. Clay read Rania's note again, puzzled over the use of his alias (she'd never once called him Declan), and her sign-off, the first letter of her *nom de plume*, which he never used. That she would have packed all her things and left her father's Koran, her most cherished possession, seemed unthinkable. The whole thing was wrong. Surely she hadn't abandoned him because of his reaction to her revelation. After everything they'd been through, he found it impossible to believe that she would just walk away, pull the cord like that. And yet it had all been there since their meeting, the repeated insistence that it was too late for them, that too much had happened, the constant undercurrent of loss and regret and things left unsaid. And then he had sealed it all by telling her that he didn't love her. Idiot. Liar.

It only took the cops five minutes. Not bad, considering Istanbul traffic. And still no Rania. Clay sat drinking his tea as two uniformed policemen ran into Erkan's building. After a couple of minutes another car came and two more cops disappeared through the glass doors. Soon after, an ambulance rolled up. He couldn't wait any longer. Clay stood, peeled off a few pulped, illegible ten-lira notes and set them on the table, put his empty tea glass on top, turned and walked out into the street.

He decided to go back to the Pera Palas. He still hoped that somehow Rania might have made her way back there to find him (stupid, illogical). And he had to retrieve Rania's Koran (soft, emotional). Arriving back shortly after nine p.m., he made his way through the empty lobby and rode the ancient, creaking elevator to the fourth floor.

Inside the room it was dark. The balcony windows were open, as he'd left them. The curtains billowed in the evening breeze. He switched on the light and stepped back in surprise.

A man sat slumped in a chair in the corner of the room, a bloody towel wrapped around his forearm, a silenced Beretta 9mm cradled in his lap. Two men lay motionless on the floor at his feet. 'Close the door,' he said.

It was Crowbar.

23

Wanted Dead

Clay pushed the door to, stood with his back to the wall.

Crowbar grabbed a half-empty bottle of whisky from the side table and poured two glasses. 'Was hoping you'd come back, Straker,' he said.

Clay stood motionless, focussing on the Beretta.

'Have a drink,' said Crowbar, holding out one of the glasses.

'Trying to quit.'

The corner of Crowbar's mouth twitched. 'Take it, Straker.'

Clay stepped over one of the bodies, took the whisky, downed it in one go and watched blood drip from the tip of Crowbar's middle finger to the carpet. 'Ever consider just knocking?'

'I need you to get me a compress, disinfectant, bandages, sutures, if you can find them, and tape,' said Crowbar, his voice wavering, stressed. 'There's an all-night chemist at the far end of the Tepebaşi road, past the Turkmen bank. Left out of the hotel. Get going.'

Clay stared at Crowbar's arm, the handgun, the blood spreading into the towel, the corpses on the floor. 'What the hell is going on, Koevoet? Come to collect?'

Confusion displaced pain on Crowbar's face. 'What the *fok* you talking about, Straker?' he said in Afrikaans.

'I'm talking about two million pounds, *broer*. Those three company men you sent to the cottage to take me out.'

Crowbar put down his glass, nodded. '*Ja, ja.* You did a nice job on those *poes*, Straker. Did I ever tell you you'd make a hell of a merc?'

'Is that why you're here? To offer me a job?'

Crowbar grunted, pushed his head to his knees. He'd lost a lot of blood. '*Jesus Christus*, Straker. What you gonna do? Stand there all night and watch me bleed to death?'

Clay widened his stance. 'Where is Rania?'

Crowbar's eyes fluttered. He looked down at the bodies leaking blood onto the floor but said nothing.

'Rania,' repeated Clay. 'Lise Moulinbecq. The woman who was in this hotel room an hour ago. Dark hair, about five-seven, knockout.'

'I know what she looks like, *broer*.' Crowbar tried a grin, winced. 'No one here but these two *poes* when I got here. I watched you leave the hotel, saw these two go in about half an hour later, followed them. Never saw Rania. Now get going, Straker, for *fok*'s sake, before I bleed out.'

Clay stepped over to the closet, pulled out his bag and patted its side. 'Everything you need, right here.'

Crowbar looked pale. He held out his arm. 'Get on with it.'

Clay stepped over the bodies, helped Crowbar to the bathroom and sat him on the toilet seat.

'Bring the whisky,' said Crowbar. His voice was faint. Clay feared he would pass out.

Crowbar took a swig from the bottle and pulled away the towel. A deep, clean gash cut diagonally across the outside of his meaty forearm. Blood welled from the wound, but he'd been lucky – they'd missed the artery. Clay poured whisky over the wound, applied pressure and wrapped the compress in place. Soon he had the arm taped up tight. The bleeding had stopped, for now.

They sat out on the balcony and watched the moon rise over the Bosphorus.

'I should get you to a doctor,' said Clay.

Crowbar shook his head. 'We have to leave,' he said.

'What the hell are you doing here, Koevoet? Tell me.'

'Looking after you, *broer*. Like you asked me to.'

'Looking after me? Is that what you call it? Fuck you, Koevoet. You sold me out.'

Crowbar took a swig of whisky, put his feet up on the railing and lit a cigarette. 'Let me tell you something, Straker. After you were demobbed, when I was still up in Angola fighting the commies, *fokken* kaffirs broke into my house back home in Jo'Berg. Killed my wife and baby boy. Gang-raped her and cut her to pieces, *ja*. They were after the TV.' His voice was steady, calm, a professional delivering a radio sitrep under fire. He filled his lungs with smoke and poured it back out through his nostrils. 'Everything I fought for all those years, gone. *Vrek*. You can't bring anything back.'

Clay stood, grasped the railing and watched the disc of the moon rise blood red behind the Sultan Selim mosque. 'Jesus, Koevoet. I'm sorry.' He felt faint.

'Don't be. I tracked them down. Killed them all.'

Clay said nothing, watched the moon go from crimson to chlorine.

'I don't sell out, Straker. Ever. So *fok* you, too.'

'Are you telling me that you didn't send those men to kill me?'

'That's exactly what I am telling you.'

Clay glanced over at Crowbar then looked back out over the city. Rania must have left minutes after he'd stormed out. Stupid. He hammered his head with his fist. Stupid. Selfish. She was in love with someone else, and she was doing what she knew she needed to do. And she was out there somewhere. He blinked off into the distance. 'How did you find me?' he said.

'I've been tracking the people who are tracking you.' Crowbar glanced over his shoulder at the bodies sprawled in the room, tipped the bottle to his lips then passed it to Clay.

Clay emptied the bottle. The whisky burned his throat. 'Medved.'

'At first, no.'

'What is that supposed to mean?'

'After word about the price on your head hit the street, I went to see Regina Medved, in Moscow.'

Clay's stomach burned. It wasn't the whisky.

'I wanted to find out what it was about, what they knew. See if the two million was for real. Played it like I was interested in the job.'

'And?'

'*Ja*, definitely. It was for real. But they didn't know who the killer was. They didn't have a target. Rex Medved had a lot of enemies. They wanted proof, and the head. Then they'd pay.'

'So those guys who came to the cottage, they were working for Medved?'

'Not as far as I can see it, *bru*. Not directly anyway.'

'Jesus, Koevoet. So who was it?'

'The tall one, the one you killed, Rutgersan, was ex 32-Bat. The one I found in the hedgerow was Kluesner, also Buffalo Battalion.'

Clay exhaled through his teeth. 'Your number was in Kluesner's phone. He called you just before they came to the cottage.'

Crowbar nodded. 'He was fishing for information. As soon as he called, I knew they were coming for you.'

'There was a third one. I clipped him, but he followed me to Falmouth.'

'Van der Plaas. Always works with the other two. A real nutter. No scruples.'

'So they weren't with the company.'

'No way, *broer*. We have standards. But Van der Plaas was with us in DCC for a while a few years back. So he knew about the cottage.' Crowbar hauled himself to his feet, swayed a moment, and walked back into the room. He picked up the bedside phone and rang down for another bottle of Johnny Walker and a complete dinner for two: kebabs, bread, dolmades, dessert, the whole affair. Then he put down the telephone and came back out to the balcony.

'I left London right after the call from Kluesner. Must have reached the cottage not long after you left. I found Rutgersan dead on the front welcome mat. Kluesner was still in the hedgerow, unconscious, but bandaged up – was that you?'

Clay nodded.

'I cleaned up the place, got someone to get rid of the body. Then I drove to the coast looking for you. I knew you'd try to get out by sea.'

Clay's mind raced back. 'The helicopter?'

'There was a storm coming. The pressure was off. I'd tipped off the cops, given them van der Plaas's description, told them he was armed. Set him up. I have friends, Straker. I wanted to warn you, let you know you had time.'

'So Regina Medved doesn't know I murdered her brother.'

Crowbar looked back into the room. 'Those are dead Russians on your floor, *broer*. They came for you. She didn't know before, but she sure as hell does now.'

Clay swallowed. His larynx felt as if it would crack. 'LeClerc. He knew the whole story. He was there that day at the capital-raising event, he knew Rania, knew about her cover.'

'Shit.'

'And they tortured it out of him.'

Crowbar inspected the bandage around his arm. It was already stained with blood, but seemed to be doing the job. 'I heard.'

'Then they killed him. That was revenge for publishing Rania's story – the one that derailed their oil operations in Yemen. Cost them millions.' Clay dropped his head to his knees, the alcohol swimming in his blood. It had been Rania's story, and Clay's, a lot of other people's too, most of them now dead. Including LeClerc. Clay shuddered.

'Makes sense,' said Crowbar.

'So who was van der Plaas working for?' Clay said. 'Who killed Eben? Who was threatening Rania before Regina Medved had even connected me to her brother's murder?'

He told Crowbar about Rania's investigations in Cyprus, the threats to her life, her disappearance a few hours ago from this very room.

Crowbar pulled a Beretta 9mm automatic from his waistband and handed it to Clay. 'Look, *broer*, I'm not sure of anything. But one thing I can tell you: the guy who was tracking you *before* LeClerc spilled it to Medved was Bulgarian, arms dealer type.'

Clay froze. 'Jesus Christ.'

'You know him?'

'Zdravko Todorov. I watched him massacre twelve unarmed

civilians in Yemen, gave evidence to the French government that led to his indictment. I also put a bullet in his knee, left him as a hostage with some Yemeni friends of mine.'

Crowbar was silent for a moment, that word hanging in the air between them like bad blood: *massacre*. 'Good reason to go after someone,' said Crowbar.

'Todorov is here? In Istanbul?'

'*Ja*, definitely. But I haven't seen him for almost twenty-four hours.'

Clay pushed the Beretta into the waistband of his trousers at the small of his back. 'Here's the irony, *broer*. Todorov did an arms deal with the Medveds during the civil war in Yemen. But the deal went bad. He stiffed them out of twenty million dollars. Regina Medved has a hit out on him, too.' He pointed at the two dead men on the floor. 'So if these guys are Medved's, then they sure as hell weren't working with Todorov.'

Crowbar laughed, lit another cigarette. 'Beauty.'

There was a knock at the door. Room service.

Crowbar stepped over the bodies of the two dead Russians and looked back over his shoulder. 'If we're going to find your *bokkie*,' Straker, we're going to have to get rid of these kills, clean up this mess and get the *fok* out of Turkey before the police invite us to stay in one of their very nice luxury prisons. Hungry?'

24

A Few Miles from Deep Water

There was something about all that blood. The wet, ferric smell of it in his nostrils, in the back of his throat. The way it seeped into the gaps between the wood and held tight, organic bonding to polar organic. That unexpectedly slippery viscosity.

On his knees, Clay towelled up the rich arterial fluid as best he could, suppressing the urge to gag. After a while he stood, stared at his arms, red to the elbows. Crowbar was stripping the sheets off the bed. He gathered them up and set to work mummifying the two Russians, winding the bundles tight with the rest of Clay's medical tape. They squeezed the bodies onto the lower shelf of the dinner trolley. With the two leaves of the table folded down, the tablecloth hung down and covered the lower shelf. Only the corpses' feet, wound in the white bedsheets, protruded. It would have to do.

They wiped down every surface as best they could, gathered up the bloody towels and stashed them in the trolley with the bodies. Clay looked at his watch. Almost midnight.

'I'll bring the car around,' said Crowbar.

'Go to the back of the hotel,' said Clay, sliding Rania's Koran into his bag with Erkan's file. 'There's a delivery bay. I'll use the service lift, bring down the trolley, meet you there.'

'Five minutes,' said Crowbar, slipping out into the hallway.

Clay took an envelope and some hotel stationery, wrote a brief note to the proprietor thanking him for all his help, regretting they hadn't been able to have that drink together. Clay stuffed the envelope with twenty-five one-hundred-dollar bills, more than enough to cover the bill and leave the proprietor with a healthy tip, one that would ensure silence and a determined cleaning of the room. He sealed and addressed the envelope, left it on the desk, took one last look around the room and started pushing the trolley towards the door.

The hallway was quiet, the lights turned low for evening. The service lift was at the far end of the corridor, near the fire escape. Clay leaned into the trolley, started to push. The casters groaned as he got the thing moving. It wasn't built for this kind of load. Its wooden frame flexed as the small, vulcanised rubber wheels caught on the carpets, dug into the floor boards, ground against their metal axles. It sounded like a freight train coming round a long bend, screaming on its rails. Some freight.

He kept pushing, past one door, then another, praying the other guests were sound sleepers. Finally he reached the service lift, pressed the call button and pushed the trolley into the car. Halfway down the lift stopped and the doors opened.

A young night porter was standing in the corridor, finger on the lift call button. 'May I help you, *Beyfendi*?' he said.

Clay flipped down the edge of the table cloth. 'No, thank you,' he said in Turkish, trying a smile.

The boy made to step onto the lift, but the trolley was blocking the entrance. 'Please, *Beyfendi*, no need for you to do that. Allow me.' He reached in, took hold of the edge of the trolley and pulled.

Clay held firm. 'Thank you,' he said in Turkish. 'No need. I wanted to speak to the chef anyway.'

The porter didn't budge. 'The kitchen is closed, sir.'

'No matter. I'll take this down, then perhaps go for a walk.'

'Please, sir. I will take it for you.'

Clay breathed deep, fixed the boy with a parade ground stare. 'Stand back, son.'

The porter stood a moment, unsure. Then he shrugged his shoulders, stepped away. The doors closed.

Seconds later, Clay pushed the trolley out into a dimly lit basement service area, concrete floors, stacks of crates and boxes, steel-framed laundry hampers, a forklift truck parked against the far wall. Just ahead was a ramp leading up to the loading bay with a wind-down metal door, closed up. Clay started pushing the trolley towards the ramp, double time. He was half-way there when something gave way. The trolley collapsed with a crack. The bodies spilled half onto the floor. Clay ran to the service door, cracked it open, looked outside. Crowbar was there with the car, a battered old Mercedes. The laneway was empty. Clay found the chain for the main door and cranked it up plate by plate.

Crowbar backed the car in, jumped out, and stared. Bodies, splintered wood, blood. '*Kak*, Straker. What a mess.'

They manhandled the bodies into the trunk of the Merc. Clay stripped the linen from the trolley, bundled it up with the towels and dropped it all on top of the corpses. Crowbar closed the trunk.

In the car, neither spoke. They both knew they'd left behind a hell of a mess.

☾

Crowbar kept to Istanbul's labyrinth of backstreets. Once clear of the city, they found the motorway and struck east into Asia Minor, then south towards the Turkish Aegean coast.

Three hours and three hundred kilometres later, Crowbar brought the Mercedes to a stop at the quayside of a small seaside village. Clay got out, stretched his legs, felt the night air cool on his skin, heard the gentle lap of waves against the seawall. A dozen fishing boats bobbed in the starlit keyhole harbour.

'Wait here,' said Crowbar, disappearing up a stone stairway.

Clay walked to the edge of the quay, stared up at the stars strobing in black emptiness. Ever since leaving the hotel, the last sentence of Rania's note had been puzzling him: *Hope you'll understand.* She hoped he'd understand. Of course he didn't bloody well understand. How could she have walked away like that and have expected him to understand? It made no sense. None at all.

Because that wasn't what she'd meant. She hoped he'd understand the message itself. *Hope*. It was obvious. Hope Bachmann. Rania was telling him to go to Cyprus. *It is no good,* she'd written. So she hadn't left willingly. She'd been forced, coerced. Whoever had done it had probably sat there and watched her write it. But why would her assailants allow her such a courtesy, when they would have known they only had a matter of minutes? Did they need her acquiescence? Or was it to mollify her, reassure her, keep her docile while they spirited her out of the hotel. He had indulged his anger and self-pity on the streets of Istanbul when he should have been there, protecting her. *Go home*. She knew he didn't have one. But she did, one that had been destroyed only days before. Another reference? *Do not try to find me.* That part was clear. She was in trouble. She needed him. Find me. That's what it meant.

Clay stood looking out across the harbour, the Beretta's grip jabbing into the small of his back, the creep of guilt black like murder up his vertebrae. He walked back to the car and reached into his bag. Rania's Koran was there. He weighed it in his hand and ran his index finger along the spine, over the long, curling Arabic emboss-ments, these ancient words that Rania so cherished, these words he'd read and tried in vain to understand, for her, for himself. Now he saw. Clarity came, a shred, a dull sliver. That was what Crowbar had meant when he'd told him about his wife and child. It was right here, in these gilded pages. *Slay not life which Allah has made sacred, save in the course of justice.*

Thirteen years ago they had violated all that was sacred, and there had been no justice to be found anywhere. But the taste of retribu-tion was sweet like mountain water, there still in his mouth from the moment the .45 slug he'd fired had pierced Medved's frontal lobe, blown the occipital all over the hotel carpet. Whatever happened now, and however long it took, he would track down the people who'd done this – taken Rania, murdered Eben, tortured and killed LeClerc – and he'd slay every last one of them. And thus, *inshallah*, would he be forgiven.

Ten minutes later, Crowbar appeared on the quay, accompanied by a stocky Turk in a woollen jumper and flat cap. The man's moustache draped around the filter of a Maltepe cigarette. It didn't surprise Clay that Crowbar knew someone here. For seven years he'd worked Europe and the Middle East for the DCC, buying arms and equipment, navigating the international embargo against South Africa, keeping the *matériel* and information flowing back to the homeland. And now, for the company, he just kept doing what he was good at. Hiring a vessel for an anonymous Mediterranean crossing was routine in Crowbar's world.

Soon they were on their way, motoring across the black surface of the Med under a moonless, cloud-brushed sky. Clay stood on the open bridge and watched the Turkish coast recede, a few scattered lights strung out along the horizon.

'Cyprus,' he said. 'That's where she is, Koevoet.'

Crowbar considered this a moment, nodded, leaned over and said something to the captain. Clay looked down into the vessel's car deck. It was a small vehicle-landing craft with straight sides, a retractable front ramp, space for about four cars. Crowbar's Mercedes, sitting low on its rear suspension, was the only cargo tonight. The first tinge of blue paled in the eastern sky, dawn perhaps an hour away.

Crowbar leaned close, shouted above the roar of the engines. 'We're only a few miles from deep water. Then we head for Cyprus. Don't worry, *broer*,' he said, putting a frying-pan hand on Clay's shoulder. 'We'll find her.'

Crowbar and the captain retreated into the wheelhouse, leaving Clay alone on the open bridge. Ahead, the darkness of the sea, the ship moving steady through the water, night air flowing cool over his face; behind, the dark coastline fading away, the last lights disappearing below the horizon. Two dead men in the car on the deck below; and above, a universe of dying stars. And in these directions there was no solidity, nothing to hold.

An hour later, the captain killed the vessel's running lights and shut down the engines. Quiet smothered them, then the breath of a light southerly, the smells of Egypt there, Lebanon, the Bekka Valley, and the pat pat pat pat of water on steel – wet, playful almost, like fucking. The ship rocked in a calm sea, a hint of dawn painting the horizon.

Clay followed Crowbar and the ship's captain down to the car deck. The captain clanked across the steel plate of the deck and started winding down the front ramp. Crowbar opened the Mercedes' driver-side door, put the car into neutral and let off the handbrake. The front ramp was horizontal now; a rush of wet air blew over them. The sea beckoned. Clay put his shoulder to the car's trunk, started pushing it towards the ramp.

'The long sleep,' said Crowbar as the car toppled off the end of the ramp, bobbed for a moment in the black water and then sank out of sight, trailing a wake of phosphorescent bubbles.

Part III

25

$F=GMm/r^2$

10th November 1994: Near Kato Pyrgo, north coast of Cyprus

It was just before sunset when they waded ashore.

Within moments the landing craft was gone, disappearing behind an iron-oxide headland towards the TRNC side of the border. They left the black shingle beach and moved inland through olive groves and scrub oak. After a while they passed an abandoned farmhouse, a charcoal kiln with a supply of logs stacked ready for pyrolysis. Clay inhaled the rich odours of the island, recent rain on the red soil of the interior plains, charred pine from last summer's wildfires in the Pentadactylos range in the north, cypress from the Troodos Mountains. Three years he'd lived here, long enough for the place to have attached itself to him somehow, a dormant virus awakened by these chemicals in the wind. He shivered, not from the cold but from something else, a realisation perhaps of what he was here to do.

They walked into Kato Pyrgo and found a pension for the night. At a local café they agreed on a course of action: Clay would go straight to Nicosia, check into the Holiday Inn near the Green Line as Marcus Edward. Then he'd find Hope Bachmann. Crowbar would head for the south coast, to Limassol. He had contacts there in the Russian 'community', as he called it.

'Be in your hotel room at five a.m. the day after tomorrow,' said Crowbar. 'I'll call you. Medved's people and this *dof* Todorov are tracking you. It's only a matter of time until they place you. So keep low.'

'Yes, my *luitenant*,' said Clay, running his fingers through his already thickening beard, thinking: I'm sorry I doubted you. It's a flaw. One of many. Trust, I mean. *Trusting*. Myself most of all.

Clay put out his hand.

Crowbar took it, tightened down hard, pumped Clay's arm a couple of times and grinned wide. 'Let's get these *fokken kaffirs*,' he said in Afrikaans, 'find Rania, and get the hell out of here. I've got real work to do.'

The bus journey to Nicosia was painstakingly slow. Narrow, twisting mountain roads lined with pine, glimpses of the Med in the distance, eventually giving way to flat inland plain, dry still, the summer's browning edge still lingering, the island's twenty-year drought now the new normal. Clay leant his head on the window glass, watched ragged roadside trees flash past like years. Thirty-four of them now, gone like Koevoet had said, never coming back. The landscape of his life lay there before him, the ridge line smoking black, the slope strewn with bodies, the mangled wrecks of vehicles, the charred stumps of trees, the ground white with ash, a winter of endings. A solitary set of footprints stretched away into the distance, wandering to some meaningless destination, the stink of death filling the air; more to come. He stopped, ash floating above his boots like fog, turned back from where he'd come, looked back across the ruin. Rania was there, standing in his footmarks as if connected to him by that umbilical of a thousand steps, her hands raised to her mouth, dark clouds massing behind her. She was shouting over the distance, calling to him, her voice thin, miles away, the slant of rain on the horizon. He wasn't sure if it was her voice he could hear on the wind, or the shapes of the words in her mouth that he could see.

Clay jerked back, his head rattling against the glass, the bus slowing through a gravel-shouldered village of fruit stands and half-built houses, the dream so clear in that instant, burned there, that he drove each part of it into his consciousness, drawing it out, frame by frame, sound by sound, the colours, the smells, until it was all there, this tableau of his life, the rain coming in the distance, Rania standing in his ashy footmarks, and he thought that maybe there was something there for him in it, and that perhaps he did know what she had been calling to him and that perhaps she was right.

That afternoon he checked into the hotel, then telephoned the University of Cyprus. He was connected to the oceanography department. One of Doctor Bachmann's grad students answered, introducing herself as Maria. Hope was running a seminar on evolutionary biostatistics over the next three days, morning to evening, she said. But if he came in early tomorrow morning, he might just catch her before the seminar. Clay thanked the young woman, then organised a rental car for the morning. He sat at the hotel room desk and looked out across the last divided city to the Pentadactylos mountains, black against the northern sky. Rain was coming, thick and cold on the night air.

He called down to the desk for room service then placed a long-distance call to his Cayman Islands banker. A message was waiting: *Flame* was in Larnaca marina, a week and a half ahead of schedule. Gonzales must have worked fast, sent *Flame* overland, to Athens probably. Clay approved the final transfer of funds to Gonzales' account. By the time the food came it was raining.

☾

The next morning, Clay stood in the hallway outside Hope Bachmann's office, brushed the rain from his coat and knocked on the door. The woman who answered was petite, dark-haired, early twenties, with a strong Cypriot nose and big brown eyes. She introduced herself as Maria Stavros, the grad student he'd spoken with the previous day. She ushered him in and closed the door.

'Doctor Bachmann is on the phone at the moment, Mister Edward,' she said, indicating the closed door at the far end of the office. She glanced at her watch. 'You'll have to make it quick. She has to leave for the seminar at ten to eight.'

Clay removed his coat and saw the young woman glance at his stump, look up quickly to his eyes. 'Are you a scientist?' she asked.

'Engineer.'

Maria glanced down at the phone, the red light blinking. 'Doctor Bachmann is still on the phone, I'm afraid. You may be out of luck. Perhaps if you tell me the nature of your enquiry, I can help you?'

'It's personal.'

'Oh,' she said with a smile, a colouring of the cheeks. '*Endaxi*. No problem.' She picked up a mug. It was decorated with embossed turtles. 'Want some coffee?'

'Thanks,' said Clay, liking this girl already.

Just then the office door opened.

Hope was nothing like he had expected. Tall, fine boned, with a square jaw and bright, aquamarine eyes that seemed to change with the light, from clear sandy-bottomed blue to murky ocean green. She looked at him quizzically, the first phase of a smile spreading across her face, a bundle of papers under her arm.

'This is Mister Edward,' said Maria, beaming at her boss. 'I told him you didn't have long. In fact, you have two minutes.'

'Thanks, Maria,' said Hope. And then, 'How can I help you, Mister Edward?'

Clay glanced at Maria. 'Can we speak alone?'

'Whatever you have to say, you can say to us both.'

'I am a friend of Lise Moulinbecq.'

Bachmann's eyes narrowed slightly, then regained their previous, wide-aperture composure. 'Please contact the seminar, Maria, and tell them that we will start an hour later today. Send my apologies.'

Maria frowned, nodded and picked up the phone.

Bachmann opened her office door, motioned Clay to enter and closed the door behind him. They were alone.

'Lise is missing,' he said.

Bachmann sat behind her desk, leaned forward. 'And you are who, exactly, Mister Edward?'

'That's not important. What matters is that her life is in danger, and I need your help to find her.'

Bachmann assessed this a moment. If she was worried about Rania, she showed no sign of it. 'It matters very much to me who you are and what your interest in Lise might be, Mister Edward.'

Clay stepped over to one of the bookshelves that lined the office walls, floor to ceiling. Here were volumes on genetics, marine biology, compendia of conference proceedings on Mediterranean sea turtles, further along a whole section devoted to political and economic philosophy, neoliberalism, Marxism, Keynesian economics. Clay picked up an illustrated volume of the fishes of the Eastern Mediterranean, put it on the corner of her desk and flipped through the pages of colourful, hand-painted drawings, the diversity overwhelming. All of this with his right hand. 'Does the name Rania LaTour mean anything to you?' he said, not looking up.

Bachmann held her hands up to her mouth, a little girl praying. She sat a moment, then stood, looked out of the office window, picked up her purse. 'Come with me,' she said.

Twenty minutes later they were walking among the tall trees of Athalassa Park, a rambling plantation of pines and eucalypts spread over more than a hundred hectares on the eastern edge of Nicosia. They'd taken his car, left it in the gravel car park, and hadn't spoken a word since leaving the campus. Now they were entirely alone.

'You must be Claymore,' she said.

So this was her, the woman Rania had fallen in love with. She'd taken off her sandals, was walking barefoot over the gravel of the pathway, her boyish hips swaying just enough under her long, cotton dress. Rania had good taste, in women at least.

'Clay.'

She smiled up at him with strong, even teeth. A flash of black at the edge of her smile. A missing tooth? 'Hope.'

'Why here?'

'I don't know how much Rania told you, but I'm under surveillance.'

'She told me enough.' Clay tried to imagine what she'd look like naked, what she and Rania would look like together. Good, probably. He pushed it away.

'My office is bugged. The government is watching me. So, it appears, are others: certain wealthy Cypriot businessmen, for instance, and of course the Russians. I'm not very popular, you see.'

Clay stopped and faced her. 'Russians?'

'They have huge interests on the island, as you probably know. Billions in offshore accounts funnelled out since Perestroika. A lot of that money is being invested in development projects, buildings, hotels, resorts, anything to clean it up. It's a travesty what's going on in Russia right now – the plunder of a nation. It's a classic case of socialism for the rich, free-market discipline for the poor.' She stopped, smoothed down her dress. 'Sorry. I get a little carried away.'

Clay nodded, allowed her to continue.

'So, yes, Russians. I know Rania was particularly interested in one group's interests here: the Medved family.'

Of course. Clay could feel the gravitational pull (F), two bodies (M and m) drawing each other in, the force of attraction proportional to the inverse of the square of the distance between them (r). The closer you get, the stronger the pull: $F=GMm/r^2$. A lot simpler to express mathematically than say, and more powerful. While he'd been hiding in the UK, Rania had been here, trying to uncover whatever she could about Medved's operations, continue the fight they'd started in Yemen, the one he'd tried to end in that hotel room in London, the best way she knew how.

'Rania was convinced that Regina Medved was the prime buyer of religious artefacts being plundered north of the border, and Erkan the chief supplier. She also had reason to believe that Medved was investing heavily in Erkan's Star Crown Resorts, the ones being developed near the turtle beaches in Karpasia. She was working on unearthing proof of these connections when she left for Istanbul.'

'Jesus.'

'You look surprised.'

'I met her in Istanbul a few days ago. She never mentioned any of this,' said Clay, thinking back. 'I guess I never gave her much of chance.'

Hope smiled, took his hand as if it were the most natural thing in the world and kept walking. They crossed the top of an earthen dam, the upstream side choked with bull rushes, a patch of green, swampy water visible near the inlet end.

'She loves you, you know,' said Hope.

The words hit him like a straight-arm to the solar plexus. Clay kept walking. After a while he said, 'Then we have something in common.'

Hope tipped her head back, opened her mouth and laughed up to the sky. 'Fairly said. I've never met anyone like her.'

There was a big gap where her left upper bicuspid should have been.

'We have to find her, Hope.'

They walked along as the sky cleared and the sun burst through the clouds. The ground steamed.

'What about you?' said Clay. 'What brought you here?'

'It's a rather banal story, I'm afraid.'

'I'm not judging anyone.'

'The turtles brought me,' she said, smiling. 'I came to Cyprus to do research for a PhD in marine biology, studying the endangered green and leatherback turtles here. As so often happens, I met someone, a Cypriot, a banker of all people, fell in love, or what I thought at the time was love. After my doctorate, we moved back to California, where I continued with post-doc research. I had a son, Alexi. But my husband didn't cope well in America. So many Cypriots are like that, you know, they pine so for this little island. I can understand why. So we came back. I got a job lecturing at the university, kept my post at the University of California, continued my research.' She paused, walked a while, still holding Clay's hand. 'And then the cliché. My husband left me for a younger woman. There was the typical nasty custody battle. Being foreign, and being female, the outcome was inevitable. Now, because of the laws in Cyprus, I am stuck here. If I leave the country, I do it alone. They will not let me take Alexi. If I want to be with my son, to retain the right to the once-a-week visits, I have to stay. Ten years it's been like that. This is my home now.'

Clay walked on in silence for some time, debating how much to share with Hope. After a while he told her about their meeting with Erkan in Istanbul, about Rania's note.

'Rania was getting close,' said Hope. 'You've seen what she's written on this, I assume.'

Clay nodded.

'If Rania's been kidnapped – if that's what you're telling me – then one of the people she's close to exposing must be responsible. That means, in order: Mohamed Erkan, who you've met, a real bastard; Chrisostomedes, my favourite – we've had a number of run-ins, he and I; Dimitriou, a government minister here, well known for venality and his favourable leanings towards big business; and finally, Regina Medved – Rania told me about your running feud with that particular family. You two know how to pick your enemies, Clay, I must say.'

They were climbing a sparsely treed limestone ridge now. At the top they looked back over the park, the city beyond, a town really, barely a hundred thousand souls, split along the middle by a snaking line of barbed wire, bunkers and crumbling, sandbagged houses.

'The common theme in all of this, Clay, is land. Coastal tourism development in particular. That's how Rania and I met. She heard me speaking at a hearing on development in the Paphos area, including Lara Beach, the last and most important turtle-nesting beach east of Akamas. Any one of the unprincipled bastards I just mentioned would have a big reason to want to keep her quiet; and me for that matter.'

Clay nodded.

'Maria, too,' said Hope. 'It's even harder for her. She's Cypriot. It's a hell of a lot easier to stand up to something you think is wrong when you're an outsider. But when you're from here, when it's your country, a place where everyone knows everyone, it's a very different proposition. She's a very brave girl.'

Clay didn't doubt it. 'Rania told me you'd been threatened,' he said.

'On several occasions. Maria, too. One gets used to it, in our line of work. The turtles are a great inconvenience to these people. A hundred years ago, the turtles nested on beaches all around the island, from Polis to Ayia Napa, up the east coast to Karpasia. Now, only the most remote beaches still support viable populations, at the two opposite ends of the island. Not surprisingly, they're also the most beautiful places in Cyprus.'

'But those beaches are protected,' said Clay.

Hope laughed. 'Not for long, if these assholes have their way. They won't stop until they've taken everything there is to take. And probably not even then.'

They began walking again, down through a stand of pine. Hope stopped, turned to face him. Her eyes were the colour of the trees. He noticed for the first time that her nose was slightly displaced, pushed to the left. It made one eye look slightly smaller than the other.

'It's all about money,' she said. 'These beaches are worth a fortune, quite literally. The marketing morons can use their favourite words – "pristine" and "unspoiled" – in their advertising campaigns, and not have to lie about it too much. And then they can bring well-intentioned but shockingly ignorant tourists to see what they are destroying.'

'Great if you're tourist number one.'

Hope smiled. 'Or even one thousand. But not so good if you come later on, because by then the things you wanted to see have been destroyed by the people who got there before you.' She reached for his left arm.

Clay pulled back.

'Please,' she said.

'What do you want?'

'Rania told me a lot about you.'

Clay allowed her to pull his arm to her. She pushed back his sleeve, examined his stump, ran her fingers over the mangled tissue, the ferocious scarring. She glanced up at him a moment, then pulled his sleeve back down.

'You probably know more about her than I do,' he said, looking down at the ground.

'Well,' she said, as they turned back towards the car, 'you're going to have a wonderful opportunity to get to know her much better.' She smiled, squeezed his hand.

Clay said nothing, hoped she was right.

'Have you thought about where you'll live, names, things like that?'

Clay stopped. 'Names?'

'Come on, silly. You were just with her. She looks great, doesn't she?'

Clay said nothing, stared at her.

'You really didn't notice?'

'Notice what?'

Hope shook her head. 'Men,' she said.

Clay blinked once. 'What?'

'She's pregnant, that's what. You're going to be a father, Clay.'

26

Dead Reckoning

Clay walked back to the car, Hope trailing a few steps behind. He opened the passenger-side door for her, closed it, walked around to the driver's side and sat behind the wheel. The gravel parking area was still empty, the eucalypts weeping onto the car's windscreen even though the clouds had broken.

'What's our best go?' said Clay. 'We're running out of time.' Rania could be dead already. Both of them, now. Jesus Christ Almighty.

Hope turned to face him, pulled one long, well-shaped leg up onto the seat, the skin of her inner thigh pale, flawless. 'I don't know, Clay. I'm sorry. It could be any of them. All of them, for all I know.'

Clay grabbed the steering wheel, clamped down. 'Best guess.' It was all they had.

Hope took a breath, held it, exhaled. 'Okay. Erkan, then. With his new development in Karpasia, he's having the most immediate impact. Rania was about to publish a piece exposing his dealings with Turkish Cypriot politicians. She'd seen documents proving that the land he is intending to build on was stolen from Greek Cypriots and that TRNC officials know about it. It will cause a firestorm, I can tell you. That's why she went to Istanbul. Now she's gone, and the story has been quashed. I'd say that's a pretty good indication.'

It made sense, to a point. Erkan had been anxious to point Rania in another direction, towards Chrisostomedes and Neo-Enosis. Perhaps put off by Clay's presence at the interview, Erkan had decided to act, snatched Rania from the hotel. But then, when Clay had showed up in his office later that evening, he'd pleaded innocence – and done it well. Maybe Hope was right, but he wasn't sure. There was only one way to find out.

'Then I have to go back to Istanbul,' he said.

Hope reached out, touched his arm. 'No. Erkan arrived in Cyprus yesterday, by private yacht.'

Clay turned in his seat.

'One of my colleagues in the north lives in Karpasia. He's a fisherman. We started working together years ago, doing turtle surveys in the north. He called me this morning. Erkan's yacht docked in Kyrenia yesterday. Erkan is now at his place in Karpasia, an old monastery that he's converted. It's absolutely beautiful.'

'You've been there?'

'A couple of years ago.' Hope straightened out in her seat.

'If he does have Rania, why would he have brought her?'

'Do you really think he would leave her behind?'

'It depends on why he took her in the first place.' Clay's mind spun then blanked, fury burning inside him. He started the car, jammed it into gear. 'What are you doing tomorrow?' he managed.

'I have a seminar. All day.'

'Cancel it.'

'Where are we going?'

'To see this friend of yours.'

Within five minutes they were on the new motorway, speeding south. Soon the city was well behind them. An ancient landscape flashed past the open side window, low crumbling conglomerate bluffs and the blunted pines of reforested terraces, each burned field and dry limestone hill a measure of time flowing in the wrong direction. Every hour that passed cut Rania's chances. It had been two days already since she'd disappeared.

Hope was on the phone to Maria, discussing the seminar. Clay checked the rear-view mirror. Traffic was sparse, a few small trucks overloaded with farm produce, a couple of cars. He took the Limassol turnoff and started the long descent towards the coast. The air warmed as they neared the sea. Soon he left the motorway and turned along a narrow, winding valley flanked by steep cliffs on one side and a cascade of terraced hillslopes on the other. Immediately after the old stone bridge he turned left onto a dirt track, past orchards and stone-walled fields, olive groves, banks of stringy eucalypts. Flocks of tiny birds, honeyeaters and finches, darted between the trees. He followed the track as it wound through the valley, eventually emerging into the narrow streets of Maroni, a tiny village in the hills overlooking olive and pomegranate groves, the Med overcast grey in the distance. In a few minutes they were on the coast road, speeding east towards Larnaca, certain they were not being followed.

'Well?' he asked.

'Maria will teach the seminar.'

'Smart girl.'

'I'm lucky to have her.'

'You trust her.'

'Absolutely I do.'

'What did you tell her?'

'That you were my lover.'

Clay looked over at her. She was smiling, playing with her hair.

'Just kidding, Clay. Don't worry.'

He kept driving.

❨

An hour later he pulled the car to a stop outside the rundown marina office in Larnaca and switched off the engine. Rain lashed the windscreen, blurring the outlines of the three dozen or so boats rocking in their pens.

'I am banned from the TRNC,' said Hope.

'Then we won't tell them we're visiting.' Clay stepped outside and walked to the office. Hope followed him.

The man behind the desk smiled as they entered, raised his considerable eyebrows, obviously impressed by what Hope's wet cotton dress now revealed.

Clay put a copy of *Flame*'s British registration on the desk.

'I've come to take possession of a vessel,' he said in bad Greek. 'She was delivered here two days ago.'

The man glanced at the registration papers, pulled out a log book, ran his finger along a column of names and dates then produced a form. Clay signed.

'Six months' mooring fees with water and power, paid in advance,' said the man. Clay hoped he wouldn't need nearly that long.

As Clay led Hope along the dock the rain relented. Clouds scuttled in low across the arc of the harbour, freighters swinging at anchor. *Flame* looked as she had that first day Punk had revealed her, brass shining, the new mast stepped, Clay's makeshift hatch replaced with gleaming new teak. Gonzales had done a good job. Clay jumped aboard and offered Hope his hand. She took it and stepped from the dock into the cockpit.

'She's beautiful,' said Hope.

'I'm looking after her for someone,' he said.

☾

By late afternoon they had cleared the Ayia Napa peninsula and were broad reaching towards Karpasia. Clay had given Hope his jacket and one of Punk's pullovers, and now she sat curled up in the cockpit, drinking a mug of steaming coffee, staring out at the coast, her long, ash-blonde hair tied in a loose knot that hung across her chest.

After a while she looked up at him. 'Did you know that turtles are one of the best examples of reverse evolution?' she said.

Clay looked up at the mainsail, reached past her and eased the main sheet a touch. He glanced at her, made eye contact.

'You don't say much, do you?'

Clay frowned. 'Depends.'

'You're worried.'

'That doesn't deserve a reply.'

Hope smiled, just a flash. 'Don't worry, Clay. I'm sure she's fine.'

'We have a long way to go,' he said, looking at his watch. 'Tell me about the turtles.'

As night fell over the Mediterranean, Hope taught. Clay could imagine her delivering a lecture, full of energy, pacing the podium, willing her students to share her passion for these strange, ancient creatures who'd been plying the world's oceans for the last three hundred million years. Sea turtles breathe air. They evolved from land reptiles, reversing evolution and returning back to the sea from where all reptiles had originally come. Laying their eggs on land was a remnant of that terrestrial past, a reproductive strategy that has served them well for countless millennia. Hope paused, looked at him full in the eyes. 'Do you have any idea how long that is, Clay? Can you imagine?'

He said nothing, looked up at the first stars shining through gaps in the cloud, the distant past there now, the calculations taking shape in his head. 'Two thousand, eight hundred billion billion kilometres, give or take. Ninety-one megaparsecs.'

Hope looked up at him over the rim of her mug. 'Pardon me?'

He pointed to the sky, swathes of stars behind a shifting screen of cloud. 'Three-hundred-million-year-old light we're seeing now. That's how far it's come. Those stars may not even exist anymore.'

Hope sat a moment, nodded. 'Rania told me about...' she hesitated a moment, smiled. 'She told me you were good with numbers.'

Clay watched the main telltale fluttering in the breeze. 'Now I'm starting to worry. Just how much did she tell you anyway?'

Hope smiled, played with her hair. 'Enough.'

'Enough for what?'

Hope looked right at him, dared him to look away. 'Sufficient for me to be mortally jealous.'

Clay looked back at her, lost.

Then Hope laughed. It was a playground laugh, full of mirth. 'Don't worry, Clay. Your secrets are safe.'

The wind rose slightly, veered. Clay trimmed the sails, got *Flame* up to six knots, the sun now just the slightest pale blush over the dark horizon.

'The turtles are dying,' said Hope after a time. There was finality in her voice, resignation. The gaiety that had surprised him before was gone.

'What's causing it?'

Hope sipped her coffee. 'Over-harvesting, pollution, entanglement in discarded plastic causing drowning, loss of critical habitat. You name it. In 1971, Cyprus passed a law protecting them, and for a while there was stabilisation in numbers. But then, about five years ago, we started to see the first cases of *fibropapillomatosis*.'

Clay trimmed the main, looked back down at her. 'Fibro what?'

'Green turtle disease. A viral infection which makes the turtles more susceptible to parasites. And now, with average sea and land temperatures rising, there's another threat. The sex of turtle hatchlings is determined by incubation temperature. Above twenty-nine Celsius, you get females. Below, males. Over a normal cycle of years it evens out. But now the population has started to skew heavily towards females.' Hope glanced up at Clay. 'It takes one of each, you know.'

'So it seems.'

Hope continued. 'We're down to the last few hundred nesting females. That's from hundreds of thousands a century ago. In the last two years, the population has gone into free-fall. And I don't know why. It's way off trend. There's some new factor at work, but we can't figure out what it is. If something isn't done soon, it's the end for the green turtle in the Med.' Her eyes glinted in starlight reflected from the sea, her face shrouded in darkness now. 'And the really sad thing is, no one seems to give a damn.'

'Not no one, Hope.'

Hope frowned. 'No. You're right. Not no one. Did you see the paper yesterday?'

'I haven't had much time for reading.'

'The UN and the EU have announced that they are setting up

a commission to investigate coastal development in Cyprus. The official enquiry starts next week. Cyprus is desperate for EU membership, and compliance with European environmental directives is a big deal. Given the country's dependence on European tourists, being seen as negligent in protecting such an iconic species and its habitat would be a huge blow. Overall, it's a major step in the right direction. And we have Rania to thank.'

'A big reason to want her silence,' said Clay.

'Or her cooperation,' said Hope. 'Erkan and Chrisostomedes will be among the first to be interviewed by the commission. I've made sure of that.'

'You'll be involved?'

'I'm chairing the enquiry.' Hope drew her knees up to her body, crossed her arms over her shins. 'What Rania has done is fantastic, Clay. Truly. I can't tell you how grateful I am for her.' Hope fell silent.

Clay held the wheel, felt the water flowing over *Flame*'s rudder, the lights of Ayia Napa now small in the distance.

After a while he said: 'She told me, Hope. About you.'

'And?'

'And what?'

'How do you feel about it?'

Clay eased off the jib, let *Flame* fall off a couple of degrees, tightened down the wheel. 'Wrong question,' he said.

☾

They sailed on through the night, making good progress in favourable but light winds. Hope slept below deck, curled under a blanket. Clay watched the stars turning in a moonless sky, felt the cold currents streaming deep and sure. After a while he opened the port cockpit locker, found the key he'd hung on a hook under the bench, went below and sat at the nav table. Clay opened his daypack, took out Rania's Koran and unrolled the chart, using Allah's words delivered to the prophet Mohamed to anchor one corner. Then he plotted a dead reckoning position using a sighting on the border post at the deserted no-man's-land town of Famagusta. Hope stirred, mumbled something in her sleep, settled. Clay took the key, reached down below the nav table, found the hidden latch for the priest hole and opened it up. The duffel bag was still there. Inside, the G21, the MP5 and the driver's H&K were all as he'd left them in Santander, clean and oiled. He figured about 180 rounds of ammunition all up, .45 and 9mm. He placed the Koran in the bag with the weapons and shoved the bag back into the priest hole, locked it up tight.

Just after dawn, the wind died and *Flame* lay becalmed on a flat, cold, November sea. Clay doused the canvas and fired up the diesel. The engine chugged to life. He opened the throttle and set course for the panhandle as the sun rose over Syria.

Not long after, Hope stirred under her blanket and sat up. Clay watched her from the wheel, looking down into the sunlit cabin as she worked her fingers through her hair, separated three long strands and started braiding. She did it absentmindedly, her eyes moving as she looked about the cabin, examining the brass instruments on the bulkhead, searching the spines of the books lining the opposite shelf. She tied the end of the braid with an elastic band and glanced up. Their eyes locked. She smiled. Clay held her gaze a moment, then looked away.

A while later, Hope climbed into the cockpit carrying two steaming mugs of coffee. She sat beside him, handed him a mug. Clay drank.

'Where are we?' she said.

Clay glanced up into the rigging, at the small Turkish flag he'd hoisted while Hope slept.

'In TRNC waters. We passed Famagusta about two hours ago.'

Hopefully, the flag would mollify any Turkish coastguard they happened to meet.

'Just tourists out for a cruise.'

Clay said nothing.

'How long until we reach Karpasia?

'By nightfall. Sooner if the winds cooperate.'

Hope reached into her purse, pulled out her mobile phone, opened the back panel and thumbed out the SIM card. From a zipped pouch in her wallet she retrieved another card, loaded it into the phone. 'I wonder if there is service out here.' She flipped open the phone, punched in a number and looked at the screen. Then she raised the phone to her ear. 'It's me,' she said, and listened a while. 'Okay.' She closed the phone, looked at Clay. 'He'll meet us tonight, just east of Dune Point. He says he's found some villagers who are willing to talk to us about what's going on in Karpasia. And he has confirmed it: Erkan is at the monastery. He can take us there.'

27

Extinction

Clay let the anchor slide into the water, paid out chain until he felt the Danforth hit bottom and start to dig into the sandy sea floor. He let *Flame* drift with the light breeze flowing out across the dunes, let out chain until a length four times the water depth lay on the sea bed, then secured the chain at *Flame*'s bow. She swung slowly head to wind as the anchor flukes bit and dug in. Clay stood at the bow, gauged *Flame*'s position against the dark rocky mass of Dune Point on one side, Rigel melting into the horizon on the other, and waited. After a while Hope joined him at the bow, her light dress rippling in the breeze. There was no moon. Starlight, aeons old, danced on the black water, bathed the beach and the dunes antique white and there was not a trace of human endeavour to be seen. The only sounds were the lapping of water against the hull and, in the distance, coming on the wind, the hooting of a pair of owls: one calling, a single rising note, short and clear, asking who, the sound drifting to them across the treed ridge beyond the dunes; and then, moments later, the reply from afar with the same question, falling. It was shortly before eleven o'clock.

They walked across the coachroof, stepped down into the cockpit. Hope went below. Clay unlashed the inflatable dinghy from the fore-deck and let it slide into the water. After a moment, Hope reappeared in the cockpit and handed Clay a mug of coffee and a bowl of hot beef stew. 'There are no labels,' she whispered, cradling her mug in both hands, letting the steam rise to her face.

'Aren't you eating?' he said.

'I'm vegetarian.'

Clay set aside his stew, went below, found a can of peaches, opened it, carried it up into the cockpit and gave it to Hope, handing her a spoon from his pocket. 'It could be a long night,' he said.

They ate in silence. Hope looked out over the water. 'You see how dark it is, how quiet?' she said. 'This is what the turtles need. Come summer, the females will return from years of wandering the seas, ready to lay their eggs. They return to the same beaches where they were born, guided by the magnetic fields imprinted on them at birth. They stand off here in the shallow water waiting for nightfall, then, when all is quiet, usually around the full moon, they come ashore. They lay three times over a six-week period, about every two weeks, clutches of about 120 eggs in chambers half a metre deep. Incubation is seven weeks.'

She looked off along the sweeping phosphorescent arc of the beach. 'This beach has the single-largest remaining population of nesting green turtles in the Eastern Mediterranean. But every year, about eighty percent of nests are dug up by foxes. So the odds aren't good. At our research station at Lara Beach in the south, we're protecting the nests and helping the hatchlings get to the sea. Thirty years from now, when they mature, with a lot of luck, a few of them will be back to continue the line.'

Clay watched the star-white crests of gentle waves curl and wash up onto the beach, listened to the hiss of water retreating across the carbonate sand, timeless.

'That's why development is the end,' said Hope, taking Clay's hand in hers. 'Any noise, any light, and the females will choose to abort their eggs at sea rather than come ashore. Each beach represents a distinct family line, a tribe if you will, going back to the darkest reaches of time, megaparsecs, Clay. Develop, and that line is wiped out forever.'

A point of light flashed on the shore, twice, three times. Clay looked at his watch. Midnight. He went below, opened up the priest hole, took the G21 from the bag, checked the mag, stuffed the pistol into the pocket of his jacket. Then he put the Beretta Crowbar had given him in Istanbul into the bag and closed everything up.

They rowed ashore, drew the dinghy up over the sand to the tide line and stood peering into the darkness. Soon after, a dark figure came sliding down the closest dune, surfing on his feet, the sand hissing like water as it flowed beneath him. Hope stepped forward. They embraced, kissed alternate cheeks. He was older, mid-sixties Clay guessed, with thick, silver hair that shone in the starlight.

'Thank you for coming,' the man said in English, the Turkish accent heavy in the consonants. 'They are waiting for us, not far from here. Five men from the village. The only ones I could find who would talk. But I warn you, they are frightened.' He looked at Hope. 'I have told them that you are from the EU, an official leading an important commission. They will only speak with someone in authority.'

'I understand,' said Hope. 'Well done.'

'The monastery?' said Clay.

'I have a car in the village. It is not far. After we speak to these men, I will take you there.' Without another word, the man turned and led them inland.

After half an hour's hard walking across country unchanged for generations, they came to a narrow, crumbling, tarmac road. Low stone walls, just ruins in places, frayed, overgrown with dark, tangled vines, lined the road on both sides. Beyond, the lighter shapes of terraced fields, more stonework, dark woodland. Clay looked back towards the beach and picked out the breast and nipple of Dune Point, the tiny black shape of *Flame* lying at anchor just beyond, barely visible. He figured they'd covered the best part of two and a half kilometres, gained perhaps five hundred metres of elevation. Hope walked barefoot, strap sandals swinging in her hand. Her friend – she hadn't given his name – pointed up the road and kept walking.

Soon they left the paved road and threaded along a narrow foot-path adjacent to a stone wall until they came to a break in the wall next to a wizened, ancient pine tree. The man stopped, crouched low. Clay and Hope did the same. The man pointed down-slope towards the dark shape of a building, what looked like an old farmhouse, about two hundred metres away, squat and square, with an open forecourt, set back perhaps a kilometre from the road. 'They will meet us there,' said the man, his voice low.

They waited. Clay glanced at his watch. Gone one-thirty. He looked out towards the farmhouse. A light flashed three times.

The man stood. 'It is them,' he said, starting down-slope.

Clay followed, Hope behind. He had just cleared the wall when lights flashed on the main road. Two cars, the hunger-bright eyes of a pair of jackals. He stopped, grabbed the man's shoulder, pointed. The headlights swerved, flashing through the trees, across fallow fields. They were coming towards the farmhouse, half-way there already.

The man stopped. '*Bok*,' he said. Shit.

'What is it?' whispered Hope.

'I don't know,' said the man. 'Perhaps the police.'

The cars had closed on the farmhouse now, painted the walls and buildings with their headlights. Five men stood in the courtyard, silhouetted against a big stone wall. The cars skidded to a halt in the gravel. Doors opened. Men emerged from the vehicles. Clay counted seven, all carrying weapons.

He didn't need to see more. He set off at a sprint down the hill towards the farm. Breathing hard, he crouched behind a stone wall, the two groups of men no more than fifty metres away now across an open field. The villagers were crowded together, five of them, up against the wall of the building, some sort of barn with big, wood-beamed sheds buttressing the stone walls, a large, oak-plank door and no visible windows. Eight gunmen he counted now, some armed with shotguns, some with what looked like Uzis. He could hear voices, the men with guns shouting, the villagers mute, blinking into the glare of the headlights. Clay's stomach lurched. He knew this, could see it unfolding as if in a dream, a nightmare he'd lived before. He pulled the Glock from his pocket, chambered a round. One mag, eight targets. Unlikely, but if he could take out two or three of them quickly, the darkness might give the villagers a chance. He'd have to get closer. He looked both ways along the wall, out across the field. Open ground, but the shortest, most direct route. That's what Koevoet had always taught them: go in fast and hard, take the most direct route. He was about to stand when Hope appeared behind him.

She'd lost her sandals. Her dress was torn at the hem. She crouched beside him, breathing hard. 'Oh my God,' she gasped. 'What are they doing?'

Voices rose in a crescendo.

'Not what it looks like, I hope,' said Clay.

Hope looked down at the gun in his hand. Her eyes widened. 'What are you going to do?'

'What I can,' he said. 'Stay here.'

By now the old man had joined them, panting, out of breath. He put his hand over Clay's gun. 'No,' he said. 'They are only trying to frighten them.'

'Who are they?'

'I don't know. They are not from here.'

'Then how can you be sure?'

'There are many of them and only one of you.' He glanced at Hope. 'We are unarmed. It cannot be done.'

One of the gunmen had opened the big door. The villagers were being herded inside the building. Two of the gunmen followed them in.

'I'm not just going to stand here and watch, *broer*. Take your hand away.'

'Please, Clay,' said Hope. 'He's right. You can't just go in shooting. You don't know what's happening here. And you certainly can't get them all by yourself. They'll kill you. Wait, please. I'm sure they'll go away.'

Three armed men now stood outside the building, lit up by the car headlights like actors on a stage. The other three had moved back to one of the vehicles, a Land Cruiser parked furthest from the barn. Clay was ready, calm, focused. A plan mapped itself out in his head. He pushed aside the old man's hand and stood.

Hope reached up and grabbed his arm. 'No,' she said. 'Don't.' Her eyes burned in the headlights' reflected glow.

A single shot, hollow and muffled by stone, jarred the night. It had come from inside the barn.

'Jesus.'

Two gunmen ran from the barn. Two more started barring the door, chaining it closed. Another had split off from the group and was doing something to the wall of one of the outbuildings, waving his arm at the plastered surface, rendering, painting. The others ran back to the cars, returned with jerry cans and started jerking them around the sides of the building, over the wooden sheds. The sharp mineral tang of gasoline filled the air.

'They're going to burn them,' said Clay.

Hope gasped.

Clay sprang forward, moved across the stubble field at an even jog. A flaming bottle arced up, crashed onto the roof, exploded. Two more followed. In seconds, the roof was ablaze. Clay was metres now from the first car. Muffled screams rose from inside the barn, incredulous, animal wails, then the dull hammering of fists on wood. Within moments the building was engulfed in fire, the flames roaring like a turbine. Orange firelight jerked across the courtyard. Clay could already feel the heat on his face, smell the smoke pouring into the night.

He was at the first car now, some sort of Japanese sedan, its lights pointing towards the inferno. Two men were walking towards the car, backlit by the fire, eyes narrowed as they looked into the car's headlights. One carried a jerry can, the other what looked like a tin of paint and a brush. Clay stepped towards them at a walk, as if he were one of them. In the darkness they didn't register him as a threat until it was too late. Clay raised the Glock from five paces and put a .45 calibre bullet into each man's chest. They toppled to the ground without a word.

Clay crouched and darted back behind the car, out of the lights. The Glock was loud. Despite the roar of the fire, the other men turned towards the sound and saw their two comrades lying in the dirt. Shouting now, a voice of command, arms waving. Two men, one taller, the other short and overweight, both armed with shotguns, detached from the group and started moving towards Clay. The others started running towards the Land Cruiser, twenty metres to Clay's left.

Clay hugged the ground, looked out from under the car, watched the men's feet approaching, the orange firelight jerking across the gravel. The others had reached the Land Cruiser. Doors opened, closed. The engine started, a tapping diesel, poorly tuned. The two men stopped next to the bodies of their comrades. A voice shouted out from the Land Cruiser. One of the men shouted back. There was a loud crash as a section of the barn's roof caved in. Embers flooded the night sky. Clay took a deep breath. Bastards. He had to get to the barn, and quickly. He bounced into a crouch then moved along the right side of the car, keeping it between him and the men. The two were right there, just inside the throw of the headlights. Tall crouching down, examining his dead colleagues, Short looking back towards the Land Cruiser. Clay stood, widened his stance, steadied the Glock on his stump, fired three times. The first bullet hit Short in the side of the head, sent him pitching backwards into the dirt. The second missed altogether, hurtled away into the night. The third slammed full force into Tall's trapezium. At that range, the heavy slug tore through the back of his neck, exploded milliseconds later from his lower back. He slumped face-first onto his prone colleague.

Short was on his back, feet scrabbling in the dirt, blood streaming from the side of his head, squinting into the headlights. The bullet must have grazed him at low angle, deflected off the skull. Still on his back, he raised a sawn-off shotgun, aimed it at Clay. A hundredth of a second later the concussion of the charge exploding, loud, very close, shot spraying the car, tearing into metal, smashing glass. Clay felt himself picked up and thrown, kicked hard in the jaw, the right shoulder and upper chest. He fell to the ground, aware he'd been hit, the pain not coming yet, just the dull ache of impact. He rolled, looked under the car. Short was standing now, backpedalling towards the Land Cruiser. Another blast from the shotgun. The car lurched as the pellets slammed broadside into the windows and door panels, smashed out the front lights. Short was at the Land Cruiser now. A door opened. Outstretched hands pulled him inside. The vehicle's engine roared. Gravel spat as the Land Cruiser swerved and sped away down the track.

Clay sat up with his back against the car, put the Glock on the ground, raised his hand to his shoulder, felt the blood there, wet, gritty. He could see Hope and the old man running across the open field toward him, their faces a blur, painted in firelight like denizens of hell. He touched his fingertips to his face. His eyes were starting to swell shut and a thick, warm liquid trickled over his top lip and into his mouth and out over his chin and neck.

He grabbed the pistol, pulled himself up and ran towards the barn.

The heat hit him like a blast wave from a Cuban rocket, sucking the air from his lungs, searing his face. Doubled over, he moved towards the barn's door. Long tentacles of flame reached out from under the door, searched their way up the planking. Clay raised the Glock and fired at the outline of the chain lock. The metal housing blew apart. He dropped the gun, pulled off his jacket, wrapped it around his hand and yanked the chain from the door. Then he stepped back, filled his lungs, the air thick and hot in his throat, grabbed one half of the door, pulled it open, and plunged into the flames.

28

The Killing Gene

Everything was burning.

Smoke and flame enveloped him. He fell to the ground, crawled forward, eyes streaming, blind, feeling with his stump. He hadn't gone far, a few metres only, when his knee bumped something soft. He reached out with his hand. It was one of the villagers, lying on the ground near the door. Clay grabbed what felt like the man's collar, staggered to his feet, started dragging him back towards the open doorway. The man was heavy, unconscious. Clay leant his left side towards the doorway, reached out into the burning air with his stump, jerked the body across the ground. His lungs screamed. He would have to breathe soon, flood his lungs with smoke. He pumped his legs, drove forward. A temperature gradient, the slightest cooling. A few more steps. He could sense an opening, feel a counter-current of air, oxygen being sucked in to fuel the fire. The doorway was close. His nervous system demanded: breathe. He groaned, let go of the man and with his last strength dove forward.

The smoke caught in his lungs as he hit the ground, an acid wail. He crawled forward, sucking in cooler night air, vaguely aware now of Hope and the old man dragging the villager free of the barn, the crash as more of the roof caved in, a burning village of embers pouring from the open doorway, scattering the ground around him, a haemorrhaging carpet of glowing cinders. He staggered to his feet, breathed deep and quickly, hyperventilating, preparing for a deep dive. Then he turned and ran back inside the barn.

This time he got further in, stuck to the same wall where he'd found the first villager, figured they'd huddle together for protection.

He moved forward in a crouch, sweeping the ground ahead with his stump, like a blind man with a cane. Still nothing. He moved right, towards the wall. He had maybe another thirty seconds left. The heat was intensifying. He could feel it raw on his face, searing his skin, see it bright-red through his eyelids, smell it everywhere, the char of wood, the singe of hair, burning rubber and boiling metal. Nothing. Shit. He pushed ahead. Still no one. The heat boiled around him, a living turbulence that threw him back. He could go no further. He spun around, aimed for where he thought the doorway was. As he did, his left foot hit something, the unmistakeable give of living flesh. Clay swung back around, reached out with his hand. It was another of the villagers, unconscious. Clay crouched low, started pulling the man free. This one was smaller, lighter than the first. In a matter of seconds Clay had him clear of the barn.

He collapsed to the ground, gasping for breath.

Hope was there, crouching beside him, her hand on the back of his head. Clay retched, spluttered, the pain already starting to cut through the adrenaline. He twisted, pushed himself to his feet, tried to open his eyes. Through narrowed, streaming slits, he could see the barn engulfed in flame, the doorway like the maw of a roaring furnace. Three men were still inside. Clay took a step forward, started breathing.

Hope grabbed him by the arm. 'Don't,' she said over the din. 'It's over.'

Clay took another step.

'Please, Clay. You've done all you can.'

He hung his head. She was right.

They stood a moment watching the fire. Then, still holding his arm, she walked him over to the shot-ridden car where the old man had laid out the two villagers.

The old man looked Clay over. 'Thank you,' he said.

'How are they?'

'Breathing,' he said. 'Thanks to you and Hope.'

Clay looked back at the barn. 'I'm sorry, I...'

The old man nodded and handed Clay the Glock. 'You must leave. The police will be here very soon.'

'What will you do?'

'I will tell them the truth. I was here meeting with my friends. Strangers came and...' He glanced over to the courtyard wall. 'Come.'

Clay and Hope followed the man across the courtyard, the fire throwing quivering shadows across the ground. They stood and stared at the wall. Scrawled in blue paint over the whitewashed surface, Clay could just make out the words: '*Remember Guenyeli.*' The Cyrillic characters were strong, almost exaggerated. Beneath the words was the symbol omega enveloping the letters N and E: the mark of Neo-Enosis.

Sirens pulsed in the distance. Clay shook the old man's hand and wished him luck.

Hope kissed the old man on both cheeks, held him a moment. Tears streaked her face. 'Come with us,' she pleaded. 'They will never know.'

'These are my friends. Someone must help them.'

'How will you explain the bodies?'

'I will say the perpetrators argued amongst themselves.'

'You will go to jail.'

'Perhaps. But I think not. How can they know? Perhaps I will be a hero.'

They could see flashing red-and-blue lights now, coming down from the village, the hum of engines.

Hope kissed him again. Clay took her by the hand and pulled her away. They started off across the empty field at a run.

☾

They kept running through the night, the pyre's orange glow chasing them, finally retreating as they neared the dunes, quiet returning like a salve, a cure. It was just gone three-thirty. A half-moon had risen, throwing silver shadows across the land. They found the dinghy, rowed out across the polished surface, the water tapping at the inflatable's stretched skin like impatient fingers. Hope clambered aboard. Clay followed, hauled up the dinghy and lashed it to the foredeck. He fired up the diesel, left it idling in neutral, went forward and started bringing up the anchor. But it wouldn't come. Clay reached over the side and tugged on the chain with his hand. It was taut, vertical.

Clay clambered back to the cockpit.

Hope was busy with the medical kit. She looked up. 'What's wrong?'

'Anchor's caught. Fouled on something. I'll use the engine.' Clay took the wheel, put the engine in gear and motored forward slowly. *Flame* started ahead, then abruptly swung head-around as the anchor held. Clay tried again, this time moving parallel to shore. Same result. With the sandy bottom, there was no way the Danforth should foul like this. They were wasting valuable time. Clay throttled back to idle, put the engine in neutral, stripped down to his shorts and jumped over the side.

The water was cold, numbing the pain in his shoulder, the burns on his face, the cuts around his eyes. It felt good. He followed the hull around to the bow, noted with admiration where Gonzales had neatly repaired the bowsprit. He grabbed the chain, filled his lungs, slipped his head below the surface and followed the chain down. He opened his eyes, letting the cold brine flood over his cornea. The water wasn't deep here, only about four metres. He looked up. *Flame*'s shadow hung above him, a dark shape against the silvery firmament of the surface. The anchor was clearly visible against the moon-pale sand. It hung half a metre above the sea floor, its flukes open like wings, snared on something.

Clay dived and reached the sea bottom. The anchor was fouled on a cable, about an inch in diameter, smooth, newish, sheathed in some sort of plastic. The anchor had pulled it up from the seabed in a loop. Both ends of the cable disappeared under the sand. It appeared to run parallel to shore, buried perhaps twenty or thirty centimetres into the sand. The cable was wedged between the blunt end of the flukes and the hinge of the anchor's stem. Pulling against it only wedged it in tighter. He would have to go back aboard, let out chain, then come back down and work the cable free. That would take time. If the police had sensed a wider involvement in the incident at the farm, patrol vessels might be on their way. They had to make miles as quickly as they could. He would have to leave the anchor behind. He pinched the anchor's shackle screw between his thumb and forefinger and turned.

A moment later he burst to the surface and clambered aboard, the chain hanging slack now in the water, the boat drifting. He went forward and brought in the remaining chain. Shivering, he returned to the cockpit and started *Flame* out to sea. Hope threw a blanket over his shoulders and began to tend his wounds, picking bits of car window from his forehead and arms, two heavily deformed pieces of lead shot from his shoulder. They hadn't penetrated far, most of their energy dissipated by the car's metal sheet and glass. It looked worse than it was. She doused the holes in antiseptic, bandaged him as best she could. She was very gentle in this, he thought, very serious.

Soon they were sipping hot coffee, the compass showing southeast, and somewhere out there, Syria.

☾

A few hours later they watched the sun come up in an overcast winter sky, burn red on the horizon then cool to yellow, softening away to a flat grey daylight. They motored on in calm seas, clear now of TRNC waters, Hope silent, brooding. A fishing boat appeared, chugging away on the horizon, and then was gone, melted into the sea, Cyprus just a smudge in the distance. After a while Clay killed the engine, tore off the bandages Hope had applied, pulled a coil of line from the port locker, cleated one end, and threw the line into the water. Before she could react he was over the side, Glock in hand.

For a long time, until he was numb, Clay floated on his back in the cold, flat sea, letting the brine lick his wounds like a dog's tongue. He let the gun slip from his hand.

Later, they struck south, and then southwest, back towards Larnaca.

Hope again dressed his wounds. 'Do you want to look in a mirror?' she said. 'You look like a stray without a home.'

Clay trimmed up the main, patted the cockpit scupper. 'This is my home.'

Hope sat with her back against the cabin bulkhead, watching him as he trimmed sail, corrected course. After a long while she looked him in the eyes. Her face was set hard. 'You know,' she said, 'I've always been taught that death is a good thing.'

Clay locked her gaze. 'So was I.'

'Do you think it is, Clay?'

'In the way I was taught? No.'

'The war.'

Clay nodded. 'It's not good or bad, Hope. You can't think that way. It's inevitable, that's all.'

She paused, hung on this a moment. 'It's inevitable because evolution demands it. Death keeps the genetic code fresh. Therefore it must be good.'

'QED?'

She drew her knees up to her chest, wrapped her arms around herself. The breeze wisped her long hair about her face. 'Our chromosomes are capped by repetitive strands of DNA that protect them from fraying. Telomeres they're called. As we age, these telomeres gradually burn out, like fuses. And when they do, we start to die. Death is programmed into us from the start.'

Clay traced the horizon with his eyes. 'Those men didn't die of old age.'

'No, they didn't,' she said in a whisper, barely audible over the wind. 'It was evolution's other imperative.'

He eased the main sheet, trimmed up the Genoa. 'Don't

overanalyse, Hope.' Not now. Later you will have time. More than you could ever want.

'The killing gene,' she said. 'A throwback to our days as hunters. We're programmed to kill.'

Clay said nothing.

'More than that, Clay. To enjoy killing.'

Clay looked out to sea, pushed this away. 'Don't, Hope.'

'It's part of you, Clay.'

He considered a reply, abandoned it. After a while he said: 'I can tell you, theory doesn't help.'

They lapsed into silence again, the breeze fluking across the flat grey sea. A couple of gulls sideslipped over them, wingtip close, then disappeared towards Syria.

'You saw what they painted on the wall,' Clay said, breaking the quiet. 'Neo-Enosis.'

She frowned, nodded. 'Chrisostomedes has been warning for months that they would take action.'

'What is *Guenyeli*?' he said.

Hope curled up against the forward cockpit bulkhead. 'On Christmas Eve 1958, Turkish Cypriot militia across the island attacked Greek Cypriots in their homes. Hundreds were killed, including women, children and old people. The village of Guenyeli was one of the worst. Thirty people, mostly children, were locked inside a schoolhouse and burned alive.'

'1958. Jesus Christ.'

'Revenge has no statute of limitations. Here especially.'

'Just what you'd expect from Neo-Enosis.'

'Absolutely.'

'But there's something I don't understand.' He'd not had time to consider it until now. 'Those men tonight, the ones with the guns.'

'Murderers.' She put her head on her knees a moment, looked back up at Clay. 'This will make the Commission's work almost impossible. If people were scared to talk before, just imagine how difficult it will be to get any credible testimony now.'

'There's something else.'

'What?'

'Those weren't Greek Cypriots, Hope. Any of them.'

'What do you mean?'

'Were you listening to them?'

'No, I…'

'They were speaking Russian.'

29

Looking Down Through Blood

They passed the Ayia Napa headlands just after noon the next day and brought *Flame* into the Larnaca marina four hours later. They'd spoken little, taking turns on watch so the other could sleep below. Now they stood by Clay's rental car, the late-afternoon sun slanting across the marina car park. Clay could see the stress on Hope's face, the circles under her eyes like bruises, the lines around her mouth deeper, more anxious than before. A few hours can change the way you see everything.

They agreed that Clay would drive Hope to her house near Paphos. It was Wednesday, Maria was looking after the seminar, and there was no reason for Hope to go back to Nicosia and the university. Weekends she usually spent working at the Lara Beach research station she'd set up almost five years ago with a series of grants from the EU and the Government of Cyprus. Clay knew she didn't want to be alone.

They drove along the coast road, watching the Med flash past, the tired fields littered with stone, the soil stripped away to reveal the island's bare white bones, the forests that once covered this place centuries gone now, hacked away by successive empires. Just after dusk, Clay stopped at a roadside *periptero*. Hope got out, stretched her legs and disappeared into the shop. Clay walked through the dust of the parking lot to a payphone booth wedged up against a lamppost.

Crowbar answered first ring. 'Where the hell have you been?' he barked in Afrikaans.

'Guess.'

Crowbar hesitated a moment. 'That was you?'

'You heard?'

'It's all over the papers today.'

'And you, *broer*?'

'We have to meet.'

Clay gave Crowbar Hope's address.

'Tonight, then.'

'Hope says it's hard to find.'

'*Fok*, Straker, you growing an old woman's beard now? See you there in two and a half hours.'

Clay put down the phone and walked back to the car. Hope was already sitting in the passenger seat, the dome light on, a copy of the Cyprus English-language daily spread across her lap. A photo of the wall, the slogan clearly legible, the burnt-out buildings in the background accompanied the headline: *Six Dead in Karpasia Revenge Attack.*

Clay started the car and pulled onto the coast road heading west.

After a while Hope folded the paper, switched off the dome light. 'It says that two men are now in hospital suffering from burns and smoke inhalation, but are expected to recover.'

Clay said nothing, drove on.

'You saved them, Clay,' she whispered.

Grey tarmac scrolled away under a myopic funnel of light.

'The Turks are making a big noise about it,' she went on. 'They say they have identified three of the dead attackers as Greek Cypriots. They are demanding that the Greek Cypriot government round up the senior members of Neo-Enosis and bring them to justice. It also says that the Turkish Cypriot police have evidence that at least two others who were involved fled the scene on foot that night, possibly to the coast and by boat to the south. They are wanted for questioning. There is no mention of my friend.'

But Clay wasn't thinking about the fire, or the shootings. He was thinking about Rania. He'd gone ashore that night hoping that the villagers might provide something that would lead him to her, perhaps tie her disappearance to Erkan. Knowing that Erkan was

there, in his monastery in Karpasia, had given him the vague hope
that he might have been able to press on, confront the *bliksem* one
more time, find her there, bring her home. Now he had nothing, just
a scared scientist and more police after him.

It was dark by the time they reached Paphos. Hope directed him
through the town to the coast and along a maze of narrow roads
that snaked through the rocky carbonate hills rising up from the sea.
After a while they came to a small hamlet, twenty houses perhaps,
perched on the edge of a rocky hillside, the coast a fractal white
line half a dimension distant, the sea stretched out across the whole
world, dark and foreboding, as if you might fall into it. The road
was barely wide enough for one car. Clay slowed and looked back
over the darkened hills. A pickup truck sauntered along the winding
valley-bottom track towards the coast road. Hope waved them on
past a series of abandoned homesteads – there were so many here,
derelicts of crumbling masonry and caved roofs, the arches slumped
and ragged, the keystones dropped like old teeth.

'Here,' she said, pointing to a narrow, tree-lined lane. 'Stop.' Hope
jumped out of the car, opened a tin postbox, pulled out a clutch of
letters and sat back in the car. 'Just down here,' she said.

Clay pulled the Beretta from his pocket and checked the action.
Then he guided the car down the lane to a rock-edged turnaround,
where he switched off the engine. Hope took him by the hand and
led him on foot through an old stone archway into a night garden of
thick underbrush and tall, swaying trees, their branches black against
a moonlit sky. The house was old, limestone brickwork casements
and corners, clay-tile roof, wood-shuttered windows, a tiled veranda
set with wicker chairs and a wooden table, and everywhere the
cascade of vegetation, as if the place were clothed in it. She opened
the front door, lit a hurricane lamp and led him through the house,
carrying the lamp before her by its handle. A black-and-white tile
floor, a stonework fireplace, flashes of framed watercolours on the
walls, hand-drawn, washed sketches of sea creatures, turtles and fish
and crustaceans of the kind you see in guidebooks. Hope handed

him the lantern, opened up a set of French doors, then unlatched and folded back floor-to-ceiling shutters. A cold breeze flooded the house. The Med sparkled under a cloud-strewn night sky.

Hope left him on the balcony and reappeared a moment later with a couple of beers, handed Clay one, put the lantern on a small side table, and turned it low. Then she crouched to a small outdoor fireplace and struck a match. Soon a fire crackled in the clay hearth.

Hope turned her back to the fire, warming her hands behind her. 'I'm off grid,' she said. 'I have a twelve-volt solar photovoltaic system, gas for cooking, and my water comes from a spring out back that runs all year. This is my sanctuary.'

Clay checked his watch. Just over two hours since he'd spoken with Crowbar. There was no way he'd find the place. Hope was curled up in her chair, arms clasped over her shins, like he'd seen Rania do sometimes.

'Okay?' he said.

She nodded.

'Don't worry. We'll find her.'

'I miss her.'

Clay bit down, said nothing, sipped his beer. Me too.

Hope opened her letters, slicing open the envelopes on their short end with a polished wooden opener, glancing at the contents, setting them aside. 'Bills,' she said. She drank some beer, then picked up the last letter, opened it, unfolded the thick bond paper, read, turned it over, and reread. She looked up at Clay and let out a little laugh, setting the paper with the others.

'What is it?' said Clay.

Hope shook her head. 'It's…' She picked up the letter, looked at it again, crumpled it in her hand and dropped to the floor. 'It's nothing.'

Before he had time to ask again, a rapping sound echoed through the house. Clay pulled out the Beretta and walked quickly to the front door.

'*Die fokken duer oopmaak.*'

Clay opened the door. Crowbar stood on the veranda, stamping his feet on the tile. He was wrapped against the cold in a thick woollen jumper and black leather jacket. '*Fokken Med, ja*? Is supposed to be *fokken* hot, *ja*? *Fok* I miss *Afrika*.' His gaze wandered over the cuts on Clay's face, the singed eyebrows, the puffy red burns on his forehead and nose. '*Fok mie*, Straker. You get better-looking every day.'

Clay shrugged and led Crowbar through the house to the veranda.

'Hope, this is my friend Crowbar. He's helping me find Rania.'

Hope looked her new guest over. 'Crowbar?'

'*Koevoet*,' said Crowbar. 'That's how you say it.'

Hope brought him a beer. 'Here you go, Mister Koofoot.'

Crowbar smiled at the attempt and took a slug of the beer. Then he reached into the pocket of his jacket and placed a folded newspaper on the table. 'She's alive, *broer*.'

Clay grabbed the paper, opened it up and tilted it towards the light. There it was, on the front page of that day's *Independent*. The headline read: '*North Cyprus Land Grab Terror*'.

Clay looked up at Crowbar. 'It only happened the night before last.'

'So she must have filed yesterday, *ja*. She's here, on the island.'

The title of the piece also clearly ruled out Erkan. A cascade of relief washed through him, like being in the field hospital and the doctor looking down at you through a blood-spattered surgical mask, the blur of people moving all around you, yelling, screaming, the moans of the wounded and the dying, and his muffled voice telling you not to worry, that you're going to make it and you believe him.

'And if she's writing and filing stories, then she must be free,' said Hope, breathless. 'She hasn't been kidnapped at all.' Her smile was big, like her name.

'Then why hasn't she contacted anyone?' said Clay, looking at Hope. 'Not even you.' He could see the words hit her, the smile die, the pain spread through her. It felt good for a second, faded fast.

Hope grabbed the paper, read the article in silence, put it down.

'Rania writes here that the murders we witnessed were made to look like the work of Neo-Enosis, but that in fact it was Erkan's men, hired guns. Not simple retaliation for some old grievance, she says, but an attempt to silence those who would speak out against the land grab in the north.' Hope frowned. 'She doesn't *want* to make contact. She's hiding. How else could she have accessed this kind of information?'

It made sense. Rania had been trained by French intelligence. Clay knew that if she wanted to disappear, she could. But then, why the note left in the hotel room in Istanbul? Had he misread it after all, willed into it some meaning that was never there?

Hope said, 'The Turks are saying that the gunmen were Greek. Rania appears convinced they were Erkan's men, Turks. You told me you thought the gunmen were speaking Russian.'

'Not thought,' said Clay. 'They were.'

Hope glanced up at him. 'Okay, then. They were.'

'Russian?' said Crowbar.

Clay nodded.

'Why would Erkan hire Russians?' said Hope.

Crowbar drained his beer. 'Why not? This place is crawling with 'em. Funnelling cash out of Mother Russia as fast as they can milk those big fat tits of hers.' Crowbar stood, wandered off towards the kitchen.

Hope looked at Clay. 'Your friend. He's … colourful.'

Clay said nothing, let the silence sit between them.

Crowbar returned with three beers clawed in one hand, set them on the table.

'Do help yourself,' said Hope.

Crowbar grinned at her and opened a beer. Then, speaking to Clay in Afrikaans, said, 'There's something I need to tell you.'

'Don't worry, *broer*. She's–' Clay stumbled, stopped. She's what? Rania's lover? Future godmother to their child? Fucking third peg in a *ménage à trois*? 'She's okay,' he said.

Crowbar looked at Hope and continued in English: 'Your research place, just down here at Lara Beach.'

'Yes?'

'You don't know?'

Hope leant forward in her chair. 'Know what?'

'It was ransacked two nights ago, destroyed. Equipment wrecked, windows smashed, documents taken, that nice new Toyota Hilux torched.'

Hope's eyes widened. Even in the dim firelight Clay could see initial disbelief give way to the body blow of bad news. Her face crumpled.

'No one was hurt,' said Crowbar.

'Jesus,' said Clay. 'Who did it?'

Crowbar stood, stretched his shoulders, twisted his torso in a slow arc back and forth, as if he were limbering up for a fight. 'I did.'

30

Tears for Wool

Hope gasped. 'You?'

Clay stood, squared up to his old platoon commander, waited for an intelligible answer.

Crowbar raised his hands and sat back in his chair. 'Look, I'm trying to help, *ja*.'

'By smashing up her research station? Are you fucking crazy, Koevoet?'

'*Ja*, definitely.'

Hope leapt up and open-palmed Crowbar across the face. The crack of skin on skin pierced the night air.

Crowbar sat unmoving.

Hope looked at Clay, back at Crowbar. There were tears in her eyes. 'Five years' work, you asshole. That's what that place was. It represents thousands of volunteer hours, irreplaceable funding painstakingly raised. And you walk in here like it's just another…' she stumbled. '…I don't know, and tell me you've destroyed it. For heaven's sake, *why*?'

'It was my employer's idea. Not mine, *ooma*,' said Crowbar in English. The attempt at respect was lost on Hope.

'You better start making some sense, *oom*,' Clay said in Afrikaans.

Crowbar rose from his chair, put a hand on Clay's shoulder. 'Look, Straker. I'm *fokken* here, aren't I?' he said, his voice calm, even.

'Who are you working for, Koevoet?'

'A friend of yours. Same one tried to kill you in Istanbul.'

Clay's throat tightened. 'Regina Medved.'

Crowbar nodded.

Clay sensed the movement of Crowbar's torso, the coil as he shifted his weight to his back foot. He just had time to turn his head through thirty degrees before the blow fell.

Crowbar's huge right fist ploughed into Clay's cheekbone, sending him spinning to the ground. Clay landed hard, his left shoulder and hip taking the brunt of the fall. To his surprise he was still conscious.

Hope screamed, started moving towards the house. Crowbar put out a big, hairy arm and stopped her dead.

Clay put his hand to his face, felt the bruise coming up. Nothing was broken; no teeth missing. Normally, a bareknuckle blow from Koevoet meant fractured bones, concussion.

Crowbar stood above him, a grin as big as the African sky spreading across his face. 'I've waited a long time to do that, *ja.*' He reached down and held out his hand.

'Jesus, Koevoet.' Clay reached up.

Crowbar hauled him to his feet, inspected the welt growing on Clay's face. 'With the burns and the shot, that looks *lekker*, *ja*?' he said in Afrikaans.

Hope stepped back, her way still barred by Crowbar's arm. She seemed to have recovered somewhat, now stood hands on hips. 'Either speak in a language I can understand, and tell me what the hell is going on, or get out,' she hissed. 'Both of you.'

Crowbar sat back in his chair as if nothing had happened, took a sip of beer. Clay and Hope looked at each other. Clay shrugged, sat. So did Hope.

In his heavily accented, stuttering English, Crowbar started to explain. While Clay and Hope had been north, he'd met with an old contact in the shipping business in Limassol. Crowbar had used him a number of times in his DCC days to ship 'goods' from Israel via Yemen to South Africa, in contravention of international sanctions. Israeli weapons, such as the famous Galil assault rifle, later produced domestically by Armscor as the R4, were the backbone of the SADF armoury during the Border War. His contact, who did a lot of work with the Russians in Cyprus ('and I mean, *a lot*,' said Crowbar) had confirmed that Regina Medved was on the island, meeting with the heads of her various businesses. Crowbar had managed to meet, if not with the dowager herself, with her number-two man, in Limassol, two days before. As a result of that meeting, he now worked 'on contract' for the Medved family empire. Smashing the research station had been his first task.

Crowbar finished his beer and put the empty bottle on the floor between his feet. 'I don't know where Rania is, Straker. But I can tell you, Regina Medved doesn't have her. She just put a one-million-dollar price on Rania's head.'

Fear detonated inside Clay's chest, tore through him like fragments of mortar casing.

'And something else. The reward for Zdravko Todorov has just gone up. Two million dead, three alive. Same as you. I think she wants to have some fun with him before they kill him.' He glanced over at Hope, leaned in close to Clay, whispered. 'They say she gets off on torture. Likes to watch.'

Clay looked up at him.

'I mean, literally. She masturbates while they torture the bastards.'

Clay sat up, took a deep breath.

By now Hope was sobbing quietly in her chair, Punk's sweater hanging from her thin frame like a lost dream.

Crowbar stood, started towards the doorway, 'Beer, Straker?' he said, disappearing into the kitchen.

Clay looked at Hope. 'No wonder Rania disappeared.'

Hope looked up through her tears. 'But she hasn't abandoned us.'

Clay nodded. Us.

Crowbar reappeared with two cold Keo grasped in one hand, a 35mm camera with an externally fitted flash hanging by its strap from the other. He handed Clay a beer. Clay put it on the table next to the other one he'd hardly touched.

'So why would Medved want me to destroy your research station?' Crowbar asked Hope, cracking the top of his beer. 'What has she got against you?'

'I've never met the woman. All I know about her is from the news. A reclusive oddball oligarch obsessed with Orthodox Christian mythology, another of the great Russian carpetbaggers.' Hope wiped her face with the sleeve of Punk's jumper. More tears for wool. She looked at Clay. 'What has she got against *you*?'

Clay shrugged.

'He killed her brother,' said Crowbar.

Clay shot him a stare.

Crowbar frowned. 'You said she was okay.'

'I *am* okay,' said Hope. 'And after yesterday, I'm not surprised either.'

'Is it because of the Commission?' said Clay.

Hope leaned forward. 'Why would Regina Medved care about the Commission?'

'Have you heard of a company called EcoDev?' said Crowbar, fiddling with the camera.

'Sure,' said Hope. 'It's one of the biggest, most successful property development outfits in Cyprus. Arch rivals of my friend Nicos Chrisostomedes.' She exhaled through pursed lips. 'EcoDev has started the application process for a major resort just west of here, at Toxeflora Beach in the Agamas. It'll never go ahead, though, because it's on Turkish-owned land that has been incorporated into the proposed Agamas National Park, and because, after Lara Beach, it's the last and most important remaining turtle-nesting beach in Greek Cyprus. So yes, the Commission is going to want to speak to EcoDev.'

'Being in the park didn't stop the Alassou Resort going ahead,' said Clay.

'That was one of Chrisostomedes' deals,' said Hope. 'Also on Turkish land.'

Clay thought back to his meeting with Erkan, right after Rania had disappeared. 'According to Erkan, that deal was "facilitated" by Minister Dimitriou. Even Erkan was in on it.'

Hope looked at him quizzically. 'Are you sure?'

'I have proof.'

Hope stared out into the night for a moment. 'If word ever got out that Chrisostomedes had colluded with Erkan, it would mean the end for his business here. He'd become a pariah. People here have long memories and they don't forgive. As for Dimitriou, his political career would be over.' Then she reached to the ground, picked up the crumpled letter and started to unfold it. 'Now this makes sense,' she breathed, smoothing out the paper and handing it to Clay.

Hope caught a breath. 'It's from Nicos Chrisostomedes. He wants me to join him for dinner the day after tomorrow at his mansion in the Troodos Mountains. He wants to discuss making a major donation to the research station.'

Clay looked at the date. Yesterday. 'I thought...'

'Yes,' Hope interrupted. 'I've been highly critical of him in the media.'

'When he wrote this he would have known that the station had been destroyed. Sounds like he wants to show you his caring, benevolent side, before the enquiry starts.'

'Obviously,' muttered Hope. 'It's so transparent it's embarrassing.'

'Are you going to go?'

'I'm not so stupid as to think I can find the kind of money he's talking about through the grants system – not a second time. Although I can't possibly imagine how this can work. He wants to develop Lara Beach, I want to protect it. But yes, I'm going. I'd be crazy not to.'

Crowbar stood, faced Clay, brought the camera up to his face. 'Put your hands behind the chair, *ja*,' he said. 'Try to look pissed off.'

'I *am* pissed off.'

'Good, *ja*.'

'What the hell are you doing, Koevoet?'

'Your hands.'

'Hand.'

Crowbar smiled. 'Your arms then, *soutpiel*. Behind, like you're tied.'

Clay put his arms behind the chair, stared into the lens, understanding.

Crowbar hit the shutter button. The flash pulsed.

Just then, Hope's mobile phone buzzed. She flipped it open, listened a moment, eyes widening. She started to speak but stopped short. 'Yes,' she said, listened again. 'I understand.' A few seconds later she closed her phone and looked at Clay. 'That was Rania's office. They've received a message from her.'

31

This, You Were Given

Hope smiled big like love. He could see it there on her face, in every contracted muscle, in the heat coming from her flushed cheeks, that exothermic reaction over which she had no control going off inside her like rockets.

'She wants to meet you, Clay,' she said, breathless. 'Tomorrow afternoon at the Mephistos copper mine waste pits in the Troodos. Three o'clock.'

'Slow down, Hope,' said Clay. 'Who was it you spoke to?'

'Someone called Hamour, from AFP's Istanbul desk. He said you knew each other.'

'Was he sure it was her?'

'He said the message came with the story that she filed yesterday. It was attached as an addendum, with my phone number, asking him to pass the message on through me. He's been trying to reach me since then. That's all he said.' Hope shook her head. 'Why wouldn't she just call me herself?'

'If she's trying to hide, she's not going to call anyone. Was there anything else in the message?'

'Nothing.'

'Are you sure.'

'That was it. Just meet her at the mine tomorrow.'

Clay looked at his watch. 'That gives us about fifteen hours.'

'Do you know this place?' said Crowbar.

'I've been there once before,' said Clay. 'A local environmental group asked me to do some chemical testing on the waste pits a couple of years ago. Rania knew that – I told her about it. It's an isolated place, on the western side of the mountains. No vehicle access. A good ten clicks walk to get in there, pretty rugged country.'

'How far from here?'

'About five hours' drive, another couple walking.'

Crowbar put his beer on the table. 'Then we'd better get moving, *broer*. Now. Anyone picks a place like that to meet, *ja*, it's because someone else is interested.'

'You have plenty of time,' said Hope.

'We're going to get there nice and early, *ooma*, make sure that if Rania does show, we have her covered. And if someone else shows up, we'll ask 'em a few impolite questions.'

Hope looked at Clay. 'What is this *ooma*?'

Clay grinned at Crowbar. 'It means old lady.'

Hope's expression hardened. She glared at Crowbar.

'*Kak, Straker, fokken roerder,*' Crowbar said in Afrikaans. And then in English, to Hope: 'No, that's wrong. It doesn't mean…'

Hope said nothing, just stared up at him.

'It's respect,' blurted Crowbar. '*Fok*, Straker. Tell her.'

Clay said nothing.

'You're not old,' said Crowbar, fidgeting now. Clay had never seen him like this, was enjoying it.

Hope played him, stood expressionless. After a moment a hint of a smile crept across her face. 'Why, thank you, Mister Koofoot. Neither are you.'

☾

They had no way of knowing from which direction Rania would approach the mine. There were at least three road access points within ten kilometres of the pits, narrow gravel firebreaks that switch-backed between ancient black-trunked pines and gnarled scrub oak, snaked around crumbling, frayed rhyolite and marble cliffs, the mountainside scarred by the centuries-old quarryings of people long dead, Ottomans, Romans.

They decided to leave Clay's rental car in Agios Psemanitos, a tiny, near-abandoned village about twenty kilometres west of the mine, and track around to the eastern approaches in Crowbar's Pajero. By the time they had hidden the 4WD two hundred metres into the forest, behind the boulders of an ancient landslide, the sun was up and the last of the shadows were edging from the deep valleys. It gave them the best part of eight hours before Rania's appointed time.

It took them less than two hours' hard walking to reach the mine site.

Clay stood beside the largest of the pits and stared down into the copper sulphate sterility of the bright-blue water. The air had that crushed, burnt smell of sulphides, the latent sweetness of molybdenum, an undertone of pine resin breaking through now and again as the breeze swirled through the valley. A faded metal sign swung from a rusted barbed-wire fence that ran with listing and fallen posts across the end of the pits towards an old adit entrance. A set of narrow-gauge rails, almost buried now, tracked from the adit across the open kill-zone that surrounded the pits and disappeared into the trees.

Crowbar was on the bank between the two smaller pits. 'Smart *bokkie*,' he said, voice bouncing over the heavy, metal-rich sludge. 'Nice field of fire.'

Koevoet was right. From where he stood, Clay had a clear view at least a hundred metres in every direction. Not a bad spot if you wanted a private conversation. And yet of all the places she could have chosen, why here?

Crowbar raised his field glasses, scanned the ridge above them, pointed up at the steep rock face. 'That's where I'll be, *broer*.'

It took them almost half an hour to scramble to the top of the ridge. The slope rock was weathered, cubed, hot already in the midday sun. It disintegrated under their boots as they climbed, trickled back down the hill in rivers. Gnarled pine trees clung to the bands of marble and gneiss that jutted from the slope like ramparts, their twisted roots spreading like veins through the barren rock. How they survived here Clay could not imagine.

They collapsed to the ground, sweating and panting. Clay looked back down to the pits, three blue sapphires sparkling in the sunshine. From here, he could see out across the whole spread of the mine workings, the old rail line snaking up the valley to the western approaches, mountains stretching away to a blue horizon in every direction.

Crowbar slung off his pack, fished out a water bottle, drank and offered it to Clay. Then he stood, walked along the ridge, disappeared momentarily behind a boulder the size of a small truck and reappeared. 'Commanding,' he said, pulling out his Beretta. 'Great lines in every direction. No better place in the whole goddamn valley.' He looked down at the pits. 'I figure 350 metres, *seun*. Too far for me to help. But I can warn you, *ja*. Two quick shots from this, time for you to *ontrek*. RV at the Pajero.'

Clay nodded at Crowbar, looked at his watch. Three and a half hours to go. He started back down the slope, the sun refracting through the edges of the treetops, strobing over him as he pushed his boots down through the rattling scree, and after all these years, that feeling again, of someone watching over you, an archangel. And, as he reached the base of the ridge and started towards the pits, he knew that everything had changed. And though he'd known it for days, it had been like so much else in his life – having the knowledge but not the understanding. You chose who you loved, or maybe they chose you. But a son, a daughter, you were given.

He sat on the middle berm, in the epicentre of the pits where he could be clearly seen. He picked up a handful of the crushed mine tailings, let the stuff fall from his hand and waited. He thought about her disappearance from the hotel that day, the note she'd left, wondered about her leaving, about Spearpoint that day on the street outside the hotel in Istanbul – had he been one of Medved's informants? Had he been the one who'd called in the assassins whose bodies were now rotting at the bottom of the Med? The things she'd said to him that last morning they were together replayed now in his head. Justice isn't an event, she'd said. It isn't something you do once. There is no end to it. Forgiveness, you earn.

In a couple of long hours, he'd see her again.

A cold wind blew through the valley. Clouds the size of mountain villages drifted high over the peaks. Shadow passed over the ridge, cooled the surface of the ponds from molten copper to glacier blue. He closed his eyes, breathed.

At just that moment, just as the unfamiliar shade of serenity began to flow over him, a shot echoed through the valley.

Then another bang, louder, higher pitched. The sound danced among the rocks for a moment then died. Clay tensed, scanned the tree line in a three-sixty-degree arc. No one. Silence. He glanced at his watch. Just gone two. The first shot was definitely Koevoet's Beretta. The second was a big charge, high velocity. Clay sprang to his feet, sprinted towards the base of the ridge.

He made it to the top about ten minutes later, quads screaming, chest heaving. He'd heard nothing since the two shots, just the jackhammering of his heart, the rail of his breathing, the loose rock tumbling behind him.

Crowbar was sitting with his back up against a slab of weathered rhyolite, hand pressed over a bloodied compress bandage that covered his lower abdomen. He opened his eyes as Clay approached. '*Kak*, Straker,' he growled. 'Bastard surprised me. *Fokken* stupid.' Crowbar raised his hand and pointed towards the back slope. 'That way.'

Clay pulled out the Beretta, sprinted to a break in the slope and scanned the valley. No movement. Nothing. Clay ran back, crouched at Crowbar's side. 'Let me look.'

'I'm good,' said Crowbar. 'He had a Dragunov, if you can *fokken* believe it. Must have been one of Medved's people. Surprised each other.' Crowbar pointed to the edge of the slope. 'He came up right there. I was side on. The round passed right through, didn't open up.' He pulled the compress away from his gut, looked down. A trough about three inches long had been sliced across his belly. The wound oozed blood. Crowbar tugged at the roll of fat that covered his midsection, stifled a laugh, winced. '*Fokken* asshole did me a favour, *ja*. Wanted to get rid of this anyway.'

'Jesus, Koevoet, hold still,' said Clay, fishing in Crowbar's pack. He pulled out a fresh compress, gauze, disinfectant. 'We're going to have to get you sewn up, *broer*. Can you walk?'

'Unless you've got a Puma handy,' grunted Crowbar.

'No Puma.'

'Then *ja*. Guess I'll have to.'

'Was he alone?'

'Didn't see anyone else.'

'Rania?' Clay doused the wound with antiseptic.

Crowbar winced, shook his head.

'Did you get a look at the guy?'

Crowbar shook his head again.

'Did you hit him?'

'I don't know. Maybe.'

'Easy shot from here for that Dragunov.'

'Good thing I came along to look after you, *soutpiele*.'

Clay ripped open a new compress with his teeth, spat out the paper and pushed it down onto the wound. 'Who's looking after whom right now, *oom*?'

Crowbar pushed him away. '*Fok* that, Straker. Go after the bastard. He can't be far, lugging that bloody great commie sniper rifle.'

'No way, Koevoet. Now hold still, for Christ's sake.'

'If that bastard has Rania…' Crowbar tailed off. 'Look, it's just a clip. I'm good. Just don't forget to come back for me, *ja*?'

Clay pushed the compress down hard on the wound.

Crowbar grabbed his wrist, held it tight. 'Go.'

Clay knelt a moment, looking into Koevoet's eyes. He knew that look. Clay stood, pulled out his Glock. 'Okay, *oom*. You win. Stay put.'

32

Twelve Years of Silence

Clay stood at the edge of the backslope and scanned the place where Crowbar's assailant had stood. Bootscuff marks in the loose, rocky soil. A brass shell casing, 7.62mm, long, fresh. And there, like moss blooming on rock, a spray of blood, viscous red drops scattered over the burnished stone, more footmarks leading downslope. Clay looked back at Crowbar, gave him a thumbs-up. 'Spoor, *oom*. Blood trail.'

'Short little *draadtrekker*. I knew I'd hit him. Go get the fucker.'

Clay reached down, touched a drop of blood onto his finger tip, raised it to his nose, inhaled the scent. He'd grown up doing this, on the veldt as a boy with his father and uncle, tracking the prey on foot, a springbok or a kudu, hours and sometimes days, the old way. Make the kill, eat the heart.

And then in Angola with Crowbar and the Battalion he'd tracked and killed human beings.

Clay checked his watch and started down the slope. Twenty minutes now since he'd heard the shots. Moving over rough country like this, carrying a heavy weapon, a strong, fit man might cover two, maybe three kilometres in that time. Judging by the amount of blood on the trail, he was also carrying a 9mm slug inside him somewhere. Clay guessed the guy had maybe a kilometre head start on him, not much more.

He moved quickly through the trees, following the increasingly ragged trail to the break in slope, then east into a valley bottom dense with black pine and remnant Cyprus cedar. Clay could tell from the scuffing of the footmarks that the man was struggling. There was quite a bit of blood. Inside the thicket it was dark and cool, the ground underfoot moss, stones, fallen rotwood. He could hear the trickling of water, smell the humic freshness of cedar. Visibility dropped in the undergrowth. Clay slowed, crouched low, moved in short bursts to cover, wary now. If the man had sensed he was being followed, he might turn, face his pursuer. Ahead, beside a moss-covered boulder, a flash of white on the ground. Clay moved forward, crouched. A paper bandage package, smeared with blood, still wet. Boot marks in the soft ground, moving away down-stream. He was close. Clay waited a moment, listened, but all he could hear was the sway of the treetops in the mountain breeze. He checked the round in the Beretta's chamber then kept moving.

About two hundred metres along the valley, the trail cut sharply upslope. Clay could see gouges in the moss where the man had slipped, deep imprints where he'd used the butt-stock of the Dragunov as a crutch. Blood hung in semi-coagulated droplets from the tips of pine needles. Up above, the torn yellow rock of the old mine road. Clay had walked this road once, about three years ago. He knew now that the guy was making for the northeastern approach, the terminus of the old mine rail line, only about a kilometre and a half away. That's where he would have left his vehicle. Clay looked at his watch. Almost an hour now since he'd left Koevoet. The guy was moving fast.

Clay scrambled up the slope towards the mine road. He'd just reached the frayed edge of the cut, was picking his way through the rusted boulders piled on the valley side of the road, fragments of ancient oceanic crust, when the tree behind him splintered, a twisting, snapping sound. He flinched, pure reflex as the second sound came, a high-pitched crack that echoed down the valley. Clay dropped to the ground, pushing himself into the rock as more rounds sent shards of wehrlite and gabbro zinging through the air around him. Then quiet. Clay stayed absolutely still. From the report of the rifle, the same one he'd heard back at the pits, he guessed a range of four hundred metres, off to the right, towards the terminus. He'd been lucky. At that range, the Dragunov was deadly accurate. But tired, breathing hard, bleeding, it would have been a difficult shot.

Clay waited a few seconds, backed away into the valley then started off at a run. He contoured the valley side about ten metres below the road, moving quickly through the trees. He guessed the sniper would be on the move again, heading towards his vehicle.

Clay had gone about three hundred metres through the trees when the valley started to shallow noticeably. He was nearing the flats, an area where four valleys met, where the mining company had chosen to build the camp and the ore-crushing plant. Derelict now, equipment dismantled, roads blocked by berms of earth, it was part of Cyprus's two-thousand-year-old legacy of copper and gold extraction, forgotten, rarely visited. Clay knew that, from this point, the road flattened out, swept around to the east in a long arc towards the camp. He kept moving, faster now, sprinting over the increasingly dry, stony ground as the wooded valley gave way to the open scrubland and dry pine of the flats. He had a clear view of the road now, tracking along the convex side of the curve. There was no spoor, no trail to follow. It was a footrace.

Clay sprinted across the open ground, still paralleling the road, between stunted scrub oak and the occasional tall, fire-scarred pine. At any moment he expected to feel the impact of a bullet, hear the sound of gunfire. And then, there on the road, not far from the berm and the old tin sheds, about two hundred metres away, a man in dark trousers and shirt. The guy was powerfully built, stocky, ran with an uneven gait, a limp, as if his left leg was strapped, held straight. Clay could see the man's left arm dangling, the white bandage tied up high near the shoulder. He carried the Dragunov in his right hand.

Clay stopped, chambered a round. He was closing. The man was almost to the sheds now, the earthen berm blocking the road. Clay called out. The man stopped, turned, stood facing him, chest heaving. A hundred metres separated them. Not more. Clay raised the Beretta, steadied it on his stump, took aim.

It was Zdravko Todorov.

'Where is Rania, asshole?' Clay shouted.

Zdravko smiled, flipped open the rifle's bipod, lowered it to the ground. 'Dead, motherfucker. Just like you gonna be.'

The words hit Clay like a spray of shrapnel, all that they meant flooding his brain at once, an overload of pain. He started walking towards Zdravko. His heart banged like a cannon.

'You lie' he screamed, framing the target in the handgun's sight. It was a tough shot. He was still too far away.

Zdravko looked back over his shoulder to the berm, no more than a few paces away. Clay knew the only way Zdravko could fire the Dragunov one-handed was from the prone position. The rifle was there at his feet, ready to go.

'Your friend too, motherfucker,' screamed Zdravko. 'I paint message for you, on wall. Did you get?'

Clay staggered, kept walking towards Zdravko, gun raised.

Zdravko raised his good arm. 'Did you a favour, Straker,' he called in his thick, Slavic accent. 'You should be thanking me. For his parents so sad, yes? Now they don't worry.'

There it was, so clear now. Zdravko had known since Yemen about Eben. As head of security for Petro-Tex, where Clay had worked as a contractor, Zdravko had undoubtedly been going through his letters, hacking into his computer. He'd murdered Eben in his hospital bed, killed his parents too. And now Rania. No, Clay refused to believe it. A wave of grief poured through him, regret, a roaring cascade that filled his head, drowning out Zdravko's words. Clay bent double, vision blurring. He could feel the turn coming on, could already see the red periphery closing in, the nausea rising inside him like a five-day fever. He swayed, tried to breathe, stumbled to the ground. Shit no. Not now.

The Dragunov barked; something tickled the back of his neck, an insect crawling there. Clay raised the Beretta towards the sound, fired once, twice, again. Cordite stung the air. He blinked hard, wiped his eyes with his stump, looked up through the dust. Zdravko was up now, running towards the berm, carrying the Dragunov by its handle. Clay pushed himself up onto one knee, raised his weapon and took aim. Zdravko was no more than a blur, wavering, fragmenting. Clay took two deep breaths. Slowly, his vision cleared. The screaming in his ears dulled. Zdravko was at the top of the berm now, his dark shape silhouetted against the tin shed beyond. Clay fired. Zdravko disappeared.

Clay scrambled to his feet, steadied himself, started running. He was almost at the berm when he heard a car engine start, rev. Then the sound of tyres spinning in gravel, stone pelting metal. He reached the top of the berm just as Zdravko's car sped away in a cloud of road dust.

☾

By the time he reached the ridge-top it was almost dark.

Crowbar was where he'd left him. As Clay approached he scowled. 'I heard shooting,' he said, his voice weak. 'Did you get the asshole?'

Clay shook his head. 'It was Todorov. He said Rania was dead.'

Crowbar closed his eyes, exhaled. 'Bullshit, *seun*. He's fucking with you.' He was pale, shivering.

'Let me look at you, *oom*.' Clay knelt beside him, pulling back the blood-soaked compress. The wound had opened up, bloomed like a flower. There was a lot of blood. Clay gave him water, pulled his fleece shell jacket from his pack and put it over his commander's chest and shoulders. 'You're not going to make it all the way back to the car like this,' he said. 'I'm going to sew you, run you an IV.'

Koevoet's eyes fluttered, opened. He nodded. '*Fokken stupid* saltdick,' he grunted. 'You never even asked me why I slugged you at the turtle doctor's place.'

Clay fumbled in his pack and pulled out his headlamp, strapped it over his head, switched it on and opened the medical kit. 'I know why you did it. Besides, I deserved it.'

Crowbar shook his head, grunted. 'You are one screwed-up individual, Straker.'

Clay ignored this, closed his mind and focused on what he had to do. He washed his hands in antiseptic, doused the wound, found the suture kit, threaded the needle. 'Lie back, *oom*,' he said. 'You need to stretch out.'

Crowbar didn't even flinch as the needle pierced his skin. Clay sewed, big ugly stitches, twelve in all, one for every year of silence. After the sewing he covered the whole thing with an adhesive suture, applied a clean compress and wrapped it all in place, winding the gauze around Koevoet's midsection and tying it off. He laid Crowbar back down, set his pack under his head and ran him an IV.

Crowbar closed his eyes. 'It was proof, Straker. That's why I…'

'Rest now, *oom*. Tomorrow, we walk.'

33

Honoris Crux

It was a long way out.

They rose early, before the sun. Clay kicked out the fire he'd kept burning all night to warm Crowbar, wedged himself under the big man's shoulder, helped him up and started walking.

By the time they reached the old mining road the sun was over the mountains and the cold was gone. They walked through a stand of gnarled pines, the trees here tall, wide at the base, somehow protected from centuries of cutting. A gust of wind blew down through the valley and Clay could hear the sound of it in the treetops. He stopped, steadied himself against Crowbar's weight and looked up. High above, the crowns of the pines swayed like mourners in the wind and the charred black trunks groaned and creaked and the air was filled with the smell of burning and pine sap as shadow branches danced on their upturned faces and over the dry haematite gravel under their boots. They kept going.

After a while, Crowbar pulled up and sat on the bench of dirt on the upslope side of the old mining track. He was breathing heavily. 'This turtle woman,' he asked pulling out his water bottle and taking three gulps. 'She married?'

'Divorced.'

Crowbar grunted and handed Clay the bottle. 'Kids?'

'A boy.' Clay drank.

'It didn't seem like much, that place we wrecked.'

'Her life's work.'

Crowbar sat there with the pine shadow moving over him, the sun streaming between the patches of grey coolness, his hand pushed down on the compress, his fingers red with the blood. After a couple of minutes he looked up at Clay and said: 'I needed to do that job to get Medved's trust. That's why I did it.'

Clay said nothing.

'Didn't seem like much.'

It never does. 'Shut up and walk, *oom*.'

It took them another hour to climb the back ridge that led to the western approach, the two of them bumping along like some semi-articulated vehicle, the sun hot now in a clear sky. The Pajero was still another two hours away.

When they reached the ridge line, Crowbar sat on a spur of rock and looked out across the next valley. 'Not much of a life, is it?'

Clay said nothing.

'This business we do.'

'Not, we, Koevoet.'

'Tomorrow and tomorrow and tomorrow. Never leaves you.'

This was a conversation Clay did not want to have. 'Let's *ontrek*.'

Crowbar didn't move, just sat gazing out over the deep green of the cedars, the browned oxides of barren ridges and rock slides, the silver clumps of oak. 'No life for a family,' he said.

Clay laced his good arm under his friend's shoulder and pulled him to his feet. 'There is always a choice,' he said.

Crowbar grunted as he got to his feet. 'We're doing a job in Angola right now. Fighting UNITA, if you can believe it. Helping the now-legitimate government of Angola, same bastards we spent ten years fighting.'

Clay shook his head. 'I don't want to talk about it.' UNITA, supposedly their allies during the war, had turned out to be the worst of the lot.

'I'm going there when this is done,' said Crowbar. 'You should join us. Get some payback.'

'Shut up and walk, *oom*.'

They made the Pajero just as the sun reached its zenith, Crowbar sweating and cursing his way over the last kilometre as a few of the stitches Clay had put in broke open.

It was nearly dark when they rolled up to Hope's place. Clay helped Crowbar from the car to Hope's front door. She greeted them in an elegant, high-necked, knee-length turquoise dress that set off her eyes. Her hair was up and a pair of silver filigree earrings shone at her neck. Her smile turned to a frown at the sight of Crowbar's blood-stained midriff.

'My God,' she said, holding the door. 'Bring him here, lie him down.' She led them through to a spare bedroom just off the main hallway. 'What happened?'

'It wasn't Rania,' grunted Crowbar.

'Your friend has a penchant for the obvious,' Hope said to Clay. 'Is he alright?'

'The bullet grazed him, went right through. He's lost blood.'

'What can I do?'

'Do you know a good doctor? One who won't ask questions?' asked Clay, lying Crowbar on the bed. 'Hot water would be good. Towels. Maybe some food.'

'Yes, of course. I'll call the doctor now.' Hope disappeared into the other room.

'Straker.' Crowbar reached out for him.

'I'm here, *oom*.'

'She's *lekker*, *ja*?'

Clay tried a smile and failed.

'Beautiful,' Crowbar grunted. 'Smart, too.'

'Rest, *oom*.'

Hope was standing at the stove, barefoot in her dress, stirring a pot of something. The kettle was on, already steaming. She looked up when Clay entered. Her eye makeup was ruined. She'd been crying. 'You both look like hell,' she said.

'Crowbar just said the opposite about you.'

A hint of a smile creased the edges of her mouth. 'I'm going to Chrisostomedes' dinner tonight. I was just about to leave.'

Clay took a glass from the cupboard, filled it with water from the tap, drank it down then filled it again.

'So it wasn't Rania,' she said.

'No.'

'And we're no further ahead.'

'No. Maybe worse.' Zdravko's words did circuits in his head.

'What does that mean?'

'Nothing. I'll explain later.'

Hope frowned. 'The doctor will be here in half an hour. He's an old dear from the village. I've known him for years. Don't worry, he won't say a word.'

'Thanks.'

Hope turned off the gas, poured soup into an earthenware bowl and produced a spoon from a drawer. She placed the bowl and the spoon on the table. Then she reached for the kettle.

'Sit' she said. 'Eat. I'll look after your friend.'

'Crowbar.'

'Yes.'

'Why don't you say it? Crowbar.'

'What kind of name is that for a grown man? What's his real name?'

'No one uses it.'

'Why not?'

'Because the few who've tried have ended up in hospital.'

'Tell me anyway.'

'Marie-Claude. Marie-Claude Van Boxmeer. His family were Huguenots, on his mother's side.'

She looked out the window a moment then turned back to face him. 'Why did he destroy my station, Clay?'

'To get close to Medved.'

She stood tall, wiped her eyes.

'He did it for Rania, Hope.' He did it for you. I know you can't see that right now, but it's true. He did it for me. He did it because that's who he is. Clay wanted her to understand this, to know what he knew, to know that as a young NCO, Crowbar had taken part in one of the first deep recon patrols inside Angola, and when the other two members of his unit had been badly wounded, he'd stayed with them, held off repeated enemy attacks until a rescue force could reach them. They counted twenty-three enemy dead scattered around his position. For it, he was given a battlefield commission and the Honoris Crux, the South African equivalent of the Victoria Cross, for bravery under fire. A stain now, yes, but an honour back then. Clay wanted her to know that Crowbar was the bravest, most honourable man he knew. And he wanted her to know that, when it had mattered, back there at the cottage in Cornwall, Clay had believed his friend capable of betrayal. But he didn't say any of it.

'Thank you,' she said, walking towards the doorway.

Clay said nothing.

Hope turned, faced him. 'Come with me tonight, Clay. Please.'

Clay looked down at his torn and bloody clothes.

'Drive into Paphos,' she said. 'It's close. The shops are open till seven. You have plenty of time.'

'I should stay with Koevoet.'

'Don't worry. I'll look after him.' Hope looked down at her feet, up into his eyes. 'Please, Clay. I need you with me.' Fear swam in her eyes.

'What happened?'

'My friend from the north, the one who was with us that night in Karpasia, he contacted me this morning, after you left. He told me that the two men you pulled from the fire were taken to hospital in Nicosia. He visited them yesterday. They seemed to be doing well, he said.'

Clay listened.

'He said that one of them, a man who has lived in the village since he was a boy, spoke to him. He told my friend that two years ago, in winter, he came across some workmen digging what he said was a long trench in the beach, above the tide line. They were laying some sort of cable, or pipe, he didn't see which.'

'The cable I snagged with the anchor that night?' said Clay.

'I don't know. It could have been. My friend said that when he approached the workmen, they told him to go away, that it was government business, a new telephone line for the area. He went back a few weeks later, but all trace of the trench was gone. He walked along the beach for miles, but found nothing. Then one day, months later, they were there again, the workmen, this time just three of them, in one truck. They weren't digging this time, he said, just working in one place. After they'd left, he went to the place they were working. All he found was a pipe sticking from the ground and a tap, like a water tap, he said.'

'It could have been anything.'

Hope frowned. 'One of the men you saved also told my friend that, since then, there's been more activity, all of it on Greek land. He says they are preparing to build. He said he knew the families who owned this land before the war, he said what Crown Star was doing was wrong, that it was stealing. That's why he decided to talk.'

Hope reached out for his hand. 'This morning, when my friend went back to the hospital, he was told that both men you saved had suffered respiratory failure and died in the night.'

'Jesus Christ.'

'They were murdered, Clay. That's what he said. To keep them quiet.'

Clay pulled the car keys from his pocket. 'Still think it was Neo-Enosis?'

Hope shook her head.

'I'll be back in an hour. Watch Koevoet for me.'

'I intend to,' she said, picking up the kettle and heading for the spare room.

34

Altruism

They arrived at the front gate of the Chrisostomedes mansion an hour late. A uniformed guard checked Hope's name against a list and waved them through. They wound their way up the gravel drive, past the dark trunks of centuries-old pine trees until they emerged onto a broad, gravel parking area.

Hope stopped the car and switched off the engine. 'How do I look?' she said.

'Brave,' said Clay, straightening his tie in the mirror. The face staring back was almost unrecognisable, bearded, bruised, cut.

She smiled. 'Got the story straight, Doctor Greene?'

Clay nodded.

They walked across the gravel towards the front entrance. The house was not what Clay had expected. Thick wooden beams swept from native rock foundations, cantilevered between living pine and cedar as tall as any he'd seen on the island. The entrance was tiled in rough slabs of Troodos lava, bordered in lush juniper, the huge, oak door seemingly a single slab of wood, the floor-to-ceiling windows framed in big, square-cut timbers. The lighting was low, intimate. Clay could hear the sound of running water nearby, a rivulet or fountain.

As they neared the door, a man in a dark suit approached them. Six foot, broad shoulders, he emerged from the shadows. Pale eyes, flattened nose, a pronounced widow's peak of dark hair. Clay's heart thudded, jumped.

'Jesus Christ,' Clay muttered under his breath.

'What's wrong?' whispered Hope, taking his hand.

'An old friend.'

Spearpoint checked Hope's purse, ran his gaze across her dress, and, satisfied nothing dangerous could be concealed there, turned to Clay.

'*Parakalo*,' he said in Greek. Please. Distinctive Cypriot accent.

Clay raised his arms, tensed.

Spearpoint ran his hands up along Clay's back, inside his jacket, along his waist. Then he crouched, frisked Clay's legs down to his ankles. Clay took a breath, another. One knee to the head and the guy would be down for a while. The last time he'd seen Spearpoint, he'd been chasing him through the streets of Istanbul. Now he was here, apparently running private security for Chrisostomedes.

Coincidences happen. Those apparently random, acausal connections that leave us shaking our heads in wonder. They happen all the time. Aristotle knew this. It is part of probability that many improbable things will happen, he wrote. But this was not a coincidence. Spearpoint stood, nodded, led them inside. Either he hadn't recognised Clay, or he was pretending he hadn't. Either way, this dinner party had just become a lot more dangerous.

They came into a broad entranceway, all stone and rough-cut wood. A wide, timber-plank staircase arched its way up to a mezzanine that stared down at them from three sides. Everywhere, indirect lighting glowed from nooks and recesses in the walls. A maid ushered them into the dining room. A massive oak table was set for five. Candles flickered, silver sparkled. Hope took Clay's left arm, laid her hand on his stump. They stepped down onto the lower-level pinewood floor, over the biggest Persian carpet Clay had ever seen, a weave wrought of tiny, delicate hands, here again the lighting low, intimate. There was that feeling that on other nights the table and carpet might be swept aside to create a ballroom where elegant guests would twirl and shimmer under crystal lights. On the far wall, dozens of gilded, metalled illuminations, individually lit, threw brass light glancing across the room. They walked to the massive picture windows, cupped their hands to the glass to beat the reflection and gazed out over the dark, undulating sweep of the mountains, the grey rumple of the foothills beyond, the shimmering lights of the coast. This was what money could do.

'Welcome, Doctor Bachmann.' Nicos Chrisostomedes stood on the upper landing and looked down at them across the gulf of the dance floor, the archipelago of dinner table and chairs. He wore a dark, double-breasted suit, an open-collared white shirt. His face was lean, cragged, cut hard like hammered metal. Unlike so many Cypriot businessmen he looked fit, as if he had time for exercise and used it. He was fifty, Clay guessed, looked forty. 'I see you have brought a friend.'

Hope smiled, twirled her hair in her fingers like a schoolgirl. 'This is Doctor Greene, a colleague. I hope you don't mind.'

Chrisostomedes joined them at the windows, kissed Hope on the cheek and shook Clay's hand. 'A colleague,' he said, looking Clay straight in the eyes. 'And with which institution are you affiliated, Doctor Greene, if I may ask?'

Clay held Chrisostomedes' stare. 'I am an independent consultant, actually.'

'And what is your field of specialisation, Doctor Greene. Turtles as well?' He glanced at Hope.

'Hydrology,' said Clay.

'I see. Yes. Water and turtles.'

Clay said nothing, kept his gaze flat, unwavering.

'And do I detect a South African accent?' Chrisostomedes continued, unfazed by Clay's stare back. 'Rhodesian perhaps?'

'Right the first time.'

'Of course.' Chrisostomedes ran his gaze over the cuts and scars on Clay's face, his empty left sleeve. He did it slowly, with deliberation, so Clay would know. 'A dangerous business, hydrology.'

'Car accident,' said Clay.

Chrisostomedes nodded as if he didn't believe a word. 'There have been some big changes in your country recently, have there not?'

'I wouldn't know,' said Clay. This guy was already starting to grate on him.

Chrisostomedes blinked once, turned away and snapped his fingers. A uniformed Philippina maid appeared. 'One more place setting,' he barked.

The maid scurried away.

'Beautiful,' said Hope, looking towards the far wall.

'Illuminations from across Christendom, since the earliest stages of the form,' said Chrisostomedes. 'May I offer you something to drink? Champagne, perhaps?'

A couple appeared on the elevated landing, a squat, overweight Cypriot in a dark-blue suit and claret tie, and a six-foot redhead in a gold-sequined mini-dress sprayed onto a porno-queen figure. They stood a moment, the woman tottering in impossibly high heels, the man blinking as if considering the mechanics of descending the three broad steps to the main level.

'Dimitriou,' Chrisostomedes called out. Big smiles from all. 'Come and meet our guests, Doctors.'

Introductions were made. Champagne came. The girl's name was Katia. Small talk cluttered the room. Weather. The beautiful house. The view in daytime.

'Please everyone,' said Chrisostomedes, 'be seated. Our last guest is running a bit late and has asked us not to wait. Dinner is served.'

Chrisostomedes sat at the head of the table. Hope was placed to his left, across from an empty place presumably reserved for the tardy guest. Dimitriou was seated next to Hope, facing the redhead. An extra place was set for Clay next to the redhead and her impossible to ignore, artificial décolletage. The housemaid brought in the first course – lobster bisque – and poured wine for all.

Chrisostomedes raised his glass. 'Ladies, gentlemen, thank you for gracing us with your presence. I would like to welcome you, and offer a special toast to Doctor Bachmann and her great work here on our island.'

Hope glanced over at Clay. Glasses clinked.

'*Kalo orexi, bon apetit.* I have the lobsters flown in fresh from Nova Scotia,' said Chrisostomedes, spooning the hot liquid into his mouth.

The redhead lifted a spoonful to her face, sniffed it once, let the spoon slip back into the bowl.

'Please tell us about your research, Doctor Bachmann,' said Chrisostomedes between mouthfuls. 'For the benefit of our other guests less familiar.'

Hope put down her spoon, dabbed the corner of her mouth with a white linen napkin. 'We are studying the two threatened species of Mediterranean sea turtle. Cyprus is one of their last nesting strongholds. Basically, we are trying to save them from extinction.'

'Surely it is not so dramatic as that,' said Dimitriou, staring at the redhead's tits.

'Absolutely it is,' countered Hope immediately. 'I won't bore you with the details, but in the last few years their numbers have gone into free-fall. A few more years of this, and they'll be gone.' She turned to face Dimitriou. 'So yes, it is as dramatic as that.'

The Minister swirled the wine in his glass. 'This may be so, Doctor. But the real question for Cyprus, for its government and people, must be whether this issue makes any material difference to our prosperity, to our economy. Frankly, I do not believe that the majority cares, or is even aware.' He smiled across the table at his improbable companion. 'What do you think, Katia?'

The redhead looked at him as if surprised to be invited into the conversation. She glanced around the table, settled her witch-hazel eyes on Clay. 'Animals have as much right to exist as humans,' she said in good, slightly accented English. 'Sometimes, I like animals better than people.'

Clay smiled at her. He guessed Poland, Ukraine perhaps, mid-twenties but she looked older.

'An emotional response,' said Dimitriou. 'Illogical.'

'Not at all, Minister,' said Hope. 'The concept of animal rights, of other species' unalienable right to exist, is firmly entrenched in modern ethics. We cannot be so arrogant as to assume that we are the only form of life worthy of the right to exist, nor can we be so ignorant as to believe that we can exist without the web of life that supports us.'

'Noble sentiments, Doctor.' Chrisostomedes motioned for glasses to be refilled. 'But here in Cyprus, as long as illegal invaders remain – invaders who have murdered our people, stolen our land – there will be few who will have the inclination to bother with such matters. Conservation is failing here, Doctor, because the Turk has no regard for nature. Examine the history of Ottoman rule, from Iraq to Lebanon, and you will find a story of plunder, waste, devastation and murder.'

Clay looked at him across the length of the table. 'Have you ever been to Kizildag in Isparta?' he said.

Chrisostomedes looked up at him. 'Pardon me, Doctor?'

'Drop the Doctor,' said Clay. 'I said: have you ever been to Kizildag in Isparta?'

Chrisostomedes took a sip of wine, placed the glass on the table, looked down at it as he twirled the stem around on the tablecloth. 'No, *Mister* Greene, I have not been to Turkey.'

'A sixty-thousand hectare national park. Some of the best remaining cedar forest in the world. Great hiking.'

Hope beamed at him. So did Katia.

Dimitriou frowned and Katia's smile disappeared. 'The point is this,' he said, clanking his spoon into his empty bowl. 'Most people are ambivalent at best. But when it becomes a choice between protecting a bunch of reptiles and economic progress, then most reasonable people are going to choose progress. That may sound harsh, but it is the truth.'

Hope hung her head. 'You know, Minister, ten years ago I would have argued against you until all the wine was gone, and then some. I would have told you that tourists come to a beautiful place to see beautiful things, to swim in clean seas, to see marvellous creatures in their natural habitat, to walk in unspoiled forests. I would have argued, and have on many occasions, that those tourists generate huge revenues, and that unlike oil, or gas, or coal, which you dig out once and then it's gone, a country's natural ecosystems are renewable assets that can continue to generate economic benefits as long as they stay healthy and functioning. But now, I'm not sure anymore.'

'I'm in that business, Doctor Bachmann,' said Chrisostomedes. 'And I can tell you that the modern tourist is too exhausted to aspire to anything more than a comfortable bed, sunshine, a pool, a white sandy beach to lie on, and a good meal at the end of the day. The vast majority have no interest in wildlife, particularly if it requires some effort to see. It's dangerous and messy. And while personally I am very fond of nature, as you can see,' he moved the blade of his hand from left to right, 'I am afraid, Doctor, that your newfound cynicism is absolutely warranted.'

Katia drained her glass, put it down. 'I love hiking,' she said. 'And scuba.'

'Shut up, Katia,' hissed Dimitriou.

'Well I do.'

Dimitriou shook his head and waved for more wine.

'So do I,' said Clay.

'I've never seen a sea turtle in the wild,' she continued, bending down to adjust her shoe. 'But I would love to.'

Dimitriou glared at her. 'Stupid girl.'

'Well I would,' she pouted.

'It's unforgettable,' said Hope. 'They are beautiful creatures, perfectly evolved over millions of years.'

'Evolution,' laughed Chrisostomedes. 'The Earth and everything in it was created, my dear, by God. Nothing evolved.'

Hope put her spoon down, open-mouthed.

Something bumped Clay's leg. He moved his hand under the table. It was a foot, bare, surprisingly soft. Katia beamed at him, wiggled her toes. There was a slip of paper between the second and third digits. Clay slid it out and put it into his pocket.

She smiled at him again, turned towards him and leant forward, inviting him to look. She seemed about to speak when Chrisostomedes said: 'I understand, Doctor Bachmann, that your Lara Beach research station was destroyed recently. Such a shame.'

The table went quiet.

Hope bristled. 'I would have thought, Mister Chrisostomedes, given our history, that you would have been quite pleased.'

Chrisostomedes looked around the table, smiling at each guest in turn. 'Not so, Doctor. As I outlined in my letter, I am prepared to fund the reconstruction and continued operation of your facility for the next five years.'

Hope sat still, lips slightly parted, saying nothing. Clay watched her reach for a strand of hair, twirl it between thumb and forefinger. She had known that something like this was on offer, but clearly this was much bigger than she had expected.

'I…' she started. 'I'm stunned. That's very generous.'

'All we would require in return would be some flexibility.'

'The conditions?' said Hope.

'But of course. This is business. There has to be something in it for me, otherwise why would I bother?'

'Of course. No altruism here.'

'There is no such thing as altruism,' said Dimitriou.

Katia pouted.

'All we ask is that you relocate the station slightly,' said Chrisostomedes.

'Relocate? To where?'

'Toxeflora Beach, in the Agamas. Just a few kilometres up the coast.'

'I know where it is,' said Hope, visibly shaken. 'You're not serious.'

'I do not joke, Doctor,' said Chrisostomedes. 'I have neither the time nor the compunction.' His face was set hard, the creases around his mouth like the dark fractures edging a crevasse.

'On Turkish land? Inside the national park?' blurted Hope. 'You're insane.'

'*Proposed* national park,' said Dimitriou.

Chrisostomedes leaned on his elbows. 'Don't look so shocked, Doctor Bachmann. I understand that you recently put in an application to do exactly what I now propose.'

Hope glanced towards Clay then looked down at her hands. 'That was years ago. I was new here, I wasn't aware of the status of the lands, the plans for a national park. Of course as soon as I was made aware, I withdrew the application.'

'Well, this time our friend can ensure the proper dispensations are made, is that not so, Minister?' Chrisostomedes inclined his head towards Dimitriou.

'Indeed,' nodded the minister.

Just like you did at Alassou last year, thought Clay.

'And what about Lara Beach?' said Hope.

'We would develop an ecologically sensitive, world-class resort: a five-star hotel, casino, water park. All with your design input, of course, to ensure minimal disruption to turtle nesting.'

Hope pushed back her chair. 'Are you crazy?' she shouted. 'It would mean the end of nesting on that beach. Forever.'

'It seems, Doctor, from what you have told us, that will happen regardless,' said Dimitriou.

'And we hope you will want to reflect our generosity in the Commission's findings,' added Chrisostomedes.

Hope pursed her lips, said nothing.

They all ate on in silence.

After a while there was a knock at the door.

'Ah, good.' Chrisostomedes rose to his feet. 'Our missing dinner guest.'

Everyone looked up. Two people had entered. A man and a woman. The man held the woman by the arm, his hand clasped over the bare skin just above her elbow. He led her across the hardwood landing to the steps. The woman was dressed in a black cocktail dress. She wore black pumps. Her dark hair cascaded down over bare shoulders.

Clay lurched to his feet. It was as if the blood had been syphoned from his head. He grabbed the edge of the table to steady himself.

Hope squealed like an excited schoolgirl.

The woman was Rania. And guiding her down the steps, Zdravko.

35

Thirty Weeks and a Hundred Years

Surely, he thought, the essence of beauty was imperfection. Four fingers to a palm, six palms to a cubit, four cubits makes a man, and in man's symmetry the universe is structured. But this seductive Vitruvian mathematics was shattered by the dark line under her left eye, the slightly off-centre dimple in her chin, the chaotic quasars spinning in her eyes. Real beauty could only exist in the immediate presence of something marred, disjointed, sullied somehow: a datum. Only complexity could create the depth that beauty required, the multiple layers and infinite variants that could build a forest, one leaf, one branch, one limb, one tree at a time, sculpt the Sierpinski carpet of a coastline, or scatter celestial dust into the utter individuality of each retina. Hers.

Chrisostomedes nodded. Zdravko released Rania's arm. She snatched it away, reached up to where his hand had been. Zdravko turned to leave, took two paces towards the door. Then he stopped, looked back over his shoulder as if he'd forgotten something. He was looking straight at Clay, his eyes like gun slits.

'That will be all, Todorov,' said Chrisostomedes.

Zdravko muttered something, adjusted the sling cradling his right arm, turned away and closed the door behind him.

Rania started across the carpet. Clay could see the changes now, her breasts heavier, her figure rounder. His feet were tingling, his legs quivering. His brain raced to process what he'd seen, what he was seeing. Rania walking towards him, his child there inside her, her hips swaying beneath the thin material of the dress, her eyes dark with makeup, Zdravko's finger marks still on her arm and Zdravko just outside the door somewhere.

Adrenaline poured into Clay's system, swamping his senses. He needed to run. Grab her by the hand and run. Through the door, out to the car. Did they have time? Maybe. His Beretta was in the car, pushed up under the passenger seat. If he could get to it, they had a chance. But he needed to settle, calm himself, think things through. What the hell was Zdravko doing here? Working for Chrisostomedes, apparently. He'd clearly been surprised by Clay's presence. Either Zdravko hadn't shared his recent attempt on Clay's life with his new boss, or Chrisostomedes hadn't yet realised who Clay was. One thing was sure: Zdravko was here, and Rania was being held against her will. That's how Zdravko had got the message to Hope, via the AFP, about the meeting in the mountains. If Crowbar hadn't surprised him on the ridge, he would have put a bullet in Clay's head. An easy shot for a marksman armed with a military-spec sniper rifle. It was intolerable, impossible to contemplate. Nausea flooded through him. He struggled to breathe. Rania was halfway to the table now, striding with that lean, elegant gait Clay had so admired the first time he'd seen her by the pool in Aden, thirty weeks and a hundred years ago.

Hope stood, ran to Rania and threw her arms around her. The two women embraced, kissed, whispered to each other and walked hand-in-hand to the table. Rania smoothed her dress under her legs, sat. Hope regained her place and sat facing Rania.

Chrisostomedes glanced at Hope and opened his arms as if addressing a congregation. 'Everyone, this is Lise Moulinbecq, the journalist.' Chrisostomedes introduced each of his guests in turn. Clay was last.

Rania leaned forward slightly, looked down the table at Clay. The candle flame danced in her eyes but her expression was neutral, hard. Her face was fuller than he remembered but dark hollows pulsed above the tops of her cheekbones like bruises through makeup. She looked tired.

'Hello, Doctor Greene,' she said, dead flat. 'I am pleased to meet you.'

'Likewise,' Clay stammered. The message was clear. They didn't know each other. 'I've read your stuff.'

'Every tenth word, I'm sure, Doctor Greene.'

'No, really,' said Clay, still struggling. 'You write well.'

'You're very kind.' A quick smile, a fraction of a second only. 'But I think you have it backwards, Doctor Greene. I hear you also write well.'

Then she turned away, began exchanging pleasantries with Dimitriou, who seemed to have met her before.

Hope sat beaming at Rania, entranced, watching every gesture, devouring every word.

'Lise has been our guest here for the past few days,' said Chrisostomedes. 'Because of the tense situation here on the island, and the sensitivity of what she has been reporting, we thought it best to provide her somewhere safe from which to work.' Chrisostomedes directed what he no doubt thought was a charming smile at Rania.

Clay cringed.

'Yes,' said Rania. 'There is a lovely view from my room.' She pointed to the picture windows, the lights of the coast flickering in the distance. 'This, but one floor higher. *Magnifique.*'

Chrisostomedes beamed.

'When can we expect to read your next piece, Ms Moulinbecq?' said Dimitriou.

'It will appear tomorrow, I believe,' said Rania. 'It concerns the joint EU-UN Commission of Enquiry on Coastal Property in Cyprus.'

'Ah yes,' said Dimitriou, nodding to Hope. 'We were discussing this just before you arrived.'

Hope leaned forward, facing Rania. 'The Minister has suggested that I direct the Commission towards favouring Mister Chrisostomedes' activities and proposals. In return, they would fund the rebuilding of my research station. There's a story for you.'

Dimitriou laughed. 'The good Chairwoman is under the illusion that her fellow panellists are, how shall we put it, *impartial.*'

Rania reached across the table, took Hope's hand, looked her in the eyes. 'I have reason to believe,' she said, 'that when the enquiry convenes in three days, the UN representative on the Commission will propose a land-swap deal, in which selected Turkish coastal properties in the south, including Toxeflora Beach lands, will be transferred to Greek Cypriot ownership, in return for Greek lands in the north, including in Karpasia, being transferred to Turkish Cypriot title.'

Hope gasped. 'That's tantamount to a green light for development.'

'Exactly,' said Rania. 'But to the public, and certainly to the Greek Cypriot Government, who, as you know, are anxious for EU membership, it's a way of demonstrating rapprochement, compromise, to show they are working for a solution to the Cyprus problem.'

'And who will gain most from this, if it transpires?' said Chrisostomedes.

'Not you,' said Clay.

Katia giggled.

Dimitriou frowned, stuffed a too-big spoonful of Pavlova into his mouth and chewed.

'Mohamed Erkan, that's who,' said Chrisostomedes, glaring at Clay.

'It would remove his last real barrier to development of the Karpasia beaches,' said Rania. 'My sources tell me that a deal is being discussed right now between Ankara, New York, Brussels and the TRNC Government that would lift UN Environment Programme World Heritage Site status from the Karpasia beaches, if this compromise can be reached. The UN desperately wants a solution to the Cyprus problem, and this is seen as a major step forward towards that goal.'

Hope slumped back in her chair. 'Shit.'

'Do you see now why we have made our offer, Doctor Bachmann?' Chrisostomedes patted her hand. 'If your station is on Toxeflora Beach, and if it is protected inside a new Agamas National Park, it blocks the deal.'

'And you can build your resort on Lara Beach,' said Katia, smiling at Clay.

'Shut up, Katia,' barked Dimitriou.

'And Erkan can't build his,' said Katia, clearly enjoying this. 'Less competition for you.'

Dmitriou glared at Katia, turned to face Hope. 'Just think,' he said, 'a new national park, new world-class research facilities, you at its head. How proud your son will be.'

Hope rocked back as if hit by a punch. She stared at Dimitriou, volts arcing invisibly in the space between them. 'How dare you–' she gasped.

Rania sat, head bowed, silent, as if drained of energy. She'd said what she had to say and now it was over.

'Please, Doctor,' said Chrisostomedes. 'What the good Minister means is that we are aware of your recent, shall we say, *difficulties*, with regard to your son's emigration status. He has ensured me that a special dispensation for your son can be made that will allow him to leave Cyprus with you, should you decide to go back to America.'

Hope stared at Chrisostomedes, then back at Dimitriou. 'Is this true?'

Dimitriou nodded through a mask of Upper House magnanimity.

'Back to America,' she mumbled.

Clay could see Hope withering under the combined assault. Rania sat exhausted, lifeless. He'd seen and heard enough. They were running out of time. He stood, dropped his napkin over his untouched dessert. Conversation stopped.

'Let's go, Hope,' he said, pulling out her chair. 'We have a lot to discuss. You can expect an answer shortly, gentlemen.'

Hope stood and took his arm, leaning into him. She was trembling, gazing down at Rania as if expecting something, a way out, a rescue.

'Perhaps Ms Moulinbecq would care to join us?' Clay tried to catch Rania's eye, but she looked away.

Chrisostomedes rose. 'I'm afraid she and I also have much to discuss tonight.'

As if on cue Rania looked up at Clay. 'Yes. Yes, that is correct,' she said. 'Perhaps another time, Doctor Greene?'

'Two days, Doctor Bachmann,' said Chrisostomedes. 'If we haven't heard from you, we will be forced to make other arrangements. And I can assure you they will not be nearly as optimal.'

Clay guided Hope across the dining room, the nature of these other arrangements becoming clear to him. 'Come on, Hope,' he whispered, 'we have work to do.'

Spearpoint appeared at the door and glared at Clay – if he hadn't recognised him before, he did now.

He met them on the dining-room landing, ushered them to the front door, and followed them out. There was no sign of Zdravko. Soon they were at the car. Spearpoint stood back, arms folded, watching them.

Clay helped Hope into the passenger seat, closed her door, then turned and faced Spearpoint, locking his gaze. 'Touch her, either of you, and you're dead,' he said.

36

Backwards from Being

'Don't worry,' Clay said, getting behind the wheel of the little Corolla. 'Nothing's going to happen to your son, I promise.'

Hope said nothing, just stared ahead. She was shivering.

Clay pulled off his jacket, put it around her shoulders and started the engine. Leaving the gate behind, Clay drove about a mile, watching the rear-view mirror. They were not being followed. He turned down a small side road leading away into the forest, found a notch in the trees where the shoulder widened, pulled the car off the road and turned off the engine. They sat in the darkness.

'Do you have your phone?' asked Clay.

'What?'

'You need to call your friend. In the north.'

'Now?'

'That thug who checked us at the door on the way in, he was in Istanbul. He was following Rania.

'My God.'

'We're running out of time, Hope. So, yes. Call him now.'

She pulled her phone from her bag, punched in a number.

'Ask him: what did the truck look like? The one his friend saw at the water pipe in Karpasia, near the beach.'

The phone engaged. Clay could hear the voice. She asked the question, listened. 'He asks what you mean,' Hope said.

'What kind of truck was it? Was it a dump truck, a van, a tanker?'

Hope spoke, waited. 'He says a tanker.'

'Shit.'

'What is it, Clay?'

'I'm not sure,' he said, the permutations spinning in his head. 'It was something Dimitriou said: "It's happening anyway". He knows it's happening, knows the turtles will be gone soon. And when they're gone, the problems are solved, for everyone.'

'Bastards.'

'They're all positioning themselves for when that day comes. And as far as they're concerned, the sooner the better.'

Hope stared at him, blank.

'Stay here,' he said. 'I won't be long.'

'Where are you going?' Her voice was thin, miles away.

Clay opened his door, turned to her. 'Call your ex. Get him to take your son somewhere safe, out of the country if he can. Do it now. Stay put till I get back.' Then he stepped out of the car and started through the woods back towards the house.

It didn't take him long to find the perimeter fence, a three-metre steel picket affair lipped with coils of razor-wire. Every hundred metres or so, a main anchor post shot from the rocky ground, topped by the roaming red eye of a CCTV camera. Clay followed the fence around, downslope first, then along the bottom side of the property, keeping to the trees, moving through the undergrowth, along the sides of boulders and volcanic outcrops. He stopped, looked up at the house cantilevered out over the cliffside on concrete piles anchored into bedrock, the lights glowing in the dining-room windows. Rania was up there somewhere. Zdravko, too.

He started moving again, skirting the perimeter beneath the cliff. There was no fence here, just the near-vertical faces of rock. There were no cameras either, and no guards – not that he could see. He moved along the base of the cliff, looking up into the underside of the house, the steel I-beams clearly visible, the cross-bracing, the concrete foundation grafted onto bedrock, pumped into fractures and faults. He stopped directly beneath what he guessed was the dining room. The rock here was cool, slightly damp, coarse-grained. It was steep, but it was not featureless. A decent climber could do it. Two hands would be good.

He stood a moment, ran his hand over the Beretta's grip. She was up there. If he went now, could he find her, bring her out safely? He needed time. They all did.

Forty minutes later he was back at the car, having completed the tour of the perimeter. Hope was standing by the side of the car, smoking a cigarette. She threw it to the ground as he approached, crushing it out with her foot. 'I was starting to worry.'

'How's your son?'

'It took some doing, but my ex has agreed to let Maria take Alexi to Greece. He'll stay with his grandparents in Thessaloniki, in the countryside. They leave tomorrow. He's excited about missing school.' Her voice cracked with relief.

'Maria?'

'My ex can't get away from work. Or so he says. Maria is the only other person I can trust. She needs a break, anyway.'

An hour later they arrived at Hope's cottage in the hills. The roads were deserted, the island quiet this time of year, empty of tourists. They hadn't been followed.

Clay stopped the car and switched off the lights. They sat a moment, the weight of all that had happened pushing down on them. The moon had risen, a pale arc that brushed the treetops and roof slates of the house in quivering grey and set black shadows scurrying like intruders through the underbrush. Finally they stepped from the car and started up the path. They had reached the front steps when Hope stopped. The front door was open.

Clay touched Hope on the shoulder, reached for the Beretta, wedged the grip between his knees and pulled back the slide, arming the weapon. 'Back way,' he whispered.

She took him by the arm and led him around the side of the house, past a huge, spreading cactus, to the edge of the patio where they'd sat with Koevoet not long ago. In the dim moonlight they could see that the outdoor furniture had been overturned, potted plants upended and smashed, the black soil strewn like bloodstains across the tile.

The house was dark, quiet. The back shutters had been forced, pried from their mounts and tossed into the hedge.

Clay stepped onto the patio, moved towards the doorway. He stopped at the kitchen window; the shutters were still intact; he pressed his ear to the slats, listened, waited. Nothing. Hope was beside him, her face luminescent and pale, carved in fear. He touched her arm with the end of his stump. 'Stay here,' he said, and then turned and walked through the doorway.

The house was empty. Crowbar was gone.

Hope lit a lantern, gave it to Clay and lit a second. It was as if a typhoon had raked through the place. Fragments of glass and ceramic lay scattered across the floor, the remnants of every cup and plate. Cupboard doors hung from twisted hinges. The stove looked as if it had been hit with a sledgehammer. They picked their way through the shambles to the sitting room. Books and CDs were strewn across the floor. The furniture had been upended. Hope's bicycle, a nice Italian road model, lay in one corner, the frame bent nearly at right angles, the delicate wheels a tangle of spokes and shattered aluminium rims. She slumped to the floor amidst the chaos, bowed her head.

Clay left her alone and moved through the rest of the house. Each room had received similar treatment, but he found no trace of blood, no sign that Koevoet had been here when it had happened. He went back to the kitchen and searched for the basket in which Hope kept recent newspapers; it was upended near the back door. He righted the kitchen table and chairs, gathered up the newspapers, dumped them onto the table, sat and turned up the lantern. In turn, he opened and smoothed out each paper, stacked them in chronological order. Then he grabbed a pen from the floor and opened up a copy of *The Independent*. An article by Rania was there on page eight; it had come out since she'd disappeared. He started reading, circling words.

Hope came into the room and stood looking over his shoulder. 'What are you doing?' she whispered.

'Every tenth word.'

'What?'

'Backwards.'

'Pardon me?'

'Rania pretended not to know me. Every tenth word, that's what she said. Didn't you hear her? That she was sure I only read every tenth word of her articles, that I had it backwards, that I wrote well. She knows the longest thing I've ever written was a letter, and that was three lines.'

He focused on the paper.

'Today, commission, a, north.' Hope read out the words as he circled them. 'Until, for, the, soon, problem. It makes no sense.'

Clay started again with the second word, counting out ten, underlining, transposing. 'The, would, comprehensive, furthermore. There's nothing there.'

Clay started again at three, boxing words now, the string emerging unintelligible again. Hope turned away, started picking things up from the floor, placing them on the counter. 'So this is what Chrisostomedes meant by "other arrangements". The bastard.'

Clay stood, gazed down on the page, distancing himself, literally decimating, looking for a pattern. 'Do you have any snorkelling gear?' he said.

Hope stood with her hands on her hips, looking around the room. 'What?'

'Mask and fins.'

'I'm a marine biologist, Clay.'

'Can you grab a couple of sets? We need to go for a swim.'

Clay was only half aware of Hope leaving the room. Something had emerged. He sat, grabbed the pen and started underlining words.

Hope reappeared carrying a pair of masks.

'Look at this,' he said, holding out the paper to her. 'The underlined stuff.'

She read them out. 'After, no, some, reaction, government, the, murder, threatening, here, relation, has, Chrisostomedes, falsehoods, writing, into, coerced, being, island, once–'

'Stop,' said Clay. Now cut out the first six words, and start backwards from "being".'

Hope stood looking at the paper. 'My God.'

'That's how they got her to leave Istanbul. They have her relation. Could it be her aunt – Madame Debret? They must be holding her somewhere, using her to coerce Rania into writing what they want – writing falsehoods.'

Clay banged the Beretta down onto the table. Was that how Zdravko had become involved? Having tracked Rania to Cyprus, had he offered his services to Chrisostomedes, realising they had a common goal? Had he been the one who had grabbed Madame Debret in Switzerland, burned down the chalet on Chrisostomedes' behalf? And then Istanbul, working with Spearpoint. If Zdravko had been watching the hotel, then he would have known Clay was there, too. Why not kill Clay then and there? Had Medved's people scared him off before he could finish the job?

'So the stories she's had published since she disappeared in Istanbul are garbage,' said Hope. 'Chrisostomedes' version of events.'

Clay nodded. 'And if Rania stops cooperating, or if we try to get her out, they do something bad to her aunt.'

'Limassol,' said Hope.

'What?'

'That's where her aunt is. She whispered it to me when we kissed, at the dinner tonight. Just that: "She's in Limassol".'

'And now you, too, Hope. They know about your…' Clay stopped, swallowed. 'About your relationship with Rania. That was the other message tonight. Run the enquiry the way they want, or Rania will suffer.'

'And my son.' Hope put her hands to her face. She was crying. 'I can't, Clay,' she said. 'I can't do what they ask.' She stood, eyes wide. 'I have to go to Nicosia.' She started towards the door.

'Now?'

'I have to see my son.'

'I need your help, Hope. Rania needs you.'

She spun around. Tears fell to the floor. 'I can't,' she gasped.

Clay stepped towards her. 'Look, Hope. Don't you see? As long as they think you're cooperating, you're safe. So is your son. We've got two days to find Rania's aunt, and get Rania out of there.'

Hope wiped her eyes. 'What if I just resign from the commission? Let someone else lead the enquiry.'

'You lose any influence you may have had. Besides, could you live with the consequences?'

Hope hung her head. 'So I chair the enquiry. If I support Chrisostomedes and that slimeball Dimitriou, I get a new research programme, with nothing to research because the turtles are all gone. And then what? Will Chrisostomedes just let Rania walk free, after what he's done to her? She'd have it all over the papers in a heartbeat.' She looked up at him through her tears. 'And if I don't support them, the UN and the TRNC make a deal with the government, and Karpasia and Lara are wiped out. Whatever I do, it's the end for the turtles. And nothing the Commission decides is going to help Rania, or her aunt.'

'By then it won't matter anyway,' said Clay, picking up the handgun. 'As soon as the enquiry starts, they're both dead.'

37

Everything They Shared

Clay and Hope left the house shortly afterwards. They found a small pension not far from Paphos, taking separate rooms. Early next morning, they drove west into Agamas. After a couple of hours of slow going on rough, unpaved tracks, Hope directed them seaward. They left the 4WD at the end of a steep track and Hope led Clay down a rocky footpath towards the lonely arc of a white sand beach. The hammered-lead surface of the sea sloshed under a wet, uncertain sky. A pair of gulls fled south across the water, kissing up feathers of white spray.

'This is Toxeflora,' said Hope. The soles of her feet squeaked as she walked over the sand. A chill gust sent her hair streaming. 'In July and August, during the nesting season, we've managed to have a team down here most nights to monitor the turtles. There have been the usual problems with foxes, but in the last couple of years the numbers of nesting females has plummeted, and the survival of those eggs that have been laid has been catastrophically low. We're very concerned.'

Clay levered off his shoes. The sand was cool and damp. 'Where do the turtles lay their eggs?'

Hope walked to a point a few metres from the edge of the scour slope.

'In winter, the storms pull sand from the beach and dump it out to sea. The profile becomes much steeper, like now. In summer, the sand is piled back onto the beach by the gentler waves, and the beach flattens out again. So in summer, it would be about here. Above the tide line.'

Clay started walking along the beach, scanning the ground between the rock and the break in slope.

Hope followed.

'When will your son arrive in Thessaloniki?' he asked, checking the rock for any signs of disturbance. So far, all he'd seen had been made by nature, not man.

'This afternoon.' Hope seemed to think about smiling, but let it die stillborn on her face. She'd been a lot more composed since she'd called Maria again a few hours ago, confirmed that her faxed letter of permission for Maria to accompany her son overseas had gone through, and most importantly that her ex had also signed a similar declaration. Everything was in order. They were now booked on the early flight, leaving Larnaca for Athens in just a couple of hours. 'What about your friend, Koofoot?'

Clay smiled at Hope's mangled attempt at the Afrikaans pronunciation. He'd managed to reach Crowbar on Hope's phone earlier that morning. After being treated by the doctor, Crowbar had locked up Hope's place and gone to Limassol to check in with Medved's people. Clay told him about Rania, the break-in at Hope's, their suspicion that Rania's aunt was being held somewhere in Limassol, probably by Zdravko Todorov. They had agreed to meet at noon in Pissouri, a seaside village halfway between Paphos and Limassol. 'He'll be okay,' said Clay. 'He's tougher than he looks.'

That got a half-smile from Hope.

'He's looking for Rania's aunt right now.'

They were halfway to the far point, about equidistant between the two rocky headlands that marked the ends of the beach, when Clay stopped. There, up ahead, in a sandy embayment in the rock, something caught his gaze. He sprinted across the sand.

'What is it?' called Hope, running to keep up.

It wasn't much, would be easy to miss if you weren't looking for it. A steel pipe, half an inch in diameter, sticking up from the ground, capped at knee height with a simple gate valve. It was barely visible, nestled in a clump of acacia.

'It's a water tap,' said Hope.

Clay opened the valve. Nothing. 'Do you remember what your friend from Karpasia said about the pipe? He said he saw a tanker truck there.' Clay took Hope by the hand. 'It's not for getting something out of, Hope. It's for putting something in.'

Hope looked down at the pipe, at the surrounding ground. 'There is no way you could get a vehicle in here.'

Clay started inland, clambering up a rocky carbonate bluff, contouring a series of prominent outcrops. Hope followed. He'd gone about two hundred metres inland when he came across a set of twinned ruts twisting away through the rocks, faint, overgrown with winter grass, not recent.

'Vehicle tracks,' said Clay.

Hope was looking back out towards the sea. 'People come in here all the time for picnics, a swim. I don't see that this means anything, Clay.'

'Maybe it doesn't.' Clay clambered back down to the beach, located the standpipe, took five paces towards the sea, dropped to his knees and started digging like a three-legged jackal looking for a carcass. 'How deep did you say these turtles lay their eggs?' he said, reaching into the deepening hole. His fingers carved away at the banded, silica-rich sand, scraped through layers of coarser, pebbly material.

'About where you are now.'

Clay kneeled back, sat looking down into the hole. 'There,' he said. 'Do you see that darker layer, just above the base. It's softer, finer grained.' He reached into the hole, scooped out a handful of the darker sand, smoothed the silt between his fingers, brought his hand to his nose and sniffed. 'Hand me a bucket, would you?'

Hope reached into her backpack, passed him one of the empty plastic ice-cream containers he'd appropriated from the hotel the night before. Clay scooped the dark silt into the container, retrieved four more handfuls, closed the lid and wrote on the lid with a black marker pen.

'What are you looking for?' said Hope, stashing the sample in her pack.

'We'll know soon.'

After Clay had collected three more samples, all from the same depth and at the same point in the beach profile, but dotted along the length of the beach, he stood and looked out over the sea. 'Fancy a swim?' he said.

Before she could answer, he stripped off his clothes, piled them on the sand and strode down to the water's edge. He stood naked in the surf, the water lapping his ankles, felt the breeze flow cold over the dangerous frailty of his body. 'Pass me a mask and snorkel, could you?'

Hope stood with a smirk on her face, looking him over. She reached into her pack. 'I don't know,' she said. 'The water's pretty cold this time of year.'

Clay turned, started wading into the sea.

'Wait,' she called, scampering down the beach with a pair of masks hanging from her hand. Clay caught a glimpse of her long, pale legs, the patch of auburn between, and then she was in, wading up to her chest. Her nipples were pale, turgid. A beam of sunlight broke through the clouds, held them a moment in its warmth, coloured her face, her bare shoulders. She handed him a mask and snorkel and fitted hers.

They swam out into the bay, the water cold then slightly warmer for a moment and colder again as they moved away from the beach. The water was clear here, so lacking in nutrients. Prisms of light searched down from the surface, scanned across the seabed for a moment, then faded away, replaced by a new cloudburst farther on. It was as if they were suspended in a dream of their own making, and there was nothing but the cold, clear water and the sky and the blue sand and everything that they shared. Clay knew what he would find. The cold and the thought of it made him shiver. He estimated a depth of four metres here. He searched the sea floor.

And there it was, a subtle ridge in the sand, running parallel to the shore, snaking in the shifting sealight. He waved to Hope, pointed along its length. She nodded, her eyes big behind the mask's lens. Clay signalled down.

He dived. Hope followed him. Pressure built. Clay equalised, released air from his lungs, reached out for the bottom. Head down, kicking to maintain position, he clawed at the ridge. Sediment erupted from the bed, hung like fog in the water before dispersing in the bottom current. He kept digging but the sand was like soup, flowed back to fill whatever depression he managed to create. Hope dropped down beside him, used her two hands.

Moments later they burst to the surface.

'It's too deep,' Hope panted. 'The winter bedload is thick here.'

'We'll follow it along,' said Clay, treading water. 'Find a better place.'

'This way,' said Hope, teeth chattering. She bit down on the mouthpiece of her snorkel and started swimming towards the western end of the beach. He followed, watching her limbs move pale and goose-skinned through the sun-strobed water.

The ridge grew in prominence, then faded. They kept going, picked it up again, moving steadily parallel to the shore, always in about four metres of water. As they approached the headlands, sand gave way to rock, dark and slick with seaweed. Clay looked at his watch. They'd been in the water for almost half an hour now. He reached out, touched Hope's thigh. She twisted to face him, popped her head out of the water.

'Let's go in,' he stuttered. 'Warm up.'

She nodded and started swimming towards the headland. He followed. They emerged from the sea, clambering naked over the rocks.

They found a ledge cradled into the headland where they could shelter from the wind and sat looking out across the bay. The sun streamed from between the ranks of drifting cumulus in thick woolly beams, scattering over the surface of the sea like chaff in the breeze. There had been some early winter rain, and now the usually barren coastal hills shimmered with life, thick ephemeral grasses, gorse, the prism points of a million dewdrops. They were completely alone.

The rock was smooth and warm to the touch. They lay on their backs and soaked up the rock's heat, water dripping cold from their bodies, pooling around them on the hard mineral surface, warming in the sun. Hope reached for his hand, took it. He closed his eyes, felt the sun's warmth on his body, heard the hush of her breathing. She rolled onto her side, traced a fingertip along the scar on his cheek, then kissed it. A nipple brushed his chest, hard and cold, then the soft compression of her breasts as she moulded to him, warm now, wet. He could feel himself hardening. Heat poured from the rock now, from their bodies. He turned his head. Her eyes were closed. They kissed. She tasted sweet, salty, like heather. She rolled onto him, wrapped herself around him, pulled him in. There were no words. They were together now, bodies joined. She moaned as he pushed into her, arched her back. He moved slowly, feeling her respond. He was close. She moaned, louder this time, gripped him tight, shuddered. His head was swimming. He made to pull away.

'No,' she breathed, holding him in. 'Fill me.'

After, they lay on the rock in the sun for a long time. Neither spoke. After a while Clay stood, glanced along the beach, turned, looked down at Hope and offered his hand. She took it, and he pulled her to her feet.

He looked into her eyes. 'I love her,' he said. To the degree I am able. Maybe not as others love, but as far as I can understand it, I love her.

Hope smiled and raised her finger to his lips. 'It's okay,' she said. 'Don't say anything. Now we're complete, the three of us.'

☾

It didn't take them long to find what they were looking for. They tracked it into the rocks, up onto the shore. Hope stood beside him, examining the black sheathing.

'It's the same type of cable we snagged with the anchor that night in Karpasia,' he said.

Hope looked both ways along the beach. 'What is it doing here? There's nothing here. No houses, no buildings of any kind. Is it a telephone line?'

Clay motioned towards the water and started following the cable out, pulling it up from the seabed as he went. As the water deepened, they took turns, one diving down, exposing a few centimetres of cable, returning to the surface to breathe, the other taking over. After half an hour, they had unearthed about twenty metres of cable. Clay's fingertips were raw from the digging, numb with the cold. He rose to the surface, breathed and looked down through the water at Hope struggling with the cable. He was tiring now, could feel the cold deep in his core. Hope looked gone. He tread water, waited for her to surface.

Something grabbed his leg. Hope burst to the surface, shouting through her snorkel. She spat out the mouthpiece, pulled up her mask. 'I've found something,' she gasped. 'Come and look.'

They spent a few minutes inspecting the thing, as much as they could manage in the cold, then swam back to the beach. They walked back along the sand, close but not touching, saying nothing. Soon they were back where they'd left their clothes. Hope turned away, pulled on her underwear, followed quickly by her jeans, a t-shirt, her big knitted wool jumper. Clay rummaged in his pack for his knife, sprinted back along the beach to the place where they'd unearthed the cable. By the time he returned, Hope was walking back down the beach towards him, phone hanging in one hand.

'That was Maria,' she said. 'They're on their way to the airport.'

Clay nodded. 'Good.'

Hope looked down at the dead thing hanging from Clay's hand, the severed arteries dripping sea water, the black body lifeless. 'Is that it?'

'One of them, yes. Do you know what it is?'

'Have you ever seen a marine geophone?'

'Sonar?'

'Same idea. Basically an underwater loud speaker.'

'I don't understand.'

'Turn those things on during the nesting season, and no turtle will come close. That strand of the phylogeny dies. Evolution stops.'

Hope pushed her fingers through her hair. Clay could see strands of grey kinking through the blonde. Her hands were shaking. 'They're doing it on purpose,' she said. Then she sat in the sand and pulled her legs up to her chest and hid her face between her knees.

Part IV

38

Trust

19th November 1994: Southern coast of the Agamas Peninsula, Cyprus

Hope pulled her phone from her bag, stared at the screen. 'Missed call,' she said. 'It was Maria. Probably just checking in.'

Clay turned the car onto the tarmacked road, headed east. Hope thumbed a number into the keypad and put the phone to her ear. Clay heard the line connect. Hope glanced over at him, speaking into the phone in excited Greek. After a while she went quiet and listened. Clay could hear the voice on the other end of the line, female. It sounded like crying.

Hope closed her phone, stared straight ahead. 'That was Maria,' she said, her voice barely a whisper. 'They were stopped at the airport by customs officials, refused permission to leave. She's back in Nicosia. My ex, the bastard, balked at the last minute. He called customs, told them Maria was taking Alexi out of the country without his permission. They were waiting for them.'

'Shit.'

'The asshole set me up.' She stamped her foot. 'Now he knows I'll never get custody. He's never trusted me, ever since–' She pushed her palms into her eyes. 'He thinks I've concocted this whole thing as a way to get Alexi away from him.'

Clay said nothing.

'Alexi is back at my ex-husband's house. I have to see my son, Clay.'

Clay nodded. He was starting to understand, just starting.

'We'll meet Crowbar in Pissouri, then go straight there. It's on the way. It won't take long.'

Hope frowned.

They arrived an hour late, drove down the narrow main road that paralleled the empty shore. Rain pounded the windscreen, blown from low clouds that stampeded across the sky like frightened buffalo. Crowbar's Pajero was parked outside the only taverna in town, an old limestone-brick building with an arched entranceway and a bare winter tangle of grapevines dripping from wire trellises. Clay had taken a circuitous route, doubling back, stopping at roadside turn-outs, scanning the traffic behind. He had learned from Istanbul just how good a professional tail could be, and just how poor had been his efforts to elude them. He was taking no chances now.

They left Hope's car in a side road and walked down the back street to the tavern. Crowbar was sitting alone at a table in the far corner, a view of the grey sea showing through closed-up windows, two empty beer bottles and a third half-full on the table in front of him. A Cypriot family, three generations, halfway through meze, were the only other patrons. The smell of food sent Clay's head spinning, opened a hole in his stomach. Crowbar stood as they approached, shook Clay's hand. Hope took Crowbar's two hands in hers, kissed him on the cheek. He smiled at her. They sat and ordered food.

Crowbar raised his beer. 'You're late, *seun*.'

'Anti-tracking, *my luitenant*.'

'No need.'

'No price on your head, *broer*.'

'I met Regina Medved this morning.'

'Does she still love me?'

'As much as ever, *seun*. Two millions worth.'

'Where is she?'

'Nicosia. South side. Dialysis machine, mobile ventilator, the whole *fokken* Moscow travelling circus. I showed her that photograph of you all banged up, told her I had you tied up nice and safe. So they've stopped looking for you.'

'With the reward you'll get, you can retire. Your friends in the company won't be happy.'

'Told her I'd hand you over day after tomorrow. Best I could do, *ja*. She's getting the cash together now. Said it would take her a day.' Crowbar sipped his beer. 'I mean, *fok*. A *day*. *Kak*, how do people get that rich?'

'By screwing people like us,' said Hope.

Crowbar smiled, took her hand, a child's fingers disappearing under a paw of hairy, scarred callous. 'Too right, *bokkie*.'

Hope looked across at Clay. 'What's this *bokkie*?'

'It's good. You know, *bok*. Antelope.'

Hope's frown approached neutral.

'Medved's *fokken gek, ja*. Crazy as a starving hyena. She's convinced the Patmos Illumination is here. Thinks it'll save her. Someone here in Cyprus has promised to deliver it to her. That's why she's here, *ja*. Nothing to do with you, Straker.'

The waiter brought their food: chicken souvlaki, unleavened bread, salad. They ate in silence. Clay turned in his chair and looked out of the window at the rainy street. All quiet.

Crowbar pushed away his empty plate. 'How was your day at the beach?'

Hope glanced at Clay.

Clay looked away.

'Someone is intentionally frightening away the turtles,' Hope said, 'preventing them from coming ashore to lay their eggs. It's genocide, plain and simple.'

Clay reached into his pack and pulled out the black cylinder about the size of a car's oil filter. Six inches of cable hung from one end like a severed tail. He put it on the table. 'They've buried these along the sea bed in shallow water.'

'Noise emitters,' said Hope. 'We've been watching that beach during the nesting season to make sure no one disturbs the turtles. They must have laid it a few winters ago, probably by ship. We never thought to check underwater.'

'*Fokken* hell.' Crowbar looked genuinely astonished.

'What about Zdravko?' Clay said, putting the device back in his bag.

'Found him.'

'Limassol?'

Crowbar nodded. 'The aunt is with him. The neighbour says she saw an old lady go into the place four days ago, hasn't seen her leave since.'

Clay's insides jumped.

'I've got a colleague watching the place now.'

'We've got to get them both out, Koevoet – Rania and her aunt. And we've got to do it soon, before Chrisostomedes moves either of them.'

Crowbar finished his beer, nodded.

'And it's got to be simultaneous. If Chrisostomedes finds out someone has snatched away his insurance policy, Rania's dead.'

'Chrisostomedes will address a Neo-Enosis rally tomorrow afternoon in Nicosia,' said Crowbar. 'He leaves for Nicosia tomorrow morning, according to my sources.'

'So it has to be tonight.' Clay looked at his watch. 'We need to get the beach samples to the lab in Nicosia, get Hope to her son. Tomorrow is Sunday. The enquiry starts on the twenty-second, Tuesday. It's doable.'

Crowbar frowned. 'You need to keep out of sight, Straker. You're supposed to be my prisoner. You can't be dropping in to labs, socialising.'

Hope reached for Crowbar's forearm. 'Maria can take the samples in. She knows the lab, the technicians there. We do a lot of work with them.'

Crowbar forced deep furrows into his brow, finished his beer. 'Do you trust her?'

Clay looked over at Hope.

'Of course, yes,' said Hope. 'I asked her to take my son to Greece, for Christ's sake.'

'How much do you know about her?' said Crowbar.

'She's worked for me for almost three years now. Before that I supervised her PhD. I trust her implicitly.'

Crowbar grinned. 'Okay, *ooma*. Good enough for me. We go tonight.'

Clay nodded.

Crowbar put a mobile phone on the table. 'Time you had your own phone, *my seun*.'

☾

The two and half hours to Nicosia hung up like a week on the front line waiting for leave. The rain persisted, coming in waves, turning the roads into rivers. Hope was sullen and quiet, wrapped in her own fears. She had called Maria and asked her to meet them outside a *periptero* just off the highway, about a mile from the lab. She had also called the lab manager and asked him to come in for an important job. By the time they reached the outskirts of Nicosia it was late afternoon and the rain had cleared.

When they pulled in to the puddled gravel parking area outside the *periptero*, Maria was already waiting for them in her silver VW Beetle.

Clay stopped the car, kept the engine running, reached into his pocket and pulled out a thick fold of US dollars.

Hope glanced at the cash. 'Not a good idea,' she said. 'Paying cash would arouse suspicion. Let me put it on the university's account.'

'We need rush service. You'll have to pay double.'

'Don't worry about it,' said Hope, pushing away his hand.

Maria was walking over to the car now. Hope rolled down her window.

Maria leaned in. Her eyes were red. She'd been crying. 'I'm so sorry about your son, Doctor Bachmann,' she said. 'I did exactly what you said. But when we tried to go through customs—'

'It's okay, Maria. Don't worry. It's not your fault. Thanks for trying.'

Maria nodded and looked across at Clay. 'Doctor Greene.'

'Thanks for this, Maria,' he said, reaching for the bag of samples in the back seat and handing them to her.

'We need rush service,' said Hope. 'Tomorrow if possible. Put them on our account. It's very important, Maria.'

The girl took the bag and nodded. She pulled out a little notebook and a pen. 'Analysis suite?'

Clay specified the analyses to be conducted.

'And tomorrow morning,' said Hope, 'I need you to go to the border crossing in Agios Demetios. A man called Berker will meet you there and give you a second set of samples.'

Maria blanched.

'Don't worry, Maria. He's an old friend. I called him and asked him to collect half a dozen samples from Karpasia Beach as soon as he could and deliver them south. The samples will be labelled *Valk*, and are to be run for the same set of chemical parameters.'

'*Endaxi*?' Clay asked. Okay?

Maria nodded and hurried away to her car.

By the time Clay and Hope reached the centre of town, night had fallen and the streets shimmered with light. Closed shop-front windows glowed, beckoned to a homeward trickle of umbrella-toting office workers. Random squares of light burned inside the dark hulks of squat office buildings, desperate bankers staring into flickering screens, the stink of alchemy oozing into the air even on a Saturday night. Money never sleeps, thought Clay, doesn't take a day off.

'What will you do?' said Hope. It was the first time she'd spoken since dropping the samples with Maria. 'The two of you. After, I mean.'

'I don't know. Go to Africa, I guess. Disappear for a while.'

She pointed left. He turned.

'I wish I could disappear.'

Clay said nothing, drove.

'Here,' she said. 'Just along this street.'

Clay slowed the car and scanned the street. Windows evening-lit, a few cars parked half up on the pavement, tree shadow swaying over rooftops, house fronts.

'This is it,' she said.

Clay stopped and turned off the engine. There was just the quiet of the street, Hope sitting there beside him, her face almost hidden in the darkness.

'Alexi is waiting for you,' he said.

Hope tried a thin smile, failed. 'Be careful,' she said.

'You too, Hope.'

'I'll be in meetings with my co-convenors all day tomorrow, preparing for the enquiry. Opening statements start at ten o'clock Tuesday morning. Erkan is scheduled to testify at two that afternoon. If he decides to show up, that is.' She paused. 'Will you be there?'

'Not a good way to disappear.'

'If you could testify, Clay, it would be very valuable. Rania, too.'

'You'll have all the proof you need. I'll give you Erkan's dossier. You don't need us.' He felt sick inside.

Hope stared at him across the half metre of darkness that separated them. After a moment she opened her door and stepped out of the car. 'Come in with me, Clay, please.'

Clay looked at his watch, nodded, got out of the car and followed her to the house.

Hope's ex answered the door. He was a big man, tall, heavy-set. As soon as Clay saw him he knew something was wrong. His eyes were red, swollen. He looked like a little boy who'd lost his mother at the fair.

'Hope,' he said, glancing at Clay. 'What have you done with him?'

'What are you talking about?' said Hope, reaching for the doorframe. 'Where's Alexi?'

'The police are on their way.'

'Police?'

'After I brought him home from the airport, I took him to the park to play. I turned my head for a minute, and he was gone. I've looked everywhere, called everyone. I know you've taken him, you and that bitch Maria.'

39

Natural Selection

Hope stood in the doorway looking as if she'd been given a dose of cyanide, could feel it creeping through her body. 'What are you talking about?' she gasped. 'Where is my son?'

'Stop the bullshit,' her ex-husband bellowed, leaning forward at the waist. 'Where is Alexi?'

Hope raised her hand to her mouth. 'My god,' she whispered. 'You think …. You think *I* have him.'

'That's exactly what I think, you slut.' He jutted his chin towards Clay. 'You and your *friend*, here.'

Hope wheeled around, her glance ricocheting off Clay like an afterthought. 'He's … He's got nothing to do with this, Pavlos. Where is my son? What have you done with him?'

'You tell me,' he screamed. 'Your bullshit story about being in danger, about needing to leave the country. Using that dyke Maria as your mule. I can't believe I almost fell for it.'

Hope withered, took a step back. 'Do you think I would kidnap my own son?'

Pavlos leaned in, only a couple of paces from Hope. 'You bitch. You fucking bitch. You've been wanting to take him from me ever since we–'

'Ever since what?' screamed Hope, counter-attacking. 'Ever since *you* left *me?* Go on, say it. You left me. For that brainless whore of yours.'

Pavlos flinched a moment and then started towards Hope, fists clenched. Clay stepped forward, interposed himself between trembling mother and heaving, near-hysterical father. He and Pavlos were inches apart. Clay could smell the foulness of the guy's breath, the fear seeping from his pores. The guy was almost as tall as Clay, probably as heavy, but soft, arms and belly like dough.

'What the hell are you doing?' Pavlos screamed, spraying Clay's face with cold spittle. 'Get the fuck out of my way.'

Clay wiped his face with the sleeve of his stump arm, said nothing, just stared back at the man. For a short moment Clay wondered if he'd try. Pavlos puffed and heaved, the muscles in his neck twitching under their layer of fat, his fists still clenched at his sides, and then it was as if everything just drained out of him at once. His shoulders slumped and his head dropped and all of a sudden he was inches shorter and the rage was gone and only the fear was left. He backed away towards the middle of the room, sank into a chair and folded his arms across his chest.

'We'll see what the police say,' he muttered.

Hope closed the door, leaned back against the wall and slid to the floor, burying her face in her hands. Sirens wailed in the distance.

Clay's phone buzzed. He put it to his ear, turning away from the warring parents.

'It's me.' Crowbar's voice was rough, hard. 'Zulu Tango left the Limassol apartment ten minutes ago.'

'The old lady?' Clay answered in Afrikaans.

'Still in there, as far as we can tell.'

'Sit tight, Koevoet. There's something I have to do.'

'We need to go soon.'

'Stand by,' said Clay.

Clay put the phone in his pocket, touched Hope's shoulder, looking over at Pavlos. 'Will you be okay, Hope? I have to go.'

She looked up, nodded. By now Pavlos was catatonic, immobilised. Clay looked right at him, made sure that he was listening. 'Call me if you need anything, Hope.'

She nodded, the sirens close now.

Clay turned and ran down the front steps and jumped into Hope's car. He rounded the end of the street just as a police car sped past in the other direction, flinging a panic of strobing blue light across the house fronts.

Clay sped down Digeni Avenue, turned past the English School towards Strovolos. Finding a broad gravel shoulder lined with dusty cypress trees, he pulled off the road, stopped, grabbed his phone and found the scrap of paper Katia had given him at the dinner party.

She answered second ring.

'Katia, it's me, Doctor Greene.'

'I know that isn't your real name.' She spoke as if she'd been expecting him.

'I need to talk to you.'

Silence for a moment, and then: 'Come to my apartment.' She told him the address.

'Ten minutes.'

'Doctor Greene?'

'Yes.'

'I'm glad you called.'

(

Katia's apartment was in one of the new blocks that had gone up on the south side of Strovolos to accommodate the influx of tax exiles, bankers and accountants who now dominated the island's economy. Eight stories, tall for Nicosia, it was square-edged, concrete and glass, all the old trees taken out and paved over.

Clay parked around the corner and buzzed at the main entrance. The door clicked open. He ran up the stairs to the third floor, found apartment twelve and knocked.

Katia opened the door. In her heels she was almost as tall as Clay. Her hair was down, big red rings freshly curled. Perfume hung in the air, something expensive. She was wearing pull-up stockings and a half-cup bra that left her big pink nipples exposed. She smiled. 'I was hoping you'd call.'

Clay closed the door, stood for a moment looking at her. Other than the hive cascading from her head and the carefully plucked curve of her eyebrows, she was hairless. She stepped closer, put her arms around his neck.

'That's not why I'm here,' he said, gently pushing away one of her arms, trying to ignore the jolt of desire fizzing through his extremities.

She looked at him a moment, unsure, as if surprised that a man had called on her not wanting sex. Then she smiled, turned and walked away. Her body was tight, pampered, the skin without flaw. She vanished into a doorway, returned a moment later wearing a floor-length, oriental-style silk dressing gown. She lit a joint and sat on the couch.

Clay sat opposite her. 'Where is Dimitriou?'

She took a long draw on the spliff, a crisp sound as the weed ignited, glowed. 'Why should I tell you?'

'Because someone has taken Doctor Bachmann's son, and I think he knows who.'

She took another drag, offered him the joint.

He waved it away. 'No thanks, Katia.'

'You're not as fun as I thought you'd be.'

'I'm not as fun as *I* thought I'd be.'

She frowned, pinched the roach end of her joint and inhaled through puckered lips.

'Where's Dimitriou, Katia?'

Katia exhaling: 'I don't know where he goes or what he does. He pays for this apartment, my clothes, expenses, and for that I do what he tells me.'

Clay nodded, understood. 'Have you heard him mention anything, anything at all, about Hope or her son?'

'I hear a lot of things. They talk all the time, he and Nicos. They think I'm stupid, that I don't know Greek. But I do.'

'Better than me.'

She smiled. 'Like the last time I was at Nicos' place in the mountains. I like that place. It's so beautiful. The pool is great. Anyway, Nicos was showing Dimitriou some of his art, all that really old stuff he has. Did you know that Nicos tags each piece with a microchip, so that if someone tries to take it, the alarms go off? I bet you didn't know that.'

Clay nodded. 'You said you liked scuba.'

'You remember.'

'There's a wreck off Polis that's good,' he said. 'You should try it.'

She looked down at his stump. 'What happened to your hand?'

'I traded it.'

She smiled. It was a sad smile. 'That woman, the journalist.'

Clay said nothing.

'You traded it for her, didn't you? You love her.'

Clay nodded. Close enough.

'I know why they were threatening your friend,' she said.

Clay looked into her eyes. They were the colour of the acid pools at the Mephistos copper mine, sterile and opaque. 'Please, Katia.'

'He lives near the Presidential Palace, on Afxentiou Street. Number five.'

Clay stood. 'Thanks, Katia.'

'He's an asshole. I hate him.'

Clay said nothing.

She stubbed out her joint, looking up at him from far away. 'If you ever, you know, want to…' she pulled at a curl, '…go diving, just call me.'

☾

By the time Clay reached the outskirts of Nicosia, it was already gone nine. Soon he was on the old Troodos road heading west for the mountains.

He called Crowbar. He was still watching the Limassol apartment where they suspected Rania's aunt was being held. Zdravko hadn't returned. No one else had gone in or out. Clay pressed on, pushing Hope's little car to the limit, speeding through the night. He could feel time start to fray, its long edges coming apart, spinning away. Everything had changed, though he could discern in the world around him no overt signs of transition. The car functioned as designed, the road unfurled before him in the myopia of the head-lights, his heart pumped blood, the mobile's green light pulsed in the darkness on the empty seat beside him. And yet change was here, all around him, and it was as if he were being carried along in a fast-moving river, the banks far off and shrouded in fog. He could feel it cooling his blood, pushing him further into the darkness. Some live, some die. Those that live pass on their genes. Modification by natural selection, Darwin had called it.

Clay closed his eyes, drove on. Time slowed. He could hear the engine screaming in front of him, feel its vibration. How long now? A second? Two? So many dead. And never with any time to under-stand, just that instant between living and not, with nothing in between, no time to prepare, to consider what was to be lost, what might have been. Binary only. On. Off. Where did the interface lie, at what limit? How long could a moment last?

He opened his eyes. The road was still there.

He jammed the accelerator to the floor, hurtled towards her.

The road steepened, Sunday-night empty. The lights of Kako-petria flashed past, vanished in the rear-view mirror. Thick stands of pine reached blackened arms out over the road. He jammed his stump down onto the wheel, picked up the phone, hit redial and cradled it between his shoulder and ear.

Crowbar answered.

'Go in twenty,' Clay told him.

Clay left the car on the side road where he'd stopped before with Hope and plunged into the forest towards Chrisostomedes' mansion. Lights flashed between the dark, upright torsos of the pines, among the pleading arms, through the needle fingers. The fence was there, the glow of the gatehouse. A single guard inside, a car parked just nearby, inside the compound. Clay stayed in the trees, moved down-slope, away from the gate, picking his way through the granite boulders, over the steepening outcrop. The house was above him now, perched on the cliff. He zipped up his jacket put on his head-lamp, unlit, and started climbing. He'd always been a strong climber – as a child in the trees outside his parents' house, before the war with friends in the Draakensburg. One-handed, unbalanced, he had to rely far more on his feet and the power of his legs, shift his centre of gravity down. The lower section was steeper and more feature-less than he'd remembered. Twice he dead-ended, had to backtrack, find a new route. Finally he found a fault zone, a near-vertical dis-continuity in the rock. It was some way out from under the house, visible from the balcony twenty metres above, within the throw of the building's lights.

Twenty minutes had come and gone. Crowbar would have gone in by now, and with any luck would have rescued Rania's aunt. Clay jammed his stump into the fault and started to climb. Able to use his left arm this way, he moved quickly up to a layer of fractured basalt. A narrow, weathered ridge marked the interface between the layers. Bird droppings dotted the rock, lines on a road. He hugged the rock face, toed his way towards the house. He was almost back in shadow when the phone buzzed in his pocket. He kept moving. Soon he had reached the lowermost foundations. He swung up over a cross brace, followed the rock to the abutment where it met the main slab. The dining room where he'd last seen Rania was directly above. He flicked his headlamp to red, ran the beam along the abut-ment wall. Nothing. He'd have to go up and over. He followed the base of the slab, gained the side of the house then extinguished the headlamp, moving along the concrete wall until he came to a recess. Inside, a doorway leading into the foundation. He tried the handle. Locked. He switched on the headlamp again, examined the handle, the locking mechanism. Light off, he stood with his back against the wall, breathing hard. The phone buzzed again.

'*Broer*.' It was Crowbar. 'Where are you?'

'About to go in.'

'She's not here.'

Clay's heart loped. 'What?'

'Gone. The place was empty.'

'Shit.'

'Go anyway, *bru*. Get her.'

'If they–'

Crowbar cut him off. 'You may not get another chance. I'm on my way.'

Clay closed the phone, jammed it into his pocket. If he managed to get Rania out, Zdravko wouldn't hesitate to kill her aunt. But every minute that passed pushed Rania further towards the edge. How long would Chrisostomedes keep her around? Now that he had Hope's son, did he still need Rania? Crowbar was right. Clay pulled out the Beretta, stood back, aimed at the door handle.

Just as he was about to pull the trigger, a muffled detonation rang through the house.

Clay stopped dead, listened. The sound of blood pulsing, of air moving through his mouth, inside his head, the wind in the pines, the squeak of twisting wood as the trees swayed in the breeze.

And then, in quick succession, two more bangs, gunshots, coming from inside the house. Clay raised his gun and fired.

40

The Ladder of Divine Ascent

The 9mm slug blew the lock to pieces. Clay kicked in the door, swung the red beam of his headlamp around the room. A storeroom: an old lawnmower, shovels, tools, a workbench of sorts, boxes, everything covered in dust. At the far end, a stairway made of rough-cut wood planking. Clay approached the bench, pocketed the Beretta, scanned the tools. He picked up an axe, ran his stump over the dullness of the blade and replaced it on the bench. A hammer, a hand-drill, a power-saw, stacks of old blades. From upstairs, the sound of someone running, a door slamming.

Clay grabbed a steel crowbar and moved quickly up the stairs. At the top, a blade of light shone from under a wooden door. The door was locked. He set the crowbar's claw to the door frame and pushed. The wood splintered and came away. He flipped the crowbar around and forced the bolt, swung the bar under his left arm, pulled out the handgun, pushed open the door with his foot.

The light hurt his eyes. He was in a corridor, empty white walls, hardwood floor, somewhere on the same level as the main dining room. He started south, towards the front of the house and the main stairway. Another retort, louder this time, close, the distinctive bark of a large-calibre handgun. A second later the alarms went off. Clay started running. The corridor doglegged left, ended. There were doors on both sides. Clay went right, south, and pushed open the door. He emerged into a narrow, dimly lit perimeter of some kind. The outside wall was solid rough-hewn stone that curved away in both directions like the interior of a cave. Towards the inside, a screen of heavy timbers, like looking into the depths of a forest at dusk, soft, butter-coloured lights shining between the trunks, and beyond, the main entranceway. Clay went left. The underside of the staircase came into view. A gap opened up in the screen work. He set the crowbar on the floor against the wall and emerged into the main gallery.

Ahead, the front door was wide open, the night staring through. Alarms screamed, lights pulsed. Clay reached the base of the stair-case. The stairs were still hidden from view by the sweeping wooden balustrade. He looked up to the mezzanine. No one. He swung around to the first step. A face stared up at him, eyes wide, mouth open. The man was sprawled across the bottom four steps as if he'd been trying to slide down head-first on his back. Blood seeped from a hole in his forehead, trickled across the hardwood, dripped to the stone flag floor. It was Spearpoint.

Clay bypassed the body and took the steps three at a time. He worked his way through the upper floor, room by room, moving quickly, the Beretta up, ready, cradled in the partial crook of his left arm. Rania's room was empty, the bed made, the closet bare. He knew it was hers. He could smell her.

She wasn't here. Damn it all.

Clay burst from the room, flew down the hall to the mezzanine, the alarms wailing in his ears. As he reached the top of the stairs he saw a man limping across the stone flags towards the front door. A black duffel bag hung from his shoulder. He carried a handgun. It was Zdravko.

Clay raised the Beretta, fired, missed. Zdravko ducked, stumbling out of the door. Clay crashed down the steps, sidestepped Spear-point's lifeless body, raced across the gallery and out into the night. Zdravko was halfway across the gravel car park now, silhouetted by the lights of the guardhouse. Clay could see the body of the gate guard lumped dark in the gravel next to a car. His pulse was slow, his breathing calm. He raised the handgun, took aim, fired. Zdravko kept running, that crazy stiff-legged limp. Clay fired again. Zdravko jerked as the bullet clipped his left thigh. He stopped, swayed, spun around, raised his weapon. Clay rolled away as rounds slammed into the wooden beam behind him. Zdravko was almost to the car, still going, dragging his leg. He reached back with his pistol, fired on the run, blind. Rock chips flew from the wall inches from Clay's head. Clay crabbed left, stood, planted his feet. Zdravko was opening the car door. He reached back again, the handgun scything wildly, fired twice more. A window to Clay's right exploded in a shower of glass. Clay steadied himself, sighted down the barrel and unloaded the clip.

Zdravko fell in a heap.

Clay dropped the spent magazine to the ground and loaded a fresh one. He used his mouth, his knees. Just like he'd practised at the cottage. Three seconds. He walked towards the car, weapon ready. Zdravko lay motionless, face down. As Clay approached, he could see the damage. He'd hit him in the neck, the upper shoulder, lower back and the base of the spine. Blood oozed to the ground. Zdravko was dead.

Clay stood looking down at the man who had threatened the woman he loved, who'd murdered his friend, others besides. He watched the blood soak into the gravel, working its way between the stones, the bubbles coming up, bursting thick with plasma. He looked at the weapon in his hand, hot still, impassive, uncaring, ready to continue.

'Only Allah decides who lives and dies,' he said aloud. 'Something a friend said to me once.' He turned over the body and looked at the face. 'But in this case, we'll make an exception.'

Lights flashed through the trees. A car was coming up the drive. Clay reached down and picked up Zdravko's bag, kicked the dead man's handgun under the car, then moved to the guardhouse, crouching against the wall.

The car came to a halt outside the gate. Clay heard the engine stop, a door open, close. Footsteps crunching in the gravel, heavy, approaching slowly. Whoever it was would have seen the bodies by now. Clay readied himself. The footsteps stopped. Seconds passed, the alarms screaming still.

'Straker,' came a voice.

'Koevoet,' he said.

'Rania?'

'Negative.'

'*Kak*.' Crowbar approached the car and turned Zdravko's head with his foot. 'The *poes* who got me with the Dragunov.' He looked up as Clay joined him. 'You okay, *seun*?'

Clay nodded and motioned towards the dead guard. 'He killed him. More inside. He was leaving with this.'

Clay put the bag on the back of Zdravko's car and unzipped it. Inside were two white towels. Crowbar picked one up and unfolded it. There was something inside, wrapped like a present. He dropped the towel back into the bag, fished a torch from his pocket, turned it on and ran the beam over the object. It was a small painting, more like an engraving, no bigger than a paperback, faded colours on heavy, dark wood. Crowbar tilted it towards the light.

Figures in single file suspended against a gold background climb an invisible ladder. Winged devils hover beneath the ladder, plucking unfortunates from the queue. Many fall. They plummet into a fiery abyss, mouths open in screams of horror, into the waiting jaws of sea monsters, drooling grotesques. A throng mills at the base of the ladder, each supplicant's eyes raised, waiting to take his turn. At the top right, a larger image, haloed in gold leaf, bearded, holds up the first two fingers of his right hand. He is reaching out to the climbers, calling to them, urging them up.

'Jesus Christ,' breathed Clay.

Crowbar looked up at him. 'What is it?'

'Like I said: Jesus Christ.'

Crowbar grinned, unwrapped the second towel. It was another icon, identical. 'Where the hell did he get these?'

'Chrisostomedes collects them.'

'Stealing from his employer.'

'Time-honoured.'

'Why kill all these people and take only this?'

'Because this,' Clay said, picking up the second icon, turning it towards the light, 'or one of these, is worth more than that house and everything in it. And it's probably the only thing on the planet that would have convinced Regina Medved to let him live. The Patmos Illumination.' Zdravko must have planned it from the beginning.

'So it does exist,' said Crowbar.

'Apparently yes, and more than one.'

Clay looked down. Something was dripping on his boot. He reached down, touched it with his finger. 'Blood,' he said.

'Where's it coming from?' said Crowbar.

Clay reached down under the rear bumper of Zdravko's car, catching a drop as it fell. 'From inside.'

Crowbar stepped back, kicked at the trunk. 'Won't open.' He raised his handgun, aimed it at the lock.

Clay pushed Crowbar's gun down. 'Wait.'

Clay ran back inside the house, grabbed the crowbar from where he'd left it and ran back across the gravel. It didn't take him long to pry open the trunk.

A face he'd seen only once before, four months ago in a café overlooking Lake Geneva, stared up at him with empty, unblinking eyes. Rania's aunt, Madame Héloïse Debret, gagged with tape, hands bound together behind her back with a plastic zip tie. She'd been shot in the chest.

41

As Good as Anything Else

Crowbar dropped him at Hope's car and they drove in tandem through the back mountain roads until they emerged in Kakopetria. By the time they saw the first police car, they were already clear of the foothills. They stopped next to a darkened roadside *periptero* under the shadow of a copse of evergreens. Clay joined Crowbar in the Pajero. They watched in silence as first one, then a second police car sped past towards Troodos. For a moment Crowbar's face lit up blue and red, his jaw hard-set, covered in stubble, his wispy hair draped across his forehead in sweat-glued spines. They sat in the darkness for a long time, watching the lights disappear into the distance.

After a while Crowbar pulled a half-empty bottle from under his seat, unscrewed the cap, swigged.

Clay couldn't see the label, but he could smell the cheap, duty-free scotch. 'Chrisostomedes must have taken Rania with him,' he said.

Crowbar took another swig and capped the bottle. 'The rally is going ahead as planned. Tomorrow afternoon in Nicosia, down on the Green Line.'

Clay looked out into the black of the trees, the lighter grey of the tired fields beyond. 'He's taken Hope's son.'

Crowbar went quiet. '*Fokken* bastard.'

Clay told him about Katia, his suspicion that Dimitriou might know the boy's whereabouts. 'We've got to find them, *oom*. Both of them. And quick.'

Crowbar nodded, patting the bag on the seat between them. 'He'll be wanting these, *ja.*'

'We'll offer him a trade.'

282 PAUL HARDISTY

Crowbar opened the whisky and took another sip. 'Do you know how much these are worth, *seun*? Medved's offering ten million dollars, no questions. I say we kill the bastard, sell the icons to the dowager, then *fokken* retire in the Seychelles.'

'No, *oom*. We trade. We give him back his icons, he lets Rania go. Rania promises to keep quiet about what happened. We leave the country quietly, vanish.'

'What about him?' Crowbar pointed his chin to the back of the Pajero where they'd bundled Zdravko's body.

'The Cypriots won't give a damn about him. We've done them a favour. But go after one of their own, a luminary like Chrisosto-medes, they'll call out the army.'

'What about Medved?' said Crowbar. 'You think you can run away with that kind of money tagged to your head? Someone will find you, *ja*. Both of you. Sometime, somewhere.'

'You said it yourself. She'll be dead in six months.'

'That's what they've been saying for the last two years. They keep finding new ways of keeping the old bitch going. But if we give her this thing she wants, we might just be doing ourselves a big favour.'

Clay took the bottle, swigged a mouthful, winced as the whisky found him. Crowbar was right. They had to end it with Medved, one way or another. If she believed in the Illumination's power enough, she might just eschew medical science and hasten her own death. It was as good as anything else they had, maybe better.

Crowbar took the bottle back. 'I admire you, *seun*.' Just the whites of his eyes glistening in the dull half moonlight. 'Even with Medved off your back, you think you can keep Rania quiet? Get her to run, leave Hope hanging? You've always been a dreamer, Straker, a *fokken* idealist. Congratulations. Now you've met someone even more stub-born and idealistic than you are.'

Clay looked away. 'That's exactly what we're going to do, Koevoet. Run. Then I'm going back.'

Crowbar raised the bottle in his hand as if to look at the label. 'What did you say?'

'I'm going back to South Africa.'

'Goddamn, not that again. They'll arrest you the minute you step off the plane.'

'New government, *oom*.'

'That's what I mean. *Fokken* ANC all legitimate now. A pack of *fokken* terrorists and thieves running the country.'

'I'm going to testify.'

Crowbar stopped breathing.

'Desmond Tutu is going to chair the Truth and Reconciliation Commission. I'm going to apply for amnesty.'

Crowbar was silent a long time, just sat there behind the wheel, staring out into the night. 'Don't do it,' he said finally.

'I have to. It's the only way I'll be able to live with myself. It's killing me, *oom*. I need to tell the truth. This thing they're doing, it's my last chance.'

'Don't be naïve, Straker. You tell the truth, they'll throw you in prison till you die. No way in hell they'll grant you amnesty. No *fokken* way.'

'I won't mention names. No one else. Just me.'

'As soon as you open your mouth, they'll know we were all lying.'

Clay breathed, worked his lungs. He was back there on the stand all those years ago, facing the military tribunal, his tie too tight around his neck, his collar chafing his skin in the stifling January heat, and that one officer, a colonel with a grey moustache, red, sun-burned cheeks and eyes like lead shot, who never seemed to blink or move but sat there for hours staring right through him with the ceiling fan turning overhead and the stenographer coughing and the way his cough would echo through the converted library they were using as a courtroom, the sound echoing off the marble floors and the colonial pillars and vaulted ceilings so that it was a continu-ous barking, like a pack of wild dogs braying at the scent of fear. And even then, he knew, from the demeanour of the officers, by the questions they asked, by the way they cut him off the moment he began to elaborate, anything more than a yes or no, that they weren't interested in the truth, only in the process, that it could be said that the enquiry had run over ten days and had questioned all twenty-one surviving members of the platoon, as well as the crew of the helicopter who'd overflown the village later that day, and the forward artillery observer and his pilot who'd come by two days later, but by then FAPLA had been in, and the jackals and the hyenas had been at the place and there was nothing much left to see.

'It was war,' said Crowbar. 'Not politics. This commission is about politics. It's the ANC's way of legitimising *their* atrocities. It's not for us. You say one word, I guarantee you can kiss Rania and that little baby she's making for you goodbye. You'll never see them again.' Crowbar banged the bottle down onto the dashboard.

'What we did was wrong, Koevoet.'

'*Goddamn*, Straker. We don't have time for this. Let it go.'

'All those people.'

'*Fokken* enemy non-combatants. They were harbouring the enemy. They attacked *us*, don't forget.'

'Kids, Koevoet. Little children.'

'*Fok*, Straker. You think you're the only soldier who has ever had to do something he was ashamed of? What about the concentration camps you English cunts put our women and children into? They starved to death or died of the plague. Thousands of 'em. You going to salve your pussy conscience about that, too?' Crowbar opened the door, got out, slammed it shut.

Clay got out of the passenger side, walked around the front of the vehicle and faced Crowbar. In the dim light he could see the fury on his face.

'Look, *oom*, I'm sorry. I shouldn't have brought it up.'

'No. Just *fokken* break your oath to all those men you fought with, let them find out when the man comes knocking at their door.'

'They won't…'

'*Fok* you, Straker.'

'What is it, Koevoet? In blood stepp'd in so far? Is that it?'

'Don't, asshole. I'm warning you.'

'Too far gone? Is that why you joined the company?'

Crowbar took a step forward, brought his face to within inches of Clay's. 'Spare me the psychobabble, Straker.'

'You think there's no way back, don't you? That's it, isn't it?'

'You want to know?' Crowbar was shouting now. 'You really want to know?'

Clay breathed in the whisky vapour that hung like a cloud around their heads. 'Go ahead,' said Clay. 'Tell me, *bru*. What are you so afraid of?'

Crowbar tensed, clenched his fists at his sides. He was looking up, his lips almost brushing Clay's chin. 'Here's the thing, *seun*. It's simple.' He smiled, stared into Clay's eyes. 'I like killing people. That's all. And I'm good at it.'

Clay stepped back, Hope's words coming to him like certainty. After a while he said: 'I'm not like you, Koevoet.'

'Yes, Straker. You are. You just haven't admitted it to yourself yet.' Crowbar reached into the car, grabbed the whisky bottle, drank then thrust it into Clay's hand. 'Go. I won't stop you. But it won't bring those people back. You've got to live with it, *seun*. Nothing else you can do.'

Clay emptied the bottle, flung it against the wall.

42

Playing House

They left Hope's car in a side road outside the village and continued on in Crowbar's Pajero. It was well past midnight when they rolled past Dimitriou's place.

'That's it,' said Clay. 'Number five.'

The house was set back from the street within a lush, floodlit garden, surrounded by a ten-foot perimeter fence lipped with razor-wire. Lights were still burning in the upstairs rooms. Crowbar did a circuit of the neighbourhood then pulled the vehicle up at the end of the street, just beyond a small bridge, and killed the lights.

'No guards that I can see,' said Crowbar. 'CCTV at the front gate, over there at the corner. Probably motion sensors around the place. Pretty basic.'

'I only need a few minutes,' said Clay.

'Don't do anything stupid, *broer*.'

Clay nodded.

Crowbar pointed back towards the bridge. 'Go in along the river-bed, around back. Plenty of cover. If the boy's there, get him and get out fast. Exfil the same way. I'll be waiting here.'

Clay nodded.

Crowbar handed Clay a balaclava hood, a pair of leather gloves and a pair of wire cutters. 'I'll look after the security system,' he said, glancing at his watch. 'Go in ten.'

It didn't take Clay long to find the back wall of the property. Using wire cutters one-handed was more difficult than he had antici-pated. Luckily the wire here was sparse, poorly anchored. At the appointed time, he dropped into the back garden and made his way to the house. The rear patio door was unlocked. He stepped inside, closed the door behind him. A thin moonlight frosted the walls, the kitchen countertops. Clay moved towards the front of the house, aware now of the smell of the place, detergent and tonight's dinner, cigar smoke, cat. He emerged into a marble-floored entranceway, the main staircase on his left, lights burning upstairs. He stopped, inhaled deep and listened. The sound of a toilet flushing upstairs, water running, the squeak and clunk of a door closing.

He started up the stairs.

That feeling deep in his stomach. Being somewhere you don't belong. Crossing a border into another's territory.

The main landing. A hallway. A kid's nightlight glowing. A door, closed, papered with cartoons – flowers, rainbows, smiling cartoon people, unicorns. Hushed voices from the end of the hallway, a half-open door, a wedge of yellow light.

Clay breathed in, out, started walking.

Dimitriou was sitting up in bed, a book in his hand, a pair of reading glasses perched on his nose. His wife lay next to him, also reading, her hair in some kind of net. They looked up as Clay entered the room.

Before they had a chance to react, Clay grabbed Dimitriou by the shirt front and hauled him out of bed. Books and a bedside lamp clattered to the floor. The wife screamed, pulled the covers up over herself. Clay slammed Dimitriou up hard against the wall.

'What do you want?' spluttered Dimitriou.

'Where is the boy?'

'Who?' Recovering now.

His wife screamed in Greek, reached for the phone on her bedside table.

Clay tightened down on Dimitriou's throat. 'Tell her to shut up and put down the phone.'

Instant compliance. The wife sobbed quietly.

'Where is he?'

'I know who you are.'

Clay let go of Dimitriou's neck and jammed his stump up under the man's chin. He pulled out his switchblade and popped the blade so Dimitriou could see. 'Where is he?'

'I … I…' Definitely scared now. The wife, too.

Clay placed the sharp point of the blade against Dimitriou's cheek so he could feel the coldness of it. 'I can start here, show you how this thing works.'

Dimitriou was shaking. 'He's … not here. Oh God, please don't.'

Clay pulled back the blade. 'Tell me, and I'll leave. No one gets hurt.'

Dimitriou nodded quickly. 'Chrisostomedes has him,' he managed. 'I told him not to, I told him. Please.' Fear swam cold and fast in his eyes.

'Where?'

'I don't know. Please believe me.'

'Guess.'

'Here in Nicosia. I don't know where.'

Clay disengaged, stepped back. 'You tell him, he touches that boy, one scratch, you'll both regret it. Understood?'

Dimitriou nodded.

Then he looked at Dmitriou's wife. 'You may want to ask your husband about the boy he's kidnapped, and about that Russian mistress he keeps. I suggest you both think twice before you call the police.'

Her eyes were already widening as Clay closed the knife and put it into his jacket pocket.

'Enjoy your evening, *Minister*.'

☾

It was fifty-fifty whether Dimitriou was going to call the cops. They needed to move fast.

Crowbar slipped the Pajero into the underground parking garage at Hope's Nicosia apartment. The streets were still quiet, dawn coming. They'd seen no more police cars. Clay grabbed his bag and they walked up the four flights of stairs to her flat. He tapped on the door twice. She opened immediately and closed the door behind them.

She kissed Clay on the cheek, touched his arm that way she did. Then she threw her arms around Crowbar's neck, buried her face in his chest and held him a long time.

Clay dropped his bag to the floor and stood there watching them. Next to Crowbar, she seemed small and frail. Her breathing was shallow and rapid. After a while she pushed herself away from him. She looked as if she'd spent the night staring into a nightmare.

'What took you so long?' she said, her voice hoarse, cracking. She pulled a tissue from her sleeve and blew her nose.

'Any news?' said Clay.

'Nothing.'

'What about the cops?' said Crowbar.

'They've put out an alert for him. Otherwise, nothing.'

'And Pavlos?'

'He told the police that I was hiding Alexi, that I was going to try to leave the country with him. So far, though, they haven't pressed charges against me.'

Clay shook his head. 'Someone must have seen him.'

'I've spoken to every neighbour, every person I know who uses that little park – it's only at the end of the street – anyone who might have been there that afternoon. Nothing. No one saw anything. I mean, how can you take a child to a park and then just lose him?' She buried her face in Crowbar's chest again.

Crowbar let her cry.

'Did you find Rania?' she said, wiping her eyes.

'No,' said Crowbar. 'Chrisostomedes has her.'

'That asshole,' she snapped, eyes flashing.

'I'm pretty sure he has Alexi, too,' said Clay.

Hope gasped. 'My God. Where?'

'I don't know, Hope. But I intend to find out.'

She turned her face away, sobbing. 'How could anyone…?'

Crowbar walked her to the couch, sat her down. 'Have you heard anything, had any communication from Chrisostomedes?'

She straightened up, took a few deep breaths. 'Nothing.'

'You will,' said Clay

Hope sleepwalked to the little open-plan kitchen, poured herself a cup of coffee and one each for them. She wrapped her hands around the cup, clasping it to her chest. 'We have to find him,' she whispered into her cup.

'Both of them,' said Clay.

'Both of them,' said Hope. 'How?'

'Chrisostomedes' rally starts in just over an hour. I'm going to pay him a visit.'

Hope put down her cup and ran her hands through her hair. 'How about some breakfast before you go?' she said, trying a smile, failing.

Soon the flat was filled with the smells of toasting bread and frying bacon. Crowbar hunched over a plate of fried eggs, bacon, tomatoes and hot buttered toast. Hope put a similar plate in front of Clay.

'Delicious,' Clay said, mouth full.

'Playing house,' she said, frying pan in one hand, spatula in the other.

'Never played that game,' said Clay, looking over at Crowbar.

'It was fun, for a while.' She topped off his coffee. 'Until he started to hit me.' She smiled wide, pulling back her lips in a full-on grin, anger there still in her eyes, the gap in her teeth clearly showing.

Clay felt a distant fury start to simmer within him somewhere then wither on a chill gust of memory. There was no question now, none at all. He had to go back. Until he did, he would never be the man Rania deserved, never have the courage to look his own son in the eyes.

Crowbar wiped the last of the egg from his plate with a corner of toast. 'I've been looking into who owns what around here,' he said, still chewing; 'the two beaches where you found the buried cables.'

'EcoDev wants to develop Toxeflora,' said Hope. 'Royal Crown, Erkan's outfit, has already started to develop Karpasia,'

Crowbar nodded. 'Trace the majority ownership of both companies back far enough and where do you get?'

'One's a Greek Cypriot company, the other is Turkish,' said Hope. 'Neither government would allow common ownership.'

'If there's enough money to be made, anything is possible.' Crowbar took a big bite of toast and a swig of coffee.

'So tell me, Marie-Claude, for heaven's sake. What's the connection?' Hope asked.

Clay looked over at Crowbar, raised his eyebrows.

Crowbar frowned. 'It looks like EcoDev is owned eighty percent by a Cyprus-registered shell company, which is majority-owned by a Bermuda holding company. According to my contact, that holding company is owned by the Medved family.'

'Jesus,' said Clay. 'That's why Rania's been digging around in this.'

'But Royal Crown is owned by Erkan, from what I've heard,' said Hope.

'Only partially,' said Crowbar. 'Proxy companies owned by Regina Medved have a controlling interest.'

Hope gasped. Despair filled her eyes. 'So that's it,' she said. 'Of course. Kill them off, blame it on some mysterious illness, or just on general environmental decline, overfishing, disease, and your problems are gone. Up go the resorts, in come the tourists who will never even know what has been lost, happy in their ignorance, and the whole fat fucking economic balloon just keeps going up and up until there's nothing left.' She stood with her hands on her hips, breathing hard. 'It's so sad. It's too much to take in. It's so unbelievably *cynical*.'

'And the other buried lines?' said Crowbar. 'What about those?'

'The samples should have been analysed by now,' said Clay.

Hope's face set hard. 'Shit, I'd forgotten all about them.' She opened her phone and dialled the laboratory. She spoke, waited, listened. Her face blanked. 'Are you sure?' she said into the phone. 'Check again.' After a while she put down her phone and stared past them.

'What is it, *bokkie*?' said Crowbar.

Hope looked at him as if confused. 'I don't believe it.'

They waited.

'They say they never received any samples. That Maria never came in. They never saw her.'

From outside on the street came the sound of dogs barking, car doors closing. Clay walked to the window and peered through the shutters. A police car was in front of the building. Two cops were walking to the front entrance.

43

The Illusion of Mercy

Clay left Crowbar and Hope in the flat and took the stairs to the roof, emerging into the smoky calm of a winter morning. The rooftops of old Nicosia spread before him like a Cubist's cry for help, a patch-work hide of red clay tile, exhaling chimneys and weeping water tanks, the whole carapace bristling with aerials, wires and cables. He found the fire-escape, descended two flights of creaking iron stairs and hopped across to the flat, tile-strewn roof of the neighbouring building. He struck east towards Ledras Street, paralleling the Green Line where the UN blue caps still conducted regular rooftop patrols across the old walled city.

Sirens wailed in the distance. Clay quickened his pace.

Moving across the jumbled rooftop landscape, he could see people in the streets below, streaming towards the centre of the citadel. Some carried placards. Blue-and-white Greek flags flapped in the breeze. He could hear it now, too, that sound of excited people gathered together, voices cancelling, adding, echoing from the walls of build-ings, channelled up like steam from the churning streets below. As he approached Ledras Street he could see a police cordon, strung out in a wide semi-circle around the Ledras Street bunker, the manned Greek Cypriot army outpost that looked out to the Turkish side of the city across a time capsule of mined and wired UN buffer zone. He crouched next to the lip of the building's façade and scanned the rooftops. The police had taken up positions on top of at least three buildings that he could see. In bright-yellow reflective vests, they were making no effort to conceal themselves. On the Turkish side, another crowd was assembling, like an opposing army, Janissaries streaming towards the epicentre of the city, drums beating, red banners flying, crescent moons. Clay checked his Beretta, secured it back under his belt at the small of his back and pulled his jacket down on top. A ragged chant rose from the Greek side, built, then was drowned momentarily by the thrum of a low-flying helicopter. It was ten-thirty. Chrisostomedes was due to address the rally at eleven.

At a crumbling concrete parking garage two streets from Ledras, Clay descended to the street and joined the river of people. Swept along, glad for the anonymity, he was now part of the crowd streaming towards the rally point. Some people carried banners or cardboard placards. A man carried a small boy on his shoulders. The boy wore Mickey Mouse ears and held a small Greek flag, which he waved back and forth. A young woman in a business skirt and tennis shoes walked beside Clay for a while, a pair of high heels swinging from one hand. She glanced up at him for a moment then disappeared in the crowd. Everywhere the excited voices and smiling faces of people expecting to be entertained. Ledras Street was packed as far back towards the old mote as he could see, hundreds of people facing the buffer zone. Flags whipped in the breeze. A few young men had shimmied up lampposts for a better view. People lined the second-floor balconies of the storefronts, sipping tea as if watching a parade. A wooden scaffold stage had been set up not far from the border. It was draped in Greek flags. Behind, a lone Greek Cypriot flag flew from the army outpost. Clay worked his way forward through the throng, towards the stage. As he got closer, he could see the security cordon. Half a dozen men – big, bouncer types dressed in dark suits – patrolled a crowd fence that ringed the platform. More lined the approach to the stage stairs and milled in the small side street that led off the main mall. This was where Chrisostomedes would soon approach by car. The police would have cleared a back route for him, would hold it open for him when it was over.

The crowd was chanting now, pushing towards the stage. Clay was close, perhaps ten back from the crowd fence. From across the divide, the sounds of the Turkish rally rose to greet them, horns and cymbals, voices joined in angry unison, drumming. The crowd surged forward. A young man moved past him, towards the border post. As he passed, he reached into a satchel slung over his shoulder and pulled out a bottle. He disappeared into the crowd.

A cheer rippled through the air, clapping. Chrisostomedes had arrived and was moving towards the stage, his entourage in train, Rania not among them. He was dressed in a dark suit and tie. His hair shone in the sun. As he climbed the steps the crowd grew louder, the clapping more enthusiastic. He reached the podium and raised his arms.

'Nicos, Nicos,' they chanted.

From the other side of the buffer zone, a Turkish chant rose until each drowned the other.

Chrisostomedes raised a microphone, tapped on it with two fingers. The crowd quietened, letting the wave of Turkish noise sweep over them.

Chrisostomedes started to speak. His tone was calm, like that night at the dinner table – rational, reasonable. In short, clipped sentences he spoke of friends, of the mother country, of enemies. Single, simple ideas. He stopped frequently. He basked in the applause that greeted each statement, each appeal.

Clay worked his way forward until he stood four back, five metres from the stage. An easy shot on the range, but difficult enough surrounded by shifting, moving people. Chrisostomedes was building now, his voice louder, the tone more insistent, theatrical. Someone jostled Clay. He turned. The man beside him smiled, murmured something then stepped away, a stone the size of a plum clenched in his fist. Chrisostomedes finished a sentence. The exclamation point hung in the air, drifted across the rooftops. The crowd erupted into frenzied cheering. Chrisostomedes stood looking out across the crowd, watching the effect of his words on his countrymen.

A sudden movement to his left sent Clay flinching instinctively right and down. A flash of orange flame, an arm whipping forward, a flaring arc smoking up towards the border post, sailing across the narrow no-man's land. Then a burst of flame, the sound of an explosion, people screaming from the Turkish side.

Someone yelled nearby. More projectiles curved into the air, stones, flaming bottles. Outgoing. Some landed short, smashed into the border post, others fell into the churning sea of demonstrators on the other side.

And then that moment of confusion when people are still not certain that what their eyes see is actually happening. Those further back were still cheering, still chanting.

Clay watched the first Molotov cocktail come in. It was a strong throw, a catapult shot perhaps, the bottle tumbling end over end, the flaming rag spinning out black smoke. He followed it as it arced up, reached its apex. The bottle seemed to hang there, waiting for Earth to pull it back down. Total time to impact: twice the initial velocity multiplied by the sine of the angle of trajectory divided by 9.81 metres per second squared (gravity). The calculations flashed in Clay's head. Three seconds to impact. Clay counted it out, watched the thing hurtle in, held his breath.

A man standing ten metres away disappeared in a flowerburst of orange flame. Glass scythed through the crowd. People fell screaming, bleeding. Others stumbled back, pushed up against the press of the crowd trying to move forward. Stones rained down, clattering off balconies, smashing roof tiles. Clay saw a woman go down, blood gushing from her forehead, a man crouch to tend her. Everywhere was panic. Unable to retreat, the crowd surged towards the stage, trampling the barrier, streaming into the alleyway, sweeping aside the security men. Chrisostomedes held his ground, the podium now surrounded with people, an island in a raging river. He was pointing towards the Turkish side, screaming into the microphone. Clay was almost at the podium now. Another Molotov cocktail sailed in. Clay watched it start its descent. It was coming straight for him. He dropped as the bottle crashed into the base of the podium, engulfing the platform in flame. One of the security guards stumbled, burning, stood waving his arms, then fell, disappearing under the crowd. The rush had become a stampede. Chrisostomedes was still on the stage, gesticulating madly as the flames climbed around him, smoke swirling thick and heavy now in the narrow street.

Clay moved closer to the podium, held his ground against the surge of panicking bodies. Chrisostomedes looked down, the microphone still glued to his mouth, his jaw still working, the sound system still pumping out his words. He was looking right at Clay now, eyes flashing. Clay pushed forward to the edge of the stage, reached up through the flames, grabbed Chrisostomedes by the leg and pulled hard. Chrisostomedes crashed down onto the platform, bounced and hit his head on the plywood edge as Clay dragged him to the ground. The flat of his back hit the pavement with a thud, then his head.

People streamed past, oblivious, blinded by thick smoke. Another volley of stones ripped into the crowd, clattered to the ground. The security men were gone, swallowed up. Clay jammed his knee into Chrisostomedes' solar plexus and applied weight. Chrisostomedes opened his eyes, blood pooling around the back of his head.

'Where is she?' asked Clay

Chrisostomedes winced. 'You.'

'Answer me.'

'I don't know.'

Clay leant into him. 'Bullshit. She's your house guest, remember?'

Chrisostomedes grunted as the air left his lungs. 'Whoever you are, you're here illegally. You won't get far.'

Smoke swirled around them thick and blue. Clay pulled out the Beretta, pushed the barrel hard into Chrisostomedes' forehead so he could feel the muzzle cutting into his skin.

'You want to talk about illegal? You kidnapped and murdered Rania's aunt. Let's start there.'

'You can't prove that.'

Clay pushed harder on the Beretta, brought his face up close. 'Still want to be President?'

Chrisostomedes' eyes wavered. 'You wouldn't dare,' he coughed.

'How sure are you?'

A drop of blood trickled across Chrisostomedes' forehead. 'It doesn't matter anyway. I don't have her.'

Another petrol bomb whooshed nearby. More screaming, more bodies flooding past, shadows in the smoke, voices raised now, shouting, Chrisostomedes' entourage calling out to him, to each other. Clay was out of time.

'Bullshit.' Clay pulled back the Beretta, pushed the muzzle into Chrisostomedes' left calf and fired. Chrisostomedes' body jerked as the bullet blew through the muscle. He howled in pain, his voice lost in the stampede, just one more scream among hundreds.

Clay pointed the smoking barrel at Chrisostomedes' face. 'Next time is the last time.'

'I don't have her,' Chrisostomedes choked through the pain, terror in his eyes. 'I … I sold her.'

Clay pushed the gun into Chrisostomedes' forehead again, felt his finger twitch on the trigger. 'What the fuck does that mean, you arrogant son of a bitch?'

'I traded her,' he gasped. 'To Regina Medved. For the reward money.'

Clay sprang back to his feet, the implications of this staggering like a drunk through his brain. Of course. Now that Chrisostomedes no longer needed Rania to write his version of events, he'd cashed her in. It had been his plan all along, probably conceived and facilitated by Zdravko Todorov, each one thinking that they were using the other, probably congratulating themselves on their cunning. Jesus Christ. Made for each other.

Clay raised the Beretta, aimed at Chrisostomedes' head, tightened down on the trigger, rage burning inside him. Clay watched his eyes open wide then close, as if eyelids could deflect bullets. Flames reached out from the stage. People stumbled past in the smoke, ghosts. Time slowed. Projectiles rained down in graceful arcs, the din of their impact filling his head to empty it. And it was like the last time, the flood of debilitating conscience, mercy's childhood grip still tight despite the dulling. His hand shaking violently now, the screaming so loud that he could no longer tell what was real and what was in his head. Then, just a few months ago, he'd walked away, let Zdravko live. And everything that had happened since, all the death and the killing yet to come, was a direct result of that single decision. Mercy. Another illusion.

Shouting close by. The shape of someone moving through the smoke towards the podium. Chrisostomedes opened his eyes, looked up as if unsure why he was still alive. A voice calling now in the smoke, very close. Another.

Clay took a deep breath, braced his arm with the crook of his other elbow and aimed between Chrisostomedes' eyes. 'Nicos,' he said. He wanted him to see this.

Chrisostomedes opened his eyes, looked up at the gun.

'Where is Bachmann's son?'

Chrisostomedes' eyes fluttered a moment. He opened his mouth as if to speak, what Clay imagined to be a vowel – was it *I*? – forming on his lips. And then his eyes rolled up in his head and he was gone, from the pain, from the fear, or both.

Clay held the gun there for a brief moment, tried to breathe. Then he shoved the handgun into his jacket pocket, spun around and walked away into the noise and smoke.

44

The Only Thing That Mattered

At first he walked, tried to stay calm. Tried to think.

Regina Medved had Rania. It was the worst possible outcome.

He broke into a run, joining the crowds fleeing the mayhem. An ambulance screamed past, lights flashing. Clay upped his pace, running through the warren of crumbling, turn-of-the-century homes, past walled courtyards and gardens gone wild, relics of a time when cities were built for people, not cars. Breathing hard now, he passed an ancient stone church, and further on an abandoned mosque, the windows and entrance boarded up and the fraying stonework covered in graffiti, and then a row of newer warehouse buildings, seemingly unfinished, square-cut with barred windows and white neon tube lights swinging naked from concrete ceiling beams. The noise of the riot receded behind him.

As the crowd thinned, he slowed to a walk, opened his phone and dialled. 'It's me,' he said.

'What the *fok* happened down there?'

'Politics.' He looked down. There was blood splattered over his trouser leg.

'Where are you?'

'On my way to you now. He sold Rania to Medved.' More on his sleeve.

Silence on the other end.

'Call Medved, Koevoet. Call her now. Tell her you want Rania, that you have the illumination, that you'll trade.'

'Understood.'

Clay put his phone in his pocket, kept walking.

Behind him, sirens echoing from both sides of the line, the smell of burning rubber drifting over the city. So much he should have asked Chrisostomedes. There hadn't been time.

Crowbar's apartment was near Paphos gate, not far now. Just beyond was the old Ledra Palace hotel. Sitting between the Greek and Turkish lines, cut-off in no-man's land, it was the headquarters of the UN peacekeeping mission, the venue for the cross-border enquiry scheduled to begin tomorrow morning.

Clay turned into the alley behind Crowbar's building, walked into the back service entrance and took the fire stairs to the third floor. The flat was at the end of the corridor, immediately adjacent the stairwell, at the far end from the lifts. Clay knocked twice, waited, heard the chain come off, the bolt pull back. Crowbar looked him up and down and closed the door behind him.

Clay slumped into a chair and poured himself a whisky from the three-quarter-full bottle on the lounge room table. The TV flickered live images: ambulances speeding down narrow streets, smoke blanketing Ledras Street, a man with a bandaged head being helped by police, aerial shots from helicopters circling overhead, the crowds still streaming away from the border on both sides, all the sounds of it pouring through the open balcony doors. A UN helicopter thudded past close overhead, the sound of dawn hangovers under canvas in the Caprivi. He looked up at Crowbar, searching for an answer in his face.

Crowbar sat opposite, picked up the bottle, swirled the contents, lifted it to his mouth and drank. 'I called Medved.'

A capacitor tripped somewhere inside Clay, emptied him. The void held, defying him. And just when he thought it would last, fear flooded in cold and fast, a glacial torrent. 'Is Rania alive?'

'I spoke to her.'

Relief exploded inside him. Like that feeling after a barrage – the smoke and dust drifting like fog, and the smell of the earth ripped up around you, and the sounds of the wounded and dying calling for help, or just crying, and you know you have survived. '*Allah akhbar*,' he said.

'What the *fok* does that mean?'

'What did she say?'

Crowbar put his hand on Clay's shoulder, glanced at the blood on his sleeve. 'She's fine. Unhurt but scared. Who wouldn't be? We meet Medved tonight, west of town, on the Green Line. She's agreed to the deal. Get cleaned up and get some sleep, *seun*.' He handed Clay the bottle.

Clay put it to his lips and felt the whisky go into him. 'I haven't slept for ten years.' Except for that one night in Istanbul.

Crowbar frowned.

'When, Koevoet?'

'Midnight. Medved will be there. She wants to see the Illumination herself. She doesn't trust her lieutenants with this. If it's the real thing, she'll give us Rania.'

'And if it's not?'

'Don't use your imagination.' Crowbar reached down and produced first one, then the second icon and placed them on the table. Side by side, the illuminations looked nearly identical.

Clay gazed at the men falling into the abyss, the terror in their faces. He picked up one of the icons and turned it over. The backing was dark hardwood, polished with age. A square hole about the size of a fingernail pierced the centre. Clay pushed his little finger into the hole up to the first knuckle. Then he looked at the second piece. The shape and thickness of the wooden backing varied subtly between the two. There was the same kind of hole in the back of the second illumination, but its outline was more in the shape of a parallelogram, as if the square had been stepped on. Near the hole was a tiny silver fleck the size of a grain of salt. Chrisostomedes' microchip. 'We better find out.'

'Ahead of you, Straker, as always. I'm meeting the curator of the Cyprus museum at six o'clock this evening. If anyone knows, it's him.'

Clay looked at his watch, still awkward on his right wrist. 'One of them is real, at least. Question is, are they more important to Medved than revenge?'

'Medved doesn't give a shit about Rania.' Crowbar picked up one of the icons. 'This is what she wants, *ja*. She's desperate. She *believes*. Fifteen million cash. That's what she's bringing tonight. Three for you, two for that dead *bliksem* in my car, ten for this. Rania was just a lucky accident as far as she is concerned.'

'It was no accident, *Koevoet*.'

Something from the TV interrupted his thoughts. Clay grabbed the remote and turned up the volume. A policeman in a blue uniform with gold braid and a peaked cap was speaking to the cameras, a waggle of microphones jammed into his face.

'–the suspect is a foreigner, white, male, with fair hair and blue eyes,' the cop said in accented English. 'He is very tall, and is missing his left hand. He is believed to have entered the island illegally with the help of the Turkish authorities, and is armed and extremely dangerous. Anyone who may have seen this individual should contact police immediately.'

'*Goddamn*,' said Crowbar. 'Very tall?'

'It's all relative, *oom*.'

Crowbar snapped a grin.

The station cut to more footage of the aftermath: broken bottles, injured people being helped by paramedics, heads swathed in white bandages, arms in slings, fires still burning. Every emergency vehicle and policeman in the city was tied up dealing with the aftermath of the riot. And then a face he knew, the hair combed quickly back, the dark suit impeccable. Cameras flashed, hands pushed microphones towards him.

It was Dimitriou: '–the result of Turkish treachery,' he said in English, pointing behind him towards a column of smoke rising into the sky. 'This was an unprovoked attack on innocent people. For twenty years we have lived with a military occupation. One third of our country appropriated and occupied, our property stolen, our people raped and murdered while the international community stood by and did nothing. Today, Turkish agents operating inside Cyprus used this disgraceful attack as a diversion for the attempted assassination of Nicos Chrisostomedes, one of our most prominent citizens. With the help of God and our prayers, he will survive. This incident has convinced me, once and for all, that our destiny as a nation, as a European nation, as a Greek nation, can only be fulfilled with the complete and permanent withdrawal of all Turkish occupying forces from our island. This is Nicos Chrisostomedes' vision: a new Hellenic renaissance here in Cyprus, a new *Enosis*: Union with Greece. I am pleased to announce today that in the upcoming election I will be endorsing Nicos Chrisostomedes' campaign for the Presidency.'

Cheers rose in the background, clapping.

'They had this all planned,' said Clay. 'They had agitators in the crowd. I saw them. They started it, sent over the first petrol bombs.'

A question from one of the reporters, something about the transborder commission on coastal development.

Dimitriou paused, looking into the camera. 'All Cypriots should see this commission for what it is: a farce, an illegitimate attempt by outside parties to dictate to us, here in our own country, how we are to manage our affairs, our economy, our own lands and property. I have been called to testify, and I say to you now that I will not be attending this disgraceful kangaroo court.'

More cheering.

'Furthermore, I will be formally asking Parliament in session tomorrow to demand that the EU and UN dissolve the Commission, and focus its attention instead on the heinous atrocities being committed here by agents of the Turkish military and the illegitimate Turkish puppet government in Northern Cyprus.'

'Congratulations, Straker. You've now joined the ranks of the Turkish army.' Crowbar pulled on a dark jacket, checked his Beretta. 'Stay put. They'll have roadblocks up, and your picture's everywhere. I'll be back by six.'

Clay grabbed him by the arm. 'Where are you going?' He'd done it too quickly, had sounded too desperate. He let go.

Crowbar put a hand on Clay's shoulder. 'It's okay, *seun*. I'm going to see Hope. I've got some bad news for her.'

'Shit. Is she okay?'

'As well as can be expected, with her kid missing. But at least the cops aren't going to charge her. That's what they came over to tell her this morning.'

'So what is it?'

'That girl, Maria. She's disappeared.'

Clay exhaled.

'I did some checking on her. Appears she's married.'

'A lot of people are.'

'True. But not everyone is married to Dimitriou's sister's son.'

'Jesus.'

'She sold us out, *seun*.'

Blood. Here, it was everything.

'Looks like she destroyed the samples. Tipped off Hope's ex, the cops too probably.'

Trust. It was the only thing that mattered.

Without it, what did you have?

45

A Question of Faith

Clay stayed put.

He showered and found some clean clothes.

He ate.

He tried to sleep. Tried not to think.

Built surfaces and shapes in his head with double and triple integrals, saddles and spheroids, ran n-1 algorithms with sequences of prime numbers, anything.

Crowbar returned after nightfall, more than an hour late. His mouth was set in a scowl. He gathered the icons, wrapped them in the towels and put them into the black bag.

'Let's go, *seun*,' was all he said. 'Get this done.'

The museum wasn't far, a short drive through the old city. The traffic was bad, the narrow roads choked with ambulances and police cars. Clay sank low in his seat and tilted his chin to his chest. Crowbar was silent at the wheel.

By the time they arrived, the museum was closed for the day. Crowbar parked around back, a property line of big cypress trees swaying evening shadows across the buildings. Clay glanced at his watch: almost eight o'clock, the meeting with Medved still four hours away. He followed Crowbar to the back of the building – a British Empire sandstone affair of vaults, pillars and arches – scanning the perimeter gardens as he went.

Crowbar knocked on a rear service door. They waited as the light faded.

'*Kak*,' Crowbar cursed. 'I said six-thirty. Maybe he's gone.' He knocked again, harder this time.

'Or maybe he called the police.'

'I don't think so. I said I had information about the Patmos Illumination. He sounded very keen.'

Clay nodded.

Koevoet grunted something, scuffed the concrete walkway with his boot.

At last the door opened. A smallish man in a grey suit and grey woollen tie peered out at them from the semi-darkness. Thick-lensed glasses perched on a substantial and very Cypriot nose. His hair was thick and wiry, the colour of winter cloud.

'You have brought it?' he said. He sounded breathless, as if he'd just struggled up five flights of stairs.

Crowbar wedged his boot into the door and lifted the black bag that Zdravko had been carrying just a few hours earlier. The curator led them down a dimly lit, tiled corridor, past a series of closed doors, up a set of iron stairs and into an office. The room could have been in a heritage-listed government building in England – stone-mullioned windows, ancient polished wood panelling, heavy oak furniture, dark with age, the smell of book must and old leather and wood polish everywhere, something out of the 1800s. It reminded Clay of the dock in the Central Criminal Court in London, coming up the spiral iron staircase from the cells below, emerging into the chambers, staring up at the judge.

The curator sat behind his desk, turned on a table lamp. Clay and Crowbar sat in leather armchairs before him.

'Gentlemen, I must tell you,' the curator began in perfect, public-school English, wiping his eyeglasses on his shirt tail, 'I am asked to look at so-called Patmos Illuminations almost every week.'

Crowbar put the bag on the desk, unzipped it, pulled out a white towel, unwrapped it and put the first piece on the ink blotter.

The curator put his glasses back on and directed the lamplight towards the piece. For a long time he sat looking at it, tilting the lamplight this way and that, not speaking. After a while he reached out and picked it up. He handled it as if it were a landmine, as if he was afraid it would blow his hands off if he jarred it. He turned it over, gazed intently at the back for a long time. Then he put it back on the blotter.

'Where did you get this?' he said.

Crowbar glanced over at Clay, back at the curator. 'We found it in a car.'

The curator frowned, thought about this for a moment, then reached out and touched the base of the illumination with his index finger and held it there a while.

'What do you know about the Patmos Illumination?' he said, staring at them. He looked like an owl, big eyes blinking behind powerful lenses.

'Not much,' said Clay.

'The *Ladder of Divine Ascent* has been missing since the invasion. It disappeared from the Church of Aya Katerina in Karpasia in 1974 as the Turks advanced through the north. It is one of the most important historical artefacts in Cyprus, a direct link between this island, the disciples, and Christ himself.'

'Is it true what they say?' said Crowbar. 'About the blood of Christ.'

'That is what some believe. There is basis for this in historical fact. The first record of the illumination itself is from Sinai in the twelfth century. It was brought to Cyprus in the fifteenth century by Celestine, an Alexandrian monk. In the early 1970s scholars from Greece took samples of the wood on which the illumination is anchored. Carbon dating confirmed that the wood was cut in what is today Lebanon, about two-thousand years ago. Ancient scrolls speak of parts of Christ's cross being carried across the region by the disciples and used to create religious icons of all kinds. The wooden backing has long been believed to be from the cross piece. It has a hole where the nail is believed to have pierced Christ's hand.'

'*Goddamn*,' Crowbar muttered in Afrikaans. 'And the healing?'

'There are rumours, stories through the centuries of miracles, of healings.' The curator took off his glasses, reached out again and touched the edge of the illumination with his fingertips. 'I suppose it is a question of faith.'

Clay's phone buzzed in his pocket. He grabbed it, put it to his ear.

'Declan, is that you?' A woman's voice.

Clay said nothing.

'Doctor Greene? This is Katia. You remember?'

'Yes, I remember.'

Crowbar glanced at him, raised his eyebrows.

'I think I know where he is,' came Katia's voice.

'Who?'

'The person you're looking for.'

A jolt. 'I'm listening.'

'Can you come over? I'm scared.'

'Tell me where he is.'

She paused. Clay waited.

'I heard them talking,' she said.

'Who?'

'Dimitriou and Chrisostomedes. Last night. I think I know what they are doing.'

'You're a smart woman, Katia.' He could hear her smile.

'Can you come to my flat?'

'Tell me where he is, then I'll come.'

'Dimitriou owns a taverna near Famagusta Gate. Xilares, near the wall. Do you know it?'

'Yes.' It wasn't far, a couple of clicks across the old city.

'He's there. There is a house in the back. I heard them. That's what they said.'

Clay put his hand over the phone, leaned over and whispered into Crowbar's ear: 'They're holding Hope's son at Xilares.'

Crowbar nodded.

Clay looked out of the window, at his watch.

'Declan?'

'Yes, Katia.'

'What's your real name?'

He looked up at the curator. 'Clay.'

'I want to leave him.'

Clay said nothing.

'Do you believe me?' she whispered.

'I believe you.'

'Will you come tonight?'

'Yes. After I get the boy.'

Clay closed the phone, put it back in his pocket, looked at Crowbar. 'We've got to go.'

'So,' said Crowbar to the curator. 'Is it the real thing?'

The curator put his glasses back on. 'The piece is genuine, gentlemen. Very old. Beautiful.'

Crowbar glanced at Clay, grinned.

The curator cleared his throat. 'It is quite valuable, actually. It would make an excellent addition to the museum.'

Clay picked up the icon.

'What are you doing?' said the curator, eyes widening until they seemed to occupy the entire area of his lenses.

'We've got what we needed,' said Clay. 'Thanks for your time.'

'You haven't let me finish,' said the curator, out of breath again.

'Finish, then,' said Crowbar.

'As I was saying, this piece is old, and quite valuable. But I'm afraid, gentlemen, that this is *not* the Patmos Illumination.'

Crowbar leaned across the desk. 'What did you say?'

'I said: this is not the Patmos Illumination.'

Crowbar slammed his palm down on the desk. '*Kak.*'

'How can you tell?' said Clay, the implications of this spinning through his head.

The curator reached out and touched the edge of the icon. 'This piece is similar in size and composition to the original, but about two hundred years younger. You can tell by the pigmentation.'

'So it's a copy,' said Crowbar.

'No. Rather, a later original based on the same theme, influenced by the earlier work.' The curator looked up at them and frowned. 'It's called *art*.'

'Art is the guy who ran the grain elevator,' said Crowbar.

The curator looked up at him as if he was crazy.

Crowbar waved his hand, looked over at Clay. 'Arthur Brooks. Ran the grain elevator in Viljoenskroon, near where I grew up.'

The curator shook his head. 'I can understand how you mistook it.'

Crowbar nodded, took the illumination from Clay and started wrapping it in the towel.

But the curator put his hand on Crowbar's arm. 'Wait,' he said. 'Please.'

'You heard him,' said Crowbar. 'We have to go.'

'This artefact should be in a museum. It belongs to the people of Cyprus.'

Crowbar pushed the curator's hand away and continued folding.

Clay reached into the bag, pulled out the second piece, put it on the desk and flipped open the towel.

For a moment, it looked as if the curator was trying to work out just how that particular sleight of hand had been executed. His gaze flicked from the illumination on the desk before him to the towel that Crowbar still held in his hands and back again. He stared a moment, then snatched up the icon, turned it in his hands, examining every part of it. 'My God,' he gasped.

'Another original based on the same theme?' said Clay.

'What the *fok* did you do that for?' hissed Crowbar in Afrikaans.

Clay ignored him. 'Well?'

'Incredible. They are subtly different, but every detail is authentic. The work of the same artist, clearly, the same period. I will need to do tests, refer to the archives, to be sure.' He wiped his hand across his brow. '*Panamaiou.*'

'That stupid *fok* Todorov took the wrong pieces,' said Crowbar in Afrikaans, taking the second piece from the curator. 'Let's go.'

And before the academic could object, they were gone, down the corridor and back to the car.

46

A Hell of a Thing

'It's a set-up,' said Crowbar as he pulled the Pajero up onto the pavement to bypass a queue of traffic waiting to turn right onto Makarios Avenue. The vehicle lurched back onto the tarmac and sped through the intersection. 'Either they've told her to call you and tell you the boy's at Xilares, or they've made sure she overheard them. They will be waiting for you.'

'Katia's scared, Koevoet.'

'Of course she's scared. Who isn't?'

'You.' He meant it.

Crowbar laughed. '*Ja*, besides me. *Fok jou, broer*. Changes nothing. They *own* her.'

But it hadn't just been fear Clay had heard in the young woman's voice. There had been defiance there, too, lithium flaring on uncertain waters. 'They *think* they own her.'

'Be careful, *seun*. Don't invent. Always see it for what it is.'

Clay turned his face into the stream of cool night air, let it wash over him. 'We have to get Hope's son back.'

Crowbar gunned the engine, sending the Pajero flashing down Elefteria Street towards the old city. 'We're running out of time.'

Clay checked his watch again. Crowbar was right. He needed to see Katia first, hear it from her straight, look her in the eyes. If it was a set-up, and they were waiting for him at Xilares, he'd know as soon as he saw her. 'Turn here.'

Crowbar skidded the 4WD into a high-speed turn, accelerated down a side street.

'Three blocks, on the right, the apartment building.'

Crowbar pulled up a hundred metres short. The street was quiet, quaint limestone homes nestled within lush gardens, the yellow lights of evening flickering between dark, swaying branches, the sounds and smells of evening meals drifting in the air, a mother's call, a child's shriek, the clinking of pots and crockery. They sat in the darkness a moment, let silence cover them.

'What do we do about Rania?' said Crowbar. 'Without the Patmos Illumination, Medved won't deal.'

'You heard the curator. They're pretty close. All we need is a few minutes. Less. By the time Medved figures out it's not the real thing, we'll have Rania out.'

'We may not get that chance.'

'It's all we've got. We're just going to have to play it out, *broer*.'

'That's if we can get to her. The RV is out of town, west of the old airport, on the border. There will be roadblocks up at all the main roads out of the city.'

'We go the back roads, then.'

'Maybe,' said Crowbar. 'Risky. We get caught up in a roadblock and you can say a long goodbye to Rania.'

Clay looked over at the dark silhouette of his friend. 'Time for you to go, *oom*,' he said. 'You're not implicated in any of this yet. I'll take it from here.'

Crowbar smiled. '*Fok jou*, Straker. You can't do it without me. Now get going. If Katia's telling the truth, we'll go to Xilares, get the boy. They won't be expecting us.'

'And if she's not?'

'We go anyway. Fight our way in if we have to.'

Clay nodded, stepped out onto the pavement, every sense tingling, endorphins flooding his system, the biggest high. 'If I'm not down in ten, come and get me.'

Crowbar nodded, looked at him a moment then drove off, disappearing down a side street.

Clay started towards the building, careful to keep his stump in his jacket pocket. At the adjacent corner he crossed the road and stopped in the shadow of a large pine tree outside the throw of the streetlights. Katia's flat was on the southeastern corner, overlooking the road. Lights blazed. Curtains fluttered through an open patio door. From where he stood Clay could see someone moving inside, a woman. Clay stood for a while in the darkness then saw her stride out onto the balcony, light a cigarette, exhaling long with her head back, blowing the smoke up into the night. It was Katia. She'd taken three puffs when she jerked her head around, looked back into the flat. Then she flicked the cigarette over the balcony and hurried back inside. Clay watched the orange end spin like a flare to the ground and land on the pavement in a puff of embers.

Less than two hours now until the rendezvous with Medved, until Rania. Jesus, he breathed to himself, if … But he didn't allow himself to continue the thought. He buried it. Destroyed it. Focused back on what he had to do right now. That's how you stayed alive. This was what Hope had been trying to explain to him that night off the Syrian coast. It wasn't that you were forced to do things for which you were not designed. It was the exact opposite. It was a hell of a thing.

A car pulled up outside the building. Clay sank back into the shadows. A couple got out. He heard voices, laughter, farewells in English. At the doorway, the man reached into his pocket, pulled out a set of keys, fumbled with the lock and opened the glass door. Clay started moving across the street. The woman giggled as the man ushered her inside with his hand in the small of her back, drifting downward. They were inside the well-lit lobby, heading for the stairs. Clay sprinted along the pathway and grabbed the door handle just before it clicked closed.

Clay stood at the bottom of the stairwell. He could hear the couple making their way up. Whispers, a slap on bare skin, more feminine giggles, then a door closing. Silence. Clay moved quickly up the stairs, emerged onto the fourth floor landing, found Katia's door. He stood a moment in the corridor, listening. The muffled sounds of Greek pop music from the flat next door, the drone of a TV further down. Nothing from Katia's flat that he could make out. He knocked twice.

Nothing. He waited a moment, knocked again, harder this time. The sound of footsteps.

'Who is it?' came Katia's voice through the door.

'Declan.' Low.

A pause, longer than he would have expected, and then the sound of a bolt sliding back, a chain. The door opened. Katia stood before him dressed as if ready for a night on the town. A wild night.

Clay stepped inside. 'You seem surprised to see me.'

'I didn't think you'd come,' she whispered, clearly flustered. 'You said that you were going to...' She stopped. Her cheeks burned red under her thick makeup.

Clay kept his gaze fixed on her eyes. 'You asked me to come over, Katia.'

She looked down at the ground, back over her shoulder. 'I ... I thought you were going to Xilares.' She was hiding something.

'Are you sure the boy's there, Katia?'

She flicked her big fake eyelashes, looked back over her shoulder, down at the floor, then started pushing him back towards the door. With the change in light he could see that her lower lip was bruised, swollen. The lipstick had been an attempt at camouflage.

'I'm going out, please leave now,' she whispered, glancing back into the apartment again.

'Is someone else here, Katia?'

She blinked, inclined her head. She looked terrified.

Clay reached out and took her hand. 'I can help you, Katia. But you have to tell me the truth.'

There were tears in her eyes. 'I'm...' she began, sobbing now. 'Clay, I'm sorry ... Please, you must go.' She pushed him towards the door again.

All of a sudden it was clear. Crowbar had been right. It was a set-up. And if the boy wasn't at Xilares, if that was just a lure to draw him in, then there was only one other logical place he could be.

Clay clamped down on her hand, pulled her close, whispered into her ear. 'The boy's here, isn't he?'

47

Hurt

Katia closed her eyes, swallowed a sob.

Clay reached into the pocket of his jacket, pulled out the Beretta. At the sight of the weapon her eyes widened, froze there big and terrified. With his stump he guided her back towards the door, putting himself between her and the main room.

'It's okay, Katia,' he whispered. 'Don't worry. I understand. I'm not going to hurt you.'

She opened her mouth as if to speak, eyes swimming in whirlpools of tears.

'Where is he?' Clay said.

She buried her hands in her face and crumpled to the floor, pointing to the bedroom door. It was closed.

'Is he alone?'

She shook her head without looking up.

Clay knelt by her side and spoke into her ear. 'How many?'

'One,' she mouthed.

'Just call out that it's okay. Make something up. Anything. A friend came by. Can you do that for me?'

Hope dawned across her face for a moment, a realisation perhaps that things could be different for her. But in an instant her expression changed. It was fear there now. Terror. She shook her head from side to side.

'No,' she said through the tears. 'No. I can't. He'll send me back to Russia. I don't want to go back. I'd rather die.' She hid her face in her hands again.

A muffled voice from the other room: 'Katia?' A man.

Clay put his hand on Katia's back. 'Look at me.'

She shook her head, kept it buried in her arms.

'It's not him you have to worry about, Katia. You'll go to prison for this. The Cypriots take a very bad view of kidnapping.'

The man's voice again, in Greek: 'Who is it, Katia?'

'Help me,' said Clay. 'Please. We can make this right.'

'Dimitriou will kill me. He's said it lots of times.'

'No, Katia. He's finished. I'm going to finish him.'

Her eyes flashed through the tears. 'You don't know him. He knows everyone here. He is very powerful. They are all together.'

'Help me. If you do, you'll be free of him. I promise.'

She stirred, hope fighting with fear in her eyes. 'Promise?'

Clay nodded.

She sniffed, took a deep breath. He helped her to her feet. Then he closed the door, loud enough so it could be heard in the other room and signalled to her with a nod.

'*Endaxi*,' she called out in Greek. It's okay.

The man's voice from somewhere inside the apartment, in English: 'Who was it?'

She snatched a deep breath, looked at Clay. 'My neighbour,' she called out, voice unsteady. 'He is going to London on a business trip. He…' She stood. Her eyes darted right and left. A second dragged out, another. Then just as Clay thought she would freeze up altogether, she blurted out in choppy Greek, 'He wants me to water his plants while he is away. I always do it for him.'

The man laughed. 'I'm sure you do.'

Katia crisped her lips. 'Pig,' she hissed. 'One of D's men. He … he *does* things to me. D lets him. As payment.'

Clay put his arm around her shoulders. 'Okay, Katia, here's what we're going to do. I want you to call the boy. Tell him you're going to make him something in the kitchen. A treat. We're going to try to get out of here without anyone getting hurt.'

She nodded, smoothed her skirt, wiped her eyes.

'Alexi,' she called out. 'Would you like some ice cream?'

'What?' came the man's voice.

'Can he have ice cream with me?'

'Bring me some too,' called the man again.

'Go to the kitchen,' murmured Clay. 'Start getting out the stuff. Then call the kid.'

'What if he comes out?' Her voice was shaking.

Clay could see the bruises under her makeup now, felt the anger rising in him, the burning shame, too, coming hard and bloodstained and stomach-emptying. He doubled over, put his head to his knees. His heart was loping. He gulped for air, fought it back. When he looked up again, Katia was staring at him, terror in her eyes.

'Go,' he said.

Katia pushed herself forward, tottering on her heels. Clay moved to the corner of the hall. From there he could see all of the apartment's main room, the open kitchen to his right, the door to the bedroom. Katia reached the kitchen, opened the freezer, banged the ice cream container down onto the counter.

'Alexi,' she called out. 'Ice cream.'

The bedroom door clicked. The sound of Greek TV. Clay took a step back, flattened himself against the wall, the Beretta's Braille grip familiar as a recurring nightmare. He watched Katia. She smiled towards the bedroom door. Then the tacky peel of bare feet on tile. Little steps. The feet moving in an irregular shuffle, a limp. The boy.

Katia stood there with the spoon in one hand and a bowl in the other, her eyes flicking from the boy to Clay and back again, and he saw, in the harsh kitchen light, her hand and the spoon and the ice cream dripping white onto the black granite counter top.

'Where's my fucking ice cream?' yelled the man, voice louder now that the door was open.

'Coming,' said Katia, staring right at Clay, eyes wide like a terrified animal.

The boy was in the middle of the main room now, about three metres away. Clay could see the back of his head, the dark curly hair, the way he swung his left leg slowly forward without bending the knee, overbalancing on the right. Clay glanced around the corner towards the bedroom. Just the television light strobing on the far wall. He pocketed the gun and stepped towards the boy.

The boy heard him coming and twisted at the waist just as Clay reached him. His face was bruised, eyes mere slits cut in the swollen purple flesh. His lower lip was three times its normal size, split and oozing blood. Clay clamped his hand over the boy's mouth just as it opened, muffling a scream, scooped him up under the knees with his stump arm. The boy was struggling, wriggling and flapping like a landed fish, strong. Clay squeezed him hard, looked at Katia. 'Let's go,' he mouthed.

Katia dropped the spoon into the bowl, started walking.

'What's going on out there?' the man's voice again.

'Sorry, just dropped something,' said Katia.

Clay was at the door now. The boy had stopped struggling, lay panting through his nose in Clay's arms.

Clay put his mouth close to the boy's ear. 'Your mother sent me to get you, Alexi,' he whispered in English. 'You're safe. We're going now.'

The boy went limp in his arms as the fear fled.

Katia was beside them now. She opened the door, trying to be quiet, but she rushed and the bolt slid back with a loud click.

'What's going on, Katia?' the man shouted from the bedroom.

Clay pushed Katia out into the corridor, started guiding her towards the fire escape at the end of the corridor. More shouting from inside the apartment. They were about halfway to the stairs when the fire door swung open. A man burst into the corridor, back turned.

Clay swung the kid under his left arm, started reaching for his gun. The man pivoted, faced them. It was Crowbar.

'Jesus,' breathed Clay.

'We've got to hurry,' said Crowbar. 'Medved won't wait around.'

Clay looked at the boy. 'Okay, Alexi?'

The boy nodded.

Time looped back on itself and he was carrying another injured boy, back in Yemen, the kid's body wracked with radiation poisoning, and Clay, through his ignorance and selfishness, somehow responsible. And that other time, many years before, when he had pulled the trigger and the boy had bled to death in his arms, Clay cradling him just like this and the dust from the helicopter covering over everything and the gunfire so loud in his head every night since.

'This man can carry you better than me,' he said, his voice far away, over mountains.

'Jesus, they sure worked him over,' said Crowbar.

'I fought them,' the boy said.

'Good man,' said Crowbar, taking the boy in his arms. For a big man he was surprisingly gentle.

'Get them to the car,' Clay said.

Crowbar nodded. 'You?'

'Give me five minutes.'

'We don't have five minutes.'

'Two, then.' Clay turned away. Someone was going to get hurt after all.

Crowbar reached out his hand, grabbed Clay's shoulder. 'No, *seun*,' he said. 'Not this time.'

48

Each Minute Has a Price

Crowbar gunned the engine and the Pajero shot down the narrow lane.

'*Goddamn*,' the glottal Afrikaans was clear over the whine of the diesel. Crowbar jerked the Pajero onto the broad carriageway of Elefteria Avenue, the centre-median palms swaying in the breeze, lights burning in the tavernas that lined the set-back lanes. Crowbar glanced over his shoulder at Katia and the boy huddled together in the back seat.

'How long do we have?' asked Clay.

'About half an hour.'

'How far from the RV?'

Crowbar leant on the horn, brushed past an old man in a vintage Hillman. 'Not sure. About that, maybe a bit more.'

Up there, not far, was the border, the Green Line, the demilitarized zone between Turkish and Greek forces. In places up to two miles wide, a meandering, twenty-year confusion of sandbagged emplacements, barbed-wire entanglements and anti-tank ditches, the farm fields and hills sown with thousands of anti-personnel and anti-tank mines. And dotted along this wandering scar, from Kato Pyrgo in the west to Deryneia in the east, a rusty wire and sandbag necklace of UN observation posts. Out there, where they were going, the blue cap patrols were few, the posts widely spaced, the lines far apart.

Clay looked back at Katia, smiled at Alexi. 'We can't take them with us,' he said to Crowbar. 'It's too dangerous. And now that we have the boy, Hope will be their target. We have to get to her.'

'We don't have time, Straker. The old bitch is jumpy as hell. I tell you, *broer*, if we're late, she flies. You can guess what that will mean for Rania.'

Clay swallowed. 'Call Medved.'

'What?'

'Call her now. Tell her you're caught in traffic. Anything. Tell her we need fifteen more minutes. That'll do. If she's as desperate for the illumination as you say, she'll wait.'

Crowbar shrugged, pulled out his phone, flipped it open, hit speed dial, put it to his ear. He spoke in Russian, listened, spoke again, straight-arming the Pajero through the midnight traffic towards the edge of the city. Then he closed his phone, frowned and pushed hard on the accelerator. The Pajero lurched forward.

For a while he said nothing, just manhandled the vehicle through the traffic. And then he said, voice flat: 'The bitch will wait. Fifteen minutes. But we don't have time to get Hope. And these two will have to come with us. Tell the girl to keep the kid quiet. They need to get down on the floor and stay out of sight. You too, Straker.'

A police cruiser flashed past in the other direction, lights strobing.

Clay twisted in his seat, faced Katia and Alexi in the backseat. 'Did you hear that?'

They both nodded, eyes wide in the glow of the streetlights, the flash of headlights from the road.

Katia unbuckled her seat belt, then the boy's, and slid down with him into the space between the edge of the backseat bench and Crowbar's chair back. As she did, her minidress hiked up over her thighs. The delicate pale skin was scarred with red linear welts, as if she had been caned. She curled up on the floor and pulled the boy to her. Except for the bruises and cuts they looked like a newborn antelope and its mother, all arms and legs, tawn and black, the pale of her skin, the boy's big dark curls.

Clay nodded to her, looked into the boy's eyes. 'We'll see your mother soon,' he said. 'Okay?'

Alexi nodded.

They were close to the outskirts of the city now, on the old Kako-petria road, the Nicosia airport on the bluff looming ahead, scene of the fiercest fighting of the invasion, now off-limits to all except the UN peacekeeping force.

'*Moeder van God*,' cursed Crowbar. In the distance ahead, flashing red-and-blue lights, white illumination, traffic tailed back. A roadblock.

Crowbar turned sharp right, towards the airport. The Pajero lurched from side to side on the road. They hit the shoulder, skidded across the gravel. Katia screamed. Stones cracked off the windscreen. The passenger compartment was full of dust, thick, choking. Crowbar gunned the engine, fighting to control the vehicle. It swerved, righted, regained the tarmac.

'Where the hell are you going?' said Clay.

'Through the UN base. With all the roadblocks up, it's our only way out of the city. I know the senior officer there. He'll take us through.'

'How?'

'Let's just say that I'm his retirement plan.' Crowbar dialled a number on his phone. 'Don't worry. We go in, come out the other side.'

'But what about Hope, Koevoet? They'll kill her.'

'Command decision.' In Afrikaans. 'Best result, cheapest price. How the *fok* do you think I got all you *fokken* babies through the war alive? I made *decisions*.'

'We still have time.'

'Not enough.'

'Call Medved again.'

'Each minute has a price, Straker.'

'Spare me the homilies.'

'*Homilies*? *Fok*, Straker, I don't even know what that means.'

'Jesus Christ, what price?'

Crowbar slowed the vehicle; they were approaching the main entrance to the UN base.

'Koevoet.'

Crowbar stretched his back, rolled the vehicle to a halt. 'The perverted old bitch said we could have as much time as we wanted.'

As he heard the words, Clay's vision collapsed, fear pushing in from all sides like nothing he had ever felt, even in the worst days.

'Each minute, one step,' said Crowbar. At the last word, his voice wavered. Just a little. If you didn't know him, it was imperceptible. But for Koevoet, it was almost panic.

Clay's heart stopped.

'Rania is blindfolded. They've sent her out into the minefield. Each minute we're late, they force her one more step forward.'

49

Dark Wells of Gravity

Led by Crowbar's contact – a Lieutenant Colonel in the British Army and commander of the base – it took them less than twenty minutes to clear the UN checkpoint, make their way across the derelict airport and discreetly emerge on the far side of the base though a little-used, overgrown exit in the wire.

Crowbar launched the Pajero along a gravel road, heading west. Minutes sped by.

'There,' said Crowbar, slowing the Pajero.

Up ahead, an abandoned farm house, barely visible in the weak moonlight, a line of old pine trees, the branches overhanging black and heavy, and the road T-ing into a gravel track that ran parallel to a barbed-wire fence. Beyond the fence, the open ground of the buffer zone.

A black panel van was parked, lights off, about twenty metres from the intersection. Ten metres behind, close to the wire, was another vehicle, a dark Mercedes saloon. Crowbar rolled the Pajero to a stop.

Clay said over his shoulder, 'Keep down and keep quiet, Katia. And whatever you do, stay put.'

Nothing.

'Understood back there?'

'Yes.' Katia's voice, scared. And then, 'Yes.' Alexi.

'Give her Todorov first,' said Clay in Afrikaans, pulling back the Beretta's action, the grip between his knees. 'We get Rania, then she gets the icon.'

'She'll want you, too,' said Crowbar.

'If she wants me, fine. We won't have much time before she figures it's not the real thing. Once you've got Rania, don't worry about me. Get her out of here, Koevoet.'

Crowbar opened his mouth to speak.

Clay cut him off. 'I know what you're going to say, *oom*. The answer is no. Get Rania. If you have to leave me, do it. I can look after myself.'

Crowbar sat there a time in the dim light from the moon and the car's instrument panel. And then he said: 'Keep your hands behind your back, like you're tied. Stay in the car till I come get you. Act like you're banged up, *ja*.'

'I *am* banged up.'

Crowbar gave him a quick smile. 'Once we're out there, play my lead, Straker. We'll get you both out, understand? Don't want the old bitch wanking herself off over you.'

Clay peered into the darkness. A lone figure was standing next to the panel van, on the side of the track near the barbed wire. He was holding an assault rifle. 'Shooter, right of the van, five metres.'

'Got him,' said Crowbar. 'Let's do this thing as quick as we can, go get Hope. Just like Angola. Okay?'

'Hope.' Clay had almost forgotten. He reached into his pocket, took out his phone and dialled her apartment. She answered first ring.

'It's Clay.'

'*Panamayou*, where have you been?'

'We've got Alexi.'

Silence. And then, 'What did you say?'

Clay passed the phone into the back. 'Talk to your mum, Alexi.'

A hand took the phone, and then hushed voices, cries of joy through the line.

After a moment Clay took the phone back. 'It's me,' he said. 'Look, Hope, without Alexi as a hostage, they're going to come after you. Is there somewhere you can go?'

Breathing down the line, deep, fearful, elated. 'Yes. A friend's place, a small flat in the old city near the Green Line,' her words were rapid, clipped. She gave the address.

'Go there. Now. We'll bring Alexi. Just sit tight, be invisible.'

'What about Rania? Is she safe?'

'We're going to get her now.'

'Thank you, Clay. Thank you.'

Clay closed the phone.

Crowbar nodded, rolled the Pajero forward, the tyres crunching on the gravel, and stopped fifty metres from the van, the wedge of the Pajero's headlights illuminating the front of the van, the rusted red-and-white sign hanging from one of the fence posts, painted with a skull and cross-bones, and the words *danger, mines*, in big red letters. The man by the wire raised a hand to shield his eyes from the light, the AK47 he carried pointing out beyond the fence, towards the Turkish lines. Clay followed the line of the man's weapon out into the darkness and across the dry, hummocky no-man's land of the minefield. A lone figure stood about thirty metres away, barely visible in the dark, facing the Turkish side, unmoving, arms wrapped around herself against the cold.

'Jesus, Koevoet,' Clay said.

'I see her.'

Clay clenched his fist behind his back. 'How the hell are we going to get her out?'

'We'll figure it out.'

'*Hulle sterf.*' They die.

'No, Straker. We get her out, clean as we can, then we get the boy out of here and we go for Hope. Okay, *seun*?'

Clay could hear the words, faint starlight blinking through a thickening night of hate, Crowbar's voice drowning in the genetic roar inside his head. He dropped his head to his knees, concentrated on the air filling his lungs, holding it there, pushing down, slowly letting it go.

And then Crowbar's voice again. '*Seun*? You okay?'

Clay sat up. The van's headlights had come on. 'Just like Angola.'

Crowbar nodded, opened his door, stepped out onto the gravel and slammed the door behind him. Clay watched him walk across the dual-lit distance between the vehicles, stop short of the van, stand arms extended at his sides. The shooter by the wire registered him with a glance, kept his weapon trained on Rania. Clay could see her dark silhouette. She'd turned now, stood facing them. She was blindfolded. He spoke the name of her god, and called on him to protect her and wished with all of himself that it could be him out there now instead of her. But just as quickly, he let it go. Such distractions got people killed. There was only now, only what it was.

The front passenger door of the panel van opened. A man got out. He was tall, slim. An Uzi hung from his neck. He walked towards Crowbar and stopped ten paces from him. Clay could see the man's mouth moving, and then, on the night breeze, the muffled sound of voices. The two men spoke for a while and then Crowbar turned away and walked back to the Pajero, long calm strides. As he passed Clay's open window he said: 'Phase one.' He opened the back of the vehicle, hoisted Zdravko's body up over his shoulder in a fireman's carry, slammed the tailgate closed and walked back towards the van. The man with the Uzi had returned to his spot and now waited for Crowbar, a metal case in his left hand. Crowbar got within about five metres, stopped and dumped the body on the ground, face up. It landed with a dull thud, that lifeless grain-sack sound that once you've heard you can never forget. Crowbar stepped back.

The man with the Uzi paced forward, shone a torch in the corpse's face and turned the head with his boot. Then he raised his hand, gave the thumbs-up back to the van and tossed the case to Crowbar.

Voices again, Crowbar pointing out into the minefield at Rania. The man with the Uzi shook his head, pointed at the Pajero, at Clay. Crowbar, shifting his stance, his voice louder now, clear on the wind, saying, 'No. The girl first. Then the Illumination. Go tell your boss.'

Damn it, Koevoet.

The man with the Uzi stood a moment, weighing up what this big Afrikaner had said, by now surely feeling the presence of this man, the sheer will. Then he turned away and walked back to the van. He leaned into the passenger window a moment then came back out to face Crowbar. More talking, voices raised. Then Uzi shouted something and the shooter by the wire raised his weapon and trained it on Rania.

Clay's heart lurched, hammered out a few panicked beats, hung there as the fractions of time that make up a second ticked by, aeons in each. And then Crowbar's voice and the rifle lowering and his heart beating normally again and Crowbar striding back towards the car.

Crowbar went to the driver's-side door, threw in the case, grabbed the bag containing the Illumination, pulled out his Beretta, came around to Clay's door and opened it.

'Out, Straker, and make it convincing. The old bitch wants you first. Who would've guessed it?'

Clay grabbed his stump in his right hand, kept his arms tight behind his back. In the darkness they would never be able to tell his arms weren't tied. Crowbar made as if to free Clay's legs, grabbed his hair, jerked him out of the car and stood behind him. 'Walk,' he said.

Clay moved across the car-lit gravel towards the van. As they got close, Uzi shone his torch in Clay's face. Clay narrowed his eyes against the light, kept his head high, let them have a good look.

'Stop,' said Uzi.

Clay complied, Crowbar behind him with the Beretta cocked and loaded and jammed into Clay's side. Convincing enough.

The van's engine started. It rolled forward and stopped beside them. The panel door slid open, engine still running.

It was the eyes that Clay would always remember. Not the platinum wig that looked as if it had come straight out of the sixties, or the crudely applied cherry-red lipstick smeared over thin, withered lips, the undertaker's rouge applied to the yellow skin slumping over the jutting cheekbones, or the plastic tube sprouting from the right nostril, the frail, slumped shoulders, the concentration-camp arms, each pierced with a catheter, the tubes recycling some fluid of horrible opacity, the lights and filters and pumps of the dialysis machine blinking behind her like an airliner's control panel. None of that.

The woman who faced them now across a thick pane of bullet-proof glass, slumped in a wheelchair set in the van's cargo platform, stared out at them through eyes of an intensity and depth such as he had never seen. They seemed afire, consumed, more determined, more enraptured even than those of the supplicants awaiting their turn on the Ladder of Divine Ascent.

'He will kneel,' said Regina Medved. Her voice was deep, almost mechanical, muffled by the glass, filtered through a speaking grille set just below her mouth, like the ones at train station wickets.

Crowbar jammed his boot into the back of Clay's knee. Clay crashed to the ground, keeping his arms behind him.

'For you, my brother's killer, all the devil's horrors.' She ran her tongue over her wizened lips, a deathly flush on her cheeks. 'Hours will pass as centuries and you will beg for my satisfaction.' She inclined her head.

Uzi opened the front passenger door, threw another aluminium case onto the ground.

'Your money, mercenary,' said Regina Medved. And then to Uzi: 'Take him.'

Uzi moved to grab Clay by the head, but Crowbar blocked his arm with his handgun. 'The woman first.'

Clay could see her, unmoving in the darkened field, the shooter still there, just a few long steps away, weapon at the ready.

Medved's index finger twitched, her hand crisped around the chair's arm. 'Our agreement is distinct from this,' she rasped.

Crowbar raised his hand, let the bag sway. 'The Illumination is right here. Give me the woman.'

Her eyes flicked left then right, narrowed. 'What is she to you, this harlot with the devil's child, next to these millions?'

'That is my business.'

'No, it is mine. I caused her to be here. She is here because she owes *me* penance.'

Clay's pulse lurched. Of course. This was not some accident of coincidence, some perturbation of chance. She *wanted* her here.

Somehow, Medved had manipulated LeClerc into sending Rania to Cyprus. Clay remembered LeClerc's cryptic tone when he'd called him from Santander, the fear in his voice, the unfinished statements, as if he'd wanted to tell him something important but couldn't bring himself to do it. To tell him *this*. Fear did hard things to a man. But it didn't matter now. Rania went to Cyprus and when Medved had got what she wanted from LeClerc, they'd killed him, slowly and brutally. If Chrisostomedes and Todorov hadn't got to Rania first, Medved would have killed her too. Now she was one step away.

Crowbar raised the bag higher. 'Do you want it or not?'

Medved's finger twitched, then swung slowly to point at Clay. 'But this one, this soon to be ash, he was with her in London, in Istanbul. *He* wants the woman.' Her eyes were burning now, two dark wells of gravity in the vacuum of space. 'Yes,' she hissed. 'Yes. Of course. She carries his child. She is fat with it.' She hung on this for a moment, and then the corner of her mouth opened and that part of her bottom lip fell away. Behind, the teeth were dark and foul. 'He is your rival.'

Crowbar shifted his feet, dropped his arm with the bag to his side, the black handgun still in the other, said nothing.

'Yes. It is this. Even polluted and stinking with another man's issue, you lust for her. She softens your mind, mercenary. She weakens you.'

Crowbar spat into the gravel, muttered something in Afrikaans. 'Let her go and you can have your icon. I had it verified by the Cyprus Museum today – it's authentic.'

'This I already know.' Medved turned her head towards the back of the vehicle.

Clay heard the rear door open, someone step to the ground. A small man dressed in a grey suit approached them. He carried a metal case identical to the one that now lay on the ground at Crowbar's feet. A headlamp was strapped across his forehead. It was the curator from the museum.

'Verify,' she said.

Crowbar slung one strap of the bag over his shoulder, unzipped it and beckoned the curator forward.

'Here we go,' Crowbar said under his breath, in Afrikaans. 'You take the one by the wire. I've got the one here close. After that, fire at will. Wait for my signal.'

Clay flexed his shoulder muscle so Crowbar would feel it in his hand, felt for the Beretta's grip.

The curator approached, blinking through thick lenses.

'Good to see you again,' Crowbar said.

If the curator was surprised, he betrayed no evidence of it. He shrugged and switched on his headlamp, reached into the bag.

Crowbar grabbed his arm, holding it firm. 'Inspect it where it is,' he said.

A hiss escaped from the curator's lips. He leaned in so that his head was inches from the bag. After a moment he stood back and Crowbar let go of his arm. The curator looked at Medved.

'Tell me,' she said.

'Steady,' said Crowbar.

The gun in Clay's hand now, behind his back.

The curator nodded. '*The Ladder of Divine Ascent*,' he said.

Either the bastard had lied to them at the museum, or he was lying to Medved now.

'The one and only,' said Crowbar, exhaling, looking straight at the curator. 'Isn't that right?'

The curator shuffled his feet, cleared his throat. 'Yes, of course. It is completely unique.'

Medved sighed. It sounded like methane escaping from a bloated corpse. She nodded to the curator, who set the case on the ground next to Crowbar and stepped aside. Then she looked at Uzi, inclined her head.

Uzi raised his weapon, and before Clay or Crowbar could react, let go a short burst. The curator slumped to the ground, riddled with holes.

'*Kak*,' said Crowbar.

Uzi smiled, lowered his weapon.

'Take it,' said Regina Medved. 'Ten million dollars.'

Crowbar glanced over at the curator's motionless body, then kicked the case away with his foot.

'You will take my money, mercenary, you will give me this Judas, and you will go.' Medved nodded to the driver, who shouted something to the man by the wire. He lowered his weapon, took a step away from the wire. 'Take the whore. She is nothing.'

The words sent dopamine surging through Clay's veins. They still had to get her out of the minefield, but at least they weren't going to be shot at while they did it. He slid the Beretta back into his belt, stared hard at the ground, willing his eyes dull and resigned.

Crowbar pulled the bag's strap from his shoulder, zipped it closed and threw it into the van. The bag landed at Medved's feet, only the glass now separating her from it. She called out something in Russian. The driver appeared, grabbed the bag, disappeared back into the van, and handed her the icon on the other side of the glass. She held it in both hands, the splinters of her fingers searching over the wood, caressing, fondling, finding the nail hole, penetrating. She looked up. Her eyes were aflame, feverish. She gasped, closed her eyes. Then she reached back behind her and flipped a switch. Dialysis lights flickered and died, pumps spun down, fluids stalled in tubes.

'The Judas who killed my brother,' she said. 'Give him to me. Two million as we agreed.'

Clay hung his head. Money being thrown around like empty beer cans at a Battalion piss up.

'Keep it,' said Crowbar, grabbing Clay by the hair, pulling his head back, putting the Beretta's muzzle cold against his temple. 'Let *me* have him.'

Uzi was to Clay's right, the shooter just beyond, still at the wire, but facing them now, watching them, the muzzle of his rifle pointing away from Rania.

Medved sat fondling the icon, staring out at them from across the glass. Clay kneeling in the road, Crowbar's handgun pressed into the side of his head, Rania still out there, blind and unable to move.

Then Medved coughed into a handkerchief, gazed down for a moment at the issue and raised her eyes. 'No,' she said, voice like iron on old splintered wood. 'No.' Then she twisted her head and faced the driver. The movement was surprisingly quick. 'Kill her,' she said.

50

The Blind and Ruthless Levers

Evolution never stops. Its time is measured not in seconds or centuries, but in generations – sex and death the blind and ruthless levers. Can a man evolve, or can he only put his hope in those that follow him, in those that he may cause to follow?

As Claymore Straker knelt in the pale illumination of the headlights, his fingers reaching for the grip of the loaded Beretta hard and clean against the base of his spine, hearing Regina Medved's muffled words projecting through the cool night air, watching the van's driver register those words and turn his head towards his colleague standing by the wire at the edge of the minefield, the moon pale and thin above the Pentadactylos in the distance, he knew that in himself evolution was retrograde. Inside him, a lower order had emerged, purer, shorter-lived.

The man by the wire turned to face Rania, started to raise his rifle.

The gun was in Clay's hand now, coming forward. Uzi had seen what was happening and had started to react, was raising his weapon. Koevoet, too, was moving, bending into a crouch, his Beretta coming up, Medved there behind her ballistic polycarbonate laminate, fondling that amputated arm-end of crucifix, finger-fucking the hole, those eyes burning with a fervour almost divine, anaerobic, watching all of this unfold before her like some *Macbeth* of the mind.

Clay fired first. The shooter by the wire spun, fell just as Crowbar's 9mm erupted behind Clay's right ear. Uzi piled into the ground, a gaping hole in his chest. Clay was already on the move, sprinting towards the wire. Behind him, the muffled sounds of gunfire, the bark of an AK, car doors slamming, tyres spinning on gravel, headlights jerking across the road, over the fallow minefield. The second car, the Mercedes, was backing away now, engine screaming. Someone was leaning from the passenger window firing a handgun. Clay could hear the pop-pop-pop, see the muzzle flashes, was even aware that the bullets were intended for him. But he was indifferent to it all. He was at the wire now, the shooter immobile on the ground, the AK's muzzle hanging oblique on the lowest strand of wire. Rania standing dark in the empty, moon-grey field, thirty metres away. More firing now, Crowbar banging away at the retreating vehicles, muzzle flashes in the darkness. A round pinged from the steel fencepost beside him. And then, from the far side of the buffer zone, a loud whoosh and a thin line of grey smoke rising into the night sky.

'Rania,' he shouted. 'It's me, Clay. Crouch and hide your eyes. Now.'

It was all he had time to say before the flare ignited. Clay crouched, the phosphorous burning above him. The ground at his feet lit up white, shadows lurching and tottering like drunks across the barren landscape. He scanned the ground for footmarks, any sign of the path Rania had taken as they'd forced her through the minefield, but there was only the hummocky ground scattered with thousands of jerking shadows. And then, from the Turkish lines, the flash of tracer, red and slow and fast, arcing towards and above and past him, followed by the thunk thunk of a heavy machine gun. Rania huddled close to the ground, illuminated by the flare, in clear view. Clay rose, took a bearing, trod on the lowest strand of rusty wire, pried the next up with his hand, crouched low and stepped into the minefield. Then he took a deep breath and started running.

If the Turks and Greeks had laid anti-personnel mines as the Cubans had taught FAPLA and SWAPO to do in Angola, they would be randomly spaced within bands of variable density running orthogonal to the expected direction of movement of enemy troops. No straight lines, no patterns, nothing remotely mathematical or predictive that you could use. It had been a Russian-made PMN antipersonnel mine that had blown off Bluey's legs that day outside

Mavinga, a steel casing wrapped around 250 grams of trinitro-toluene, about the size of a can of tuna. That's all it took. One minute you were walking through the tall grass of the *chana*, waving the flies from your eyes, watching the late-afternoon sun slanting shadows across the wind in the grass, the next you were on the ground staring wide-eyed at the charred stump of bone where your thigh use to be. This minefield was laid twenty years ago. Clay could only guess at the tactical circumstances of the time. And even if any of that could be known or deduced, there was no time.

Clay moved fast, kept his stride long. Twenty footfalls between them now, the calculations automatic, unwanted, each kiss of the ground a Poissonian process, independent of the one before, mine or no mine, anywhere from a one-in-twenty to one-in-thirty chance, he figured. The closer he got to her, the better the odds, the past of no statistical bearing on the future. Tracers flashed above his head, swip swip. Close. The sound of the machine gun hammering. He was fifteen metres in now, halfway, still going, limbs still intact. In the flarelight he could see her struggling with the blindfold, trying to push it from her eyes with her shoulder. Only ten metres from her now, Clay moving fast, feet barely touching the ground.

'I'm coming Rania,' he shouted. 'Straight line from the dead guy by the wire. Stay low.' Blindfolded, she would have no way of knowing which way she had gone in. Another burst of tracers, closer now. Last warning.

She looked up in his direction just as the flare died. Darkness enveloped them. Silence. A few more strides now only, flying over the ground as if he could somehow minimise contact, skim over its surface. He was going to make it. They were going to make it.

And then, behind him as his trailing foot left the ground, a click. He knew that sound, knew what would come. His stomach con-tracted, anticipating the blast. He was moving fast, almost to her now, would shield her from the blast. She could walk back out, follow his line, step where he'd stepped. Koevoet would be waiting for her, would talk her through it. Down, he yelled to her. His body

PAUL HARDISTY

tensed, started curling, instinctively minimising surface area. A second passed, another. Seconds? Fractions? Time playing tricks on him now, slowing to a near stop, his demise witnessed in absolute clarity. But no, a second. Another. Jesus, a dud. Can you believe it? After twenty years in the ground, yes, a dud. Thank Christ. Still nothing. Some luck. He smiled, Rania there now, close. He slowed and spoke her name.

The force of the blast ripped into the back of his legs, lifting him and hurling him into her.

51

Violence Having Been Done

This proximity, dreamed of, so long anticipated. The feeling of her close to him, their bodies pressed together so that he could not tell which was her and which was him, arms and legs and lips and hair, short, fast breaths and fingertips and hearts going hummingbird-fast, so close each to each, and he could smell her hair and that smell of wild veldtgrass and lemon blossom that would always be her, and the other too, freshly opened earth, that spade-cut, brown-wet clay smell, like a trench or a grave, and the flint-spark sharpness of deto-nation, the drifting cordite from the Turkish lines, and now, sweet and heavy, the smell of blood.

As his head cleared he reached for her, opened his eyes. He'd been thrown into her and he'd hit her hard. She was pinned beneath him. He reached out with his stump, pushed himself up, rolled off her onto his side, facing her. Pain shot through his legs, a searing that spread from the backs of his knees to just above his tailbone where the shrapnel had caught him, and the familiar wet-glue feeling of blood on skin.

She lay on her side, knees to her chest, head to her knees, unmoving.

'Rania.' He reached over and pulled off her blindfold, untied her hands. Her face was streaked with mud, tear tracks through the earth.

She opened her eyes.

His heart stopped.

'Claymore.' Her voice was wire thin.

Shouts from the Turkish line, scattered rifle shots. At the wire, the dark shape of the man Clay had killed. Beyond, the gravel track and three other bodies prostrate and dark on the silver gravel. Medved's van and the Mercedes were gone. There was no trace of Crowbar or the Pajero.

Clay pushed himself up on one elbow, looked back to the dark, low ridgeline that marked the Turkish line. There had been no more flares, no more shooting for a couple of minutes now. They would have seen the vehicles depart, seen and heard the mine go off. It wouldn't be long before the Greek Cypriot Army would be on the scene, or the UN. The nearest post couldn't be far.

Silence reigned, the quiet of violence having been done.

'We're going to get out of here,' he said.

'*Mon dieu*,' she gasped. 'You are hurt.'

Clay tried to move his legs. It hurt like hell, but they were working. He got to one knee, bit back a groan, let the coarse deluge flow through him. He looked out over no-man's land.

'Okay, Rania. Here we go. Just take my hand, follow me close. Walk in my foot marks. It's going to be *lekker*.'

He reached for her hand. It was cold, her grip weak.

'Here we go,' he said.

He stood, stayed in a crouch, pulled her gently up.

She gasped, hissed between clenched teeth, stood doubled over at the waist, her hands over her abdomen, legs trembling.

'Rania, what's…'

She sank to her knees, cramped over.

Clay knelt beside her, pulled one of her hands away from her abdomen. It was covered in blood, thick and viscous.

She collapsed into him. 'I'm sorry,' she whispered, and then she was gone.

There was no time, there were no options. Clay reached his good hand behind her shoulders, levered her body up, slipped his stump under her legs, cradled the backs of her knees in the crook of his elbow, pushed himself to his feet and started towards the road.

If the Turks had seen them, and he had every reason to believe that they had, silhouetted in the moonlight on that barren field of fire, staggering a few steps, resting, another step towards the wire and the road and the edge of the buffer zone, then they had decided they were not a threat. They would have the high-powered night vision lenses on them now, would see that they were unarmed and injured.

Clay swayed, rebalanced, stepped long for the next footmark. Blood squeezed between his toes as their combined weight compressed his boots. Sweat ran cold down the gutter of his spine. Voices drifted from the Turkish emplacements as he carried the only person he'd ever truly adored, limp and so pale in his arms like a new bride, her head thrown back, her long hair swaying with each stride. Another step, her delicate, powerful, beautiful, damaged body heavy through his legs. One more. Again. Two more steps. Almost there. He could see Crowbar now, standing on the other side of the wire, urging him on. The Pajero was there behind him, lights extinguished.

By the time he reached the wire, Clay's arms were wet with Rania's blood. He collapsed his weight into the top strand of the wire and passed Rania over to Crowbar. The barbs cut through his jacket, dug into his abdomen. Crowbar carried her to the Pajero and lay her in the backseat. Clay scrambled through the wire. In the distance now, a flash of red and blue lights, police or military approaching.

Clay staggered into the Pajero, squatted on the floor beside Rania, felt the shrapnel dig into him. Through the encroaching pain he could see Katia and Alexi staring up at him with wide eyes. And then they were moving, Crowbar speeding the Pajero through the night.

Clay touched Rania's face. She was still breathing, but unconscious. He pulled open her blouse and exposed the wound, a puncture no bigger than a milk tooth just below the base of that fine rib cage. He reached around behind her, moved his hand along the smooth silk of her back, could feel no exit wound. Not a bullet. She had been facing him when the mine had exploded. He hadn't taken it all. Somehow a piece had reached her.

'Shrapnel,' he shouted over the din of the engine.

'*Moeder van God,*' said Crowbar. 'Hold on.'

Clay could feel himself drifting away, the pain in his legs dominant now, crowding out any control he had left. 'Get her to a hospital,' he managed. 'Keep her safe, Koevoet.'

Part V

52

Should Have Been Twenty

23rd November 1994: Just outside Nicosia, the Green Line, Cyprus

He was walking on the morning edge of a sandstone cliff. He stopped and looked out over a splitting chasm, the rock face disappearing in a vertical plunge to the wadi floor. Through the heat haze, he could see the thin, drawn-metal thread of a river, a cluster of mud-brick buildings, more scattered along the base of the far cliffs, patches of greenery following the places where water might be, everything as seen from the window of an airliner, drifting past in pressurised serenity. He knew this place, or parts of it, the broad trench of the Wadi Hadramawt, and down there now, suddenly close, a column of people moving in slow cadence across the dry plain. Tiny figures in black, throwing up a wake of dust. Men and women, dozens of them, trudging towards the cliff. He knew these souls. Each individual's gait and dimensions of limb, each tilt of head, was known to him. Rania was there, and Abdulkader, though Clay knew he was dead, and Eben too, at the start of the war when he was still Eben, and Kingfisher and Bluey with both his legs, and others dead and living from that place and others. They were looking up at him now through the mist, eyes wide, calling to him, their mouths dark voids opening and closing, though he could not hear what they were trying to say. He called out to them from the clifftop, but they could not hear him. A drum banged in the distance. He searched the valley bottom for the drum but could see nothing, just the column moving closer to the cliff and the dust rising from their feet. Again the sound of the drum echoed from the valley walls, up the miles of smooth, red sandstone and he knew it was calling him. Clay leaned out over the edge, arms wide. The current of air rising from below held him suspended above the void like an invisible pair of hands so that he could see clear down, the whole cliff-face there below him and the faces looking up at him and the bang of the drum and the wadi floor so far below that it would take a lifetime of falling to reach it.

He jumped.

And suddenly the cliff edge was the cargo door of a Hercules and he was falling away from it, and as the ground floated up towards him, he knew that he could not go back, that even here time moved in one direction only and its tyranny was absolute. His right hand moved instinctively for the rip cord but he knew no canopy would blossom above to carry him gently to Earth, and he knew Eben was not there behind him, nor Koevoet, nor any of *Valk 5*, living or dead, and the ground pulling him down was not the green of Angola now but the dead, dry dune ground of some other place, and then, closer, voices, faint at first, louder now, blunted somehow, muffled.

You killed them.

Yes, he heard himself answering. I killed them.

And the woman?

Rania.

Who is Rania?

She's there. I can see her.

Where is she?

There, in the wadi, looking up at me.

Did you kill her too?

Clay opened his eyes.

He was lying face down in a hospital bed. Sweat covered every part of his body. He could smell the laundry-fresh smell of the sheets, the antiseptic clean of the linoleum floor, the smell of his own sweat. Daylight shone white and diffuse from a louvered bank of windows. He tried to move his legs, but they were as if made of softwood, spongy and unresponsive. His skull ached. Clay ran his tongue around the parched desert of his mouth, tried to swallow.

Slowly, his vision sharpened. A private room. Whitewashed walls. A stainless-steel wash basin, a chair, an IV stand beside the bed, tubes running into his arm. Outside, the washed afternoon sawing of palm fronds, a couple of derelict, single-storey buildings, the paint peeling, windows boarded up.

And that little red puncture set in such a pale and gentle landscape.

He had to find her. He closed his eyes a moment, pushed himself up on his elbows, tried to swing his legs to the edge of the bed. As he did, something mean clawed at him, pushed him down. He collapsed back to the bed, panting with the pain, sweat blooming from his pores.

Not long after, a doctor came. He was clean-shaven, hair close-cropped, fibred with silver. There were deep, good lines around his eyes and mouth, a father perhaps, mid-career. He glanced a moment at Clay's chart, opened and closed his mouth.

'How long have I been here?' asked Clay, his own voice muffled, bubbling through a fathom of seawater.

The doctor mouthed a reply.

'Can't hear you,' Clay croaked, pointing to his right ear. Clay turned his head so that his right ear was against the mattress. 'Try now.' Koevoet's Beretta going off right next to his head, back at the minefield, must have damaged his eardrum.

The doctor shifted to the other side of the bed, facing him again. 'Don't worry about your ear,' he said. His voice was gentle, the accent English, vaguely West Country. 'There's a bit of bleeding, but no permanent damage. Your legs are a bit more problematic.'

Clay's insides tightened. Ever since seeing Bluey's legs blown off in Angola, his nightmares had regularly featured the inability to walk. Strangely, his left hand was almost always present and working in that same irrational shadow-world.

'You were unconscious when they brought you in,' said the doctor. 'We operated right away. You've been asleep for thirty-six hours.'

Clay fought back a curse. 'There was someone else with me when I was brought in. A woman. Is she here?'

'Yes, she's here,' said the doctor. 'She was stable when I left last night, but I've only just come back on shift. I'm sorry, I don't have any more information than that.' The doctor checked Clay's IV, told him that he'd removed nineteen mine fragments from his legs, that the scarring would be extensive but that the damage had been mostly superficial. He was already healing well and could expect to make a complete recovery.

'Only thing, it should have been twenty,' Clay said.

'Pardon me?'

'Nothing, doctor. If you hear anything…'

The doctor nodded and left.

An hour later, Crowbar appeared. He was wearing a new suit. His hair was slicked back and he was carrying a black leather briefcase. 'More improvements, I see, Straker,' he said, taking a seat next to Clay's bed.

'How's Rania?'

Crowbar coughed, adjusted his tie. 'The operation was long, but she's hanging in there, *seun*. She's tough.'

'And the baby?' He could barely say the words.

'Look, Straker, I won't bullshit you. They're both alive, they're both fighting. That's all you can expect for now.'

A deep ache twisted inside him, obliterating the pain in his legs. He tried to breathe it away, thought that a mathematical scale for the measurement of pain was needed, some Fahrenheit of hurt, the dolors of the heart so much worse than any of the flesh.

'Where is she?'

'Here, at the UN hospital. At the end of the hall. They're better equipped than anywhere on the island, especially for this type of wound.'

'*Al hamdillulah.*'

Crowbar frowned. 'Still on with all that Muslim shit?'

'She's Muslim.'

Crowbar blinked, said nothing.

'Nice suit.'

Crowbar grinned wide. '*Ja*, not bad. Looks more official, coming in here.'

'I thought it was a dud,' said Clay. 'Delayed detonation.'

'Those mines have been in the ground for a long time. Lucky for you. You were far enough away when it went off.'

'Not far enough.'

'You did everything you could.'

'Not everything.'

Crowbar said nothing.

'How's Hope?'

Crowbar dropped his head, seemed to settle himself a moment. 'She's–' He stopped, pursed his lips, gaze wandering around the bare walls. 'She's *lekker*. Strong. Running the Commission like a pro. Kicking arse and taking names. Opening statements were yesterday.'

'Alexi?'

'Back with *ma*. Well hidden.'

Clay nodded. 'Good, *oom*. Good.'

'Chrisostomedes is getting desperate. Hope has put his operations and his candidacy under close scrutiny. It's already causing a *grande* political shit-fight. Chrisostomedes and Dimitriou are trying to turn the hearing into a referendum on the President's authority to involve the EU and the UN in the internal affairs of Cyprus. Fun.'

'Rania's the key. They know that. They're going to try to get to her.'

'Don't worry, Straker. As far as Chrisostomedes knows, Rania is dead. But we can't take any chances.'

Clay tried to turn over. As he did, a blaze of fire filled his vision, like looking eyes-closed into the inferno, the twitching capillaries suddenly everywhere, blinding him. He gasped. Crowbar reached for his arm, held it.

'*Goddamn* that hurts,' said Clay through clamped jaw.

'Stop being such a pussy.'

'*Fok jou, Koevoet,*' he said, trying to force a smile.

Crowbar waved this away, pulled a newspaper from his briefcase and put it on the bed. 'It's all in there. Hope is going to need you to testify.'

Clay looked around the hospital room. 'The minute I set foot in that hearing room, Dimitriou will have me arrested.'

'It's not going well, Clay. Chrisostomedes is trying to discredit Hope. He's claiming that she intended to develop Toxeflora Beach, and he's produced documents to prove it. She's going to need your help.'

'They'll charge me for assaulting Chrisostomedes, probably for the murders at the minefield, too. I could get ten years.'

'More like fifteen,' said Crowbar. 'If Chrisostomedes becomes President, it could be more.'

Clay shook his head. There were an infinite number of primes. Euclid had proved it in 300 BC. Enough to keep him busy a long time. 'I'm getting out of here, Koevoet. As soon as she's strong enough, Rania and I are going to disappear. Go somewhere the world can never find us.'

'Back to Africa,' said Crowbar.

Clay nodded. 'Something like that.'

Crowbar closed his eyes a long moment. 'You'll have to get off the island first. At least you can afford the top lawyer in the country.'

'You got the money?'

Crowbar grinned wide. 'Fifteen million.'

Clay breathed out, held it a moment. It was a lot of money. None of it worth anything without Rania. 'Something important you have to do for me, *oom*. Paper and pen?'

Crowbar fished in his briefcase and pulled out a chewed, inch-long stub of HB pencil and a paperback – a yellowing fourth-hand copy of *The Brothers Karamazov*. He riffled the pages, opened the back cover, tore out a blank endpaper and handed it to Clay.

Clay glanced up at this man who never ceased to surprise him, set the paper on the book and scribbled instructions. The pencil was so dull and his hand so shaky his writing came out looking like a six-year-old's doodle. 'My boat's in Larnaca harbour. There are some documents on-board Hope is going to need. With them, she won't need me.'

Crowbar took the paper, folded it and slipped it into his inside breast pocket. Then he dropped the Dostoyevsky into his briefcase. 'Got to go, *seun*,' he said. 'Can't stand here staring at your naked arse all day. I'll be back soon.' He turned to go.

'Koevoet.'

Crowbar stopped, faced him.

'*Dankie.*'

Crowbar waved it away and closed the door behind him.

Clay pumped himself a dose of painkiller and opened the Cyprus English language daily and held it over the edge of the bed.

Since his attempted assassination by a Turkish agent (predictable), Nicos Chrisostomedes' popularity had surged. The latest pre-election polls now put him eight percentage points ahead of the incumbent. Neo-Enosis was on everyone's lips. Tensions with the TRNC and Turkey hadn't been this high since the war.

The Commission had heard the latest scientific evidence on the current state of the marine and coastal environment in the eastern Mediterranean and Cyprus. And the news was not good. Inappropriate and poorly managed coastal development in particular was causing long-term environmental damage, pushing several species towards extinction. Chrisostomedes had accused Turkish developers, including Mohamed Erkan (mentioned by name) of illegally acquiring and developing Greek-owned coastal land in the occupied north. Chrisostomedes denied having any plans of his own to develop on Turkish-owned lands at Lara Beach.

Clay closed his eyes, let the paper fall to the floor. He breathed in the night air, held it, let it go, felt the deadening work of the anaesthetic. None of this mattered. Not the pain, not the money. The political issues of a nation divided were of no importance. His life was nothing.

Rania and the baby were still alive, still fighting.

Nothing else mattered.

He drifted into a shifting territory of thousand-second minutes and the half-deadened flutter of palm fronds swaying in the Mediterranean breeze. There were grains of clarity there, too, grasped for the briefest moment and then scattered across wandering moonlit dunes. Time stalled, restarted, and then disappeared altogether.

A hand shook him awake.

He opened his eyes. The doctor was looking down at him, his face drawn into tight lines, the whites of his eyes shot through with burst blood vessels.

'What is it?' said Clay, awake now, riding adrenaline. 'What's wrong?'

'The young lady you were asking about. She's...' The doctor caught his breath, seemed to compose himself a moment. 'We must hurry. She's asking for you.'

53

The Future Spread out before Them

By the time Clay had crutched his way the fifty metres down the night-lit corridor to her room, Crowbar and Hope were already there. The nurse had cranked up Rania's bed so that she lay propped up against the pillows, pale and gauntly beautiful, her night-black hair accentuating the bloodless white of her skin. Dual heartbeat monitors pulsed behind her.

She smiled at him, the merest brightening of the eyes.

Dopamine flooded his system. He gasped, swayed on his crutches. Crowbar took a step towards him, but he raised his hand and Crowbar backed away. Clay went to her, took her hand.

'*Oh, chéri*,' she whispered to him across galaxies. 'With us it is always this way.'

Clay said nothing, just stood looking into her eyes as if in this alone he could drown.

'You are healing well?' she said, her voice a thread.

'Jesus, Rania. I'm so sorry.'

'Do not apologise.'

He sank his chin to his chest. 'I didn't think. I just ran.'

'*Ridicule*. You did the only thing possible.'

'If I'd taken more time, thought it through…'

'Please do not worry.' She looked very tired.

He straightened. 'We're going to get out of here, Rania. Disappear. Raise our son, together.'

She shook her head, the barest movement. '*Non*, Claymore.'

'Please, Ra.'

That hint of a smile again. '*Non, chéri. Une fille.*'

Electrochemical reactions flared inside him, cascading. A daughter. Not something he'd ever imagined, being a father to a little girl. So much he'd have to learn. So much to fight for.

'I am sorry to interrupt,' said the doctor. 'But we must take her now.'

Clay spun around. 'Take her where?'

Crowbar put his hand on Clay's shoulder. 'Easy, *seun*.'

'We missed something,' said the doctor. 'She is losing blood. The baby is in distress. We must operate again. She wouldn't let us start until she saw you.'

She squeezed his hand, the faintest pulse. '*Chéri*.'

Clay looked into her eyes, those dune-swept planets skidding away.

'Those things I wrote,' she whispered. 'He forced me.'

'I know, Rania. It's okay.'

'Héloïse? Is she alright?'

Clay hesitated. 'She's dead, Rania. I'm sorry. We couldn't save her.'

Tears welled in her eyes, spilled down her cheeks.

Urgency in the doctor's voice now. Orderlies unlocking the caster brakes and starting to push the bed, he still holding her hand, trying to walk with her.

'*Sura Al Ma'idah*,' Rania said, the Arabic coming like breath, choking in her hallucination.

'I don't understand.'

Her eyes fluttered, opened. 'Promise me, Claymore.'

'Promise what?'

'*Talion*,' she whispered.

And then she was gone.

☾

Crowbar and Hope walked him back to his room in silence. Dawn bled flat and grey through the half-shuttered windows. An orderly helped him into bed, reconnected his IV, left. Hope sat by the bed.

Mascara scarred her cheeks. Crowbar hovered by the door, alert. Clay stared at the wall, trying to process all that she'd said, the catastrophe of his psyche unable to cope.

After a long while Crowbar said: 'Dimitriou filed charges against you today in the criminal court. Two counts of assault with a deadly weapon. Four counts of murder, including the curator of the Cyprus museum and Rania's aunt.'

'Jesus,' breathed Clay.

'You're in luck, *broer*. No death penalty here.'

Death. For so long, after the war, he'd welcomed it, sought it even. Now, suddenly, there was something to live for. 'Did you get the documents from *Flame*?' he asked.

Crowbar opened his briefcase and passed the red folder to Clay. 'Nice boat, by the way.'

Clay handed the folder to Hope. 'It's all in there,' he said. 'Everything you need. It proves Chrisostomedes and Dimitriou colluded with Erkan to illegally develop Turkish-owned land in the south. Proves that everything Chrisostomedes is saying is a lie.'

Hope started leafing through the document.

'Chrisostomedes' thugs followed us again last night after the hearing,' said Crowbar. 'Had to lead them all the way to the Troodos, lose them in the mountains. Come daylight they vanished, like roaches.'

Not for first time, Clay marvelled at the ability of some to dismiss mercy, as if being spared was simply a right, a matter of destiny. 'I should have killed the bastard when I had the chance.'

Hope brushed a strand of hair from her face. 'Chrisostomedes is trying to implicate me in this conspiracy he's fabricating.' She shook her head. 'He's trying to tie us together, Clay, you – the supposed Turkish agent – and me. They have photographs of us, together.'

'At Toxeflora Beach,' said Crowbar. 'They've shared them with the newspapers, apparently.'

Clay said nothing.

Hope blanched, continued. 'And today Dimitriou testified that you had threatened to kill him if he didn't support my plan to develop Toxeflora. *My* plan, Clay. Can you believe it? He said he had witnesses, CCTV footage.'

Clay swallowed hard. 'He does.'

Hope opened her mouth a moment as if to speak, closed it.

'I needed to find out where they were holding Alexi.'

Hope slumped. 'Shit.'

'Why would a Turkish agent be helping to push development on their own land?' said Crowbar. 'It makes no sense.'

'Easy,' said Hope. 'If the development went ahead, it would prove that Greek Cypriots are actively stealing Turkish-owned land in the south. That would directly and negatively affect the south's application for EU membership, something the Turks bitterly oppose.'

'And something Chrisostomedes opposes,' said Clay.

'Exactly,' continued Hope. 'And it would provide the Turks with justification for accelerating their own illegal confiscations of Greek-owned land in the north. That's what Chrisostomedes is claiming, anyway. The bastard's been reading out excerpts from Rania's articles to support his case. And my fellow commissioners are buying it, warped though it is.'

'Then he still thinks Rania's dead,' said Clay.

Crowbar nodded.

Clay pointed to the dossier on Hope's lap. 'Get that to the press and Chrisostomedes' bid for the Presidency is ruined.'

Hope shook her head. 'Alone, it's not enough. We need testimony to back it up, Clay – yours or Erkan's.'

'Not a great position,' said Crowbar. 'Erkan has refused to testify, and if Straker testifies he goes to jail.'

'We could run,' said Clay. 'All four of us. Cut out through the north.'

'I know some good places,' said Crowbar. 'We have money.'

Clay shifted up onto his elbows. 'Of course, if we do run, Chrisostomedes gets his way, probably becomes President, and Medved keeps jerking the strings. They'll come after us. We'll be running for a long time.'

Hope folded her arms across her chest. 'Does either of you honestly think that you will be able to convince Rania to run away from this? Do you think I'd abandon my own son, for god's sake? You can run if you like. But I'm going to stay and find a way to bring these assholes down.'

Hope's words settled over them like an attack order, each contemplating his or her impending role and what fate might bring.

Crowbar was silent, back to the wall.

'What if we could get Erkan to testify?' said Clay. 'Is he still on the island?'

Hope nodded. 'As far as I know.'

'How are we going to do that?' said Crowbar.

'Convince him.'

Hope leaned forward in her chair. 'If we don't come up with some credible evidence in the next two days, the commission is going to wrap up proceedings. We won't get another chance to expose what Chrisostomedes is doing, especially if he wins the election.'

'Erkan's just as guilty as Chrisostomedes,' said Crowbar. 'Why would he willingly expose himself?'

Clay pointed at the dossier. 'He was going to share this with Rania. At least that's what he told her.'

'Did Rania believe him?' asked Hope.

'I think so, yes. She was determined to find out.'

'Erkan was adamant,' said Hope. 'He will not testify.'

Clay thought back to the last time he'd seen Erkan in Istanbul. 'He's terrified, Hope. If I can find out why, there's a chance I can convince him. I have to try.'

'There's isn't much time,' said Hope.

'I'll go tonight.'

'Jesus, Clay. You can hardly walk.'

'Better I go,' said Crowbar, predictably.

'No, Koevoet. I was with Rania when she interviewed Erkan. I was the one who took the dossier. He knows me, if nothing else. Maybe I can get through to him. Rania certainly thought she could.'

Crowbar coughed. 'I hate to break it to you, *broer*, but you're not Rania. I've seen more diplomatic creatures cleaning a day-old buffalo carcass.'

Clay ignored this. 'Look, the UN airport wire is unguarded on the Turkish side, like here. If your friend in the north can meet me with a car, Hope, we can drive to Erkan's place in Karpasia, pay him a visit.'

Crowbar nodded. 'And if you can't convince him?'

'Then I'll testify. Do the time.'

Crowbar turned to Hope. 'What do you think, *bokkie*?'

'We don't have a lot of options,' she answered.

'Okay, Straker, you go north,' said Crowbar. 'I'll find Maria.'

Hope hung her head. 'I still can't believe that she betrayed us.'

Crowbar put his bear paw on her shoulder. 'Blood is thick, *bokkie*. Nothing you can do.'

'I'll arrange it with my friend in the north,' said Hope, taking Crowbar's hand. 'We'll meet you back here tomorrow morning, Clay, and go straight to the hearing.'

'And I'll speak to the base commander,' said Crowbar. 'Until then, sit tight, *seun*.'

Clay switched to Afrikaans. 'Last time you said that, three guys came to kill me.'

Crowbar reached into his briefcase. 'Let's hope history doesn't repeat. Regina Medved is very pissed off right now, by all accounts. She's kept her dialysis machine off and spends all day talking to the illumination.' He produced a clean Beretta and handed it to Clay. 'I doubt even she'd be crazy enough to come after you here, but you never know, especially now.'

Hope glanced at the handgun, frowned. 'What was Rania saying, Clay, just before they took her in?'

'It was something from the Koran, I think. In Arabic. I don't know what it meant. A promise she wanted me to make.'

'*Talion*,' said Crowbar. 'It's not Arabic, it's Latin.'

'What does it mean?'

'She wants you to apply the law of talion, Clay.'

Clay and Hope looked up at him.
'Legal retribution. An eye for an eye.'

☾

After Hope and Crowbar had gone, the orderly checked Clay's bandages and administered another dose of anaesthetic. Clay stared out across the derelict airport. He wondered about Rania, about the new person inside her, about how strange that was, how foreign to him, the creation of life. A vision of his parents came to him, a distant memory, camping in the Cedarburg mountains when he was young, nine or ten, hiking up to a waterfall, his mother tall and athletic with her long, pale legs and high-veldt hair and the way her long braid swung back and forth like a cheetah's tail as she walked, his father surging ahead as always, broad-shouldered, invincible. It took them a long time to reach the top. The waterfall thundered from the cliffs above, fed by recent rains. The rocks were slippery. Looking down you knew that if you fell you would fall a long time, have time to think about what was coming as the rocks rose up to meet you. He'd taken off his shoes, walked right up to the edge, stood with his toes curled over the lip of the rock. He'd wondered if he would be brave enough to keep his eyes open all the way down, or if he'd close them before he hit. His mother and father had taken off their shoes, too, had come and stood beside him, one on each side, there on the edge looking down into the chasm. A rainbow cradled them as they stood in the spray, the three of them alone on that mountainside with the whole world and all of the future spread out before them.

54

The Price You Paid

As soon as they arrived he knew something was wrong.

Clay had slipped through the UN wire as planned, shortly after sunset. Crowbar had arranged it all with the base commander, the only stipulations being that Clay make his way back to the egress point in the wire by 0500 hours the next morning, and that he not attract the attention of the Turkish Army. Any later, or any commotion, and he was on his own – the wire would remain closed. The base commander was already treading a dangerous line harbouring them, and Crowbar had been forced to up the inducement, in the form of a cash 'signing bonus' as he called it, sourced from Medved's death money.

Hope's friend, the old man who had led them inland from the coast that night of the fire, so long ago it now seemed, had met him on the other side of the wire, and together they'd driven north to the coast under a star-strewn sky.

They arrived just before eleven o'clock, left the car hidden on a small track off the main road and walked in overland. Despite the doctor's additional bandaging and the extra painkillers, Clay's legs burned with every step. It was as if each of the sixty-seven stitches were tearing out in turn, like a zipper being undone along the back of his legs.

He followed the old man up through a tangled thicket of scrub oak, limping along at half speed with short, stilted strides. When they reached the crest of the ridge, the trees ended. They looked down at the sea across long-denuded fenlands of juniper and wild caper.

About a mile away, set on a rocky spur overlooking the sea, the walls and grounds of Erkan's mansion glowed like a bonfire. Miles of empty, moon-washed coastline strung away in either direction. Clay could hear the waves foaming on the beach, see the phosphorescent glow of the surf against the cold black of the water. The smell of wild oregano and charred pinewood came strong on the air.

As they approached, they could make out the double layer of security fencing, and beyond, the ancient, walled grounds of the converted monastery. King palms, centuries old, scythed in the night breeze, sending bladed shadows ricocheting from the floodlit monastery walls. Once, this had been a place of peaceful contemplation and spiritual cleansing. Now, red-eyed CCTV cameras swivelled their paranoia from atop steel towers at every bend and crook in the fence-line.

They reached a small pinnacle of boulders that overlooked the main gates and provided a partial view into the gardens and of the main building itself.

Hope's friend tugged Clay's sleeve. 'Look.'

The main gate was wide open. Two cars were stationed at the floodlit entrance. Armed men hovered around the vehicles. Clay counted at least four. And in the ditch at the side of the road, in partial shadow, a pile of what appeared to be animal carcasses.

'Erkan's men?' whispered Clay.

'Perhaps. I do not know.'

'Is there another way in?'

'There is an entrance on the beach side.'

And then, above the gentle shunting of the sea, the sound of gunshots – two, three muffled cracks from somewhere inside the monastery.

Clay pulled out his Beretta.

The old man put his hand on the gun. 'There is nothing we can do.'

Clay pushed the old man away. 'I'll meet you back at the car.' He was about to start off towards the beach to find the second entrance when he heard the sound of car doors closing, engines starting.

A third car had appeared at the entrance. It had come from inside the compound, and now rolled to a halt. One of the armed men approached the vehicle and spoke to the driver. Moments later all three cars were speeding away along the narrow, gravelled drive towards to the main road.

It was just gone midnight by the time Clay and the old man reached the main entrance. The big steel doors were splayed open. Bullet holes riddled the guard shack and blood stained the white, floodlit gravel. Heaped in the ditch nearby were not the animals he thought he'd seen, but men, five in all, their limbs splayed and entwined to give the appearance of four-legged beasts. Clay checked them each in turn, pulling them free, laying them on the gravel, pushing his fingers into the flesh of their necks, searching for a pulse, knowing already from the cold in their bodies that they were all dead.

The old man was staring at him.

Clay wiped his hands on his trousers. 'What is it?'

He paused, looked into Clay's eyes. 'You frighten me, young man.'

Clay ignored this. 'I am going to find Erkan.'

The man smiled a sad smile. 'I will go back and bring the car.'

Clay nodded. '*Çok teşekur*,' he said. Thank you. And then the things he did not say: I do not expect to see you again, but thank you, old man. In bringing me this far you have taken a huge risk. Honour to you.

Clay started towards the monastery.

Floodlit shadows jerked epileptic across the pathway, fell twitching onto the arches and towers and limestone walls. Gravel crunched under his feet, and in his mind the path was fashioned from the smashed and brittle shards of dried bones, femurs and ribs and the concavity of shattered hips. He felt the gun's weight in his hand, the familiarity of a grafted prosthetic. The blood of strangers on him, too, its smell thick in his nostrils.

He was thirty-four years old. At eighteen he'd gone to war, lost his parents a year later in a car crash. Since then he'd travelled through the world alone, Koevoet the closest thing he'd had to a father, to what his father had tried to be to him, to what he would now have to be if the baby lives: guide, conscience, uncompromising compass swung on wisdom and courage, impossible to live up to. As an adolescent, Clay had come to see his father as a wizened mystery, with so much of what he'd done unsaid and unshared. Once in a while a story had emerged, almost by accident, as afterthought, like the time he was caught in a mine collapse in one of the deep reef mines near Jo'berg and survived three miles underground for five days and got his men to safety, most of them anyway. And as Clay climbed the stone steps to the arched atrium, he wondered if he would share any of this – these events occurring right now – with his daughter, or if he too would keep it all hidden away, and if he might be around long enough to try.

He found them on the second floor, in a grand room with sweeping views of the sea and the coast, a fire dying in a huge stone fireplace. Two bodyguards lay face-down by the door. Furniture was strewn across the room, upended. Broken glass sharded oriental rugs, shimmered on polished marble tile.

Clay knelt, turned one of the bodyguards over. It was Hum, his face still swollen from Clay's strike of a few days ago. There was a deep gash over his right eye, fresh, weeping blood, but no other visible wounds. He was still breathing. Clay moved to the other body, a woman: Ho. She groaned as he turned her over. Her jaw was wired up. She opened her eyes a moment, just a flutter, and mumbled something that Clay could not make out. She'd been shot in the thigh. Clay cradled her, examined the gash in the back of her head, the brush-cut hair beaded with blood. Like Hum, she was alive and breathing.

Clay threaded off his pack and pulled out his water bottle. He cut Ho's trouser leg open and exposed the wound. It was low down, close to the knee, in the fleshy part of the quadricep. Blood leaked from the hole. He couldn't see an exit wound. Clay irrigated the area then pushed a compress down onto the wound and tied it in place. He was applying a tourniquet to the leg and winding it tight when something hard jabbed into the back of his head.

'Don't move.'

He didn't.

'Turn around. Slowly.'

It was Erkan. He was bleeding from a deep gash in his lower lip. There were abrasions around both eyes. His nose was swollen to twice its normal size. His right arm hung limp from the shoulder. A .357 Magnum revolver shook in his meaty left hand. '*You*,' he said, voice hollow, constricted. 'What do you want?'

Clay kept his hand open, in plain view. 'She's bleeding.'

Erkan motioned for him to continue.

Clay tied off the tourniquet, laid her down. 'Call an ambulance,' he said.

'I already have,' said Erkan. 'The police, too.'

Clay stood. He figured he had ten, maybe fifteen minutes until the cops arrived. Assuming the old man hadn't already fled. 'What happened?' he asked. 'I saw them leave.'

'You can see very well what happened.'

Clay glanced at Erkan's shoulder. 'That's broken.'

'Compassion does not suit you.'

'Let me set it.'

Erkan laughed, waved the pistol at him. It was a good effort at bravado, considering the pain he must be in. 'What do you want?'

'How about lowering that gun?' said Clay.

'I would rather not, under the circumstances. Say what you have to say and leave.'

Clay filled his lungs, held it then exhaled slowly. 'We need you to testify at the commission on coastal development.'

Erkan shifted his feet, grimaced in pain. 'I have already given my answer to the commission.'

'If you don't help us, Chrisostomedes is going to walk away blameless from this. He'll probably win the election, too.'

Erkan shook his head. 'Help you? Your friend Moulinbecq has spent the last month trying to destroy me. Judging by what she has written, Chrisostomedes is a saint.'

'Chrisostomedes was coercing her. But that's over.'

Erkan was quiet a moment. 'Look around you,' he said. 'This was a warning. Even if I wanted to help, I cannot.'

And suddenly, it all made sense: Erkan's cornering of the illegal market in religious antiquities; his apparent desire to share the Alassou dossier with Rania, 'off the record'; his chauffeur's attempt to capture them shortly afterwards; the fiery murders that night in Karpasia; the cable Clay had pulled up with *Flame*'s anchor as they fled, the burns on his face not yet blistered. All of it.

'Rania – Lise – told me what happened to your wife and son. Those were warnings, too, weren't they?'

Erkan called over his shoulder. A woman emerged from behind one of the couches that hadn't been overturned. She was tall and slim, with thick black hair. Her face was horribly disfigured, the skin stretched in angry pink ridges across her lovely cheekbones, the eyes inert, glass.

'*Gel*,' he said to her. Come.

The woman approached, found Erkan with her hands and tucked herself in beside him.

'My wife.'

'I am very sorry for what happened,' said Clay.

Erkan's wife inclined her head.

'The interview,' said Clay. 'You were trying to help us.'

'The only way I could.'

Erkan's wife gripped her husband's arm, put her lips to his ear, whispered something. He patted her arm, continued. 'They were going to kill Mademoiselle Moulinbecq, after she returned to Cyprus. I tried to warn her. I thought you were…' He trailed off. 'I thought you might be one of *hers*.'

'Medved.'

'The Devil, Mister Greene. There is no other explanation.'

Clay closed his eyes. You don't understand, he thought. I didn't either, for a long time. For years I searched for someone else to blame. But now it is clear. There is no devil. There never was. There are only *people*. 'That's why you insisted Rania come alone,' he said.

'Yes. But I was betrayed by one of my oldest employees.'

'The chauffeur.'

'Never would I have believed it. He had been with me for over twelve years. I haven't seen him since that day.' Erkan winced in pain, indicated the two body guards lying on the floor. 'These, at least, are loyal.'

'Help us now,' said Clay. 'You can make it right.'

'I didn't want to do any of it,' Erkan said. 'The Greek properties were not ours to take. I tried to tell her, but she insisted. They were the best sites, the best beaches, the most valuable. Regina made it happen. She bribed politicians here in the north, silenced dissenters. That's how she works. No one is safe. And when the environmentalists started bringing pressure through the EU and the UN to protect the nesting beaches, she developed a plan to make that go away, too.'

'The poison dosing lines.'

Erkan nodded. 'And the acoustics.'

'Are they still in operation at your sites in Karpasia?'

Erkan hung his head. 'You must understand. This is where I spent summers as a boy. These beaches, the sea,' he waved the gun in a long arc, 'all of this. It is God's holy creation, his perfection. What I have done is a sin, and I will burn for it, I know. But I had no choice.' There were tears in his eyes.

'There is always a choice.' Something Rania said to him once.

'No, Mister Greene. You are wrong.' Erkan twisted half around, faced the back of the room. 'Anastasia, come out.'

A girl appeared from behind the couch. She was wearing a pink-and-blue flowered party dress. Her dark hair was pulled back and tied with pink ribbons. Tears streaked her pre-adolescent face. She had her mother's beautiful bone structure and light complexion.

'This is why they were here, Mister Greene, or whatever your name is. They have already taken my son. If I do not continue to serve, they will take my daughter.'

How young she looked, Clay thought, how frightened. 'Testify,' he said. 'Tell the world what Regina's doing here, doing to your family. The authorities will be forced to act. It's the only way.'

Erkan raised his chin, Turkish for 'no'. 'Impossible.'

'Help me, and I'll help you.'

'How can you possibly help me?'

'She wants me dead, Mister Erkan. She's put a price on my head.'

Erkan's eyes widened.

'I killed her brother.'

'Then you are already dead.'

'Maybe,' said Clay. 'But not if I kill her first.'

For just a moment, Clay thought he saw a glimmer in Erkan's eyes. But then it was gone and Erkan was staring at him, lips pursed, jaw clenched. 'No, Mister Greene. You cannot help me.' He raised the pistol. 'Now, get out of my house.'

This was the price you paid. A cost quoted in options foregone, in freedoms lost, in principles and beliefs abandoned. It would be so easy from here: hire a boat, sail to Turkey or one of the Greek islands, and disappear. He had money, documents, weapons. He knew places where no one would ever find him, not Medved, certainly not the government of Cyprus. But he no longer had a choice, just as Erkan didn't have a choice. And he could no more fight against it than change his blood type or the colour of his eyes. He had to go back. And he would have to testify.

Clay put his open palm on his chest. 'None of us are saints, Mister Erkan. And she's not the Devil.' And then he turned his back on the father and the mother and the daughter and went out the way he came in.

55

Death Comes Soon Enough

The old man did come back with the car. Three and a half hours later they reached the eastern outskirts of Turkish Nicosia – much smaller and less built up than the Greek part of the city. They trundled through deserted, half-lit streets, the twin grafted minarets of the Semiliye mosque – previously the Cathédrale Sainte Sophie – reaching heavenward from the clutter of the sleeping city. After a while they left the town behind and emerged into a country of crumbling stone walls and ancient dust-covered olive groves. The old man turned south, towards the border. A kilometre or so on, he left the paved road and switched off the headlights, continuing in darkness along a twisting, barely discernible track that skirted the base of a rock-strewn mesa. Progress was slow. The car lurched and scraped over ruts and potholes. Clay winced with each creak of the old car's suspension, each crash of stone against steel, clamour enough to wake every Turkish soldier in Cyprus, to bring spirits up from their tombs.

And then, finally, silence. They sat side by side in the old car, nestled in the moon-shadow of a clutch of tangled cacti.

'I can go no further,' said the old man. 'Follow this track.' He pointed into the night. 'The UN wire is not far. You must hurry. It is almost five o'clock. Go with God, young man. You are in need of him.'

Him again.

They shook hands in the darkness, the barest hint of grey showing in the eastern sky. Clay thanked the old man for all he had done in this matter, for the risks he had taken, and wished him long life.

The old man smiled, his teeth and the whites of his eyes gleaming in the darkness. He put his hand on Clay's cheek and held it there a moment as if Clay were a little boy, a grandson. The smell of tobacco smoke seeping from his long, bony fingers.

'Find peace, young man,' he said. 'Death comes soon enough.'

They shook hands again and the old man drove away, leaving Clay alone in the moon-altered country contemplating the veracity of this last statement and the kindness from which it had sprung.

☾

Hope met him as planned back inside the UN base. She was alone. Her hair was up, her eyes set off by a shallow-water scarf and sea-blue jacket. He got into her car, and soon they were through the main gate and into the Nicosia backstreets.

'Erkan isn't going to testify,' Clay said after a while. 'I think he wants to, but he's scared.'

'Damn,' said Hope.

She reached into her purse and produced an envelope. She handed it to Clay. 'This is your Presidential special executive order,' she said

It was all in Greek. 'Not a full pardon, I'm guessing?'

'It allows Declan Greene to testify. When you are done, you'll be taken into custody by the Cyprus police.'

Clay pulled in oxygen. 'You were expecting this.'

Hope nodded as she shifted gear, turned onto Digenis Avenue. 'It was the best I could do.'

'Where's Crowbar?' he said.

'Still looking for Maria.' Ten minutes later they were approaching the Ledra Palace Hotel, now HQ of Sector 2 UNFICYP and the venue for the joint commission. A throng of protestors crowded the wire on both sides of the Greek Cypriot guard post, shouting and waving placards.

Someone hammered the side of the car with an open palm as they passed.

'They are for Chrisostomedes,' said Hope. 'People are very upset about the rumoured deal to swap Turkish and Greek land.'

At the gate, Hope showed her pass. They'd just been waved through when her mobile phone rang. She raised it to her ear, glanced at Clay as she turned the car into a parking space marked 'reserved – commissioner'. The lot was nearly full.

'Rania's still in intensive care,' she said, dropping her phone in her handbag and shutting down the engine. 'They'll call me as soon as there is news.'

Clay stared out through the car window at the hotel's crumbling façade, let this uncertainty churn through him. He'd tried to see Rania when he'd got back to the base, but the doctors weren't allowing her visitors.

Hope reached over and took his hand. For a long time she didn't say anything, just sat there beside him, running the palp of her thumb back and forth over the calloused ridges of his third and fourth knuckles as they watched the last few invited guests trickle into the hotel.

'Ready?' she whispered, finally.

'Not really,' he said, opening the door and stepping out onto the gravel.

Hope led him past the throng of protestors towards the Islamic-arched front entrance of the hotel. Once the pinnacle of luxury in Cyprus, twenty years of boot heels and neglect had left the place looking and smelling more like a rundown Cairo train station. They passed through the lobby, over scuffed, unpolished marble, past milling delegates. An attractive young woman in a dark jacket and slit skirt, a pile of documents clutched to her breast, schoolgirl-style, followed him with a smile in her eyes. Her thick, dark hair and something about the way she stood and held her head reminded him of Rania. He met her gaze for a moment, but she glanced at his stump and looked away with a frown.

At the conference room doors, Hope stopped and touched Clay's elbow. 'I can't tell you how much I appreciate what you are doing, Clay.' She went up on her toes and kissed him.

The conference room was full. Easily a hundred and fifty people seated in rows of chairs, more lining the walls, half a dozen TV cameras on tripods trained on the main front podium. Someone had pried open a couple of windows along the garden-facing wall behind the podium, but the thin gasp of air that managed to slip into the room was quickly lost in the claustrophobia of sweating bodies.

Hope led him to the front of the audience and indicated an empty chair. Clay lowered himself slowly into its sculpted concavity, feeling the sutures on the backs of his legs stretch and then compress against the hard plastic.

Hope stepped up to the podium, sat behind the cloth-draped head table and faced the audience, the glare of the TV camera lights illuminating her face. Behind the podium, the flags of Cyprus, the UN, the EU, and the red-and-white stripes, star and crescent moon of the TRNC. To her left, a fine-jawed man with dark hair and severe eyebrows scribbled something in a notebook. The name plate before him read: Duplessis, European Union. To her right, Thornton of the United Nations, grey haired, mid-sixties, Clay guessed, a man of obvious experience.

Off to the side of the podium was an elevated wooden platform arranged with a single white plastic chair and a microphone – the witness stand.

Thornton blew into the microphone, invited the audience to turn off their mobile phones and opened the day's proceedings. The first witness of the day was called.

Dressed in a dark jacket and tie, his left leg in a cast, Nicos Chrisostomedes planted and swung his way to the stand on a pair of crutches. His mouth was set in a flat line of pain. Sweat pooled in the deep parallels channelling his forehead. He sat, stated his name and was invited to continue his testimony.

The audience fell quiet.

'Commissioners, ladies and gentlemen, I apologise.' Chrisosto-medes adjusted the microphone. 'Yesterday, I was unable to attend because I was in hospital. I have received some bad news. My doctors have told me that without these,' he raised one of his crutches for all to see, 'I may never walk again.'

A moan from the audience, then silence. Cameras whirred and clicked.

He continued: 'I tell you this not to gain your sympathy, but because it is of immediate relevance to these proceedings. The well-known journalist Lise Moulinbecq has for some weeks now been conducting her own investigations here in Cyprus. Her findings have been widely published. They corroborate all of my earlier testimony, including the devastating effect of coastal development in the north on sea-turtle populations. I have just heard from the police that Ms Moulinbecq disappeared a few days ago. During several interviews that she conducted with me, she shared with me that she feared for her life, that she had received death threats from Mohamed Erkan.'

Murmurs from the audience.

'In fact, I have just learned that Mademoiselle Moulinbecq's aunt was kidnapped and brought to Cyprus by agents acting for Erkan. But Moulinbecq refused to be blackmailed, and continued to write the truth. Police found her aunt yesterday, in Limassol, dead in the boot of a car.'

Chrisostomedes turned and faced Clay. 'Today you will hear from a new witness, a close colleague of Doctor Bachmann, a Mister Declan Greene. He is in the audience now.' Chrisostomedes pointed at Clay and glared. 'Less than a week ago, this man held a loaded gun to my head and threatened my life.'

A hundred indrawn breaths.

'And after a desperate struggle, he shot me in the leg, before fleeing like a coward.' A long pause, Chrisostomedes letting it sink in, basking in the sympathy. 'He is a Turkish Islamic agent.'

Two police officers, stationed at the back of the room, started to move through the crowd towards Clay.

Clay took a deep breath. Shit. Here we go.

Hope covered her microphone, leaned towards Thornton and spoke into his ear, sliding a document across the table to him.

Thornton glanced down at the paper a moment and then asked the policemen to approach the dais. The cops considered the paper and then moved off to one side. The pair stood with thumbs looped in belts, staring at Clay.

Chrisostomedes now produced a thick manila folder. An orderly shuttled it to the dais and placed it before the commissioners. 'Before you is the official police record of Mister Declan Greene. As you can see, he entered Cyprus illegally ten days ago. And where do you suppose he came *from?*' A pause for effect now, long enough for the obvious to dawn. 'He came, ladies and gentlemen, from Turkey, where he was observed meeting with Mohamed Erkan.'

The audience erupted like a geyser, shouts and jeers flooding the room.

Chrisostomedes continued. 'He is wanted by Cyprus police for four murders, including the horrific slaying three nights ago of the curator of the Cyprus museum.' He paused for effect. 'The name he uses, Declan Greene, is an alias. By cross-referencing their records, the police have determined that his real name is Claymore Straker. Three years ago, he moved to Cyprus and set up an offshore business here. He was provided a legal work visa at the time. Four months ago, Claymore Straker was reported to have been killed in Yemen. At the time of his supposed death, Claymore Straker was classified by Interpol, the CIA and the Government of Yemen as a known Islamic terrorist, and was wanted for at least a dozen murders.'

The room was silent. Just the whirr and click of cameras and voice recorders. Clay sank back in his chair. If he wasn't before, he was truly fucked now.

56

Life

Thornton tapped the microphone, faced Clay. 'The witness will please state his name. His real name.'

Clay knew there was only one course he could follow, one that ten years ago he had chosen to forsake, and had regretted ever since. Crowbar had been there that day, too, at the military tribunal, had shared in the lie they'd all told. He searched through the crowd for Crowbar, couldn't see him. 'My name is Claymore Straker.'

'The Mister Straker recently reported killed in Yemen?'

'Yes.' Clay narrowed his eyes against an explosion of flashbulbs.

'You should know, Mister Straker, that this Commission expresses great reservation in having you appear as a witness, given your status as a suspected murderer, both here and in Yemen. And while I stress that this Commission's role is to investigate coastal development in Cyprus, and judging your previous actions will be left to a court of law, we will need to ask you questions which, should you choose to answer, may incriminate yourself.'

A low grumble from the audience.

'I understand.'

Thornton leaned forward.

'Did you assault Minister Dimitriou in his home, as he claimed yesterday in his testimony?'

Clay looked around the audience, all those people staring at him, the expectant looks on their faces. He breathed in, let it go. 'Yes.' A year for assault.

Outrage from the crowd.

'Did you shoot Mister Chrisostomedes in the leg as he claims?'

'Yes.' Two to three more for grievous bodily harm.

More derision.

'And Mister Straker, did you kill the four men who were found dead near the Green Line five days ago?'

'Three of them, yes. But not the curator.' Life.

Thornton glanced at Duplessis, then at Hope. 'So you agree with the account of events that Mister Chrisostomedes has given to this commission.'

'I roughed up Dimitriou, yes. I shot Chrisostomedes. Other than that, everything they've told you is false.'

Clay pushed his mouth to the microphone, spoke over the rising din. 'Chrisostomedes kidnapped Lise Moulinbecq's aunt, forced Lise to write a series of articles blaming Erkan for stealing Greek land in the north. When he no longer needed her, he killed her aunt and sold Lise to Regina Medved, the Russian oligarch. Medved had put a one-million-euro price on Moulinbecq's head.' He glared at Chrisostomedes, his best death-row stare. 'God knows what's become of her.'

Chrisostomedes and half the audience were on their feet now, shouting, the other half seemed locked into a bemused silence. Thornton hammered the gavel and called for order. After a time the crowd settled, and Thornton took the microphone.

'Mister Straker,' he began, 'you have confessed before this public enquiry to two assaults and three murders, all perpetrated here in Cyprus within the last few days. And now you produce for us a version of events diametrically opposed to that described to us by one of the nation's elected officials and one of its most trusted businessmen. This Commission cannot consider you a credible witness.'

Thornton leaned to his side and Duplessis whispered something into his ear, to which Thornton nodded. 'In addition, and for the record, I find your story highly unlikely. In effect, you are calling a candidate for the Presidency of this country an extortionist. This Commission cannot and will not tolerate slander.'

The audience erupted in a wave of cheering and clapping.

Hope put her hand over her microphone and leaned towards Thornton. They spoke for a long time, back and forth, Thornton shaking his head, Hope animated, pressing her point. Finally Thornton took the microphone and peered down through smudged bifocals. 'Mister Straker, I am told you have information regarding the decline in turtle populations in Cyprus.'

'I have physical and documentary evidence,' said Clay.

'You may continue, on the condition that you restrict your testimony to this evidence.'

'May I be allowed to present exhibits?' he asked.

Thornton nodded.

Clay reached into the duffel bag, pulled out the marine loudspeaker and held it up for all to see. The dark cabling hung from its body like severed tentacles.

'Four days ago, I recovered this device from Toxeflora Beach.' He explained its placement and intended function. 'There is a similar system in Karpasia,' he said. 'Doctor Bachmann can confirm what I'm saying.'

The crowd was hushed now, attentive.

An orderly shuttled the exhibit to the dais. Thornton examined the object, passed it to Duplessis, then leaned over, covered his microphone and spoke to Hope at length.

'No turtles, no reason to protect the beaches,' said Clay.

Thornton looked up. 'We understand the implications, Mister Straker.'

Chrisostomedes stood, glanced at Dimitriou and addressed the dais. 'May I be allowed to comment, Mister Chairman?'

Thornton nodded.

An orderly handed a spare microphone to Chrisostomedes. 'How do we know this item was taken from Toxeflora? It could have come from anywhere. Are there photographs, eye witnesses?'

'Mister Straker?' said Thornton.

'I don't have photos,' said Clay. 'But Doctor Bachmann was there with me when we found it.'

Chrisostomedes laughed. 'The photos in the newspapers today suggest that Mister Straker and Doctor Bachmann were doing something else that day at the beach.'

Laughter skittered across the room.

Thornton again: 'Anything to add, Mister Straker?'

'Only what I saw. Someone had also installed some sort of pipework system along the beach. Doctor Bachmann and I collected samples of the sand adjacent to the piping.'

'Do you have any results to share with us, any data?'

Clay shook his head. 'No. No I don't.'

Chrisostomedes raised his hand, was given permission to speak. 'I would invite the Commission to immediately send a team to investigate whether such a system exists. I have no knowledge of Karpasia, of course, but I assure you no such system will be found at Toxeflora, either onshore or offshore.'

'Mister Straker?'

'Of course you won't find anything now. As soon as they realised we'd discovered what they were doing, they went back and took it all out.'

Chrisostomedes pointed at Clay. 'The very idea that anyone would do such a thing is preposterous. This man has no credibility whatsoever.'

Thornton nodded. 'We shall do exactly as you have suggested, Mister Chrisostomedes. We will send a team to investigate the site. Thank you for the suggestion.' And to Clay: 'Do you have any further evidence, Mister Straker?'

As Clay scanned the audience, all those expectant faces, Dimitriou smug, Chrisostomedes with arms crossed, triumphant, he realised that coming here to testify had been a colossal error in judgement. Without hard evidence, it was their word against his. And here, his word wasn't worth shit. Not only that, but by revealing Clay's past and associating him with Hope, Chrisostomedes had ensured that Hope's own testimony was devalued. Every time Clay opened his mouth he was weakening Hope's case.

'We're waiting, Mister Straker. Do you have any more evidence to present?'

Clay reached into his bag, touched Erkan's dossier. If Hope wanted to use it, she would have to do it herself. He closed his eyes, fought back the despair crushing his lungs. 'No,' he said. 'No, I don't.'

A murmur echoed through the room. Clay could hear the voices refracting from the bare walls and the window glass and the hard tile floor, the individual and distinct becoming dull amalgam. He opened his eyes. Hope was staring past him, towards the back of the room, her mouth open in a half-formed word. Clay swivelled in his chair, followed her gaze.

The big back doors to the conference room were open. Half a dozen people, TV cameramen and reporters, turned to look. There, silhouetted against the light streaming in from the big lobby windows, stood Crowbar. He had a folded-up newspaper in one hand. The other was clamped around Maria's arm.

57

Her Dark Insanity

The future remains hidden, waiting for our triggers. Or, as Rania believed, was Allah the determiner of all things? As Clay watched Maria squinting into the lights, saw her raise her hand and flick a wisp of hair from her face, he considered that perhaps life was nothing more than a battle between fate and determinism, each side gaining ground and then losing it again to counter-attack in a war of attrition neither side could win.

Crowbar escorted Maria down through the crowd to the front row of seats, whispered something to her, and ushered her forward. She looked as if she'd been camping in the mountains for a week, living in a tent. Her clothes were stained. She'd put her hair up, and what spilled from under her cap was tangled and laced with leaves and twigs.

Hope beckoned her forward. Maria approached the dais, clutching a small backpack to her chest. The two commissioners spoke to her for a long time. Then she turned and walked to the witness stand.

Clay stepped aside and retook his seat in the front row, next to Crowbar.

'Did you hear?' Crowbar said. A strong whiff of whisky.

'Hear what?' said Clay.

'Medved died this morning. That little icon was better than a bullet.' Crowbar handed Clay a newspaper. It was a copy of the *International Herald Tribune*, dated today. Crowbar jabbed his finger onto a page two piece. 'Read this.'

Clay read, reread, looked up and tried to catch his breath. 'Jesus. When did she do this?'

'Must have been between operations.'

'She never said anything about it.'

Maria sat and adjusted the microphone. She stated her name, listed her qualifications in marine biology and chemistry, her position at the university. Then she reached into her bag and produced what looked like a medicine phial. 'This,' she began, holding the thing up, 'is one of a dozen samples of sand collected at Toxeflora Beach in the south, and from the UNESCO World Heritage beach in Karpasia, in the north.'

Maria handed the phial to an orderly, who shuttled it to the dais along with an envelope and a sheaf of papers. She continued: 'Each of these samples was collected at the depth and position where female turtles lay their eggs. Each sample was collected adjacent to a perforated irrigation pipe that had been buried along the beach, connected to a stem input valve, as you can see in the photographs before you.'

A growing silence crept over the assembled, the interested public, the paid supporters and coerced witnesses, the press and the politicians, the guilty and less guilty. Thornton looked over the photographs one after the other, passed them to Duplessis and Hope in turn.

'After obtaining the samples from Doctor Bachmann, I halved them as a standard precaution.' She paused a moment, glanced up at Hope, then continued. 'As instructed, I went to submit one set to the commercial laboratory here in Nicosia for rush analysis. But before I could do so, I was confronted by two armed men who took the samples and warned me to keep quiet. They made it very clear what would happen to me if I said anything.'

Maria looked shaken, but she kept her composure, spoke clearly and with authority. She explained how she'd decided to go into hiding. With the help of her boyfriend, she'd gone to Toxeflora, found the buried lines and taken photographs. Realising the danger, she'd decided to analyse the duplicate samples herself at the university laboratory. She found that the samples all contained significant concentrations of organochlorides and organophosphates, along with residuals of xylene and ethylbenzene. All the samples were similar, at Toxeflora in the south and Karpasia in the north.

'That system of pipes,' said Maria, 'is for pumping diesel laced with pesticides, DDT, and chlorobiphenyls into the sand, just above the tideline.'

The room was completely silent.

'Could it affect the turtle eggs, if they were in contact with this mixture?' asked Duplessis.

'Yes,' said Maria. 'Definitely. These are highly toxic chemicals. There are studies in the literature that have looked at the effects of organic pollutants on turtles. Exposure decreases hatchling success, increases deformities, and makes hatchlings more susceptible to disease. Hatchlings born in this environment would have little chance of survival.'

By the time she was done, a new kind of murmur was rippling through the audience.

'This represents a deliberate attempt to kill off the remaining turtle populations of Cyprus,' said Maria. 'With the turtles gone, the main reason for protecting these beaches goes away. Developers on both sides of the border are the big winners.' She looked out at the crowd, locked her gaze on Dimitriou. 'This is my country. If I don't look after it, who will?' She sat and folded her hands in her lap.

Pandemonium. Flash bulbs going off. Everyone speaking at once.

Chrisostomedes, visibly shaken, stood and was granted permission to speak. 'With respect, commissioners,' he began, adjusting his tie, 'even if such a horrific thing has occurred, any suggestion that I have been in any way involved is pure slander. Anyone could be responsible. Indeed, the fact that a similar system supposedly exists in the north would point the finger squarely at the Turks.' He took a deep breath. 'My record on conservation stands for itself.'

Clay reached into the duffel bag at his feet and grabbed the dossier. He stood, holding it above his head. Bemused silence from the audience, a few whispers from the back of the room. Thornton waved Clay forward.

Clay placed the folder on the dais. 'Mohamed Erkan gave me this, two weeks ago in Istanbul,' he said to the commissioners. 'Have it verified. It's absolutely authentic. These documents prove that Chrisostomedes has been colluding with Erkan for years, with Dimitriou's help, to illegally develop Turkish-owned coastal land in the south. It's all in there: bank details, names, places, dates.'

Thornton took the dossier, opened it and started leafing through the pages. After a moment he handed the folder to Duplessis. 'Astounding,' he said.

'Same systems, north and south,' said Clay. 'Chrisostomedes took care of the southern beaches, Erkan the north. Erkan told me so himself.'

Duplessis looked up from the dossier, wide-eyed. 'If this is true…' he said, stopped.

'I have one more exhibit,' said Clay.

'Proceed,' said Thornton.

Clay turned to face the audience. Most of them seemed to be staring at his legs, the floor around his feet. 'It wasn't only about land.' Clay reached into the bag and pulled out the Patmos Illumination, held it up for all to see.

A few in the crowd recognised it instantly, most sat perplexed. Chrisostomedes looked ashen, pre-cardiac. Clay let him look at it a good while.

'This is perhaps the most famous of all the iconic Greek Orthodox artefacts that disappeared during the 1974 invasion,' said Clay in a clear loud voice, taking his time, letting it hit home. 'For twenty years Greek Cyprus has been blaming the Turks for its loss. I recovered this from the home of Nicos Chrisostomedes five days ago.'

'Mister Straker,' said Thornton into the microphone.

Clay turned and faced the dais.

Thornton pointed to Clay's feet.

Clay looked down. The floor around him was covered in bright red shoe prints. Blood pooled at his feet, soaked the cuffs of his trousers, filmed his shoes. He reached for the back of his right leg, felt the wet tackiness there. A few of his stitches must have ruptured. He hadn't even noticed.

He looked back up at Thornton, shook his head. Then he stepped forward and placed the illumination on the dais, turned back to the audience. 'If you look at the back of the icon, near the lowermost nail hole, you will see a tiny silver square. It's a microchip. Every piece in Chrisostomedes' private collection has a chip like this. I'm sure if you have it analysed, you'll see his name there, quite clearly, and if anyone is interested, they can match the chip to the ones on all the other pieces in his collection. Who knows what you might find.'

The room was silent, the implications of this whirring in brains and beaming through live TV feeds.

'So,' Clay continued, 'in July 1974, when the Turkish Army was advancing through Northern Cyprus, what do you think the young Nicos Chrisostomedes was doing? Fighting to protect his country as so many others did? No. He was busy raiding every church he could find, carrying off as many valuable artefacts as he could. And ever since, he's been blaming the Turks for their disappearance.'

It was time for the final shot. Clay opened up the newspaper, handed it to Thornton and pointed to the article. His finger left a smudge of blood on the page just above the byline.

Thornton took the paper, read, looked up and passed it to Hope. After a moment, Hope leaned in and whispered something to Duplessis, then to Thornton.

She held up the paper. 'Ladies and gentlemen,' she said, 'before I officially close this morning's proceedings, I would like to read you something from today's *International Herald Tribune*. It is entitled: "The Evolution of Fear". It was written by Lise Moulinbecq.'

In a clear, sure voice, Hope read the words that Clay had already committed to memory. Rania's words. Written from her hospital bed just a few hours before, wired across the world to make the deadline, published and printed and sent back out around the world in time to be here, now. It was all there, in her wonderful prose, everything that had happened to her since Istanbul, the compromised stories she'd been forced to write, itemised and corrected, Chrisostomedes' coercion, his abduction and murder of her aunt, Regina Medved's dark insanity, all of it.

And as Clay listened, heard Hope declare the session closed, watched her raise her phone to her ear, Crowbar moving through the crowd towards her now, he saw her mouth open in a noiseless scream. Then her phone falling to the floor and shattering into pieces as she stumbled from the dais, tears pouring down her face, Crowbar folding her into his arms and them both turning to face him, Crowbar's big jaw quivering on its hinges, Hope reaching out for him now, grief pouring from her eyes as the policemen pulled him away, started cuffing his only hand. It was over.

58

What You Had To Forsake

Seven months later

Clay walked along the outdoor corridor of the old, British-built Lefkosia Central Jail, breathed the cool air coming heavy with pine and cedar from the unseen mountains. He looked through the barred arches across the empty courtyard to the whitewashed crosses of thirteen EOKA fighters killed by the British during the liberation struggle of 1955. The British buried them inside the prison to avoid the uproar of public funerals. Incarcerated even in death. Clay stared at the pale, straight geometry of the grave curbs; to save space, the men were buried two to a pit. The white Cypriot flags hung motionless in the dead air, the nimbus of razor wire glowing on the crest of the penitentiary wall above the words: 'A brave man's death is no death at all.' Clay thought that when he died it would be good to share a grave with a brother. He also knew, with absolute certainty, that he would die alone.

Crowbar was waiting for him outside on the pavement. It was a sunny day, clear and blue with the scent of lemon blossom and charred pine strong on the breeze from the Pentadactylos Mountains. Clay walked away from the prison gate for the last time, took Crowbar's offered hand and clasped it hard.

'You look good, *seun,*' said Crowbar.

'You too, *oom.*'

'How do you feel?'

Clay stood on the pavement, breathed in the free air. 'Older,' he said, glancing back at the prison gates.

'That's what prison is for.'
'How's business?'
'Booming. Someone's always got a war to fight.'
'Angola still?'
'Long-term contract. You should join us.'
'No, Koevoet.'
'You know where to find me if you change your mind.'
They started walking along the pavement towards the old city.
'Thanks for getting me out, *oom*.'
'Not me, *seun*. Hope. She arranged it.'
'Thank her for me.'
'How was it?' Crowbar said after a while.
'Rough at first. After that everyone pretty well let me be.'
'Hit first, hit hard.'
He had.

In the end, it had gone pretty quickly. A few weeks after Regina Medved's death, Erkan had come forward and admitted to colluding with Chrisostomedes. His testimony had led not only to the destruction of Chrisostomedes' by then shaky political career, but to his arrest and indictment for the theft of the Illumination, and for kidnapping and conspiracy to commit murder. Erkan also provided information to TRNC police that led to the arrest of two Russian men for the fiery murders of the Karpasia villagers. The men had admitted to being in the employ of Regina Medved at the time. With no one left to hold it together, the Medved family empire was in ruins.

Clay's trial had been swift. He'd been acquitted of the murders of Todorov and Medved's men due to lack of evidence. The curator's murder had been firmly attributed to Uzi. Clay's lawyer had performed admirably. Responsibility for the death of Madame Debret was rightly placed with Todorov. For the assaults on Chrisostomedes and Dimitriou, Clay had received a two-year sentence, reduced to six months by Presidential decree, thanks in part to an anonymous donation of half a million euros to the President's re-election campaign.

They reached the roundabout at Paphos gate, continued past

the old sandbagged bunkers and derelict guardhouses, through the warren of narrow streets in the old city.

'Did you distribute the money like I asked?' said Clay.

'Two hundred thousand to Katia, a million to Hope's foundation, a million to Hope, two million in a trust fund for the establishment of a National Park in Agamas. Goddamn overgenerous in my book. The rest I split between us, gave your half to Rania. Oh, and I gave her back her Koran, like you asked.'

Clay nodded. 'And the second icon?'

'A gift to the grateful people of Cyprus.'

'Good, Koevoet. *Dankie.*'

They passed a boarded-up mosque, the minaret covered in vines. Beyond was an old Ottoman house, the ground floor of which had been converted into a bar.

'Drink?' asked Crowbar.

Clay shook his head. 'Can you take me to where she's buried?'

☾

They drove west in Crowbar's rented car, across the broad, flat inland plain and up into the Troodos mountains, cooler here now, the Mediterranean summer approaching its full fury, and then down along the dirt tracks that threaded through the pine and cedar country towards the deep blue of the west coast, the bleached shingle beaches just visible now through the trees, the white surf seemingly static, held in place by some faithful attractor.

Crowbar geared down as the track steepened and they started downhill towards the abandoned Turkish village of Gialia, unchanged for two decades, the stonework crumbling, the road through town still a narrow single track, the trees rampant, the fields overgrown. And then they were at the sea, the long coast road south to the Agamas. A hot breeze buffeted the car as they drove, bent the scrub trees and the wheat in the fields.

Crowbar guided the car to a stop in a gravel pullout at the edge of a limestone bluff and turned off the engine. Below them, the arc of Toxeflora Beach spread from rocky point to narrow windswept peninsula.

Crowbar started down a narrow chalk footpath towards the beach. Clay followed. Soon they reached a small terraced meadow, once a farmer's field, the grass close-cropped, the stone walls frayed. Crowbar stopped next to a stone marker. Beside it, an evergreen seedling swayed in the sea breeze. Beyond, the blue Med stretched away to a cloud-strewn horizon.

'As good a place as any,' said Clay.

'Rania chose it.'

He could see the line along the beach where they'd excavated and removed the poison dosing lines and, further out, the place where he and Hope had first discovered the cable, the rocks where they'd made love, warm in the late-afternoon sun.

'I thought she might have been here today,' said Clay.

Crowbar stood looking down at the tiny plot.

'Did she try to contact you?'

'I haven't seen her since the day she was discharged from the UN hospital,' said Crowbar. 'She left the next day.'

A deep pang flowed through him, heavy and thick, loss and guilt and bewilderment in unequal parts and a thousand other things he could neither name nor understand. Clay looked down at the grass under his feet, the pitifully small grave. 'Did she give her a name?'

Crowbar just shook his head, looked away.

'She never even got a chance…'

'No.'

They both stood looking out to sea. After a long time, Crowbar said: 'What will you do?'

Clay reached into his pocket, ran his fingers over the envelope, the letter she'd written him while he was in prison. He'd answered, twice, to a post office box in Switzerland, but she'd never replied. He had no idea if she'd even received his letters. 'Go south, I guess. Sail to Africa.' Like she'd said in the letter, he had to work it out, alone. So did she.

Crowbar nodded.

'Then, maybe…'

'*Miskein*,' said Crowbar. Perhaps.

'You?'

'I'm going to marry Hope, *seun*. I asked her and she said yes.'

Clay turned, smiled for the first time in six months. 'I'm happy for you, *oom*. Happy for you both.' He was.

'She's going to have a baby.'

'That's great news, *oom*. *Lekker*.'

Crowbar turned, faced him and put his hand on Clay's shoulder. 'I want you to know something, *seun*.'

'Shoot.'

'Hope told me about what happened, about you and her and Rania. Everything.'

Clay said nothing, just looked into those diamond-blue eyes.

'And I want you to know that I'll look after him as if he was my own.'

Clay stood a moment, searched within the depths of Crowbar's eyes, within himself, then looked out to sea. And then he understood what Rania had meant, all that time ago in the hotel room in Istanbul overlooking the Bosphorus. This was the true measure of things: what you had to forsake. And what you might, one day, regain.

Acknowledgements

Deep thank-yous to everyone who has helped to bring this book to publication. My fantastic, gutsy publisher Karen, James West for his great editing, and everyone at Orenda Books (including the other fabulous Orenda authors). None of this of course happens without the support of my family, Heidi, Zac, Dec, Mum and Dad, Matt and Mark. Thanks also to my agent, Broo, and to Eve Seymour and Gary Pulsifer, and to all of the great passionate booksellers around the world who are willing to take a chance on new authors. And many thanks to you, the reader, above all.

An exclusive extract from Paul E. Hardisty's *Reconciliation of the Dead*, published in spring 2016 by Orenda Books

I

No Longer Knowing

22 June 1981. Lat 16° 53' S; Long 18° 27' E,
Southern Angola

Claymore Straker looked down the sight of his South African Armscor-made R4 assault rifle at the target, and waited for the signal to open fire.

For almost a year after leaving school to enlist, the targets had been paper. The silhouette of a man, head and torso, but lacking dimension. Or rather, as he had now started to understand, lacking many dimensions. Blood and pain: surely. Hope and fear: always. But more specifically, the 5.56 mm perforations now wept blood rather than sunlight. The hollowpoint rounds flowered not into wood, but through the exquisite machinery of life, a whole universe of pain exploding inside a single body – infinity contained within something perilously, ultimately, finite.

Just into his twenty-first year, Claymore Straker lay prone in the short, dry grass, listening to the sound of his own heart. Just beyond the tree-line, framed in the pulsing pin and wedge of his gunsight, the silhouette of a man's head moved through the underbrush. He could see the distinctive FAPLA cap, the man's shoulders patched with sweat, the barrel of his rifle catching the sunlight. The enemy soldier slowed, turned, stopped, sniffed the air. Opal eyes set in skin black as a level-five drift. At a hundred metres, less, it was an easy shot.

Sweat tracked across Clay's forehead, bit his eyes. The target blurred, disaggregated. He blinked away the tears and brought the man's chest back into focus. And for those few moments they shared the world, killer and victim tethered by all that was yet unrealised, the rehearsed choreography of aim and fire, the intended ballistics, the engineered destruction. The morning air was kinetic with the hum of a trillion insects. Airbursts of cumulus drifted over the land like a year of promised tomorrows, immediate, step-wise, each instant unfolding like heartbeat. Now. And now. And above it all, the African sky spread whole and perfect and so blue, a constant and eternal witness.

A mosquito settled on the stretched thenar of Clay's trigger hand, that web of flesh between thumb and forefinger. The insect paused, raised its thorax, perched a moment amidst a forest of hairs. It looked so fragile, transparent there in the sun, its inner structure revealed in x-ray complexity. He watched it flex its body, raise its proboscis, hover its tip above his skin, and then lance it into his hand. He felt the prick, the penetration, the pulsing injection of anaesthetic anti-coagulant, and then the reversal of flow, the hungry sucking as the insect started to fill itself with his blood. Clay filled his sights with his target's torso, caressed the trigger with the palp of his finger as the insect completed its violation.

Come on.

Blood pumping. Here. There.

Come on.

The mosquito, heavy with blood, thorax swollen crimson, pulled out.

What are we waiting for?

He is twenty, with a bullet. Too young to know that this might be the moment he takes his final breath. To know that today might be the date they print his one-line obituary in the local paper. To understand that the last time he did something – shook hands with his father, kissed a girl, swam or sang or dreamed or loved – could be the last time he ever would. Unable yet to comprehend that after he was gone, the world would continue on exactly as if he had never existed.

It was a hell of a thing.

The signal. Open fire.

Clay exhaled as he'd been taught and squeezed the trigger. The harrowing detonation slamming through his body. The lurch of the rifle in his hands. The bullet hurtling to its target. Ejected brass spinning away. Bullets shredding the tree line, scything the grass. Hell unleashed. Hades, here. Right here.

The target was gone. Clay had no idea if he'd hit it. Shouting coming from his right, a glimpse of someone moving forward at a crouch. His platoon commander. Muzzle flashes facing, off to the left. Rounds coming in. That sound of mortality shooting into the base of his skull, crawling back out to his extremities, little mouthfuls of the sound barrier snapping shut all around him.

Clay aimed at one of the muzzle flashes, squeezed off five quick rounds, rolled left, tried to steady himself, fired again. His heart hammered in his chest, adrenaline punching through him like a teenage drunk, wild, uncontrollable. A round whipped past his head, so close he could feel it on his cheek. A lover's caress. Jesus in Heaven.

He looked left. A face gleaming in sweat, streaked with dirt. Blue eyes wide, staring at him, perfect white teeth, huge grin. Kruger, the new kid, two weeks in, changing mags. A little older than Clay, just twenty-one, but so inestimably younger. As if a decade had been crammed into five months. A lifetime.

'Did you see that?' Kruger yelled over the roar. '*Fokken* nailed the *kaffir*.'

Clay banged off the last three rounds of his mag, changed out. 'Shut up and *focus*,' he yelled, the new kid so like Clay had been when he'd first gone over, so eager to please, so committed to the cause they were fighting for, to everything their fathers and politicians had told them this was about. It was the difference between believing – as Kruger did now – and no longer knowing what you believed.

And now they were up and moving through the grass, forward through the smoke, *Liutenant* Van Boxmeer – Crowbar as everyone called him – their platoon commander, shouting them ahead, leading as always, almost to the trees, Kruger on Clay's left, Eben on his right, sprinting across the open ground towards the trees.

They'd been choppered into Angola early that morning, three platoons of parabats – South African paratroopers – to rescue a UNITA detachment that had been surrounded and was under threat of being wiped out. A call had come in from the very top, and they'd been scrambled to help. UNITA, *União Nacional para a Independência Total de Angola*, South Africa's ally in the struggle against communism in Southern Africa, were fighting the rival MPLA, the *Movimento Popular de Libertação de Angola*, and its military wing, FAPLA, *Forças Armadas Populares de Libertação de Angola*, for control of the country. UNITA and MPLA were once united in their struggle for liberation from Portugal. But when that was achieved in 1975, they split along ideological lines, MPLA supported by the Soviet Union and its allies, UNITA by South Africa and, some said, America. That was what they had been told by the Colonel of the Battalion, anyway. The Soviets were pouring weapons and equipment into FAPLA, bolstering it with tens of thousands of troops from Cuba, East Germany, the Soviet Union itself, transforming FAPLA from a lightly armed guerrilla force into a legitimate army. As a consequence, things were not going well for UNITA, and it was up to *them* to do everything they could to help. South Africa was in mortal danger of being overrun by the communists. Their whole way of life was threatened, and this was the front line. This was where they had to make their stand. Everything they held dear – their families, their womenfolk, their homes and farms – all would be taken, enslaved, destroyed if they were not successful. It was life or death.

Clay remembered the day he left for active service, waiting at the train station, his duffel bag over his shoulder, his mother in tears on the platform, his father straight and tall and strong, proud. That was the word he'd used. Proud. He'd taken Clay's hand in his, looked him in the eyes, and said it. I'm proud of you, son. Do your duty. It was just like the in books he'd read about the Second World War. And he had felt proud, righteous too, excited. He couldn't quite believe it was happening to *him*. That he could be so lucky. He was going to war.

That was the way he remembered it, anyway.

Clay reached the trees, scrub mopane, Kruger and Eben still right and left, on line. They held up, took a knee. It was the middle of the dry season, everything withered and brown, the wood here tinder dry. Crowbar was about twenty metres ahead, standing beside the body of a dead FAPLA fighter, the radio handset pushed up to his ear, Steyn, his radio operator, crouching next to him. By now the shooting had stopped.

'What's happening?' said Kruger.

Eben smiled at him. 'That, young private, is a question for which there is no answer, now or ever.'

The kid frowned.

Eben took off his bush hat, ran his hand through the straw that passed as his hair. 'And the reason, kid, is that no one knows. The sooner you accept that, the better it will be. For all of us. Read Descartes.'

Clay glanced over at Eben and smiled. Another dose of the clean truth from Eben Barstow, philosopher. That's what he called it. The *clean truth*.

Kruger looked at Eben with eyes wide. 'Read?' he said.

Eben shook his head.

Crowbar was up now, facing them. He looked left and right a moment, as if connecting with each of them individually. And then, quickly, hand signals, precise, urgent. Hostiles ahead, this way, through the trees, two hundred metres. Large force. More than a hundred. We are upwind, so be aware. Take the airstrip. Secure a perimeter. We go up the middle. *Valk* 3 flanking right, *Valk* 2 flanking left. Follow me. And then he was off, moving through the scrub, the radio operator scrambling to keep up.

Jesus. Kruger looked like he was going to shit himself. Maybe he already had.

'Here we go, kid,' said Eben, pulling his hat back on. 'Stay with us. Keep low. You'll be fine.'

And then they were moving through the trees, everything underfoot dried out and brittle, snapping and cracking so loud as to be heard a hundred miles away, a herd of buffalo crashing towards the guns.

The first mortar round hurtled in before they'd gone fifty metres.

It landed long, the concussion wave pushing them forward like a shove in the back. They upped the pace, crashing through the underbrush, half-blind, mortar rounds falling closer behind, the wind at their backs, smoke drifting over them. Clay's foot hit something, a log, a root. He fell crashing into a tangle of bush. Something smashed into his stomach, doubling him over, collapsing his diaphragm. He rolled over, gasped for breath. And then, moments later, a flash, a kick in the side of the head, clumps of earth and bits of wood raining down on him. Muffled sounds coming to him now, dull thuds deep in his chest, felt rather than heard, and then scattered pops, like the sound of summer raindrops on a steel roof, fat and sporadic so you could hear each one, and something else – was it voices?

He lay there a moment, this strange symphony warbling in his head, and tried to breathe. Dirt and sand and dead leaves in his mouth and face and hair. He spat, moved his hands over his body, checked the most important places first. He was intact, unhurt. Jesus. He opened his eyes. He was alone.

Smoke everywhere, the smell of burning vegetation, cordite. He pushed himself to his knees, groped for his R4, found it half-buried. He pulled it free and staggered to his feet. The sounds of gunfire clearer now, somewhere up ahead. He checked the R4's action, released the mag, blew the dust free, reinserted it, sighted. The foresight was covered in a tangle of roots. Shit. He flipped on the safety, inspected the muzzle. The barrel was clogged with dirt. He must have spiked the muzzle into the ground when he fell, driven the butt into his stomach. Stupid. Unacceptable.

Ahead, the grind of *Valk* 2's MAG somewhere on the right, the bitter crack of AK47s. Smoke swirling around him, the smell of it thick in his head like a childhood memory, a flicker of orange flame behind him, to the right, the bush alight. He moved towards the sounds of battle, staggering half-blind through the smoke, defenceless. There was no way his R4 could be fired without disassembling and cleaning it. He felt like a rookie. Crowbar would have a fit.

By the time he reached Eben and the others, the fight was over. It hadn't lasted long. *Valk* 3 had caught most of the FAPLA fighters in enfilade at the far end of the airstrip, turned their flank, rolled them up against *Valk* 5. It was a good kill, Crowbar said. And *Valk* 5 had taken no casualties. One man wounded in *Valk* 3. Pretty seriously they said. AK round through the chest, collapsed lung. Medevac on the way. They counted sixteen enemy bodies.

Crowbar told them to dig in, prepare for counter attack, while he went to meet up with the UNITA *doffs* they'd just rescued. The platoon formed a wide perimeter around the northern length of the airstrip, linked in on both flanks with *Valk* 3 and *Valk* 2. Their holes were farther apart than they would have liked, but it would have to do. After all, they were South African paratroopers, the best of the best. That's what they'd been taught. Here, platoons are called *Valk*. That's Afrikaans for hawk. Death from above. Best body count ratio in Angola.

Once the holes were dug and the LPs set, they policed up the FAPLA dead and piled the bodies in a heap at the end of the airstrip. A few of the parabats sliced off ears and fingers as trophies, took photos. Behind them, the trees blazed, grey anvils of smoke billowing skywards. Clay stood a long time and watched the forest burn.

'Once more ejected from the breach,' said Eben, looking out at the blaze.

Clay looked at his friend, at the streaks of dirt on his face, the sweat beading his bare chest. 'Where's Kruger?'

Eben glanced left and right. 'I thought he was with you.'

'I got knocked down before we got fifty metres. Never saw anyone till it was all over. Never fired a shot.' He showed Eben his R4.

'I never took you for a pacifist, Straker.' Eben jutted his chin towards the pile of corpses. 'You must be very disappointed to have missed out.'

Clay stared at the bodies, the way the limbs entwined, embraced, the way the mouths gaped, dark with flies. This was their work, the accounting of it. He wondered what he felt about it. 'I better get this cleaned or the old man will kill me,' he said, deciding not to wonder.

Eben nodded. 'I'll go find Kruger. No telling what trouble that kid will get himself into.'

Clay nodded, went back to his hole. All down the line, the other members of the platoon were digging in, sweating under the Ovamboland sun. He dug for a while and was fishing in his pack for his cleaning kit when Eben jogged up, out of breath.

'Can't find Kruger anywhere, *bru*. No one's seen him.'

'Crowbar said no casualties. He's got to be around somewhere. Did you check the other *Valk*?'

'Not yet.'

Clay stood, shouldered his R4. 'Maybe he's with Crowbar. Let's go find him.'

They found *Liutenant* Van Boxmeer towards the western end of the airstrip, radioman at his side. He was arguing with a black Angolan UNITA officer dressed in a green jungle-pattern uniform and a tan beret. The officer wore reflective aviator Raybans and carried a pair of nickel-plated 1911s strapped across his chest. Beyond, a couple of dozen UNITA fighters, ragged and stunned, slouched around a complex of sandbagged bunkers. As Clay and Eben approached, the two men lowered their voices.

Clay and Eben saluted.

Crowbar looked them both square in the eyes, nodded.

'Kruger's missing, my *Liutenant*,' said Eben in Afrikaans.

Crowbar looked up at the sky. 'When was he seen last?'

Eben looked at Clay.

'Just before the advance through the trees,' said Clay.

Crowbar's gaze drifted to the muzzle of Clay's R4. Clay could feel himself burn.

'Find him,' said Crowbar. 'But do it fast. FAPLA pulled back, but they're still out there. Mister Mbdele here figures we can expect a counterattack before nightfall.'

'*Colonel*,' said the UNITA officer.

'What?' said Crowbar.

'I am *Colonel* Mbdele. *Colonel* Mbdele.' He spoke Afrikaans with a strong Portuguese accent. His voice was stretched, shaky.

'Your *mam* must be so proud,' said Crowbar.

Eben smirked.

The Colonel whipped off his sunglasses and glared at Eben. The thyroid domes of his eyes bulged out from his face, the cornea flexing out over fully dilated pupils so that the blood-veined whites of his eyes seemed to pulse with each beat of his heart. 'Control your— your men, *Liutenant*,' he shouted, reaching for the grip of one of his handguns. A huge diamond solitaire sparked in his right earlobe. His face shone with sweat. 'We have work here. Work.'

Crowbar glanced down at the man's hand shaking on the grip of his still-holstered pistol. 'What work would that be, exactly, *Colonel*?' he said, jutting his chin towards the FAPLA men lounging outside the bunker. As the Colonel turned his head to look, Crowbar slipped his fighting knife from its point-up sheath behind his right hip.

Mbdele was facing them again, his nickel-plated 1911 now halfway out of its holster, trembling in his sweat-soaked hand. The metal gleamed in the sun. Crowbar had closed the gap between them and now stood within striking distance of the UNITA officer, knife blade up against his wrist where Mbdele couldn't see it.

'FAPLA will attack soon,' shouted Mbdele, his voice cracking, his eyes pivoting in their sockets. He waved his free hand back towards the bunker. 'This position must be defended, must be defended at all costs. At all costs.'

Crowbar was poised, free hand up in front of him now, palm open, inches from Mbdele's pistol hand, the knife at his side still hidden. Clay held his breath.

'And what's so *fokken* important that you brought us all this way, *meu amigo*?' said Crowbar in a half-whisper.

Mbdele took a step back, tried to disengage, but Crowbar followed him like a dance partner, still just inches away. Close in, a knife was far deadlier than a gun, if you knew what you were doing.

'I said, what's so *fokken* important?'

'Classified. Not your business,' shouted Mbdele, spittle flying. 'These are your orders. Your orders. Check. Call your commanders on the radio.'

Crowbar stood a moment, shaking his head and muttering something under his breath. 'And here are your orders, *Colonel*,' he said. 'You and your men get the *fok* out there and cover our left flank, in case FAPLA tries to come in along the river,'

The Colonel's hand was shaking. Sweat poured from his face, beaded on his forearms. '*Não, Liutenant*,' he gasped as if short of breath. 'No. We stay here. *Aqui*.' He pointed towards the bunker complex. '*My* orders are to guard this. And *your* orders are to protect us.'

Clay glanced over at Eben. It was very unusual for a UNITA officer to question his South African allies. The Colonel was treading a dangerous path with the Old Man. And just as odd was UNITA clinging to a fixed position. They were a guerrilla force, fighting a much larger and more heavily armed opponent. They depended on movement and camouflage to survive.

Eben frowned. He was thinking the same thing: whatever was in that bunker, it must be pretty important.

'Our orders are to assist,' said Crowbar. Clay could hear the growing impatience in his voice. 'That means we help each other.'

The Colonel glanced back at his men. 'I am the ranking officer here, *Liutenant*,' he screamed.

Crowbar's face spread in a wide grin. 'Not in my army, you ain't,' he said. Then, without taking his eyes from Mbdele, he said: 'Straker, tell the men to get ready to move out.'

Clay snapped off a salute.

'What are you doing?' blurted the Colonel, eyes bulging. 'You … You have orders.'

'Help us, Colonel, and we'll help you,' said Crowbar, calm, even. 'We're short-handed here. Outnumbered. Get your men out on to our flank or we *ontrek*. Your choice, *meu amigo*.'

The Colonel tightened his hand on his pistol grip. 'This is unacceptable,' he shouted. '*Inaceitável*.' He rattled off a tirade in Portuguese.

Crowbar stayed as he was, feet planted, knife still concealed at his side. 'Try me, asshole.'

The UNITA Colonel puffed out his cheeks, tapped his thigh with his free hand. He stood a long time, glaring at Crowbar, trying to stare him down.

Crowbar jerked his head towards Clay and Eben. 'Move out in ten. Get going.'

Clay and Eben hesitated.

'Now,' said Crowbar.

Clay and Eben turned and started back to the lines at the double.

They'd gone about ten metres when they heard the Colonel shout, 'Wait.'

Clay and Eben kept going.

Then Crowbar's command. 'Halt.' They stopped, faced the two officers.

'I will send half my men to the left flank,' said the Colonel.

Crowbar muttered something under his breath. 'Tell them to report to *Liutenant* DeVries.' He pointed towards the bush beyond the bunker. 'Over there.'

The Colonel stood staring at Crowbar. For a moment he looked as if he was going to speak, but then he swallowed it down.

It happened so fast Clay would have missed it if he'd blinked. Mbdele was down on the ground, his gun hand in an arm lock, the point of Crowbar's knife at his throat, his 1911 in the dirt under Crowbar's boot heel. Mbdele wailed in pain as Crowbar wrenched his arm in a direction it was not designed to go.

'You ever *think* of pulling a weapon on me again, *meu amigo*,' said Crowbar, loud enough so that Clay and Eben could hear, 'and it will be the last thing that goes through that fucked-up brain of yours.'

And then it was over and Crowbar was walking away, leaving Mbdele sitting in the dirt rubbing his arm.

'*Fokken* UNITA *bliksem*,' muttered Crowbar, falling in beside Clay and Eben. 'I trust those *fokkers* about as much as I trust the whores in the Transkei. '

Eben looked over at Clay, grinned. 'Quite the get-up. Those forty-fives.'

Crowbar glanced at Eben, said nothing.

'Did you see his eyes?' said Eben. 'He was wired up tight.'

'*Fokken vrot*,' said Crowbar, slinging his R4. '*Fokken* pack of drugged-up jackals.'

'What's so important about this place, my *Liutenant*?' said Clay.

Crowbar stopped, squared up to Clay. 'What's it to you, troop?'

Clay stood to attention. 'I just meant, those bunkers…'

Crowbar stood glaring. 'They're important because I say they're important, Straker.'

'They don't seem like much.'

Crowbar leaned in until his mouth was only a few inches from Clay's face. 'The only thing you need to know is right there in your hands. Understood?'

'*Ja*, my *Liutenant*,' said Clay, rigid.

'And that goes for you too, Barstow. Couple of *fokken* smart arse *soutpiele*.' Saltdicks. English South Africans. 'Now get out there and find Kruger. Take that black bastard from 32-Bat with you.'

'Brigade,' said Clay. 'His name is Brigade, Sir.'

'I don't give a *kak* what his name is,' said Crowbar. 'He's our scout, he knows the country. Take him with you.'

Clay nodded.

'And do it quick, Straker. Cherry like Kruger, you don't find him by nightfall, he's as good as dead.'

Clay and Eben glanced at each other and started moving away at the double.

'And Straker,' Crowbar called after them.

Clay turned, stood at attention.

'I catch you again with your weapon in that state, and the commies'll be the last thing you have to worry about. I'll shoot you myself.'

South African Truth and Reconciliation Commission Transcripts.
Cape Town, 13 September 1995.

Commissioner Ksole: And you are here why, Mister Straker?

Witness: To tell the truth.

Commissioner Ksole: The truth. Why now, Mister Straker? It was a long time ago.

Witness: Because, Sir, it's killing me.

Commissioner Ksole: Do you wish to apply for a pardon, Mister Straker?

Witness: If that's possible, yes.

Commissioner Ksole: Can you please tell the commission, are you the same Claymore Straker who is wanted for murder and acts of terrorism in Yemen?

Witness: Those charges have been dropped, Sir.

Commissioner Ksole: And Mister Straker, Cyprus, also?

Witness: I served time in prison in Cyprus, yes, Sir.

Commissioner Ksole: And you provide this testimony of your own free will?

Witness: Yes.

Commissioner Ksole: And you understand, Mister Straker, that any new information provided here can, and if necessary will be used against you in a court of law if the circumstances warrant?

Witness's answer is unintelligible.

Commissioner Barbour: Speak up, Mister Straker, please. Do you understand the question?

Witness: Yes Sir, I do. Can and will be used against me.

Commissioner Barbour: And this incident, this series of incidents, occurred on the, ah, the border, during the war in Angola. Is that correct?

Witness: Yes, Sir. While I was serving with the First Parachute Battalion, SADF.

Commissioner Barbour: And the UNITA Colonel, Mbdele. Did you know him by any other name?

Witness: No, Sir. Not then.

Commissioner Barbour: And later?

Witness: Yes, Sir. The people called him *O Coletor*.

Commissioner Barbour: Sorry?

Witness: It's Portuguese, Sir. The Collector.

Commissioner Barbour: Thank you. Did you ever find out what was in the, ah, the bunker?

Witness: Yes, Sir. We did.

Commissioner Barbour: What did you find, son?

Witness does not answer.

Commissioner Barbour: Son?

Witness: The truth, Sir. We found the truth.

Commissioner Nkele: It says here, in your records, Mister Straker, that at the time of your dishonourable discharge you were suffering from mental illness, including extreme instability, episodes of random violent behaviour, complex and consistent delusions, and persistent hallucinations. Do you know what the truth is, Mister Straker?

Witness does not respond.

Commissioner Nkele: Answer the question, please.

Witness: Yes.

Commissioner Nkele: Yes, what?

Witness: Yes, Sir.

Commissioner Barbour: That's not what he meant, son.

Witness: Yes, I … I've learned to …
Commissioner Nkele: Learned to what, Mister Straker?
Witness: I've learned to distinguish.